Praise for the novels of Rick Mofina

"*Their Last Secret* is Rick Mofina at his edge-of-your-seat, can't-stop-turning-the-pages best as he dives deep into questions of truth, justice, and ultimately redemption. A riveting, moving read."
—Lisa Unger, *New York Times* bestselling author of *The Stranger Inside*

"Well-developed characters and an intense pace add to this gripping novel. This latest from a gifted storyteller should not be missing from your reading pile."
—*Library Journal* (starred review) on *Missing Daughter*

"Rick Mofina's books are edge-of-your-seat thrilling. Page-turners that don't let up."
—Louise Penny, #1 *New York Times* bestselling author

"A pulse-pounding nail-biter."
—*The Big Thrill* on *Last Seen*

"*Six Seconds* should be Rick Mofina's breakout thriller. It moves like a tornado."
—James Patterson, *New York Times* bestselling author

"*Six Seconds* is a great read. Echoing Ludlum and Forsythe, author Mofina has penned a big, solid international thriller that grabs your gut—and your heart—in the opening scenes and never lets go."
—Jeffery Deaver, *New York Times* bestselling author

"*The Panic Zone* is a headlong rush toward Armageddon. Its brisk pace and tight focus remind me of early Michael Crichton."
—Dean Koontz, #1 *New York Times* bestselling author

"Rick Mofina's tense, taut writing makes every thriller he writes an adrenaline-packed ride."
—*New York Times* bestselling author Tess Gerritsen

RICK MOFINA

HER LAST GOODBYE

mira

ISBN-13: 978-0-7783-1172-0

Recycling programs
for this product may
not exist in your area.

Her Last Goodbye

Mira
22 Adelaide St. West, 41st Floor
Toronto, Ontario M5H 4E3, Canada
www.Harlequin.com

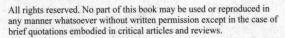

Printed in U.S.A.

*This book is for
Wendy Dudley,
who has been a guiding light*

HER LAST GOODBYE

Don't say that there is no escape
And that your troubles wear you out.
The darker the night, the brighter the stars.
The deeper the sorrow, the closer to God.

From an untitled poem by Apollon Maykov, 1878

BOOK ONE

One

The horror that was coming for Greg, Jennifer, and Jake Griffin could not have happened to another family.

Yet, like other families, they were living everyday lives in an everyday suburb.

It could've been greater Boston, Chicago, or Toronto—any metropolis with freeways webbing from crowning skylines, stretching to new communities where farm fields had been churned to yield a crop of template neighborhoods. All of them served with the same assortment of Walmarts, McDonald's, Home Depots, and other big box outlets.

It could've been Calgary, Denver, or Detroit.

Any big city with planned subdivisions, schools, playgrounds, parks, man-made lakes and protected forests. Neighborhoods of curving streets with names like Spring Breeze Way, Sunshine Rise, or Blue Willow Crescent. They were the kinds of places where kids pedaled their bikes, or skateboarded around the block, or played basketball or road hockey; where gardens were tended with love, where SUVs were washed in driveways. They were places where the houses had double garages, pools, decks and patios, big kitchens; home offices, en suite bathrooms, and fireplaces. They were the kinds of places where people pursued their dreams while trying to hang on to reality.

But behind the closed doors of their home, the Griffins held secrets, kept them unseen, buried below the surface, so that on the night the horror began, no one—not Greg, Jake, or Jennifer—knew what was coming for them.

There was no shriek, no immediate alarm, because it came upon them silently, the way an anaconda captures its prey, slowly coiling around it, squeezing until escape is impossible.

The Griffins lived in the Buffalo-Niagara region of New York, in Trailside Grove, a newish and serene neighborhood not found on any map.

On that night, everything started to unravel sometime after nine, when Greg wheeled his Ford F-150 into his driveway. After shutting it off, he sat there in the late spring twilight, the engine ticking down, dragging his hands over his whiskered face and reflecting on the evening's events.

What have I done? I should've put a stop to it.

Exhausted, yet his mind raced.

Did I let it go too far? No, relax. It'll be all right.

Taking a breath, he pressed the button on the remote opener. His double-garage door came to life, rising before him. The interior automatically illuminated.

Jenn's Corolla was gone.

She's at book club tonight. That's why she's not home.

Grunting, he climbed out of his truck and entered through the garage, smelling the usual mix of rubber, engine fluids, and fresh-cut wood, looking at items neatly placed there: the snowblower, the lawn mower, the ladder, Jake's hockey sticks, Jake's bike, Jenn's bike, her gardening stuff, his tools, workbench, table saw, and the recycle bins.

Stepping up to the interior door, he hit the wall switch and the garage door rumbled closed.

Greg entered his home with a sense of accomplishment because he'd built it. Well, he and his crew had built it, several years ago. They were among the contractors framing houses when Trailside Grove was in its infancy.

Where All Your Dreams Come True, the developer's billboard had said, the banner arching like a rainbow over an artist's concept of a world of new homes and blissful families.

For Greg and Jenn, this was their dream home.

"Our forever home," Jenn had called it.

There were still things Greg would change—a contour here, window size there, maybe the placement of a door. All right, it was well-constructed. But bottom line: he was damned proud of this house. It took a lot of their hard-earned savings, the little money they'd inherited, and a lot of sweat, but he and Jenn had done it.

Our forever home.

The strong scent of laundry soap greeted him as he moved by the washer and dryer through the laundry room. He walked into the living room, softly lit by the lamp Jenn had left on. He'd also leave it on because she wouldn't be home for well over an hour.

That's how it was on her book club nights.

He made his way to the kitchen. It was spotless. The counters gleamed in the dimmed cabinet lighting, and Greg welcomed the tranquility.

He opened the ceramic jar with the peanut butter cookies Jenn had made then went to the fridge for milk. Crunching on a cookie, he read notes written in her neat script on the calendar pinned to the wall next to the fridge door.

Jake was at Carter's tonight for a sleepover.

Right. Jenn had told him about that yesterday. Jake had a dental appointment coming up. Greg shook his head, recalling Jenn's warning: "He may need braces."

A big expense when things are getting tight.

Taking another cookie, Greg saw that Jenn had school meetings, a yoga class, then some kind of seminar-conference thing in Tonawanda with the optometrist she worked for.

Finishing another cookie—*man they're so good*—he drank milk directly from the bottle, something Jenn forbade. But she wasn't home, so...

Greg grabbed more cookies and, milk bottle in hand, went down the hall to his office. Standing at his desk, he looked over his copies of the drawings, to familiarize himself with the next stage of the job tomorrow at Phase 2 of Pine Castle Park.

Then he glanced at the printout of Kyle's email. He was continually urging him to move to Phoenix. "The building biz is booming in AZ, bro." The notion of steady work and no snow was appealing to the point that Greg and Jenn had considered moving there. But they weren't sure because Buffalo was their home.

Greg glanced at the other letters and printed emails officially informing him of the contracts his company had bid for and lost out on. Sure, the region's economy had taken some knocks over the years, but with that never-say-die attitude of Western New Yorkers, Greg believed things would improve. Still, missing out on contracts deepened his fear that if things didn't pick up for his crew soon, they'd be in real trouble.

His phone vibrated. There was no name displayed, but he knew the number and read the text.

Think about it Greg. We'd be great together.

He didn't respond.

He didn't move, still looking at the photo of Jenn with Jake on his desk. They'd known each other since high school. They'd built a good life together, shared so much. She was so beautiful, so loving, but lately, little by little, she'd become distant and he didn't know why. He closed his eyes. He was too tired to think about anything. He had to get up early to get to the job site. He left the text unanswered, turned off his phone, then connected it to the charging cable in the kitchen.

Wearily, Greg hauled himself upstairs.

He passed Jake's room, looking at his posters for the Bills and Sabres, pictures of the three of them at Six Flags in Darien, and Bills Stadium in Orchard Park.

He smiled.

Greg took a quick, hot shower, checked his hands—no splinters to pull out tonight. He brushed his teeth, got into his sweats and a T-shirt, then climbed into their king-size bed.

The green numbers on his bedside clock showed 9:59 p.m. His alarm was set for 4:35 a.m.

He usually went to bed before Jenn, especially on book club nights. Sometimes he woke when he heard her come home, most times he didn't.

In less than five minutes, Greg sank into a deep sleep. He began dreaming before surfacing through a foggy stage of near wakefulness, glancing at the clock.

One twenty-one a.m.

No, get back to sleep. I need sleep.

In his sleepy state, he turned over to Jenn.

But she wasn't there.

Two

Greg lifted his head.

Jenn's side of the bed was still made.

It hadn't been slept in.

What the—

Greg snapped awake.

Where is she?

He looked to their bathroom, the door was open, no lights on. She wasn't there. He looked to their closet. He'd left the door open. It was dark.

Maybe he'd been snoring again; "like a wild beast," she called it, forcing her downstairs to sleep on the sofa. That happened sometimes.

His thoughts then went to the cordless landline phone on his bedside table. If Jenn had called, he would've heard; he had the ringer set to its loudest level. He grabbed it.

No messages.

Where is she?

Greg got up, first looking in the other upstairs bedrooms. All were empty. He padded downstairs.

The sofa was empty.

He went through every room on the main floor, flipping on lights, looking for her in vain. He went downstairs to search their finished basement, the guest room, his man cave, the spare room.

She wasn't there.

Climbing up to the main floor, a tiny warning bell pinging in a corner of his mind, he went through the laundry room and opened the door to the garage.

Jenn's Corolla was not there.

He pushed the button on the wall control, raising the garage door.

His pickup stood alone in the driveway.

Cursing, he rushed back into the house for his phone on the counter. Yanking off the charge cord, he called Jenn's phone. It rang to voice mail and he left her a message: "Where are you, honey? Call me!"

He texted her with the same message, then checked his phone for any calls, texts, or emails Jenn may have sent earlier that he may have missed.

There was nothing.

Driving his hands through his hair, his mind raced.

This had never happened before.

All right, okay, she'd gone to her book club meeting at her friend's house in Ripplewood Creek, a hamlet, what, some three miles away, if that. And they always finished around 10:00 p.m., or 10:30, and she always came home and went to bed.

So why wasn't she there?

Did her car break down? Was she in an accident? Wouldn't someone have contacted me?

Staring at his phone, Greg had an idea. He hurried into his office and switched on his tablet. Their plan came with an app to help locate their phones if they were lost, or track them if they were stolen.

If I find Jenn's phone, I'll find Jenn.

Greg tapped on the app on his tablet. He wasn't good at this stuff. Taking a breath, he followed the instructions and a map of their neighborhood appeared on his screen, locating his phone at their house, but nothing current on Jenn's. The last location of Jenn's phone was old, placing it at their house. But her phone was not plugged into her charger on the kitchen counter, where she always kept it.

That meant she had her phone with her.

He went through the help pages to find the contact number for the twenty-four-hour support line and called. After the prompts, he was put on hold, then a live person came on the line.

"I'm trying to locate my wife's phone. It's kind of urgent," Greg said.

"Yes, sir," said the agent, whose name was Taj. "Just a few security questions about your account."

Forcing himself to stay calm, Greg answered the questions.

"Okay, sir. I've verified your account." Taj was pleasant. "Did you try signing into the advanced browser online?"

"No, I don't know how—look—" After Greg explained his situation, he said: "I need your help."

"Yes, sir. One moment."

Greg could hear the rapid clicking of a keyboard for several moments.

"Sir, I'm sorry but we're unable to provide an updated location for that phone."

"What? Why not?"

"It could be any number of reasons, such as a dead battery, no internet connection, or a SIM card issue…"

"I need to find her phone."

"I would advise you to keep up with your efforts. Your wife could resolve the issue at her end, and then you can locate the phone. Is there anything else I can help you with today, sir?"

"What?" Stunned, Greg then said: "No."

He was at a loss.

It was now 2:46 a.m.

He thought for a moment.

Jenn's book club.

He'd call whoever hosted. But who was it? A small wave of shame rolled over him. He knew little about his wife's book club group, other than a few first names, and that most of them lived in Ripplewood Creek.

Wait.

Greg went to the kitchen calendar, where Jenn had noted the meeting: "Book Club. L."

That had to be Liz. Greg had met her at the mall. It was last year. Jenn introduced her as being in the club. Liz was a retired bank teller. But what was her last name? He thought for a moment. It started with an M…for Martin! No—Meyer! No—Miller!

It was Miller.

Liz Miller.

He needed her number.

Greg went beyond the kitchen to the alcove that was home to Jenn's desk and computer, where she handled all their household finances. It was a foreign land to him. She kept it ordered, tidy. Jake smiled from a framed picture she kept on one corner.

Greg had seen Jenn with her little blue address book many times. Did she keep it here? The first desk drawer he opened had envelopes, bills, statements, warranties. The next drawer had a stapler, tape, pens, stamps, sticky notes, paper clips, and there—a blue address book! He flipped through it, coming to Jenn's handwritten entry for Liz Miller, including her address in Ripplewood Creek and phone numbers for her landline and cell.

Gripping his cell, Greg called.

As it rang, he wrestled with the absurdity of his situation, the imposition, the embarrassment. Then, touching Jenn's desk, looking into their son's face, Greg confronted the break from the order of their lives.

A man answered, his voice groggy, bordering on a growl.

"Hello?"

Greg let out a breath. "Mr. Miller?"

"Yes."

"I'm sorry for waking you. I'm Greg Griffin. My wife, Jennifer, was at your house earlier, for a book club meeting."

Miller said nothing.

Greg continued, not believing the words as he spoke them aloud.

"Jenn, my wife, hasn't come home."

"What?" Miller's voice was tense and he coughed.

"My wife hasn't come home from your house."

"What? She what? It's three in the morning."

"Mr. Miller, could I talk to your wife, please?"

Greg heard another voice in the background, then a rustling.

"Hang on." Miller was less tense. "Hang on."

More talking, then a woman's voice, full of concern.

"Hello?"

"Liz Miller?"

"Yes."

"This is Greg Griffin, Jenn's husband. Was she at the book club meeting at your house tonight?"

"Yes, she was. What's wrong?"

"What time did it end?"

"Ten thirty, maybe a bit later. Why?"

Greg tightened his hold on his phone.

"Jenn hasn't come home."

"She hasn't come home?"

"Did she leave with the others?"

"Yes, they all left. It was after ten thirty. Greg, it's only a ten-minute drive from my house to yours."

"I know. Liz, could you call the others who were there? Maybe Jenn said something to one of them?"

"Yes. Yes, I will."

"Thank you. I'm sorry to wake you."

"Not at all. It's all right."

Ending the call, Greg stood there, almost numb.

Staring at Jenn's address book, he considered a potential scenario: Jake was sick, or hurt. Jenn picked him up from Carter's house and took him to the hospital. Maybe her phone died and she hadn't called him yet, or it wasn't that serious and she didn't want to wake him.

Grasping at the possibility, Greg flipped through Jenn's book. He knew Carter's family, the Wileys. They lived two blocks over. Holly Wiley was an assistant manager at Walgreens. Her husband, Nate, was a welder, who coached kids' softball and hockey. They'd had a couple of backyard barbecues together.

Greg called. Holly answered.

"Holly, this is Greg."

"Greg?" Her voice was low, heavy with sleep. "What is it? Why're you calling so late? Is everything all right?"

"Is Jake okay?"

"Jake? Yes, he's fine. The boys are sleeping. Why?"

"Have you heard from Jenn tonight?"

"No."

"Nothing at all?"

"I saw her when she dropped Jake off. Why?"

Greg hesitated.

"Greg, tell me what's going on," Holly said.

"Jenn hasn't come home from her book club meeting."

"She hasn't come home? Oh my God, Greg!"

"Listen, don't tell Jake. Or anybody. I've got to sort this out."

"Maybe she had a flat tire or something?"

"Maybe. I don't know. Listen, Holly, call me if you hear from Jenn."

"Absolutely. Do you want me to send Nate over?"

"No. No, thanks. Please call me if you hear from her."

Greg hung up, took a breath, went upstairs, got dressed, then grabbed the keys to his truck.

Three

Greg backed his pickup out of their driveway, shifted from reverse to drive, then headed down their street.

At this hour, Trailside Grove was tranquil.

He rolled by houses with parked SUVs and sedans reflecting streetlamps or the peaceful glow of garden lights. While his neighbors slept, he traveled deeper into his nightmare, dragging the back of his hand across his stubbled face.

Why can't I reach her? Did she have a breakdown? Was she in an accident? Where is she?

Greg glanced at his phone in the holder on his console.

Not a word from her, or anyone.

With each driveway and house he passed, each corner he turned, he looked at every vehicle, searching for Jenn's blue Corolla.

He dropped his windows to let the flow of cool night air keep him sharp as he set out to follow her path. He was taking the route she would most likely have followed to Liz Miller's house and back.

He kneaded his temple.

This can't be happening.

No other traffic was in sight as he left his neighborhood and drove along Taconic Street, a straight two-lane road of homes built on larger lots in the sixties, most of them owned by patriotic, flag-on-the-porch people retired from blue-collar jobs.

Why didn't Jenn come home?

At the intersection, he turned left onto Sentinel Trail, upgraded a few years ago to accommodate the growing suburbs. It was now a four-lane road, two lanes running in each direction. Heading west, he passed the U-Haul rental and storage, the Sunoco and Mobil gas stations, strip malls, offices for legal, accounting, and dental services. All of them closed.

There were few cars in sight. He continued on Sentinel, its gentle curves flowing to the larger outlets where he and Jenn shopped—Walmart, Lowes, and Wegmans. All of them were closed, their vast parking lots empty. At the twenty-four-hour windows of the Wendy's and McDonald's, he spotted a trickle of cars in the drive-through lanes.

No Toyota Corollas.

Stopped at a red light, worry gnawing at him, Greg called Jenn again and sent another text, to no avail. Then he flipped through her address book and typed in Liz Miller's address in Ripplewood Creek.

The light turned green.

He passed more strip malls with Fancy Paws Pet Grooming, Make My Day Florist, Big Louie's #1 Pizza, then a Bank of America branch before leaving the commercial zone.

He accelerated as Sentinel Trail continued west, bordered by shrubs and a long line of high wooden fencing, concealing backyards but not rooftops as the artery divided Trailside Grove to the south and Noble Haven to the north. After half a mile, the fence line gave way to Bluebird Park, a dense forest that stood as a natural border between the newer suburbs and the hamlet of Ripplewood Creek.

Greg knew the area, had a good idea of where he was going, and the directions on his phone affirmed it, indicating he turn right. He did, glancing at the sign that said: Welcome to Ripplewood Creek. Est. 1845.

It had originated as a farming settlement, was surrounded by forests and undeveloped rural expanses. Now, with its newer communities, Ripplewood had a population of nearly ten thousand people.

Will I find Jenn here?

The exit put Greg on Ripple Valley Boulevard, the two-lane main street through the hamlet. Parts of its eastern edge backed onto Bluebird Park. He passed St. Bartholomew's church. Its electrically lit cross was bright in the night. He took his eyes from the road to examine the church parking lot.

It was empty.

Then he came to the long, lonely stretch of the boulevard; it had no houses, no stores, no buildings as it curved through the woods. He looked into them, dense and dark for an extra moment—

BUMP-THUMP!

His truck jolted. He'd hit something with a vibration, a thudding, then crumpling and scraping under him.

He stopped, got out, and looked under his pickup. In the ambient light, he saw it. He'd run over an orange plastic traffic cone.

Didn't even see it!

Cursing, he yanked at it but it was wedged solidly in the undercarriage. He crouched and, half-crawling, seized it, pulling repeatedly, his hands slipping, grating against the steel frame, peeling his skin as the cone came free.

He tossed it to the shoulder, then pulled his shirt up and wiped his face with it. Looking down the road behind him, he saw, lying on its side, a blinking yellow beacon that someone had knocked over. It and the cone had been set to caution drivers of roadwork—a patch of new asphalt.

Greg went into the brush off the shoulder, picked up the cone, replaced it, stood up the beacon, then resumed driving along the long, uninhabited stretch bordering the forest. It continued for some distance before coming to a line of houses, the fire hall, more houses, the school, the child and day care center, the gardening center, and more houses.

He was certain this was the route Jenn had taken.

There was no traffic, no one on the street.

For a moment, he wondered if the toppled beacon and roadwork had something to do with Jenn.

How could it?

He dismissed it.

Rethinking things, he stopped, turned around, parked near the work area and got out with a flashlight from his truck. He raked the light over the grassy ditch and along the fence line and overgrowth that marked the border of a closed-off wooded area. It belonged to the county or state; he couldn't remember. Greg probed the dense forest with his light.

There's nothing here.

He got back into his truck and continued deeper into Ripplewood, studying every parked car he saw, his spirits lifting when he spotted a blue Corolla but it wasn't hers. It had a peace-sign bumper sticker on it. He glanced up at the Wood Creek Apartments, a complex of twin ten-story buildings. Then he passed the Bluebird Retirement Manor and came to the commercial center.

At its heart stood the hamlet's original town hall, a two-story stone building with a clock tower and fluted columns. Nearby, with their colorful signs aglow, was a Trader Joe's, a Citizen Bank, a Rite Aid, a Valero gas station, and a Korner Fast convenience store. All were closed, except the Korner Fast.

Not a car or person in sight, as if all of Ripplewood were deserted.

At the traffic light, Greg turned left onto Appleleaf Road. Passing Ripple Hill Elementary, it curled deep into Auden Glen, a sedate neighborhood, lush with mature trees that deepened the darkness.

Houses here were built in the 1970s on larger lots, sitting farther back from the street. Greg slowed, and in the glow of exterior house lights, he scanned driveways and the shoulder for Jenn's car.

A blue Corolla was parked near a crosswalk, but it was an older model with a crumpled fender. Not Jenn's.

His directions chimed, alerting him to turn right onto Oak Shade Drive. He slowed again, rolling through the section of pretty homes, going a block when his phone confirmed he'd arrived at his destination on the right.

There it was: Liz and Calvin Miller's ranch-style home with a wide paved driveway, treed lot, flourishing lawn, and flower garden.

Greg parked in front and stared.

She'd been here a few hours ago. What could've happened?

He looked to his phone, his heart pounding faster now.

No messages, nothing. He checked the time. It had taken him a little over twelve minutes to get here. He went online to check for any recent traffic accidents, found nothing in the area. He couldn't bring himself to see the Millers, not now, and he couldn't sit here. Turning his truck around, he set out to retrace Jenn's path to their home.

Where is she? There's got to be some explanation.

He left Oak Shade Drive, headed back down Appleleaf, coming to the business section at Ripple Valley Boulevard when he had an idea.

Greg pulled into the all-night Korner Fast convenience store and went inside. The clerk behind the counter was playing a game on his phone.

"Can you help me?" Greg said.

The clerk, Dallas, according to his name tag, was over six feet, and could've been a high school football player. He had a wispy blondish beard and acne on his face, wiry hair pulled into a ponytail. Raising his head, he paused, sizing up and assessing Greg before he said: "Sure, what's up?"

"I'm looking for my wife. Was she in here tonight?" Greg held up his phone with a picture of Jenn, beautiful smile, arm around Jake, taken last week on their deck. "She's driving a blue Corolla. Did she stop in here?"

The clerk looked at Jenn then at Greg and shook his head.

"You're sure?" Greg asked. "Could've been after ten thirty?"

"If she came in before midnight, I wouldn't know. I started at midnight, and she hasn't been here since then."

Nodding slowly, Greg thanked him.

Back in his truck, Greg dragged his hands over his face.

She always comes straight home after book club.

His pulse picked up as he resumed driving, leaving Ripplewood Creek along Sentinel, passing the stores and offices, turning onto Taconic, then home, hoping to see her Corolla in the driveway, or in the garage as he watched the door rise.

Nothing.

Sitting in his truck, he tried calling and texting Jenn again.

Nothing.

Then he checked her Facebook, Twitter, and Instagram accounts for new postings.

Nothing.

Tossing his phone onto the passenger seat, he resumed searching. This time he went to the twenty-four-hour windows at the Wendy's and McDonald's, showing Jenn's picture to the workers, asking if she'd been there. He did the same with the clerks at the twenty-four-hour Sunoco and Mobil gas stations.

No one had seen her.

He drove behind the big retail stores, searching the delivery bays. He drove behind the strip malls, checking their service lanes for Jenn's car.

Nothing.

He searched and drove for miles and for hours, his heart hammering, knowing that with each minute and hour that passed, the horror was slowly twisting around him as again and again, he followed the path to Liz Miller's house in Ripplewood and back home.

Finally, he parked in his driveway, looked to the east.

Where are you?

Watching the sky turning pink and orange, he was overcome with helplessness.

This can't be happening—and after what I was doing tonight—please, no. Please come home.

But his hope sank as the sun rose and with it, every fear.

Staring at his phone in his dirty, scraped hands, he shuddered then, steadying himself, raised it and made a call.

It was answered on the first ring.

"This is nine-one-one. Where is your emergency?"

Greg hesitated, reaching inside to form the words, clearing his throat.

"I'm in Trailside Grove. My wife is missing."

Four

The emergency dispatcher took the last of the information she'd requested from Greg then said: "We'll send a car to you, sir."

The call ended.

Staring at his phone, he swiped to Jenn's picture and her smile.

Looking into her eyes, his skin prickled.

This is really happening.

Several houses down his street, a neighbor he didn't know was getting into his SUV. Watching him head off to work, Greg ached for Jenn to return and restore the routine of their lives. Maybe it was exhaustion, or fear, enveloping him, but when Greg got out of his pickup, he entered his house in a trance. A quick shower and coffee might help him focus before police arrived, if he had time, he thought.

He managed to get the coffee started when his phone rang.

"Hi, Greg, it's Holly. Any word on Jenn?"

"Not yet. I've been out looking for her all night. Police are coming."

"Police?"

"I just spoke to them."

"Well, the boys will be up. Would you like me to keep Jake here?"

"Could you, please?"

"There's no school today, a superintendent's conference or something. I'll keep them busy."

"Thanks and please, Holly, don't tell Jake anything just yet."

"No, I won't. But listen, Nate's calling the neighborhood watch captain. They're prepared to get a search going."

"Okay, thank you, Holly. I'll keep you posted."

Greg let out a breath, glanced at the time. Remembering his crew, he texted Al Clayton, his right-hand man.

Can you take over? I won't be at the site today.

A few seconds later, Greg got a response.

Too many beers and too much fun?

Greg suppressed a rush of emotion then, shaking his head, he texted.

Got a personal emergency. Need you to take over, Al.

A moment passed.

No problem. Can I help?

Thanks, I'll let you know.

After he finished texting, Greg thought he had to tell his sister because he might need her help. Before he could call her, his phone rang.

"Greg, this is Liz Miller. Is everything all right with Jennifer?"

Hesitating, Greg said: "She still hasn't come home."

"Oh no. I reached everyone in our book club. They all saw Jennifer getting in her car to drive home. One of our group, Nicole Pitcher—do you know her, Greg?"

"I maybe—I know the name."

"She's a teacher at Jake's school—"

"Right."

"Nicole suggested getting some people together to help you with whatever you need, Greg. I mean, I'm sure everything's going to be fine, but—"

"Yes, I know, Liz." Greg swallowed. "It's thoughtful. I've got to sort a few things out and I'll let you know."

"Of course. We're here to help. Stay positive. It's going to be fine."

So much was happening. Greg steadied himself against the counter. *She can't be missing. She can't be! She's going to show up with a wild story and we'll laugh it off.* The coffee had finished brewing. He made a cup, cooling it with milk, gulped some, then called his sister.

"Hey," she said, recognizing his number.

"Kat, I need you to come over. I need your help."

"I'm headed to work. What is it?"

"Jenn's missing."

"What is it, really?"

"Kat, she didn't come home from her book club last night."

"Are you serious?"

"She always gets home around ten thirty but she didn't come home. I've been searching for her. I can't find her. I've got police coming."

"Police! Jesus, Greg."

"I don't know what's happening, Kat."

"Okay, okay, where's Jake?"

"Sleeping over at his friend's house."

"Okay, look. I'll call my supervisor, then I'll get Dad and—"

The doorbell rang.

Through the window, Greg glimpsed a marked patrol car on the street in front of his house.

"I gotta go. Police are here."

Greg opened the door to an officer wearing a gray uniform and a tan Stetson. He appeared to be in his late twenties and was holding a binder.

"Sir, are you Greg Griffin?"

"Yes."

"I'm state police trooper Rob Menza." He held Greg in a brief, fixed stare. "You reported your wife missing?"

"Yes."

"I need to get some information from you. May I come in?"

"Yes, of course."

Menza inventoried the house as Greg led him to the kitchen. The trooper's utility belt made a leathery squeak when they sat at the table. Greg picked up a trace of Menza's cologne as he slid his tablet from his binder and switched it on, declining Greg's offer of coffee.

"Could I see your driver's license, sir?"

Greg hesitated then pulled it from his wallet for Menza, who gave it a quick review, looked at Greg, and photographed it.

"Routine verification," he said, returning it to Greg. "Have you had contact with your wife since you called us, sir?"

"No, nothing. Absolutely nothing. This is not like her at all. Something's not right."

Menza took a quick assessment of Greg, unshaven, hair messed, and continued.

"Trailside Grove falls to our jurisdiction out of Clarence," Menza said, "but active alerts arising from your call are circulating with the Erie County Sheriff's Office, Buffalo PD, and every law enforcement agency in the region."

Greg nodded.

"We need more information for the detailed report we'll submit to a number of databases, to aid in locating her," Menza said.

"Okay. Whatever you need," Greg said. "Let's go."

Menza began by obtaining Jenn's full name, date of birth, several recent photos of her; a detailed physical description, such as any scars, tattoos, or jewelry she was wearing.

"Maybe a necklace that she likes and her rings," Greg said before glimpsing a glint of gold. Jenn's wedding and engagement rings were near the canister set on the counter. "No—the rings are over there. Guess she forgot them."

"Does that happen?"

"Sometimes after she does the dishes, she forgets them."

Menza asked about the clothing she was wearing. Greg didn't know because he hadn't seen her leave for book club. Menza asked if Jenn had any medical conditions, or required medications, if she was suicidal or violent.

"No."

"Is she receiving any kind of therapy?"

"No."

"Has she ever done anything like this before?"

"No."

"Describe her demeanor, state of mind prior to your report."

Greg thought. "A little preoccupied, maybe, I mean she's got a lot on the go. She works full time at Crystallo View Optical—she's an optometric assistant. She's also a member of a parents' committee at our son's school, and she's involved in other community groups. She goes to yoga class, her book club... She seemed a little distracted lately, but she's also an expert at multitasking."

Menza then requested Greg sign forms giving police permission to check Jenn's phone and computer through their carrier and internet provider, as well as access to all of her credit cards and bank accounts for activity. He signed.

Menza took down details on Jenn's Corolla, including the year, color, model, plate, registration, mechanical condition, and then collected photos of the car, as well.

"All right, sir," Menza said, moving on, "tell me what happened with a timeline."

Greg related the last twenty-four hours, how he went to work, how Jake went to school, how Jenn went to work then dropped Jake off at Carter Wiley's house for the sleepover, then went to book club in Ripplewood.

"I didn't expect anyone to be home. So, after work at the Pine Castle Park site, I went for burgers and beer with my crew at the Mulberry Bar in Depew. I got home about nine thirty."

Greg explained their routine, how he went to bed early and Jenn always got home from book club around 10:30 p.m. But when he woke around 1:30 a.m., he found she hadn't returned.

"She's never been late before?" Menza asked.

"Never."

"This is out of character?"

"It's not like her at all. It's all wrong. I couldn't reach her on her phone, so I went out looking for her."

"You searched alone?"

"Yes." Greg listed everywhere he'd searched with Menza taking notes.

"Who was the last person to see your wife, sir?"

"It would be Liz Miller in Ripplewood, and the women at book club."

"Can you get me Liz Miller's contact information?"

"Sure."

"As well as the names and numbers of the people you were with at the Mulberry Bar in Depew?"

"The bar?" Greg met Menza's stare, letting a moment pass. "Why?"

"Might be helpful."

Greg hesitated, then said: "Okay." He picked up his phone.

"One last thing." Menza looked at Greg's shirt, streaked with grime and what appeared to be dried blood, then at Greg's scraped hands. "How'd you hurt yourself?"

The question hung in the air between them before Greg told Menza he'd run over a traffic cone while looking for Jenn, wedging it under his pickup before removing it.

"And this was on Sentinel Trail?" Menza said.

"No," Greg said. "Ripple Valley Boulevard."

"Right," Menza said. "Sir, would you consent to me photographing you, your hands, and shirt?"

His request launched a whirlwind of new concerns, with Greg battling to realize the implications fueling it. Suddenly he wondered about requiring a lawyer, unable to think clearly, clinging to his need to find Jenn.

"It's routine, sir," Menza said.

"Routine?"

"No obligation, but it is routine."

"Go ahead."

Using his phone, Menza took several photographs.

"With your permission," Menza said when he finished, "would you allow me to take a walk-through of your house and property outside?"

Overwhelmed by the lack of sleep and worry pulsing through him, Greg was on the brink of snapping. *Why search the house? That's an epic waste of time. She's not here!* But he needed to cooperate.

"There's no obligation," Menza said, "but it helps."

"Go ahead. Do you want me to go with you?"

"No, I'll take a quick walk around. I'll start upstairs."

Alone in the kitchen, Greg's hands were shaking. He got more coffee. Listening to the sound of a state trooper walking around upstairs like an intruder in their bedroom, in Jake's room, then throughout the main floor and the basement, hammered home the reality.

My wife is missing.

Menza appeared again with Greg nodding the way to the garage. Menza passed through it on his way outside to walk around the house, the side yards, and the back, the deck…

What's he looking for?

Greg dragged both hands through his hair.

He checked his phone for any word from Jenn. Nothing.

Again, he called and texted her.

Again, it was futile.

Menza returned through the garage.

"Okay, Mr. Griffin. I'll be submitting a report and I'll email you a copy."

"So what's next?"

"We'll put out an appeal online, requesting the public help locate your wife. You might get media calls."

"Media?"

"Sometimes it can help resolve a case like this. Then, depending on how this goes, our detectives will assume the lead in this case."

"Detectives?"

"That's the next possible step. And it's likely our search people and volunteer groups will be involved, but let's not get ahead of ourselves."

Greg swallowed and nodded.

"Sir, would you like me to call anyone to be with you? It can be comforting at a time like this."

"No, my sister and dad are on their way."

"Good, sir. Everything that can be done to locate your wife is in motion. Thank you for your help." Menza touched the brim of his Stetson and left.

Alone at the window, Greg felt the tightening in his gut spread to his chest as he watched the trooper return to his patrol car.

Then Greg clenched his eyes.

I didn't lie. I didn't tell him everything. But I did not lie.

Five

Buffalo, New York, Trailside Grove

Minutes after state trooper Menza pulled away, a familiar purple Jeep Wrangler whipped into Greg's driveway, brakes squeaking as it parked next to his pickup.

Stepping from it was his sister Katrina. Everyone called her "Kat." She was wearing a Bills hoodie, jeans, and sunglasses perched atop her head. She was with their father, Vince. He was dressed in a plaid L.L. Bean shirt, jeans, and his worn ballcap. They came straight into the house.

Kat put her hands on Greg's shoulders and looked into his eyes.

"We're going to find out what happened to her, all right?"

Greg's jaw clenched and he nodded.

Kat gave him a crushing hug then went to the kitchen.

Vince clasped his son's forearm. At sixty-six, the retired bricklayer had a firm grip.

"This isn't like Jenn at all," Vince said. "I don't get it."

"I know, Dad."

A rush of water issued from the kitchen sink. Kat had removed her hoodie. Under it, she wore a faded Rolling Stones T-shirt. She was dumping coffee, rinsing the carafe.

"This stuff is awful." She nodded to the two cupboard doors she'd opened. "Where's the coffee I brought back from Jamaica that you like?"

"I don't know where Jenn put it."

Kat was taking charge like she always did, Greg thought, watching her look through cupboards.

Vince cast a glance around. "Is Jake home?"

"No, he's still at his friend's house."

"Does he know?" Kat asked, poking in a lower cupboard behind a stack of plastic containers.

"Not yet."

"You're going to have to tell him," Vince said.

"I know."

"Got it," Kat said, pulling out the barely used bag of Blue Mountain. "Sit down, Greg."

She got a fresh pot going then joined Greg and Vince at the table and said: "Now, tell us what happened."

Greg retold the history of Jenn's disappearance and his all-night search, the same story he'd given to the trooper. At one point, Greg rubbed his fingers and winced, then he explained about the traffic cone. As he continued, Kat and Vince listened, nodding and frowning, saying little, occasionally asking questions. When he'd finished, Vince shook his head.

"And what did the police say?" Vince said.

"Not much. The trooper took down all kinds of information and asked me for pictures for alerts. He said detectives could get involved."

"What do you think happened?" Vince asked.

"I don't know. Maybe she was carjacked? I don't know."

"Want to know what I think?" Kat said. "I think maybe she's—" Kat stopped herself.

"What?" Greg said.

"No, I don't know." Kat shook her head. "Could be a carjacking, but God, I hope not."

Greg looked at her because he thought something had flickered on Kat's face, something subtle. Or was he wrong, being punchy from lack of sleep? Or was it a nearly imperceptible manifestation of something—*of knowing*?

"What? What were you going to say, Kat? You think maybe she's what?"

"Maybe a carjacking, like you said. Stop staring like that. I don't know what to think."

Greg didn't know either. He wasn't sure about anything because he was drained. Shifting matters, Kat reached for her phone.

"Send me the photos of her and her car that you gave to the police," she said.

Greg sent the images to Kat.

"I'll flip them to my dispatcher at Ready Quick's shipping center. We'll get all the drivers looking."

Greg nodded. Kat left the table to make the call.

Greg and his father sat in silence for a moment before Vince broke it.

"Maybe she blew a tire and rolled off the road?"

"I looked for her all night, Dad."

"How's her Corolla running?" Vince said. "I remember she told me it clunked a little when she turned the wheel."

"That was a long time ago. We had the tie rod ends replaced."

"Let's look at the maintenance records," Vince said.

"Her car's fine, Dad."

Kat was done with her call. "They're circulating everything and they'll ask the competition to help, too," she said before fixing them cups of the fresh coffee.

Greg drank some, then raked his fingers through his hair. Kat and Vince looked at his dirty shirt, scraped hands, the lines carved into his face.

He was a portrait of anguish.

"You look like hell," Kat said. "Go take a shower and I'll fix you some eggs."

Needles of hot water failed to soothe Greg.

Steam clouds rose, overwhelming him with fear, guilt, and a thousand thoughts.

Where are you, Jenn?

He went numb imagining scenarios, and with Kat acting like maybe *she knows something.* But was he imagining that too? Maybe all Kat did was stop short of saying out loud what was clawing at the pit of his stomach.

Was Jenn murdered?

Greg pounded his fists against his temples, biting back his emotions.

No, she can't be dead.

He couldn't think like that. He had to stay strong for Jenn, for Jake. Gasping for air, he forced himself to be positive, grateful he had his dad and Kat to help him.

We're not perfect. We've got our problems. But we stand by each other.

Look at how Kat had jumped in, taken control like she always did, ever since their mother died. Greg was ten and Kat was fifteen when Evelyn Griffin collapsed from heart failure on the tile floor of Angelo's Diner where she waited tables.

It blew a hole in their world.

Vince never recovered from the loss.

He used to take Greg duck hunting, but it was no longer the same. One cold morning, a couple of years after his mom's death, as Greg and his father waited in the peace of the clear predawn by a marsh of a river, his dad finally spoke about her.

"I'm not the same without her. I'll never be the same man, son. This kinda thing changes you." Greg couldn't see his face, could only hear him.

In the years after that, Vince never remarried, or even dated. Sometimes, he would go off hunting, or just spend time alone, camping in the woods. "To clear my head, think of her, and maybe find myself," he told Greg.

After her mother's death, Kat took on her role in the house, going from teenager to a young woman, doing what had to be done to hold together what was left of their family. Then Jenn came into Greg's life and on some level, Kat may have felt displaced. Maybe it's why Jenn and Kat didn't always get along. It broke Greg's heart because Jenn's life had also been tragic, and from the day they'd met, Greg had been protective of her.

But in recent months, it was as if a switch had been thrown, with Jenn growing distant. Withdrawn.

He didn't know what was wrong. Whenever he tried to talk to Jenn about it, she'd deny there was a problem then she'd change the subject.

Stepping from the shower, Greg cleared a window on the fogged mirror and questioned his reflection.

Could Jenn have known what was going on with me—known of the war raging inside me? Could her disappearance be related to that, to her withdrawing, to any of this? No... How could it? It doesn't make sense. I've got to keep myself together.

Six

In the kitchen, Kat set down a plate of scrambled eggs, sausages, and hash browns for Greg.

"Thanks but I'm not hungry," he said.

"You gotta eat. I fixed it the way you like it."

"I'm going out looking again."

"We'll go with you, but first eat, Greg."

Kat's phone rang.

"If he's not hungry, he's not hungry." Vince had finished toast and coffee.

"Yes?" Kat answered her phone, listening. "Great, thank you." Ending her call, she turned to Greg, who was finishing the last of his coffee. "That was my dispatcher," she said. "FedEx, UPS, and a couple of others have blasted out Jenn's picture and information. I've got some friends with the ride share and taxi companies I can try."

"Good, thanks." Greg's phone rang and he answered.

"Greg, Doug Tucker, neighborhood watch captain for Trailside Grove."

"Yes."

"I got your number from Nate Wiley. We're co-ordinating a neighborhood canvass. Police have issued an e-alert through the watch network."

"When?"

"Like, now. But I was already talking with Nate about getting ready. Our watch teams in Ripple-wood and Noble Haven are on board. We're reaching out to community groups in the region. All of them have indicated they'll participate. We'll follow our search protocols with social media and on the ground."

"On the ground?"

"Volunteers will go door-to-door with flyers. We're setting up marshaling points at the Rite Aid parking lot in Ripplewood, the Walmart parking lot on Sentinel Trail, and the Empire Shops lot in Noble Haven. Would you like to join us?"

"Yes."

"How about in Ripplewood? I'll be there shortly. You'll see our table and flag."

"I'll be there."

Buoyed by the support and action his neighbors had taken, Greg updated his sister and father, but before talking further, he called Holly Wiley.

As the line rang, he'd found a measure of as-surance that alerts for Jenn were getting out fast, but he was concerned about Jake learning that his mother was missing. Greg was relieved that he and Jenn had not yet given Jake his own phone. He begged for one but they'd told him that at eight, he was too young, that he'd have to wait until he turned ten. Jake had his own laptop, but they'd set parental controls on it, limiting his access to what he saw online. Greg wasn't sure if Jake had taken it with him to Carter's sleepover.

Holly answered.

"It's Greg again."

"Hi, Greg. Any word?"

"No."

"You know a search has started? Nate's gone to Walmart to help organize."

"Yes, I'm heading to Ripplewood. Holly, the situation is, well, more people know now, but I don't want Jake to learn about this from anyone until I'm ready to tell him. I'm hoping it will be sorted out soon. If not—" Greg stopped, unable to remove the dread in his voice, the underlying tone of a man flailing, trying to delay the inevitable. "If not, I'll tell Jake later today when he comes home."

"Of course, I understand."

"Listen, Holly, I'm sorry to impose but I was wondering if you would take the boys to the Falls for the day, to the arcade, go-karts, and maybe to a movie and pizza, all on me? I need more time, you know?"

"Yes, of course. It's no imposition. I'll do whatever I can. We're all praying for you, for Jake, for Jenn."

"Thank you, Holly. I can't tell you how much this means right now. Is Jake near you?"

"No, the boys are downstairs having cereal and playing a video game."

"Could I talk to Jake?"

"Hold on."

In the muffling, he heard Holly calling for Jake, then the thud of running, then his son's breathless voice. "Hi, Dad."

"Hey pal, you having fun?"

"Yup, two more levels and I slay the demon!"

"All right. Good luck."

"Carter already got the demon once."

"Very cool."

"Dad, can I stay a little longer before Mom comes to get me?"

"Well, I think Carter's mom's got a surprise for you guys."

"What is it?"

"I'm not sure, but you could be in line for some major fun today. Guess that means you get to hang with Carter longer, and I'll get you when you're all done later today."

"Can you tell me the surprise? Am I getting the drone I wanted? A cell phone?"

"No, nothing like that. Carter's mom will tell you. Just be safe and have fun, okay?"

"Okay, Dad. Is Mom there?"

Greg hesitated, something caught in his throat.

"No, son, I'm sorry. She's not home right now. You have fun, okay?"

"Okay. Love you, Dad."

"Love you, too. Bye, son."

Greg stood there, inhaled a breath, let it out, then went to the fridge door where Jenn's business information was on a magnet shaped like eyeglasses. He tapped a number into his phone. His call rang to the recorded message for Crystallo View Optical. He pressed the prompts and left a message:

"This is Greg Griffin, Jennifer Griffin's husband. Jennifer won't be in today because—uh—because by the time you get this message, you'll likely know that, she's, uh, she's missing. If you hear from her you can reach me at…" Greg left his number then turned to Kat and Vince.

"Let's go look for Jenn."

Seven

Buffalo, New York, Ripplewood Creek

They took Kat's Jeep.

She drove. Vince was in the passenger seat.

Greg sat in the back, watching his neighborhood rolling by—joggers, dog walkers, neighbors talking in driveways, life going on while his world had come to a dead stop. Jenn looked at him from her picture on his phone. His stomach knotted with the undeniable fear that she'd been abducted, assaulted, left for dead.

And where was I last night?

At a freakin' bar.

Greg tingled with shame before his father spoke.

"It has to be a breakdown," Vince said, scanning the houses along Taconic before they headed west on Sentinel. "Her Corolla broke down somewhere."

Biting her lip, Kat nodded and said: "Or some simple explanation." Then Kat found Greg in her rearview mirror and continued. "That's what I think. She'll emerge with a simple explanation."

Greg returned Kat's gaze.

"What's that supposed to mean?"

Kat's attention went to the road then flicked back to the mirror at Greg.

"I know we're going to find her."

"You think so?"

"I do, Greg."

Nodding, he turned away, his heart lifted by Kat's support. But to some extent he was mistrusting of it because he knew that deep down, Kat held hard feelings for Jenn.

He looked out at the commercial strip. A lifetime had passed since he'd driven up and down Sentinel, looking for Jenn throughout the night. Now, in the light of a new day, there was more traffic and activity.

"Look." Kat pointed at Walmart. "That's one of the search groups. Want to stop?"

In a far corner of the parking lot, a few cars were parked and people were gathered at a table with an orange flag. Greg was encouraged.

"Nate Wiley's group," Greg said, scrolling through recent texts, including one from Liz Miller. "No, don't stop. Let's get to Ripplewood. That's where the women from Jenn's book club will be."

They traveled the section of Sentinel Trail that separated Noble Haven and Trailside Grove before it evolved into Bluebird Park. In the bright morning sun, Greg considered the thick forests of the park, its trails, streams and rugged terrain, but not for long because when they reached the exit for Ripplewood Creek, his phone rang.

Al Clayton was calling from the Pine Castle job site.

"I just heard. Damn, why didn't you tell me about Jenn this morning?"

"I'm still processing everything."

"What could've happened to her?"

"I don't know, Al."

"And police are on it?"

"Yes."

"Okay listen. I was talking to the guys. We'll shut things down here and help look for her."

"No. Don't," Greg said. "We're joining a search right now."

"You're sure you don't want more people?"

"Yes, thanks, but we've got lots of help. Al, we have to keep the job going. We have to meet the deadlines."

There was a pause on the line.

"You're serious?"

"Yes. Al, keep things moving on nine-seventy-five and nine-seventy-six. The footings should be done. Get the subs moving on the drainage and waterproofing, then get pouring concrete right away."

"All right," Clayton said. "Let me know if things change. Keep me posted."

Al Clayton's call pulled Greg back to the previous night with his crew at the Mulberry Bar. They'd pushed tables together in the section that was a few steps higher from the rest of the bar. They were eating wings, nachos, and burgers, and analyzing the virtues and faults of the Bills and Sabres.

Then what happened? I can't think about that. Not now.

"Here it is," Kat said.

Greg heard the rhythmic ticking of the Jeep's turn signal as they arrived at the Rite Aid parking lot.

A canvas canopy had been erected over a couple of large folding tables. A breeze waved through an orange flag affixed to one of the metal poles as they walked to it, joining the two dozen people there. Several men and women wore fluorescent green vests, with IDs and ballcaps; most had walkie-talkies clipped to them.

Kat and Vince went off to talk to the volunteers while Greg was led to Doug Tucker, the retired firefighter who'd called him and was heading the effort in Ripplewood. He gave Greg a firm handshake.

"We're only getting started. I'll show you."

Tucker took Greg to a table with maps and laptops. The reality hit Greg again when Tucker peeled a single page from the stack on a table and gave it to him.

The word *MISSING* stretched across the top over a color picture of Jenn, then her description, a summary of when and where she was last seen, and a color photo of her blue Corolla. A police number to call was at the bottom.

Greg looked at it without speaking.

"We got the information from the police," Tucker said. "We're also posting it on our sites, emailing it, texting it, getting it out everywhere on social media, Facebook, Twitter, Instagram, you name it."

Greg swallowed.

Then Tucker pointed to maps of Ripplewood.

"We're dispatching teams to canvass door-to-door with the flyer along the route police think she traveled. Then we'll expand it."

"What about Bluebird Park?" Greg asked.

"We'll send teams from Ripplewood to walk through the park from west to east." Tucker's finger traced the area on the map as he detailed the search. "In all, we should have nearly a hundred volunteers involved."

When Greg turned to look at the others, who were preparing to set out, a woman approached him.

"Greg, I'm Nicole Pitcher, a teacher at Tall Elm."

"Hi." Greg recognized her from the times Jenn hosted their book club.

"We've got people from the school. We're excused from today's conference because we know Jenn." She took him to meet them; most were strangers to him. "This is Monica Todd and Juan Perez—they're teachers. Viola Johns supervises the cafeteria. Bert Cobb is one of the custodians, Thelma Clark is in the admin office. Anita Overhauser is with the parent advisory committee and Porter Sellwin is with the school board."

"We'll find her, Greg. I live here in Ripplewood, and we've got a lot people coming out to help." Sellwin shook Greg's hand.

Sellwin was a good-looking man. Greg recalled rumors about him being a player, even though he was married. And Greg had a vague recollection of seeing Bert Cobb a couple times before, maybe helping prep the field at one of Jake's soccer games.

He thanked each of them then asked Nicole

Pitcher about the people from Jenn's book club, and she took him aside to meet them. They were near an SUV and dressed in hoodies, fleece vests, and jeans. Again, his memory of the women was hazy, having only glimpsed them briefly whenever Jenn hosted, which was once every few months. Nicole Pitcher, aware Greg was stressed, went ahead with introductions, starting with Liz Miller, who hugged him while blinking away tears.

"I'm so sorry. This is terrible," she said.

Then Rita Spencer, a retired Realtor, said: "We're going to find her, Greg."

Maria Ortiz, who helped manage her father-in-law's appliance store, took Greg's hand and patted it. "We won't give up until we get her home."

Retired nurse, April Kent, nodded to Greg.

"We're all praying we'll find her."

Basha Kominski, a receptionist at a law firm, smiled warmly. "We're going to find her."

"Please tell me—" Greg looked directly at the women "—you were the last people to see Jenn last night. Did she say anything to suggest she might not be heading home?"

Heads shook.

"Did she do or say anything that seemed odd, or out of place? Anything about her car?" Greg asked, trying to maintain eye contact with each of them, one by one, unable to conceal his desperation.

"No," Rita Spencer said, "nothing like that."

"She was fine," Maria Ortiz added.

"The state trooper came to my house this morning," Liz Miller said.

"Menza?" Greg said.

"Yes. Trooper Menza. He said he'd spoken with you," Liz Miller said. "I told him there was nothing different about Jenn, or the evening. Everyone left at the usual time. After I gave him their numbers, he said he would talk to the others in the club."

"He called me," Basha Kominski said. "I was the last to see Jenn. Our cars were parked on the street. We talked for half a minute. She was going to send me a recipe for pecan pie. Then she gave me a little wave, got into her car, and pulled away, with me following her down Appleleaf Road to the intersection with Ripple Valley Boulevard. Then I turned right and she turned left for Trailside Grove."

"That's it?" Greg said.

"That's it," Basha Kominski said.

The other women nodded.

Frustrated, Greg drew both hands to his face and kneaded his jaw, noticing that April Kent focused on the scrapes on the backs of his hands until he made eye contact with her. She hadn't said much.

"Can you remember anything at all, April?" Greg asked.

April Kent, her face betraying no emotion, shook her head.

"Jenn didn't say anything out of the ordinary to me, and I sat beside her all evening," she said, her eyes lingering on the scrapes on Greg's hands.

Eight

Greg thanked the women of Jenn's book club then observed other volunteers, heading out to canvass.

Kat and Vince joined teams moving east, covering the north and south sides of Ripple Valley Boulevard.

At that moment the sky thudded and everyone looked up as a red helicopter passed overhead.

"That's the chopper from Erie County Sheriff's Office," Doug Tucker said.

Watching it, Greg's gut roiled with hope and fear at the increasing magnitude of the response.

Then he went with the teams retracing Jenn's drive from Liz Miller's house. They started on Appleleaf Road, moving into Auden Glen. He was paired with Sue Kelston, who had a walkie-talkie clipped to her belt and wore a fluorescent vest, ball-cap, and an expression of determination.

"I've been with the watch for five years," she said. "Been involved in all kinds of searches. Our last one was a Silver Alert."

"Silver Alert?"

"A ninety-year-old woman with dementia had wandered from her nursing home in Noble Haven. We found her."

"Alive?"

Kelston looked at Greg.

"Yes. Somehow she'd made her way to the cemetery where her husband was buried," Kelston said. "We'll find your wife, trust me."

The helicopter made another pass before Greg's phone rang. It was state trooper Rob Menza.

"Sir, I'm following up to advise you that alerts have been issued, searches with community groups are underway, and we've put out a public appeal for help. The Erie County Sheriff's Office has dispatched its helicopter to search the area traveled by your wife."

"Thank you. Have you received any new information?"

"A few calls have come in."

"Someone saw Jenn?"

"It's premature to confirm anything."

"What do the callers say?"

Menza hesitated.

"I want to know," Greg said.

"Some claim to have spotted your wife in Walmart. Others say they saw her car downtown."

"You're jumping on those tips, right?"

"Sir, they lack details or specifics. But yes, we're assessing and following up every lead, I assure you."

Greg absorbed the information without speaking as the helicopter circled for another pass and his call ended.

They continued going house-to-house, placing flyers in mailboxes, wedging them in doors, or tucking them under windshield wipers because most people weren't home. For those who were, Kelston took the lead.

"We need your help to find a missing mom," Kelston always started. It usually got a resident's attention and removed suspicion that they were peddlers. Then, showing them the flyer, she'd tell them what happened, asking if they recalled anything that might help.

Most people said they'd noticed nothing, or were asleep, or not home. Then Kelston would tap her pen to a paragraph on the flyer Greg had missed, one asking if the resident had a home security recording system. If they did, would they agree to share any footage with police?

That was good, Greg thought, but he couldn't stop feeling that time was slipping away.

Moving between houses, Kelston would tape flyers to lampposts, or staple them to trees. Teams across the street were doing the same. They'd canvassed about two blocks when Kelston's walkie-talkie crackled with transmissions.

"Nothing at the gas station, or the corner store. The store was the only all-night business," a voice said.

"What about their cameras?" Doug Tucker's voice came across the air.

"We've got to go through corporate channels for them to release."

"I figured," Tucker said. "We'll pass that to police, but I'm sure they're on it."

Absorbing the setback, and taking in what suddenly seemed futile—walking through the neighborhood sticking paper on trees—Greg battled the anger rising within him.

My God, Jenn's missing. I should rush to the store, the gas station, to every business she could've passed and demand they help us with their cameras. My wife's missing and every minute that ticks by could make a difference—

"Mr. Griffin? Greg Griffin?"

Greg turned.

"Yes?"

A woman in her twenties had stepped from a small car with call letters and a logo. "WJBV News Pulse Radio."

Approaching him, she was carrying a microphone.

"I'm Brandi Chang, with WJBV." She gave Greg her card. "Could I have a moment, for a brief interview about your search for your wife?"

Before Greg answered, another car came to a halt across the street. A tall bearded man got out and trotted to them.

"Dylan Pepper, with the *Bulletin*, the online community paper. You're Greg Griffin?"

"Yes."

"They told us at the tent where to find you," Pepper said.

"Would you talk to us?" Chang said.

Looking at the two reporters, Greg remembered the state trooper telling him how media coverage can help a case.

"Yes," Greg said.

Chang moved her microphone closer and Pepper began recording a video with his phone.

"Have you heard anything from your wife since you reported her missing?" Chang asked.

"No."

"When and where was she last seen?" Pepper asked.

"About ten thirty last night. She was leaving her book club meeting on Oak Shade Drive."

"And you live in Trailside Grove?" Pepper said.

"Yes, we do."

"So it's a short drive?" Chang said.

"About three miles, maybe ten minutes."

They paused as the helicopter made another pass.

"What do you think happened?" Chang asked.

Looking around at nothing, Greg swallowed.

"I don't know. A breakdown, a carjacking. I don't know. But we're asking anyone with information to contact police."

"What are police telling you?" Pepper asked.

"They're investigating and the community has come out to help."

"Does your wife work outside the home?" Chang asked.

"She's an optometric assistant at Crystallo View Optical."

"And you?" Pepper asked.

"I'm a carpenter, a framer. I build houses with Solid and Strong Contracting."

"Do you have children?" Pepper asked.

"One. Our son, Jake. He's eight."

After the helicopter circled again, the reporters thanked Greg and left.

* * *

Morning became afternoon.

Greg canvassed with Sue Kelston all the way to Liz Miller's house on Oak Shade. Then they continued deeper into Auden Glen. As the day wore on, Greg's stomach yowled. He'd refused sandwiches and fruit brought by volunteers. He got by on coffee and energy drinks.

Later in the afternoon, word circulated that the neighborhood watch teams had covered the entire route Jenn would've taken in Ripplewood and Trailside Grove. Parts of Noble Haven and Bluebird Park were covered, too. Another shift of volunteers would be coming on to recanvass, focusing on addresses where no one was home during the first canvass.

Greg was determined to keep working with the second shift when Kat and Vince met up with him.

"Greg," Kat said. "You need to go home."

"I'm not quitting."

"You need to eat and get some rest," Kat said.

"I'm fine."

"I called Holly Wiley," Kat said. "She's on her way back from the Falls with Jake."

Vince gripped Greg's shoulder.

"Son," he said. "You're going to have to tell Jake about what's happened to his mother."

Greg's face sobered at the realization. He stared at his father, then his sister.

In Kat's Jeep, driving home to Trailside Grove, Greg unfolded the flyer and stared at it.

In a flash, he pictured Jenn at sixteen on that

day in West Grove High School when he saw her, *really saw her*, for the first time.

She was sitting on that corner bench that was easy to miss in the main lobby by the interior garden at the entrance to the cafeteria. She was hugging her books, head lowered, crying.

He only knew a little about her—that her parents had died when she was young and she had to live with her grandmother.

Greg thought Jenn was shy and quiet. There were the times he'd pass her in the hall, those moments when she pulled back her hair and glanced at him. He liked her smile.

But on that day, when he saw her alone and crying, he was concerned, even though he didn't know her. He didn't think she was crying about her parents because they'd died quite a few years before.

He didn't go to her; it would've been awkward. But later, after asking around, he'd learned that she'd been dumped by her boyfriend, leaving Greg with one thought: Who'd be stupid enough to break that girl's heart?

That's when he'd decided to ask Jenn out.

Now, as Kat wheeled the Jeep out of Ripplewood and onto Sentinel, Greg looked at the flower box that had replaced the developer's billboard for Trailside Grove. While the billboard was no longer there, its promising message haunted him.

Where All Your Dreams Come True.

Nine

Buffalo, New York, Trailside Grove

A front bumper, small front wheels rolling, hands working the steering wheel, guiding the go-kart along the twisting, turning track, closing in on another go-kart, its rear bumper, roll bar, driver's helmet, all coming into view.

"That's Carter ahead of me!" Jake pointed to the video filling Greg's flat-screen in the basement. "He's winning but I'm going to pass him."

Jake had returned from his day in Niagara Falls, bubbling with excitement, telling Greg how Carter's mom got the video option for the boys at the go-kart track and put it on his laptop.

Greg had picked up tacos and nachos for supper, Jake's favorite, and now they were playing Jake's video and eating at the coffee table in the man cave with Kat and Vince.

"Wait, is Mom here? Mom!" Jake stared at the screen. "Look!" He munched and pointed. "It's so awesome! The karts and helmets got dragons and rockets and sharks painted on them! I've got rockets! There! I'm passing Carter! LOSER!" Jake shot his fist into the air then reached for another nacho. "Mom's gotta see this!"

Jake's gaze was welded to the TV when Greg glanced across the room to Vince, and then to Kat, who mouthed the words *Tell him.*

"Isn't it cool, Dad?" Jake said when the video ended. "Can we go back there? Let's play it again." Jake picked up the remote control, restarted the video then bit into a taco. "I want Mom to see it. Where is she? Mom!"

Greg didn't answer. He couldn't find a way to begin.

"Where's Mom, Dad?"

Jake turned from the TV, his concentration shifting to the adults, stopping to read their faces, picking up a troubling vibe.

"Hey, why're Aunt Kat and Grandpa here anyway?"

Greg looked at Jake, his heart wrenching at how he resembled Jenn so much. He had her eyes, her cheeks, and her goodness. As he searched his son's face, he saw that Jake also had his mother's quick mind, her intelligence, because it was clear that awareness was dawning on him.

"This is weird," Jake said. "Something's wrong."

Greg took the remote, shut off the TV, and patted the sofa beside him.

"Come up here and sit with me," Greg said.

Jake hesitated, looked at his dad then sat with him.

"Did I do something bad?"

"No, son."

"What is it?"

"It's Mom," Greg said.

"Something bad about Mom?" Jake's voice quavered.

Greg put his arm around Jake, pulling him close.

"She didn't make it home last night from her book club."

"What do you mean? Where is she?"

"We don't know," Greg said.

"Where'd she go? What happened to her?" Jake's voice cracked.

"Her car may have had a breakdown, a flat tire, or someone took it, or a medical problem and got lost, or something. We don't know."

Jake's eyes pinballed to his aunt, his grandfather, then back to his dad.

"No," Jake said.

"It's true," Kat said.

Jake looked at Kat, then at his grandfather.

"It's true, Jake," Vince said.

Jake's breathing quickened, his face crumpled, and he began crying.

"Listen to me," Greg said. "I need you to listen. We're going to find her." Greg held Jake tight, looking at Kat and Vince. "Son, I looked all night. Then Aunt Kat, Grandpa, me, a whole bunch of people looked all day. Police are helping. They're using a helicopter."

"A helicopter?" Jake said. "Is Mom dead? Isn't that what they use a helicopter for? To find a dead person? Did somebody kill Mom?"

"No, no, honey, of course not!" Kat said, rushing

to Jake, dropping to her knees before him, rubbing his legs. "It's just that people are searching, people are looking, right now. The news is out there for people to help find her, and we're going to find her, Jake."

Vince joined them, patting his grandson's back.

"You've got to be strong, Jake," Vince said. "Hang tough. We're going to find your mom."

Wiping at his tears, Jake pulled away, his expression changing as he looked at his father, aunt, and grandfather. Sniffling, his eyes narrowed and his face hardened when he arrived at a cold thought.

"You're lying!"

"No," Greg said.

"Yes, you are!" Jake broke free, stepping away from the adults. "You're getting a divorce!"

"What? No!" Greg said.

"Mom moved away and you're just saying this to trick me!"

"Jake, no, honey," Kat said. "Nobody's getting divorced."

"My friends' parents got divorced, and they said their mom and dad lied about lots of stuff! I heard you and mom fight about money and talking about moving to Arizona and stuff. I think she got mad because she didn't want to move away and wanted a divorce!"

"Oh God no, Jake, we were only talking about maybe moving to Arizona. She wasn't mad. It's complicated grown-up stuff." Greg reached out for Jake, but Jake stepped back. "Son, listen, Mom's missing. We don't know why and that's the truth. I wish to God it wasn't."

"You're all lying!"

Jake fled the room, tearing up the stairs with jackrabbit speed. Greg followed Jake as he raced through the kitchen, calling for his mother.

"Mom!"

Then Jake ran through the house, to the door to the garage, opening it to look for Jenn's car.

It wasn't there.

"Mom!"

Jake then ran back through the house, flying up the stairs to his parents' bedroom.

"Mom!"

He searched their closet. Her clothes and suitcases were there. He looked in their bathroom. Her makeup and hairbrushes were there. He looked in the other upstairs bathroom, the bedrooms, every closet, every storage room, calling for Jenn before standing at the top of the stairs, looking down at Greg.

"Come down, son. Please."

"No! You're a *fucking* liar!"

Jake had never cursed and hearing it, with the anguish in his voice, was another piercing for Greg.

"Son, please come down."

"No! Liar!" Jake shouted then ran to his room, slamming the door behind him.

Greg started up the stairs after him before Kat tugged on his wrist.

"Let me handle this one, Greg," she said. "He needs time to absorb this. I'll talk to him."

Greg raked his fingers through his hair and nodded.

Ten

Buffalo, New York, Trailside Grove

Greg was confident Kat could calm Jake down.

Over the years, she had watched him more times than Greg could remember, often at the last minute when they couldn't find a sitter. Here was Kat, coming through again when he needed her. Greg left the stairs with his thoughts scattered, and he returned to the basement where his father was trying to decipher the remote.

"Where's Jake? How's he doing?" Vince asked, staring at the TV screen, scrolling through commands.

"In his room. Kat's talking to him."

"He's going to need time. I forget—how do I get this back on the TV?"

Greg took the control, switched the mode, muted the sound, then showed his dad how to surf channels, which Vince liked to do.

In the time that followed, Greg's phone rang, chimed, and vibrated with calls and messages of support from Jenn's friends, including updates from state trooper Rob Menza and watch captain Doug Tucker. Greg responded to as many as he could as Vince flipped through channel after channel. Everyone who'd contacted Greg was going all-out helping, or was searching, or was hopeful, or was praying, or was thinking of Jenn, Jake, and Greg.

But no one had discovered a single piece of information pointing to where Jenn was.

Suddenly her face appeared on the TV screen, over a graphic that said:

SEARCH FOR MISSING WOMAN

Greg took the control from Vince and turned up the volume on a Buffalo news channel report in time to catch the anchor saying: "...Jennifer Griffin, a thirty-six-year-old woman reported missing after attending a book club meeting in the Ripplewood, Trailside Grove area. According to police sources, it's too early to say if foul play is suspected in the case..."

The report showed the video recorded by the reporter from the *Bulletin*. There was footage of the canvass in Ripplewood, the helicopter, then Greg looking drawn and exhausted, talking to the reporters. A graphic below gave his name and the words HUSBAND OF MISSING WOMAN.

"What do you think happened?"

"I don't know. A breakdown, a carjacking. I don't know..."

The camera cut to the news anchor who said: "The search for Jennifer Griffin continues and any-

one with information is asked to contact police...
In other news, the fifty-million-dollar redevelopment project set for..."

Greg's chest tightened. He muted the TV and leaned forward.

"Foul play?" Greg cursed. "I don't know what to do, Dad."

Vince picked up the control and switched off the TV.

"That's the way they report these things," Vince said. "You hang on, do not lose faith. We're going to find her."

Greg said nothing.

"Is it possible she took off?" Vince asked. "Maybe had, I don't know, a nervous breakdown, and needed to get away, or something?"

"What?" Greg looked at his father. "No. You know Jenn. She'd never leave Jake. No."

Vince nodded.

"What did you and Jenn argue about? Jake said you fought about money?"

Greg shook his head.

"Competition for contracts is getting tough. I've got business loans for the truck, equipment. I'm carrying some debt. Now, Jake's going to need braces. Stuff like that, nothing serious."

"Sounds a little serious," Vince said.

"All right, I admit it. I get a bit stressed about work, but it's not going to make Jenn run away."

Vince's eyes swept over the scrapes on the backs of Greg's hands as if he were deciding on what, or what not, to think of them before shifting his attention to the stairs.

Jake came down into the basement dressed in pajamas. Kat was behind him, and he went right to Greg and threw his arms around him. Jake's skin was soft, his hair damp and he smelled of soap. Kat must've got him into the tub. Jake was always calmer and sleepy after a hot bath.

"I'm sorry I swore, Dad."

"We'll let it go."

"Aunt Kat says we're going to find Mom. She's going to come home, right?"

"We're doing all we can to make it happen."

Kat rubbed Jake's shoulder.

"He wants Dad and me to stay here tonight, okay?" Kat said.

"That'd be good," Greg said. "Okay with you, Dad?"

"You bet."

"We're going to go pick up some things. We'll be back soon," Kat said.

After they left, Greg offered to play Jake's go-kart video for him. Jake shook his head then he started crying again.

"Dad, can I sleep in your room tonight?"

"Sure."

"And in the morning, can I go with you, Aunt Kat, and Grandpa to search for Mom?"

"We'll see what the situation is in the morning. I'll have to talk to the teachers at your school. Some of them were helping us today."

Jake brushed at his tears.

Greg got the TV remote, pressed the commands to get online, and found a video of a beach with waves rolling over the sand in the moonlight. It was soothing. They watched without speaking. Jake fell asleep and Greg carried him to his bedroom, putting him on Jenn's side of the bed.

Greg went to the kitchen and resumed reading messages on his phone, coming to one that said:

If there's anything I can do for you, please reach out to me. Anything, at any time, Greg.

There was no name with the text, but he knew the number.

He took a breath and let it out slowly before texting back with one word:

Thanks.

Kat and Vince returned.

Within minutes, Kat began cleaning up the remnants of the tacos and nachos from downstairs. At the sink, running water, cleaning plates and utensils, she turned to Greg and Vince at the kitchen table.

"You need to go to bed, Greg," Kat said. "We'll search again in the morning."

He didn't argue.

In his room, Greg connected his phone to a charger cord and without removing his clothes, got into bed next to his son. Shutting his eyes, his body felt heavy as if under thousands of pounds of pressure at the bottom of the ocean, drowning in an abyss.

He woke, looked at the clock. He'd slept for a couple of hours.

Adrenaline was surging through him, words blazing across his mind.

"...too early to say if foul play is suspected..."

His heart hammered in his chest.

Where's Jenn? Where is she right now? If she were alive, she'd call.

Horrifying scenarios burned in the darkness.

And where was I? What was I doing?

His stomach writhing with guilt and fear, Greg dragged his hands over his face.

This is wrong. I can't rest. I've got to find Jenn before it's too late!

He got up and left a message for Kat and Vince, who were sleeping in the extra rooms.

For the second time, Greg went out alone before dawn to search for his missing wife.

Eleven

At sunrise, Al Clayton took in Phase 2 of Pine Castle Park and the streets of new houses in various stages of completion rising from the gouged earth.

He thought of how Greg was always the first to arrive at the building site, but not this morning.

Jenn was missing; it ate Clayton up. He shouted a curse as he navigated his truck deeper into the site because Greg was more than his boss—he and Jenn were friends. Clayton stopped, shifted into Park, gritted his teeth, and whispered a prayer that Jenn would come home to her family.

Then he grabbed his hard hat and got out.

Clayton didn't know how Greg could do it—demand to keep the job going—but on another level, he understood. They needed to keep the crew working.

We've got contractual deadlines, and projects are tough to get these days.

Taking care to watch his step along the dried, mud-rutted trails left by trucks and equipment,

Clayton walked alongside the different models of houses, their wooden skeletal frames evolving and taking shape. He continued past areas cleared to store building materials, insulation, shingles, framing lumber, roof trusses, and other preframed sections, eventually coming to lot #975 and #976, the two Greg had noted in their call. The subcontractors were on schedule.

Clayton knew #975 and #976 were ready to go, but would make another visual inspection.

The two lots had been excavated and were bordered with diminishing piles of dirt, in the process of being hauled from the site. The lots were ready for the next stages in the basement foundations. Forms for the footings had been installed, staked to the ground, waiting for concrete to be poured.

Twelve

At that same time, miles from where Al Clayton was in Pine Castle Park, Jayne Hicks was stretching on the porch of her friend Dianne Carr's house in Noble Haven.

A moment later, the door opened.

"Hey," Dianne said.

"Ready?"

"All set."

Dianne locked her front door and the two women, dressed in sweatpants and pullovers, headed off for their weekly ritual.

Jayne and Dianne had first met five years ago in the Wegmans parking lot where they struck up a friendly conversation. That meeting evolved into a friendship. Since then, Dianne and Jayne would set out weekly for a one-hour walk, even in Buffalo winters, varying their course depending on the weather, enjoying the serenity of the early morning. With the exception of a lone jogger or dog walker, they encountered few other people. As always, they used the time to catch up on each other's lives.

"Jeff's getting audited," Dianne said of her husband's auto parts business.

"Ouch," Dianne said.

"The accountant's not worried. She said everything's in order."

"Fingers crossed," Jayne said.

"Any word on Della?"

"Yes! She was accepted at Columbia and offered a scholarship!"

"Wow! Congratulations!"

"She's not sure she wants to go."

"Why?"

"She wants to start a pet grooming business."

"Maybe she's nervous about leaving home."

"We're going to talk about it this weekend. Let's go through the park."

The sun had risen.

Dawn washed over Noble Haven's western side as they left it, entering Bluebird Park. They followed a trail twisting through the forest, birdsong echoing in the still air. Moving deeper into the park, they enjoyed the rush of the stream that wove through the forest, punctuated with wooden footbridges.

"Did you see the news about that woman from Trailside Grove?" Jayne said.

"Yes, it's awful. Do they know what happened?"

"I don't think so."

They neared the park's western edge, which was bordered with a timeworn chain-link fence, overrun with brush and sagging in places. The fence separated the park from the expanse of forest that divided it from Ripplewood Creek.

Far off, part of the expanse spilled into the eastern side of Ripplewood, running parallel to Ripple Valley Boulevard, where the fence was in better shape, and the entrance gates were still secured with locks.

Jayne and Dianne were uncertain about the exact history of the expanse, which locals called Blueripple Woods. Going back, some said it was first federal property used for marshaling forces during the civil war. Then it was transferred to the state as timber stands; then passed to the county, which had used it to store park benches, tables, playground equipment, and other supplies years ago.

These days, it was largely neglected, not used in any official capacity, allowed to return to its natural state of dense forest. It held some mystery because it was laced with paths once used by the Union Army and old, dirt service lanes once used by public works trucks, now shrouded in overgrowth.

It was inviting to teens, to hikers, birdwatchers, and nature lovers, like Jayne, who loved the wildflowers that flourished there. She indicated a downed section of the chain-link fence, offering them access.

"Want to go through Blueripple today?" Jayne asked.

"I don't know," Dianne said. "They haven't found that missing woman."

"Oh, they must've searched in here," Jayne said,

reaching into her pocket, pulling out a pocket-size stun gun. Then she touched the panic alarm in the band wrapped around Dianne's upper arm. "Besides, we're together, we're equipped, and it's brighter now."

"I'm not sure." Dianne stared at the thick, waiting woods.

"I'll protect you," Jayne said. "Come on, it's been a while since we've gone in there. It's so pretty. Where's your sense of adventure?"

"All right."

They stepped carefully through the fallen fence, disappearing into the dense forest. Soon, they found the path they were familiar with, one that looped the area for under a half mile, before returning them to Bluebird Park.

The sun had climbed, and they'd progressed for some twenty minutes. At times, branches and scrub tugged and slapped at them, but the way the light filtered through the trees was their reward. It gave the forest a celestial aura.

"Look." Jayne, an amateur expert in local flora, pointed. "There's buckbean, and over there we have some goldthread."

"Pretty."

Jayne took out her phone to get some pictures, then they moved on.

"Oh no." Dianne halted. "I broke a lace. Hold on."

Dianne bent over to fix her shoe.

"Oh." Jayne reached for her camera. "There's some mayflowers. Oh—and dewdrops over there."

The flowers were on the shoulder of a narrow earthen road. As Jayne got closer to them, she froze, her gaze traveling beyond the shoulder of the road, to the edge of the bush.

Her lace fixed, Dianne stood.

Puzzled by Jayne, rooted to the ground, she went to her.

"What is it?" Dianne said.

Jayne raised her arm and pointed.

Dianne said, "Oh my God!"

Thirteen

Buffalo, New York, Trailside Grove, Blueripple Woods

Before Al Clayton got to the job site, before Jayne Hicks and Dianne Carr walked into Blueripple Woods, Greg drove mile after mile, through Trailside Grove, through Ripplewood Creek, down every street, alley, and service lane, searching the night for Jenn.

With every house and building he passed, his heart raced as he ran through scenarios: Did her car break down? Did she have a medical situation, or get disoriented with amnesia or something and drive away? Was she carjacked? Abducted?

Was she murdered?

Oh God. Jenn, where are you?

Greg was not a religious person. He'd turned away from his faith after God took his mother but now, as he confronted the awful, relentless fear he might never see Jenn again, he prayed.

He prayed as he guided his pickup out of his suburb, into the rural area on this side of Buffalo.

For what reason, he was unclear, only that he was drawn here by his unyielding need to find his wife.

Greg knew these paved country roads, navigating them as they climbed, cutting and turning through forests and pastures of farmland. The Ford's headlights reached into the darkness as he came to a lonely plateau on a hilltop, a sweeping curve with a view of the city lights below.

He pulled over and stopped.

This was Jack Pine Hill.

He'd find Jenn here.

In his memories.

This was where they'd come when they started dating. When he turned seventeen and borrowed his dad's truck, they'd come up here to watch the twinkling lights and talk, opening their hearts to each other in ways they'd never done with anyone before.

Looking at the lights, he was pulled across time and was with Jenn again, telling her about that day at Blessed Saints when his world stopped.

He was ten.

Sister Roberta had asked the class to draw and color a map of South America. Greg was coloring Brazil, trying to imagine a place without snow when he saw Sister Roberta meet the principal, Sister Mary, at the door. They talked in low voices, looking at him. Then Sister Roberta came to his desk, touched his arm, and whispered, "You must go now with Sister Mary."

Not knowing why his principal had summoned him, Greg went to the door. As he walked down the hall with Sister Mary, he heard Sister Roberta tell the class: "Stop your work, please. Now we're going to pray for Greg..."

Greg didn't need to keep remembering.

Sitting alone on Jack Pine Hill, looking at the lights, he knew what followed when he got to the principal's office.

He refused to think about it now, choosing to remember how Jenn had taken his hand when he'd first told her about it, and how she'd understood because of what had happened to her, her mother and father.

Greg could hear Jenn now...

My mom was a cashier at the old Colby Food Mart, working long hours, standing on her feet for each shift. But she still had time to make dresses for me... I remember she'd talk about things she'd learned in life, like how it was important to keep every promise you made to the people you love...

And I remember her smile, but it always seemed to be tinged with sadness... I don't know why... There were days I'd see her sitting alone in the kitchen, all quiet, like in her mind she had gone somewhere. She'd be drinking, rum and Coke, and sometimes she'd start crying, and if she caught me watching her, she'd pull me close, hug me so tight and say: "I love you more than anything in the whole world, Jenn..."

My dad worked hard, too, always driving his cab, or cleaning it. "Customers expect it to look and smell new, Jenn," he used to tell me on the days I helped him wash it. I thought it smelled like lilacs. And when he wasn't driving, he'd work on the doll house he was making for me. Sometimes he'd show me a card trick or other magic tricks. He was such a gentle man. He'd laugh so hard, watching my face light up whenever he'd pull a quarter from my ear then make it disappear into thin air.

Then one night, around Christmas, I woke up to screams... Our house was on fire. I couldn't get out of my bedroom, the hall was filled with flames, and the screaming... My mom and dad were screaming. I couldn't get to them... A firefighter smashed my bedroom window and saved me, but they couldn't save my mom and dad. I don't know why I survived. Why me? I'll never forget that night... I had no brothers, no sisters, no other relatives but my grandmother. I went to live with her. I was eight years old...

Jenn's tragedy broke Greg's heart.

When she first told him about it that night on Jack Pine Hill, he fell in love with her, wanting to protect her, believing they needed each other.

Now, gazing at the city lights, his heart surged.

I can't lose Jenn.

But Greg couldn't extinguish their tragic family history of losing parents, and he thought of Jake.

He needs his mother.

Then Greg's thoughts shifted to how in the last few months Jenn had grown detached but refused to acknowledge it, even denied it.

Could she have known about me? Is this all somehow related? Am I being punished somehow? I don't know. I don't know anything anymore.

Greg shook his head.

The rising sun had turned the sky to coral.

He sharpened his focus.

In the distant galaxy of the suburbs below, flashing emergency lights sped like a satellite through the streets. He dropped his window; the wailing siren flowed into his truck. Trying to locate where the vehicle was, he saw a second one, lights strobing as it zipped from the opposite end of what Greg realized was Trailside Grove.

He started his truck.

Watching for a moment longer, he saw the two emergency vehicles converge on the area where Bluebird Park bled into Ripplewood Creek.

He slid his transmission into Drive, wheeled the pickup around, and descended the hill.

Something's happening.

Greg pushed his Ford beyond the posted limit.

In a matter of minutes, he'd left the countryside, returning to the suburbs. Entering the fringes of Trailside Grove, thankful there was little early morning traffic, he blew through a few solid yellow lights.

Maybe it's a car accident? Maybe that's the emergency, he thought, rushing westbound on Sentinel Trail. As horrible as a crash would be, it gave him a measure of hope.

Then his phone rang. It was Kat. He grabbed it.

"Where are you?" she asked.

"I'm looking for her."

"Greg." She sighed, dropping her voice. "Jake's up. He's asking for you."

Greg adjusted his hold on his phone.

"Have there been any calls to the house in the last few minutes?"

"No. Why?"

"Something's going on around Trailside Grove and Ripplewood."

"What?"

A brilliant starburst flared in Greg's rearview mirror before the squawk of a siren.

"Hang on," Greg said to Kat, pulling over, slowing down, letting an Erie County Sheriff Deputy's car roar by, lights wigwagging.

"I heard that," Kat said. "Greg, what's going on?"

"Something with police. I have to go."

Ending the call, Greg accelerated on Sentinel, his eyes locked on the Erie County car as he pursued it. They tore out of Trailside's commercial strip, barreling along the divide between Trailside Grove and Noble Haven, then Bluebird Park. Greg's heart skipped as the Erie County car came upon Ripplewood Creek, taking the exit for Ripple Valley Boulevard with Greg following.

They passed St. Bartholomew's.

Up ahead, he saw a state police SUV, lights strobing, well off the street, alongside the edge of fencing on the isolated curve that bordered Blueripple Woods. It had driven on a short earthen entrance lane, concealed with overgrowth. The state car blocked the entrance at an opened chain-link gate. The Erie County Sheriff Deputy's car pulled to the shoulder near it, and the deputy got out and hurried into the woods.

Whatever was going on in there, was happening now.

Glancing at a man walking his dog, who'd stopped to watch, Greg parked his pickup nearby, got out, and went over to the two police cars.

No one was with them.

He maneuvered around the state police car, making his way along a narrow dirt road into the forest, noticing how the overgrown brush had been recently flattened. The air carried a jingle of keys, then crackled with dispatches over police radios. Blue-and-red light flashed among the gaps in the branches. Moving quickly, Greg followed the road to it.

As he came upon another state police SUV, he saw a trooper unspooling yellow plastic tape. Near it, two other uniformed officers were talking. One was using his radio, and as he turned, his eyes found Greg's.

It was Trooper Rob Menza.

In that instant, Greg caught a glint of sun reflecting on glass behind Menza, recognition dawning as he suddenly beheld it, nearly swallowed by thick covering branches and leaves, the familiar shape of a Toyota Corolla.

A blue one.

He knew the plate number.

Jenn's car.

"Mr. Griffin." Menza held up a palm stopping Greg's progress.

"That's my wife's car!"

"Sir, you have to leave." Menza called to the others. "We have to keep him away."

Two other officers emerged, each taking one of Greg's arms.

"Is she there?"

"Sir, you can't go in there," Menza said.

"Jenn!" Greg called out, struggling against the officers, radios crackling with calls concerning K-9 and crime scene techs. "Jenn!"

"We have to get you home," Menza said.

"Is my wife in there?"

"Mr. Griffin." Menza locked eyes with Greg. "You have to go home. There's nothing more you can do here."

His mind reeled, pulling him back to that day when he was ten.

Now we're going to pray for Greg.

Fourteen

Clarence, New York

That morning, in the Bureau of Criminal Investigation offices of the New York State Police Clarence Barracks, Claire Kozak was reviewing notes on a year-old harassment complaint when a shadow fell across her desk.

Lieutenant Phil Becker stood before her with an envelope in his hand.

"Erie's tossing the Trailside Grove missing mom case to us," he said.

"I thought that one was the county's."

"Jurisdictional gray zone. It's ours now and it's taken a turn."

"A turn?"

"There's a scene, a fresh one, just discovered."

"Where?"

"Blueripple Woods. Not sure what we've got, but I'm putting you and Ned on it. You're the lead, Claire."

"All right." Kozak closed her folders.

"Where's Ned anyway?"

"Kitchen, getting coffee."

Becker waited then nodded. "You two get out there. Access is from Ripple Valley Boulevard. I'll send you Trooper Menza's reports. He's there. Erie County's assisting."

"Okay, Phil." Kozak gathered a few items to leave.

"Oh." Becker, remembering, handed her the brown envelope. "This came for you late yesterday. Tracy put it on my desk."

Kozak paused, recognizing the return address. It was from her lawyer. She slid the envelope into her top drawer and closed it.

"Thanks, Phil."

After Becker left, Ned Carillo emerged.

"The Sabres need to make some trades for next year," he said, setting his coffee on his desk, "starting with—"

Kozak pulled Carillo's jacket from his chair, tossed it to him.

"Hey," he said.

"We've got to go."

"What's up?"

"We've got a new case."

Kozak updated Carillo on the way out. By the time they got to their unmarked Taurus, their phones and tablets pinged with the file from Becker. Kozak took the wheel while Carillo read aloud through Trooper Menza's missing person report for Jennifer Griffin. Upon finishing, Carillo showed her photos of Jennifer Griffin.

"She's pretty," Kozak said.

"So, she never made it home from her book club meeting."

Kozak nodded.

"And from Menza's preliminary look, no luck locating her phone, no activity on her cards or accounts," Carillo said.

Kozak nodded without commenting, and they retreated into their thoughts. As seasoned investigators, they knew not to get sucked into the frenzy of cases like this because that's when mistakes were made. You had to remain calm, cool, emotionally distanced, in control.

This was their case.

They'd been partners for over two years and Carillo knew just about everything about Kozak, from how she only drank cold Diet Coke in cans to the fact that you should never, ever, silence a Springsteen song on the car radio in her presence. And Kozak knew more than she cared to about Carillo. He was a fanatical Sabres fan, and loved spicy sausage with raw onions, making it Kozak's policy to keep Tic Tacs and Juicy Fruit gum in her bag, her desk, and the car.

As she drove, she was pleased to see Carillo had started a log with times, dates, locations, and running notes.

Nearing Ripplewood Creek, they stopped at a red light. While waiting, Carillo pulled out his phone to look through photos of Charlie, his retriever. How long had it been since his dog died?

Kozak turned away, giving him the moment. In that fragment of time, she thought of the brown envelope waiting in her desk. It held her final divorce papers. All she had to do was sign them to end her twenty-year marriage to Wade.

We just grew apart, Claire, Wade had told her.

That was after she'd discovered he was having an affair with their neighbor, Jessica. *A woman I used to have over for coffee.* Wade and Jessica moved to Brooklyn. Kozak kept the house. So much for vows, hopes, plans, and dreams. Their two teenage boys would live with her, and she'd live her life as a stronger, wiser woman.

She had no choice. That was the hand she was dealt.

Vanity of vanities; all is vanity, Kozak thought.

The light changed. Reflexively she tightened her hold on the wheel.

A short time later, they entered Ripplewood, got onto the boulevard. In the distance, they saw the flashing emergency lights and pulled up to the tangle of police vehicles, news cars, and vans.

Kozak parked on the shoulder.

Collecting what they needed and starting for the scene, they glanced at press people talking to the clutch of locals watching from across the street. Carillo nodded further off, where news camera operators were tight up alongside the chain-link fence, recording whatever they could. The investigators went to the trooper in the state car posted at the entrance gate, now cordoned with yellow tape.

"We're looking for Trooper Rob Menza," Carillo said.

The trooper's back stiffened at the plain-clothed couple before his eyes saw the badges clipped to their belts. He touched the brim of his hat, then pointed.

"In there. Follow the path."

The investigators lifted the tape and proceeded along the narrow, earthen road, overrun with brush, bent by recent traffic. Up ahead, strobing lights painted the forest red, white, and blue as they came to another knot of police vehicles, troopers, and deputies.

Menza was among them.

The trooper knew Carillo and Kozak, knew they outranked him and were going to assume command of the scene.

"Come over to my car. I'll get my notes, bring you up to speed on what we have."

Carillo and Kozak glanced toward the bright yellow crime scene tape, and the rear of the blue Corolla, nearly concealed by shrubs and branches. Then Carillo shook his head at all the police vehicles.

"Too many cooks in the kitchen here, Rob. We need to protect the scene."

"Well, it unfolded pretty fast, and the county was quick to help."

"No more people in here, unless we authorize," Kozak said.

"Got it," Menza said.

"Who's been tromping around the car?" Carillo said.

"Just me."

"And who's out in the woods around it?"

"Erie County's dog team, seeing if they can pick up anything."

"That's it?" Kozak asked. "You protected our scene?"

"I did. Erie County will put up the helicopter. And I notified FIU. They've been dispatched from Batavia and should be here anytime now."

"All right, let's go," Kozak said.

Menza began debriefing the detectives, relating the short history of the case, how Greg Griffin first reported his wife missing after a futile all-night search for her, how state police put out alerts, the subsequent canvass and search efforts, up to this morning's discovery by two walkers from Noble Haven.

"Jayne Hicks and Dianne Carr," Menza said.

Carillo cast around, looking in police cars.

"And where are they now?"

"I let them go home."

"You let them go home?" Carillo said.

"I have their statements and information."

"Was there anyone else present at the scene?" Kozak asked.

"Greg Griffin, the husband, arrived, like, within fifteen minutes of me."

"That fast?" Carillo said. "And where is he now?"

"He was pretty distraught, so I had Paulsen take him home."

"Is Paulsen sitting on the husband's house?" Kozak asked.

"Yes."

Carillo threw a look of frustration to Kozak, who absorbed it as they finished taking notes and tugged on latex gloves.

"All right, Rob," Kozak said. "Show us the exact way you traveled to her car."

Menza pointed to the route he took and the investigators followed it, alone, single file.

"Can you believe it, Claire? He lets key witnesses leave before we can talk to them."

"Nothing's ever perfect, Ned. We'll deal with it."

They stopped at the tape to survey the entire scene, assessing the stretch of pathway from which the car had been driven into the dense wild brush that swallowed it—or was used to conceal it.

Kozak used her camera to make a short video even though FIU, the Forensic Investigations Unit, would make recordings of everything. She preferred to make her own, as well.

They lifted the tape and inspected the car, confirmed by the plate as belonging to Jennifer and Greg Griffin. Brushing against the overgrowth, Kozak made another video as they first inspected the exterior for damage, or signs of violence. Finding none, she opened the driver's door to the immediate beep-pong chime indicating the keys were in the ignition.

The interior was empty.

No one was inside.

The chiming continued as Carillo searched the back and Kozak took the front. She found the registration in the glove box, studying it for further confirmation that this was Jennifer Griffin's car. The inside was clean. No immediate sign of a struggle or violence. On the passenger seat was a paperback copy of *Crime and Punishment* by Fyodor Dostoevsky.

The book club choice, Kozak figured.

Sliding her gloved fingers in the seats, looking under them, in the car's side pockets, Kozak found nothing.

No sign of Griffin, her bag, or any items.

Keys in the ignition, but she's gone.

"Anything back there, Ned?"

"Crumbs and some stains, maybe chocolate, like someone's eaten in the back seat."

"Likely her son," Kozak said, while making a video of the interior. When she was done, she said: "Maybe FIU will tell us more."

They closed the door, welcoming the end of the chiming, looked at the car and the dark forest, glancing in the direction of barking nearby.

"Okay," Carillo said, "so the husband reports her missing and goes out alone and looks all night, then calls it in, in the morning."

"Right."

"Menza talks to him at his house. He's got small, bloodied scratches."

"Yup."

More barking, then the crackling of chatter on radios.

"Then today, minutes after her car's found, he appears on the scene."

"Right."

"What do you make of that, Claire?"

"We'll be talking to Greg Griffin."

The barking continued. Then the investigators turned. Menza was approaching, waving to them.

"The dog team's found something!"

Fifteen

She can't be dead.

Seeing Jenn's Corolla, swallowed by the dense growth, gave way to Greg's imagining that she was out there, deep in the darkness, taken by the abyss.

What happened to her?

Still shaken, he used both hands to steady his hold on his coffee mug while he sat at the kitchen table across from Kat. The BLT she'd made him was untouched.

"Greg, did you actually see her?"

Looking at Kat, he said: "No."

His phone vibrated again. This time a text from a TV news channel requesting an interview. He ignored it.

"Did any cop actually tell you anything?" Kat asked.

He shook his head, turning to the window, eyes glistening as his sister looked him over. Hair mussed, face unshaven, worry lines from not sleeping, or eating.

And now this.

Greg had been out all night looking for Jenn. Then after daybreak, Greg followed police to Blueripple Woods, where they'd found Jenn's car. They'd held him back when he tried to look for her, upsetting him so much he was driven home in the back of a state trooper's car, nearly two hours ago.

"So no one said they'd found her?" Kat asked.

Greg shook his head.

Kat placed her hand on his.

"Then there's hope we'll find her," Kat said.

"Alive?"

"Yes, alive."

"How can you say that? I mean her car, the way it was when I saw it—I just don't—" His voice broke and he buried his face in his hands.

Kat moved to him and rubbed his shoulders.

Greg's phone rang. It was Liz Miller. He let it go to voice mail. Vince returned to the kitchen.

"That trooper's still parked out front, but a Channel 2 News truck pulled up."

As if cued, the doorbell rang.

"That'll be Channel Two," Vince said.

"Nobody talks to them," Greg said.

"But they may know something," Kat said.

"No," Greg said. "If there's something to know, I want it officially, privately, from police. Not while a news camera's rolling. Go tell them no comment, Kat. I mean it."

Less than a minute after she answered the front door, Kat returned.

"I told them we're not making any statements right now."

"Good. What did they say?"

"Here." She handed him a business card for Shayna Ward, Reporter. "She said they'll wait out front on the street, and that they know about Jenn's car, that police have an active crime scene at Ripplewood."

"An active crime scene?"

Greg shook his head. Police and press were waiting out front, friends and reporters calling. *An active crime scene.* He looked around at nothing, helpless when he thought—

"Where's Jake?"

"I told you. Downstairs," Kat said. "He's playing a video game online with Carter. He's got a headset on."

Greg left, opened the door to the basement, went far enough down the stairs to see his son engrossed in his game. Jake didn't see him. Greg returned to the kitchen, trying hard to form a clear thought, something he could anchor himself to.

"Kat, could you drive me to Ripplewood so I can get my truck? Dad, could you stay here with Jake?"

Kat and Vince looked at each other then back at Greg.

"You don't need to do that now," Kat said. "We could get a neighbor, or one of your crew, to do that."

The doorbell rang.

Greg frowned, figuring it was another reporter.

"I'll get it," he said.

At the front of the house, through the narrow pane of glass beside the door, Greg glimpsed two people on his doorstep. A man with short, neat, gray hair, wearing a jacket and loosened tie, and a woman with a jaw-length bob, dressed in a navy blazer and pants.

Both were sober-faced.

When Greg opened the door, they held up badges.

"Are you Gregory Griffin, husband of Jennifer Marie Griffin?" the woman asked.

"Yes."

"I'm Claire Kozak. This is Ned Carillo. We're New York State Police investigators, now in charge of your wife's case."

Now in charge.

"May we come in to talk, sir?"

Kozak held Greg with a steady gaze while Carillo made a quick, intense head-to-toe audit of his appearance and demeanor. Greg's thoughts whirled back to Sister Mary walking him down the hall, then he tried to remember his last moments with Jenn, the last thing he said to her. Squeezing the door handle hard, his knuckles whitened as he found the words.

"Did you find my wife?"

A few seconds passed; Kozak's eyes were locked on Greg.

"No. We found her car and we still have people working the scene. We'd like to come in and talk to you—"

Greg licked his lips.

"—and," Kozak continued, "we understand you have a son, Jake. Is he home now?"

"Yes. Why?"

"We'd like to talk to him first. Alone."

"Why? He doesn't—he's only eight. I should be there."

"You're not required to be present," Kozak said. "We can talk to him alone."

"I'm sure you want to cooperate, to help us locate Jennifer," Carillo said, casting a slight glance over his shoulder to the news cameras—now there were two crews—that were trained on them.

Greg opened his door wide, inviting the investigators inside.

Sixteen

Buffalo, New York, Trailside Grove

Greg led Carillo and Kozak to the kitchen where they introduced themselves to Kat and Vince.

They declined Kat's offer of coffee, and when Vince asked them about finding Jenn's car in Blueripple Woods, they revealed little, other than repeating what they'd told Greg.

The investigators' eyes went around the room, taking a quick inventory of everyone and everything before following Greg to the basement door.

Descending the stairs, they saw Jake, sitting on the floor at the coffee table working the controller for his game. He stopped, swept off his headset, and eyeballed the strangers who stood nearby while Greg went to the sofa.

"Sit with me, son," he said, shutting off the screen. "These people are with the police."

Jake stared at them, his face blank.

Kozak smiled. "I'm Claire."

"I'm Ned. Like your shirt." Carillo indicated Jake's Sabres T-shirt.

"They're going to help us find Mom," Greg said.

Jake looked at them, grappling to decide whether these strangers were on his side or if he should fear them.

"They're going to talk to you for a while."

Jake's blinking and breathing quickened with apprehension.

"You be a good boy and help them, okay?"

"But Dad, I'm—"

"It's all right, son. I'll be upstairs with Grandpa and Aunt Kat."

Greg hugged Jake, kissed the top of his head, tousled his hair softly then went up the stairs. Once the door closed, Carillo sat in the chair, and Kozak took Greg's place beside Jake.

Like most detectives, they knew kids were like barometers, able to give them an accurate reading of the pressure areas in a family. It's why their preferred strategy was to start with them.

"It's okay to be a little nervous," Kozak said. "We understand. I'm a mom, too. I have two boys, a bit older than you."

Jake looked at Kozak then Carillo, taking in the way they were dressed.

"Are you real police officers?"

"We are," Carillo said.

"You don't have uniforms. Do you have guns and badges?"

Carillo looked at Kozak, who nodded. They both showed him the grips of their holstered guns then their badges.

"We're detectives," Carillo said.

Jake's eyes widened. He swallowed hard, his chin creased, and he started crying, tears rolling down his cheeks.

"Is my mom dead?"

Kozak touched his shoulder and looked directly into his eyes.

"Oh, sweetheart, we have nothing that tells us she's been hurt, okay? It's our job to find her and bring her home, okay?"

Jake nodded.

"But we need your help. Do you want to help us find your mom, Jake?"

He nodded.

"Hey," Carillo said. "I really do like that shirt. You like the Sabres?"

Stretching his sleeve to wipe his tears, Jake nodded.

"Me too. Ever been to a game?" Carillo asked.

"A couple times with my dad."

"So, did your mom ever go to a game?" Carillo said.

"Just me and Dad."

"Jake," Kozak said. "I bet your mom likes going to her book club meetings, doesn't she?"

"She likes reading books."

"And I bet everybody likes your mom, too," Kozak said.

Jake nodded.

"Okay, this is where we need help. Can you think of anyone who might want to be mean to your mom?"

Jake thought, then shook his head.

"Maybe a time at a store, or in the neighborhood, or while driving, anything like that?"

Jake shook his head.

"All right, Jake. If you had to guess, why do you think she didn't come home from her last book club meeting? What do you think happened?"

Wiping at his face, he said: "Dad said that maybe she had a medical problem and got lost, or maybe she got a flat tire."

"All right. That's what Dad said," Kozak said. "Are there any other reasons you—*you, Jake*—can think of?"

He took a moment, then looked at the investigators as if unsure of how far he could go—what he could reveal.

"Don't worry," Kozak said. "Whatever you tell us stays with us." She pointed between him and herself. "It's confidential, you understand?"

He nodded.

"But it's very important you tell us what you think, what you feel, or what you know. And that you tell us the truth. That's how you can help us bring your mom home, okay?"

"Okay."

"So can you think of any other reasons why Mom didn't come home from her book club?"

He blinked back new tears.

"Maybe she was mad at me."

"Why would she be mad at you?"

"I keep forgetting to put the toilet seat down and she yelled at me."

"Yup." Carillo nodded seriously. "Moms don't like that."

"Okay," Kozak said, "is there anything else? Did she ever get mad at your dad? Or did he ever get mad at her?"

"I was thinking they wanted to get a divorce."

Kozak and Carillo let a beat pass before Kozak said: "What made you think that?"

Jake looked at Kozak and Carillo for a long moment.

"I heard them arguing about money and stuff."

"Did they tell you they were getting a divorce?" Kozak said.

"No. Dad said it wasn't true, about the divorce."

"They argued in front of you?" Kozak said.

"No, I was upstairs but I heard them."

"When was this?"

"For the last couple of months or so. They would argue about bills, my dad's business maybe moving to Arizona and stuff…"

"What about his business?" Kozak asked.

"I think Dad was saying that he was losing jobs and we were spending too much money and things would be better in Arizona with his friend."

"Did your mom like the idea of moving to Arizona?"

"I don't know."

"Did you?"

"No."

As Kozak took a moment, Carillo asked: "Your dad has some fairly new scrapes on the backs of his hands. Did you see them?"

"Yes."

"Did he tell you how he got them?"

"No, but I would guess from work."

"Do you know if your dad ever hit your mom, Jake?" Carillo asked.

"Hit her?" Jake shook his head. "No!"

"Is there anything else you think we should know about your mom?" Kozak asked.

"Well, sometimes, in the last couple of months, she'd just sit alone, not reading a book or looking on her phone. Just sitting alone all quiet."

"Did she ever tell you why?"

"No, but it was like she was sad about something."

Kozak nodded and Jake continued.

"So I think Mom was mad at me and Dad and wanted a divorce and she ran away from us."

Jake lowered his head and cried.

"Oh, sweetheart," Kozak said. "These things are always complicated. You're very brave to help us."

"You did a good job," Carillo said.

Jake sniffed while staring at his feet.

"I want Mom to come home. I've been putting the seat down every time now. I just want her to come home."

Seventeen

Buffalo, New York, Trailside Grove

Greg's hands were clenched fists as he stared across his desk at Carillo and Kozak.

They'd closed the door before sitting down in his home office.

"Is my wife dead? Tell me right here and right now."

"We don't know," Kozak said.

"You must know something. How the hell did her car get in Blueripple? No way she'd drive in there after a book club meeting. It makes no sense."

"That's what we're investigating," Kozak said, touching commands on her phone, setting it on his desk. Greg had agreed to allow them to record their conversation.

"You must've found something besides her car, something to tell you what or who or—"

Greg looked away at nothing while the investigators stared at him for several seconds, their faces blank.

"Greg," Kozak said. "We can't disclose if we

found anything, or not. At this time, we haven't located Jennifer, but we're stepping up our search and our investigation."

"We need your help with some questions," Carillo said.

Jenn smiled at Greg from her picture on his desk, her disappearance like a sledgehammer, pounding the truth into his gut.

She's gone. She's gone. She's gone.

He looked at the drawings for the Pine Castle job, the invoices, emails, and contract bids, all neatly organized on his desk. The importance of his work was melting in the heat of his torment, but he had to be careful.

"We understand you're a contractor and Jennifer is an optometric assistant?" Kozak said.

"She works at Crystallo View Optical and I run Solid and Strong Contracting."

"We have your statement from Trooper Menza, but let's go over that night. After work at Pine Castle, you went to the Mulberry Bar in Depew with your crew?"

"Yes."

"Now, after the bar, you got home about nine thirty, your wife was still at her book club. You went to bed, but when you woke up around one thirty, she wasn't home. You searched for her alone until you called police about four hours later."

"Yes."

"Did Jennifer have any issues at work?" Carillo asked.

"No, nothing that I know of."

"And how's business going?" Carillo asked.

"Things are tight."

"Are you facing a large debt load?"

"We're handling things."

"Would you say you're facing some financial stress?"

"Yes, but I'm looking at options to help get us through—what's this got to do with—"

"What about Jennifer? How're things going for her?"

"Fine. No problems. That's why this makes no sense." He shook his head. "It's—just so—damn—"

"Greg," Kozak said. "We have no evidence to confirm she's been hurt. At this point, she's missing."

"Under suspicious circumstances," Carillo added. "So you must brace for anything."

Greg shut his eyes for several seconds. When he opened them again, the detectives asked him to give them a timeline of his search leading up to the moment he called police. Again, Greg related the history of Jenn's disappearance with Carillo and Kozak asking questions and taking notes.

"Do you know of anyone who might want to hurt her?" Kozak asked.

"No."

"Is there anyone she doesn't get along with? Any long-standing or recent feuds, or enemies?"

Greg shook his head.

"Everyone loves Jenn. She's involved in everything—her book club, yoga class, parent-teacher stuff and committees at Jake's school, neighborhood charities, the church... Everyone loves her."

"Has she received any recent threats at home, at work, socially, any run-ins with anyone?" Kozak asked.

"No."

"Any unusual phone calls, hang ups, wrong numbers?" Carillo asked.

"No."

"Anyone lost, looking for directions?" Kozak added.

"No."

"Any strangers coming to the door, door-to-door salespeople, or tradespeople recently in the house?" Carillo asked.

Greg thought then shook his head.

"No, no one that I know of. Wait, I think we had a cable service guy come a few weeks ago. Maybe last month."

"Do you have the name?" Kozak said.

"I'll look up the invoice and send it to you."

"All right," Kozak continued. "Does Jennifer have any medical conditions, or recent surgeries?"

"I already answered much of this for the trooper."

"That was preliminary work. Bear with us."

"No medical conditions, no surgeries."

"Is she currently under a doctor's care, for any physical or mental treatment?" Kozak asked. "Is she taking any doctor-prescribed medication?"

"No to all of that."

"Has she been despondent lately? Has she been

having suicidal thoughts, or is she seeing a therapist?"

Greg hesitated.

If he told them Jenn had been withdrawn, distant, they'd want to know why, and that was a door he couldn't open.

"Greg?" Kozak said.

"No."

"Does she have any addictions to any type of drugs?"

"No."

"Gambling?"

"No."

"Any large debts?"

"No, I told you."

"Could she have met someone online?" Carillo asked.

"No, I doubt that."

"How would you know?"

"I know my wife."

"Could she have been scammed online?" Carillo said.

"No, I don't think so. She's smart and careful. Her activity with social media was only with people she knew, or tied to her activities with the school, book club, that sort of thing."

"A lot of careful and very smart people are getting taken in by some pretty elaborate schemes," Carillo said. "Before they know it, things get out of control, they get embarrassed, keep it quiet, try to get ahead of it, or there are threats against them or the family if they tell anyone."

"Are you telling me that's what you think happened?" Greg said.

"It's a possibility," Carillo said.

"No, oh no."

"We have no evidence of that," Carillo assured Greg. "It's only a possibility."

Kozak adjusted her position in her chair.

"Greg, how would you characterize your marriage?"

"Good."

"Did the subject of divorce ever come up?" Kozak asked.

"Absolutely not. Is this from Jake? Look, he's eight, his mom's missing, and he's scared. Jenn and I are not getting a divorce."

"Do you argue?"

"Yes. Don't all married couples argue?"

"Did you argue in the time before you reported Jenn missing?"

"No."

"Did you ever lose your temper in an argument?" Kozak asked.

Greg stared at her.

"Ever strike your wife?" Carillo asked.

Greg's jaw muscles pulsed.

"No."

"Do you own a gun?" Carillo asked.

"No."

"Do you possess any firearms?" Carillo asked.

"No."

"Is it possible Jenn was having an affair?" Kozak asked.

"No."

"Maybe she met someone on a dating site or in one of her many activities?" Carillo said.

"No."

"Can you be certain?" Carillo asked.

Almost whispering, Greg said: "No."

"How did you get those scratches on your hands?" Kozak asked.

"I told Menza. A traffic cone got stuck under my truck."

"When you were on Ripple Valley Boulevard, not far from the entrance gate to Blueripple?"

"That's what I told Menza."

"Is there a life insurance policy for Jenn?" Kozak asked.

Greg didn't answer immediately. "Yes, for three hundred thousand dollars."

"And who's the beneficiary?"

"Me."

Kozak nodded, then said: "Greg, you've already volunteered to let us check Jenn's phone—"

"Wait, did you find her phone in her car?"

"We're not disclosing what we found," Carillo said.

"We need her computer," Kozak said. "Our forensic people will come over to get her computer and your devices too, your phones, computers, accounts. We'll get warrants."

"Warrants—what? But why—"

"It's all routine, procedural. And we'll have them get your fingerprints, as well," Kozak said.

"Greg—" Carillo leaned closer "—are you involved in any way in your wife's disappearance?"

"God no!"

"Do you know or suspect anyone who might be involved?"

Greg shook his head.

"One final matter," Kozak said. "Would you agree to submit to a polygraph, if we requested it?"

"A polygraph? Why?"

"Again, it's routine," Carillo said.

"Greg, we want to cross you off the list as soon as possible," Kozak said.

"What list? I don't get it."

"Greg, you were the one who reported her missing."

"But I'm her husband."

Kozak and Carillo looked at him, their expressions betraying nothing.

"Yes, you are," Kozak said.

A long moment passed. Kozak picked up her phone, then she and Carillo left Greg alone to stare at Jenn's face in the picture on his desk.

He thought of the girl who'd broken his heart that day, crying near the school cafeteria. He thought of their dreams and this house—*our forever home*—that he built for them, and how now, the walls were closing in.

Eighteen

Vince kept turning his ballcap over in his hands, which were creased by a lifetime of laying brick. He stared blankly, blinking several times.

"Jenn is like my second daughter."

Carillo and Kozak had taken him aside to interview him in one of the bedrooms, where they'd closed the door and for thirty minutes asked questions about his daughter-in-law.

"The last time I saw Jenn?" He thought. "About four or five days ago, she was driving in town. I'd gone to Walgreens to pick up my prescription. She was in her Corolla at a traffic light on Cordoba Avenue."

"What was her demeanor?" Kozak asked.

"She seemed happy, wiggling her fingers, waving at me."

Vince looked at the floor.

"You found her car," he said. "What does that mean? What happened to her?"

"We're doing everything we can to answer that," Carillo said.

"And we're hoping for the best," Kozak added.

As they wrapped up, they asked Vince if there was anything he thought they should know.

"I tell you, she's a saint. She loves my son. She's devoted to my grandson. She doesn't have an enemy in the world."

He cleared his throat.

"I know she's had a hard life. My family's had a tough time, too." He covered his face and his voice broke. "We gotta do everything to find her. If we lose Jenn…"

"It's true," Kat said. "Everybody loves Jenn."

Greg had gone to the basement to be with Jake, so Carillo and Kozak used his office to interview her.

Kat looked at the photo of Jenn and Jake on Greg's desk as they took her through a range of questions, including Jenn's relationship with Greg.

"I don't know if there were any issues with their marriage," Kat said. "But, does anyone really know what's going on with a married couple?"

"Did Jenn ever confide any problems to you?" Kozak asked.

"No, we didn't have that kind of connection," Kat said. "But, to be honest, when you look at all the possibilities, the way you just listed them, yeah, anything's possible."

"What do you mean?" Carillo said.

"She could've been having an affair. Who knows?

I might be wrong, but I get the sense that Jenn might not have been happy."

"What makes you say that?" Kozak asked.

"I don't know. A feeling, I guess. She just seemed a little sad to me," Kat said. "But in my heart, I believe we'll find her. I believe she'll come home."

When Carillo and Kozak left the Griffins' house, a dozen newspeople were waiting for them on the street.

Shouldering their way through, they recognized some of the reporters who knew them from other cases. Extending microphones and recorders, they called out questions.

"Hey, Ned, did you find Jennifer Griffin?"

"No comment," Carillo said.

"Claire, do you have a suspect?"

She didn't answer.

"Any arrests?"

No response.

"Come on, Claire."

"Give us a break, Ned."

The detectives got into their Taurus with Kozak at the wheel.

They'd gone about four blocks in silence, Ned watching the suburb roll by before saying: "Those scrapes on his hands bother me. I think he's hiding something."

Kozak turned to Carillo.

"Of course he is. We never get the whole truth in the first round."

Nineteen

Buffalo, New York

*O*ne more time.

Laila Price switched on her living room TV to a blast of static and snow. Pressing buttons on her remote, she went from channel to channel only to find the same hissing blizzard.

Nothing had changed.

The cable was still out.

So was their internet.

Switching off the TV, Laila looked at her phone. At least it had a connection. She scrolled through her calendar, relieved somebody from Distinctly Connex, the cable company, was coming between one and three this afternoon. Her husband, Darrell, would be home by then. He could deal with the cable person.

It was almost 9:30 now.

She'd put the laundry away later. Looking forward to her day off, a day of errands, shopping, and coffee with a friend, Laila got ready to go out. Grabbing her keys and her purse, she went to the garage, pushed the button. The door lifted. She went to her car but stopped. A white van with no markings but a flashing yellow light had just parked in her driveway, blocking her exit. A man studying his clipboard looked up and gave her a little wave from behind the wheel.

Laila went to the driver's door. The window was down.

"Are you the cable guy?"

"Yes, ma'am."

"They told us you were coming this afternoon."

He paged through his clipboard. She noticed the name on his ID tag was Zoran Volk.

"My job sheet says from nine to twelve. A mix-up, maybe." His eyes took a quick walk over Laila, her bag, keys in hand. "It's no problem, if you want to reschedule. You have to call in."

"Mmm," Laila said.

"It might be ten days or longer before we get back."

"That long?"

"We're backed up."

"How long do you think it would take to fix it now?"

"All I got on my sheet is your cable and internet are out."

"That's right."

"Well, I gotta check outside, then inside, all your connections and signal levels."

She noticed a glint of a gold filling as he sucked air through his teeth.

"Forty-five minutes, give or take. Depends on the problem," he said.

"Forty-five minutes?" Laila knew Darrell would not survive being TV-less for ten days. "We'll do this now. Come to the front door."

"I'll check outside first."

"Okay, ring the front bell when you need to come in."

Laila returned through the garage and closed the door. She went to her living room sofa and sent messages on her phone, rearranging her errands and coffee date with Alicia.

This was not the morning she'd planned. They'd set it up for Darrell to be here. She preferred having her husband around whenever service people had to work in the house. But she had to get this done. Reaching for her tablet, she resumed reading the thriller she was enjoying.

She heard the faint jangle of a tool belt and through the window glimpsed the cable guy outside, walking around the house. Knowing he was out there made it hard to concentrate. Everything soon went quiet. She was starting to get back into her book, was halfway through a chapter, when she jumped.

The doorbell chimed loud and clear.

Exhaling, Laila opened the door.

"Hi again," the cable guy said, his tool belt laden with pliers, screwdrivers, and other items. He was holding a device that looked like a credit card reader. "Everything looks good outside."

He was tall, taller than Darrell, who was six

even. His sleeves were rolled. His arms were muscular and tattooed. He had thick, wavy hair, was unshaven with what looked like a three-day scruff. His cool, deep-set eyes took a lightning-quick appraisal of her body before meeting hers.

"I need to look around inside. It could be a bad splitter, or a system problem. My sheet says you have two TV hookups and one for internet. Where are they?"

"There's a TV in the living room." She nodded toward it. "And upstairs there's a TV in the bedroom, and I think the internet's hooked up in the office upstairs too."

"I need to start with the network box."

"I don't know what that is, or where it is."

He smiled. "They're usually in the basement. I can find it if you show me the way."

After pointing to the basement door, Laila returned to the sofa. She tried to resume reading but couldn't, not while she could hear him working. She started to text Darrell to let him know what was happening but stopped. Why not wait until it was fixed, or let him be surprised when he got home? It wasn't long before she heard the clink of his tool belt as Zoran Volk climbed the stairs.

"Hello?" he said before finding her in the living room.

"Right here."

"It's all good down there now."

"Great."

"I need to check the other connections. I'll work on the TV here, then go upstairs."

"Sure. I got some things to do in the kitchen."

The house had an open concept. While farther from him, Laila could still see him in the living room as she took inventory of the contents of the fridge, cupboards, and the pantry to make a grocery list.

"—get on the road to success with the new—"

"—Don't miss the next episode of—"

"—are you certain of the diagnosis, Doctor—"

The TV had come to life. Laila went to the living room. He handed her the remote, and she flipped through some channels before shutting it off.

"This is great. Thanks."

"I've got to check your connections upstairs. You said you had two?"

"But it's fixed?"

"I have to be thorough, make sure a problem in the system doesn't reoccur."

Laila didn't feel comfortable and suddenly remembered the laundry, which had slipped her mind.

"Well, things are a mess up there."

"There isn't anything I haven't seen. My supervisor's been—" he started then caught himself. "Ma'am, it's my job. I gotta check."

"Sure."

She led him upstairs to her cluttered home office and the bedroom where the clothes she'd taken out of the dryer earlier were still in the laundry basket, waiting on the bed to be put away.

"That is one huge bed," he said. "What kind is it?"

"It's a Texas King."

His voice lowered, as if talking to himself. It

sounded like he said: "I bet you have a lot of fun on it…"

"Excuse me?" Laila looked at him.

An icy second passed between them then her phone rang, and she pushed her attention to it. The number came up for Laila's downtown office. "I'll take this in my office. I have to move stuff around my computer out of the way for you anyway." She looked at him with a flicker of bewilderment as her phone continued ringing.

"Sure, I'll start here," he said.

She nodded.

Stepping into her office, she answered her phone. It was her girlfriend, Carlotta, and while still taken aback by what she'd thought the cable guy had said, Laila welcomed her call.

"Hey, Laila, I just had to call you. You won't believe what bossy pants did today…"

Phone to her ear, she turned to close the office door.

She had nearly shut it all the way when she froze.

She couldn't believe what she saw in her bedroom.

"Oh my God!"

The cable guy had reached into the laundry basket, plucked out Laila's underwear, then pressed his nose into it, sniffing it before putting it back.

Laila turned her back and stepped farther into her office.

"What? What is it, Laila?" Carlotta asked.

Grappling to think, she said, "I spilled my coffee. It went everywhere."

"Oh no! Why don't you call me back?"

"I'm sorry, Carlotta."

"No worries. Call me when you can."

Laila cupped her hands over her mouth, not believing what she'd seen.

Standing there for a long moment, taking deep breaths, she tried to think. Her eyes went to her scissors. She slid them into her pocket then cleared the clutter from her desk. She opened her office door to leave and caught her breath.

He was standing there.

"Done in the bedroom."

"Sure." She pointed to her computer. "There you go. I'll wait downstairs for you to finish."

Laila hurried down the steps, her mind racing.

Oh God, oh God. I want him out!

She went to the closet near the garage door and rummaged through a drawer filled with small tools, batteries, string, and all kinds of tape. She hated guns. There were no guns in her house. Darrell had got her a key-chain mini can of pepper spray last year for Christmas. Laila found it and clenched it in her hand.

Stay calm. Be cool. He likely doesn't know I saw him. Go through the motions and get him out.

She was near the door when she heard his tool belt as he descended the stairs.

"All done. You're all good," he said.

"Thank you." She opened the door for him. "Thank you very much."

"One last thing," he said. "I need you to sign my job sheet. Tablet's in my truck."

"I'll walk out with you."

He opened the passenger door of his truck, got his tablet, began typing several commands, then turned the screen to her. He extended a stylus pen.

"At the bottom," he said, holding the tablet for her.

Laila signed, hoping he couldn't see the pepper spray she was concealing in one hand. She held out the pen for him. Taking it, he brushed his fingers over hers, sending a shiver coiling up her spine.

"You got a nice house," he said.

"Thanks." She tightened her grip on the pepper spray.

"A real nice house and that bed—wow."

He tossed the tablet in his truck, walked around, climbed in, switched off his flashing light, started it, then backed out of the driveway, waving at Laila standing there, watching until he vanished down the street.

What just happened?

She went back into her house, closed the door, leaning back against it, stifling a sob, numbed by the sense of violation. She looked at the spray can then withdrew the scissors.

Get a grip. It's over. He's gone.

After taking a long moment to regain her composure, she texted Alicia, then got into her car, intending to meet her for coffee.

Still shaken, Laila took several more deep breaths as she drove through her neighborhood of Cardinal Hill, which bordered Trailside Grove.

She was unaware that Zoran Volk was following her.

Twenty

"**I**'m scared to death," Liz Miller said, tapping a curled knuckle to her lips and looking at April Kent.

They were at Liz's house getting ready to join the growing number of volunteers in the ongoing search for Jenn.

"It's frightening," April said, reading news updates on her phone.

The discovery of Jenn's car had intensified the investigation. Areas to be canvassed and searched had been widened, encompassing more neighborhoods, schoolyards, parks, and forests. A page offering a reward fund for information to help find Jenn had been established online. Social media posts of support increased along with rumors and speculation about her disappearance.

Liz continued tapping her knuckle to her lips, glancing around her house, pushing back tears.

"I feel so guilty because the last anyone saw of

Jenn was here—in my house, in my living room, right there, in that chair!"

Outside, the hammering of an approaching helicopter rose as April looked at the chair, remembering how she had sat beside Jenn. The helicopter's thrumming grew louder, pulling her back to their book club meeting.

They'd been discussing *Crime and Punishment* before taking a break to dig into the cheese, crackers, veggies, and pastries Liz had arranged on her kitchen counter. April and Jenn were the first to return to their seats with theirs while the others were still making selections and talking at the counter.

"These raspberry tarts are incredible, Liz!" Jenn called out, holding her plate close as she bit into a tiny pastry.

Jenn was wearing a mauve turtleneck and blazer. When she reached for her drink, her cuff receded and April saw the bruise. Then Jenn brushed at her hair and April saw a second bruise on her neck, peeking from the edge of her collar.

Concern swirled in April's heart.

How many bruises did Jenn have?

As a retired nurse, April had seen this so many times. She was skilled at identifying the signs of domestic violence; knew it was far more prevalent than most people realized.

Jenn caught her staring.

"What is it? Do I have food on my face?" Jenn asked.

"I like your outfit."

"Oh thanks. I love your shirt and that necklace."

April smiled, acknowledging her compliment, then glanced to ensure the others were still out of earshot.

"What happened, Jenn?"

"What happened? What do you mean?"

Ensuring no one was near, April touched her own neck and wrist area.

"Oh." She blinked fast, chuckling. "It's funny. I was playing football in the backyard with Greg and Jake, and Greg tackled me and Jake piled on. Too many boys in the house and I bruise so easily. I'm such a marshmallow."

April glanced to the others, who were breaking from the table.

"Jenn," April said, keeping her voice low, "if ever you'd like to talk in complete confidence, just call me."

Jenn shut her eyes and let out a breath.

"I love you, April. Thank you. But don't be silly."

The helicopter had passed over them and now sounded like distant thunder.

"We have to find her," Liz said. "We just have to. I can't bear to think of the agony Jake must be going through."

"He's such a sweet boy," April said.

"And Greg," Liz said. "He looked traumatized. He must be going out of his mind, that poor man."

That poor man?

April said nothing, prompting Liz to look at her until a memory surfaced.

"When Greg talked to us, you seemed a little reserved," Liz said.

"Did I?"

"Yes, a little cool to him, I thought."

"Did you see the scrapes on his hands, Liz?"

"Yes. Why?"

"They looked, well, fresh, and I was wondering how he got them."

"Likely from his work as a carpenter, contractor, you know."

Liz's phone rang and she answered it while April returned to her phone and the news stories and social media posts on Jenn. The whole time she scrolled, she couldn't subdue her unease about Greg's scrapes and Jenn's bruises. As far as April knew, no one else in the club had spotted them.

"That was Basha," Liz said. "She and the others will meet us at one of the new search sites—the Empire Heights School in West Trailside Grove."

"All right."

"Basha said the police are arranging to talk to her some more. This time it'll be the detectives who are now in charge of the case because she was actually the last person to see and talk with Jenn. Basha said the detectives will likely talk with us, as well."

"Good," April said.

Twenty-One

Buffalo, New York

Why is that guy familiar?

Kat watched the man moving among the volunteers at the Empire Heights School, greeting people with a consolatory look on his face.

He was a handsome man.

Kat tried to place where she'd seen him before. Yes, he was at the previous search in Ripplewood, but that wasn't it. Kat had definitely seen him somewhere before that—but where?

"We can't go through this again, Kat."

She turned to her father and saw the anguish in his eyes.

"We can't lose another member of our family."

Kat put her arms around him.

"It's going to work out, Dad."

Kat and Vince had come to the school to take part in the day's search while Greg stayed home with Jake, awaiting police who—as Kozak put it— "would go through the formality of executing a warrant" to take the phones, tablets, and computers from the house for analysis. It left Greg scrambling to get replacements so he could continue communicating with his family, friends, and work crew.

From the news stories online that Kat had seen, the investigation had escalated. A couple of miles away in Ripplewood, police had sealed a large section of the woods. They'd taken control, using dogs, ATVs, drones, officers, and helicopters to scour the forest where Jenn's car had been discovered, while forensic experts processed the scene.

In Trailside Grove, Noble Haven, and half a dozen other neighborhoods across the suburbs, police guided an army of volunteers in the growing search, encompassing parks, playground service lanes, alleys, vacant lots, fields, ravines, and creeks.

The Empire Heights School was less than half a mile from Greg and Jenn's house. It was adjacent to soccer fields, tennis courts, a basketball court, a playground, and a flat, green expanse vast enough for a football field. Close to a hundred volunteers had gathered and more were arriving.

"See?" Vince took in the sight. "Everyone loves Jenn. Look at this outpouring of support."

As Kat surveyed the activity, she was stabbed with raw emotion.

This would not happen if I was missing.

Her thoughts twisted and scraped, like an old key in a lock, opening to her true feelings for Jenn. On the surface they were friendly to each other, but deep down, Kat disliked Jenn. Sure, the world thought Jenn walked on water, but as far as Kat was concerned, Jenn was far from perfect.

Kat's feelings went back years, to Greg and Jenn's wedding.

Jenn never invited Kat to be matron of honor, or even a bridesmaid, at their wedding. All of it was made worse when some offhand comments Jenn had made on the reason got back to Kat; Jenn saying something about how, "Kat's got a lot on her plate and seems to be struggling right now. Besides, we want the wedding to go smoothly, right?"

It was true. At the time of the wedding, Kat's marriage to Neil was crumbling. But, dammit, was that a reason to shut her out of her brother's biggest day—a day that would have made their mother so happy? Being involved would've given Kat some happiness at a time she was struggling. It would've meant so much. Why didn't Jenn see that?

Kat was devastated. The hurt was the first of many Jenn had inflicted on her. There were times when Jenn had made Kat feel unwelcome when she visited their home. Jenn always seemed to grow a little colder whenever Kat, trying to be helpful, mentioned little things about Greg's likes and dislikes about food, about clothes, and so on. And when Kat and Neil were headed for divorce, there were times when Jenn gave her unsolicited marriage advice, to Kat's chagrin.

"Did you consider Neil might be…" Or "Kat, I read this article and thought of you…" Or "Maybe you and Neil should go to…"

Then, after her divorce, Jenn offered more unsolicited advice, even tried to set her up on a few dates. All of it may have been unintentional, or innocent, but Kat was rankled by it. She hadn't re-married. Her life, it seemed, had been a string of less-than-stellar men, and relationships that always dead-ended. Kat was constantly examining her-self as a divorced courier driver, worrying about her looks as she got older, concerned that she may never find real love and get married.

Yes, other people had it worse.

And Dad was right. Jenn, orphaned by fire as a child, had certainly had a hard life.

But so have I.

Kat was fifteen when her mother died. The cat-aclysmic loss nearly destroyed her, but she found the strength to carry on, to honor her mom. Her father was broken. Greg was lost. While grieving, Kat did everything she could to keep her family together by assuming her mother's role, watching out for her little brother and their dad. She went from being a teenage girl to an adult. Part of her life had been taken from her. Maybe that's why her relationships went nowhere. Maybe that's why she secretly resented Jenn.

Stop it! Jenn's the closest thing I have to a sister. Look around. This is real. She's missing.

"Are you okay?" asked Bert Cobb, a custodian at Jake's school.

Cobb was part of the school search contingent. Vince had stepped away to talk to some of them. Brushing at her tears, Kat smiled at Cobb. She'd made deliveries to him at the school a few times. He seemed like a nice guy.

"Thanks. I'm just worried, you know."

"We'll find her," he said.

"I'm praying we do."

"Just look how massive the searches are getting." Cobb cast around. "Where's Greg?"

"Home with Jake. Police stuff."

"How's Jake doing?"

"Oh, the best he can."

"I guess they won't be moving to Arizona. I mean, with this happening."

"Arizona?" Kat was now looking toward the group of searchers from Jake's school and that good-looking man again, talking to some officials.

"Jake was talking about it at school a little while ago."

"Oh yeah, they were thinking about it," Kat said. "Say—" she nodded to the man in the distance "—who's that guy, greeting everybody there from Jake's school?"

Cobb looked.

"Porter Sellwin. He's on the school board." Cobb leaned closer to Kat. "I understand he's quite the Casanova."

Kat stared at Sellwin for a long moment as it became crystalline.

She'd definitely seen Sellwin before.

He'd been with Jenn before she disappeared.

Twenty-Two

Buffalo, New York

Coffee rolled over the brim of Laila's cup and dripped on the table.

"Goodness, honey, be careful." Alicia reached for napkins, laughed then looked at Laila.

She wasn't smiling.

Laila's gaze flitted around the restaurant. The cable guy's surprise arrival at her home had forced her to rearrange her errands. Some took longer than she had expected. It pushed her coffee date with Alicia at The Pink Mist Mountain Café well into the afternoon. Laila had thought that keeping busy would keep her mind off what had happened.

She'd thought wrong—she was still a bit shaky.

Alicia set the damp, balled napkins aside, her smile fading as she studied her friend.

"What's eating you? Ever since you got here, you've seemed rattled."

Laila looked at her hands, twisted her rings.

"Something happened this morning, something…disgusting and a little scary." Tears came to her eyes.

"What?" Alicia put her hand on Laila's. "Tell me."

Laila looked at Alicia. They had become friends years ago in college. Laila became a copywriter. Alicia Hughes was now an editor with a New York publisher; she was a smart, kindhearted woman who was one of Laila's closest friends, someone she trusted.

"Go on," Alicia said. "What happened?"

Laila bit her bottom lip then began describing what had taken place with the cable man in her house. She included everything she saw, everything she felt, and everything she did before he left. Her hands were shaking when she finished.

Alicia's mouth fell open slightly in disbelief.

"Oh my God. You've got to report him."

"To the cable company?"

"To the police."

"Police? But he didn't hurt me."

"Not physically. *Not this time.*"

"What do you mean 'not this time'?"

"What if he comes back? He's been in your house, knows your address. What if he was just scoping your place and came back some night when Darrell wasn't home?"

Laila fell silent, twisting her ring.

Alicia recognized she'd unintentionally frightened her friend, so she pulled back. "Okay, I'm sorry if I scared you," she said.

"Well, he sure scared me."

"Look, I know he didn't hurt you physically, but

what he did must constitute a crime, some form of assault that needs to be reported."

"After it happened," Laila said, "I was thinking he must have some kind of sniffing fetish, that he gets a thrill from smelling underwear."

"It's so, so yuck, so perverse, makes my skin crawl. You've got to report him. You're probably not the first person he's done this to," Alicia said.

"Probably not."

"Think of the other women he could've done this to, *or worse*."

"Worse?" Laila said.

"In one of the true-crime books I was handling, the author, a psychologist, said that some serial killers have the fetish of smelling women's underwear."

"Serial killers? Jeez, Alicia."

"I'm sorry. I'm scaring you again. But honey, you've got to report him."

Laila nodded. They tried shifting to another subject, to catch up and talk about other things, but it was futile. Their conversation kept coming back to what happened to Laila, until it was time to leave.

Yes, Alicia's right. I should report it, Laila thought later, while driving home. *But I'm not sure I will. I'm not sure I can.*

Maybe Alicia had forgotten, because it never came up, why Laila was reluctant to deal with police about the cable guy incident. It was because of what had happened the last time Laila reported a man to police.

Her senior year in college, after meeting friends

at a bar one night, she was walking home alone. No one had wanted to leave when she did. A man started following her.

She walked faster. He walked faster.

She ran. He ran.

He caught up to her, grabbed her arm, and tried to pull her into an alley. Terrified, she'd reached into a pile of trash and hit him with a glass bottle, twisted free of him, and ran home.

That night, she reported it to police. They told her to come in the next morning to file a complaint. She went in to recount the incident but couldn't believe the officer's reaction as she reported the attack.

"Maybe you just had a bad date? Did you know this guy? Were you flirting? Did you say something to tease him in the bar? What were you wearing? How much did you have to drink?"

His questions made Laila feel like it was her fault.

She left the police station humiliated, belittled, embarrassed, and convinced her report hadn't been taken seriously. Nothing ever came of it. Not even a follow-up. She vowed never to deal with police again.

And now this.

Stopped at a light, scenarios blazed through her mind.

What if I misread everything? What if I reported the guy and he lost his job? Maybe he has kids? Maybe he's just a jerk with a sickness? Maybe I don't know anything. Maybe I'm afraid?

A horn sounded.

The light was green.

Laila brushed at her tears and continued driving, biting back on her frustration of not knowing what she was going to do.

She was oblivious to the fact that a few cars behind, a white van was following her.

Twenty-Three

Buffalo, New York, Trailside Grove

"I'll start with your right thumb."

Greg placed his thumb tip on the postage-stamp-sized platen of the fingerprint scanner, a mobile device that looked like a cell phone.

The forensic tech was absorbed in her work while Greg withdrew into his desperate hope that this was not real.

This isn't happening.

He ached for the hum of the garage door opening; Jenn parking her Corolla, entering the laundry room; her keys jingling as she placed them on the counter; then she'd walk up to him saying: "You are just not going to believe what happened, Gregory! You're just not going to believe it!"

And their nightmare would end.

Because she would be home.

But Jenn wasn't home.

The nightmare was deepening because it was late afternoon and here he was, sitting at his kitchen table while state police investigator Twyla Wilton collected his fingerprints—later she'd get Vince's, Kat's, and even Jake's—to use as elimination prints in the case of his wife's disappearance.

Just like they did with homicides.

Warrants to take his cell phone, obtain phone records for it and their landline, take their laptops, and all devices with internet connections, sat on the table near him while the questions the detectives threw at him earlier that day echoed in his mind.

Ever strike your wife?... How did you get those scratches?... Is there a life insurance policy for Jenn?... Are you involved in any way in your wife's disappearance?

"Sir?"

Greg looked at Wilton.

"Next finger. Place the tip of your forefinger on the platen."

"Sorry."

During the procedure, Greg's phone, sitting on the table next to the warrants, vibrated with calls and messages. When Wilton finished, the two other investigators, who were there to execute the warrants, allowed Greg a moment to respond to them before starting the process of taking his phone and all the devices in the house.

Greg took a call from Kat.

"Any news there?" she asked.

"Nothing. Anything there?"

"No, sorry," she said. "I guess they didn't take your phone yet."

"They will right after this."

"I'll pick up a temporary one for you and a laptop."

"Get one for Jake, too. I think he should have one, given what's happened."

"Okay. Hang in there," Kat said.

Greg scrolled through texts and emails. Most were from friends offering support, some were reporters requesting interviews; Al Clayton texted from the Pine Castle job.

Everything's running smoothly on-site. Everyone here's pulling for you. We're standing by to help.

Greg texted his thanks, then saw one of the stone-faced investigators glance at the time on the kitchen clock. Greg prepared to shut his phone off and surrender it when it pinged with a new text. He tensed. He knew the number, knew who it was from.

Praying for you, Greg. I'll do anything to help.

Greg didn't respond.

He shut down his phone and handed it to the investigators, who then went through the house with him, collecting and documenting the seizure of his computer, Jenn's computer, and their tablets.

"Where's your home video gaming system?" asked Rex Neller, the investigator whose expression never wavered from a grimace, making Greg wonder if it was permanent.

"In the basement. My son's playing."

"We have to take it."

"You're going to take an eight-year-old's video game system?"

"It's got internet access. It's covered by the warrant."

Greg shook his head in defeat.

"Let me talk to him."

As Greg went down the stairs, Jake turned from his game, pulled off his headset, eyeing Neller and the other investigator behind him.

"Did you find Mom?"

"No, son. These police officers have to take your video game and the officer upstairs needs to get your fingerprints."

"Why?"

"To help find Mom."

"But why take my game?"

"Because it's connected to the internet."

"And why my fingerprints?"

"It's complicated, son, but it will help."

Jake stared at the TV screen, eyes welling with tears.

"They have to take my fingerprints, my phone, and our computers, too," Greg said. "Listen, do you want to go to Carter's and play there?"

Jake shook his head.

"I want to stay here in case Mom comes home," Jake said, sniffing. "Can Carter come here and watch *Star Wars* movies with me?"

"All right. I'll call his mom." Greg turned to Neller. "Can I use the landline or my phone to make the call?"

Neller nodded to the wireless landline in its base next to the sofa, and Greg called Holly Wiley. She was eager to help.

"We're on our way over," she said.

After the call, after Wilton took Jake's prints, after watching the investigators leave with his phone and the computers, Greg swallowed the sting of suspicion. Minutes later, he welcomed Holly and Carter at the door and the fact that Jake seemed happy to have his friend with him made him smile.

"I can stay with the boys downstairs if you like," Holly said. "Give you a chance to get some rest. Greg, you look like you haven't slept."

He nodded.

Accepting her offer, he sat alone in the living room, switched on the TV, surfing channels, stopping on *The Big Sleep*, an old Bogart and Bacall movie about a disappearance and murder. Greg muted the sound but he couldn't silence the relentless roaring in his mind.

Numb and helpless, he went upstairs to their bedroom to lie down. He wanted to see Jenn's face, but the most recent picture he had of her was on his phone.

Now that was gone.

Gone, like her.

Unable to sleep, he searched their closet, rummaging through a flimsy shoebox where he'd kept old pens, broken watches, keys, and keepsakes he couldn't throw out, including a folded newspaper clipping of their wedding.

There was Jenn, the beautiful bride.

Holding the clipping tenderly in his hand, weakened by emotion, he sat on the bed. Looking at her radiant smile, the light sparkling in her eyes, full of hope, the memories pulled him back.

They'd continued going out together through high school. Then, being blue-collar kids, they both went to Erie Community College where Jenn studied vision care at the Williamsville campus. He studied building trades at City Campus in Buffalo. After college, they found good jobs, saved their money, started thinking about the future.

One night, after cheeseburgers and shakes, they drove up to Jack Pine Hill in Greg's pickup. As they looked at the city lights, he reached into his pocket then held out a diamond ring. It glistened like Jenn's eyes as she cried and said yes before he slipped it on her finger.

Their wedding was in a country church. Vince danced with Jenn's grandmother, Bee. Kat came. Alone. And while she was happy for them, there was an unstated tension between her and Jenn that never really subsided over the years.

Greg remembered going to Florida with Jenn for their honeymoon and the glorious turquoise water as they drove through the Keys.

Life was sweet then.

Jenn loved her job, telling him how she loved helping people, especially children, see clearly, sometimes for the very first time. And he loved building houses for people. He'd get up at dawn, drive to a job site, always studying every aspect of the craft and the business, until he eventually started his own small contracting company.

Not long after they got married, Bee died.

Her name was Beatrice, but everyone called her Bee. She was a bighearted woman, and a brilliant cook, who Greg had grown to love in the time he'd been with Jenn. Her death left Jenn completely alone as far as her biological family was concerned.

She had no one else.

Bee had left her a small inheritance, which included some insurance money from her parents' deaths that was held in a trust fund. Greg and Jenn continued working and saving and a few years later, Greg and his crew built their "forever home," in Trailside, the new subdivision.

During the planning and construction, Jenn had insisted Greg install a state-of-the-art sprinkler and fire alarm system that exceeded any codes. Jenn also insisted there were to be fire extinguishers throughout the house.

Even while they were dating, TV news stories about fatal house fires upset Jenn, causing her to change the channel. Greg understood her distress arose from her being the sole survivor of her family's tragedy.

But as time went by, and they had Jake, Greg realized that while they had achieved their dream, their lives were not perfect.

Jenn would have moments where she would fall silent, usually around the anniversary of the fire. Or she would go by herself to the cemetery in Clarence to visit her parents' graves. Other times, Greg would find her at home alone, staring at the little framed picture of her with her parents. He never said anything, unable to imagine the horror of that night.

And there was the challenge of his contracting business with its ups and downs, making him consider Arizona. Would it be a good or bad thing for them to move there? And now he was dealing with a more enticing option. Complicating everything was the fact that a few months ago, Jenn had suddenly become detached, almost disinterested.

This is not like her.

He had no idea what was wrong, but something was going on with her. Jenn hid it when they were with other people, or in public. But at home, she was aloof. Whenever he tried to talk to her about it, she'd deny anything was wrong and change the subject. They were barely intimate anymore; when they were Jenn seemed uninvolved, going through the motions. Greg mentioned therapy. Jenn shut him down. Greg tried to reach her but she would not let him in and he didn't know why.

He was concerned.

He was frustrated.

It tore him up inside because of the other things he was facing.

He'd grown angry with Jenn.

So freaking angry.

"Greg!"

Kat called to him from downstairs. She and Vince had returned. Greg joined them and the boys came up from the basement, with Holly in tow.

"They're hungry and they want to get pizza," Holly said.

The burst of energy in the house had a semblance of normal. Greg thanked Kat for getting the new, inexpensive cell phones and laptops for him and Jake, promising to reimburse her.

"For me?" Jake couldn't believe he now had a cell phone.

"There'll be some rules, son," Greg told him. "We'll activate it later."

"Wow. Thanks, Dad."

"And we got you this." Vince reached for a shopping bag, withdrew a colorful box with a drone. He handed it to Jake.

"A Firelight Mega Striker!" Jake said. "Look, Carter!"

"Awesome!" Carter said.

"We have to get it registered online. We'll read the instructions and try it out later," Greg said, nodding his thanks to his dad.

Then, just before the pizza arrived, Kat signaled to Greg that she wanted to speak with him privately.

They went to his office and closed the door.

"Was Jenn happy, Greg?"

"What do you mean?"

"Were you guys having problems?"

Greg thought hard. "What is this?"

"I just want to know."

He stared at her, his eyes narrowing. "Has this got anything to do with you thinking you know what happened but stopped short of saying it out loud?"

"No."

"Because if it does…" Greg stepped closer to Kat. "If you know something, Kat—"

"No, Greg, stop. I'm just trying to understand what could've been going on with Jenn at the time."

"Don't you think I've run every freaking scenario through my mind a million times?"

Kat was silent.

"Look," Greg said, "if we argued, we argued, like everyone else. But it's got nothing to do with this. My God, Kat, look where and how they found her car! I mean—" Greg's voice broke.

Kat hugged him.

"I'm sorry," she said. "Everybody's being pushed to the limit."

Greg nodded as he collected himself.

"Do you want me and Dad to stay again tonight?" Kat asked.

"I think it'd be best if it's just Jake and me, you know?"

"Okay, call us if you need anything."

The pizza came, everyone ate, then Kat and Holly cleaned up. It got late, time for everyone to leave. At the door, Vince took hold of Greg's forearm and pulled him close, speaking softly in his ear.

"Be strong. Don't give up hope. We're going to bring her home."

Everyone left and the quiet in the house was overwhelming. Greg moved fast to get Jake to take a bath.

They went to bed.

Greg used his new phone to get on Jenn's social

media pages. He found an older video he'd taken of her laughing while holding up live lobsters at a harbor during a vacation in Maine.

Jake laughed. "They're all wiggly."

Greg looked at Jenn, her beautiful face, until dread strained his chest.

"Will Mom come home, Dad?"

"That's what we're all working on and praying for, son—for her to come home."

Jake slid his arms around Greg's neck, holding tight as if he didn't want to lose his dad. Greg held him and they stayed that way for a long time, until Jake fell asleep.

Greg repositioned him carefully and shifted, his body trembling from stress when his last received text pinged in his mind.

I'll do anything to help.

Exhausted and terrified, Greg used his hand to smother a sob as he stared into the night.

He couldn't shake the image of Jenn's car, not knowing where she was, if she was alive, his fears circling like wolves, moving toward him from the darkness.

Twenty-Four

Location Unknown

Jennifer Griffin looked at the naked bulb in the ceiling.

She didn't know how long she'd been here.

She had no phone, no way to measure time. Not even a sense of night and day. There were no windows in this room.

Again, her terror-fueled anger erupted.

"Please!" she screamed. "I didn't see you! I don't know who you are! Let me go back to my family! Please!"

No one responded.

She kicked, pounded, and clawed at the door until her fingers and feet ached. Tears rolled down her face; she slid to the floor.

Her nightmare began after her book club meeting at Liz's house. She stopped at the Korner Fast, unable to find her favorite blueberry yogurt. She was driving home along Ripple Valley Boulevard at the long, isolated stretch curving through the woods when—*I can't remember what happened next*—everything went hazy as if her memory had been wiped out while fragments still flickered.

She pulled her car over to the shoulder. Then there was a blinding bright light in her face, a sudden electrical snap-crackling at her neck, pain shaking her brain like a marble in a glass, grinding her teeth, her body going into spasms, leaving her without control. Totally helpless.

She couldn't cry out, couldn't move.

A sack with breathing holes slid over her head.

She was hefted from her car, placed on a floor, felt a cloth gag cover her mouth, heard the peel of duct tape binding her ankles and wrists. Felt an adjustment made to align her nostrils with the breathing holes. Heard a door shut, movement, driving and driving, motor and wheels droning; breathing hard through her nose, her blood thumping.

Who's doing this? Why? What're they going to do?

Drifting in and out of consciousness, no way to know how long or how far they'd traveled before they stopped. She was placed into something hard and open. It tilted and she was moving and bouncing, a wheel squeaking.

A wheelbarrow.

She was moved in a wheelbarrow.

I'm going to be killed and buried!

A loud crackle of another electrical zap. Quaking with pain, she passed out. For how long, she didn't know.

She woke in darkness.

Her gag, hood, and bindings were gone. She was on a mattress; her body ached. She had to pee. For a long time, she didn't move or speak, then, hearing a soft click, she turned over, saw a tiny red light and heard the gentle drone of a fan. The room filled with light. She shut her eyes, taking a moment, adjusting to the single bulb in the ceiling.

That's how she came to be in her prison.

It was square, about ten by ten feet, smelling of fresh-cut wood. It seemed newly built; sawdust laced parts of the floor. The windowless walls were solid planks. There were no cameras watching her. The door had a sliding viewing port built in. The entire place felt insulated, to absorb cries for help. A small, screened vent for air was atop one wall. A small space heater—the source of the tiny red light—was built into a wall and covered by a steel mesh screen. The light bulb and heater would come to life intermittently, likely set on timers.

She had a clean mattress, pillow and blankets. They smelled new.

Beside the main door, at floor level, were two small doors side by side, like pet doors. She could open them from her side, but there were heavy metal doors on the other side that were locked.

And there were THE RULES.

They were taped to the wall next to the big door, printed in a bold black font on a single sheet of paper.

THE RULES:
THEY MUST BE FOLLOWED
BLACK PAIL FOR TOILET & WASTE—
ALWAYS REPLACE

WHITE PAIL FOR WASHING—ALWAYS REPLACE
FOOD, WATER, ETC., WILL BE PRO-VIDED

The plastic pails and other essential items were transferred to her through the small doors, usually preceded by the sudden, cold snap of her captor sliding open the viewing port. Eyes would look at her from the shadows, then movement at the lower doors and she'd receive whatever her captor delivered. So far it had been a clean toilet pail, a roll of tissue, and then food. Other times, toiletries, sanitary napkins, plastic utensils, bottled water, clean underwear, sweatpants, T-shirts, a hoodie, a notepad and pen.

Jennifer had used the pad and pen to continue pleading with her captor.

Please, I don't know who you are. Just leave the door open. I'll go back to my family.

She left her note with the pails. It disappeared without a response.

There were no other sounds here. No indication of other prisoners, no distant hum of traffic, no trains or jetliners. Nothing but her gloom and the sense that something was going to happen to her.

She hadn't been sexually assaulted.

Not yet.

She hadn't been beaten.

Not yet.

No demands had been made.

No one had spoken to her.

Will I be killed?

She flinched.

The door of the viewing port slid open.

Jennifer looked into the pool of darkness, at the eyes watching her.

Then there was activity at the lower transfer doors. An exchange of pails and then again, food was left, a store-bought ham and cheese sandwich, potato chips, bottled water, two apples, and a folded page of paper.

She opened it to the words:

YOU'RE NOT READY. BUT SOON YOU WILL KNOW WHY YOU'RE HERE.

Twenty-Five

Clarence, New York

The next morning, Lieutenant Phil Becker nodded to his law enforcement colleagues from Buffalo PD, Erie County, and the FBI.

They'd come together at the New York State Police Clarence Barracks for the first multiagency meeting of the Griffin investigation. Laptops, tablets, phones, and notebooks were positioned at the ready on the room's large table. The air held a mingling of coffee, cologne, and solemn determination.

"Let's get to it," Becker said. "Everyone's received our updated reports. This is a missing person case. While not yet confirmed, foul play cannot be ruled out given the known aspects, which we'll get to. Now, I'll throw it to the lead investigator, who most of you know, Claire Kozak, and her partner, Ned Carillo."

Kozak worked at a laptop, linked to a large screen on the wall at the end of the room. She directed everyone's attention to it, and Jennifer

Griffin's face filled the screen, along with a set of details.

"We're at the very early stages of this investigation."

Kozak began with a timeline encompassing approximate times, locations, and names on maps, arising from when Jenn was last seen leaving the book club meeting; to when Greg Griffin searched for her, then reported her missing, up until two walkers discovered her Toyota Corolla. Then aerial photos appeared on the screen, pinpointing where the car had been found, then maps with distances from Liz Miller's house to the Griffin home.

"The car's been trailered to Batavia where FIU will process it," Kozak said. "In addition to the car, a dog team made a key discovery at the scene."

Another aerial photo and map appeared.

"In dense forest, some forty yards from the car, we found a woman's purse. Among the items it contained—Jennifer Griffin's driver's license, other identification, her wallet with cash and credit cards, a personal calendar, contact list, and her phone, which had died. Forensics tells us that her phone's battery strength may have been low earlier in the evening. The phone will be analyzed and information extracted and examined."

New images of Jenn's purse and its contents, including her phone, appeared, and notes were taken by investigators. Kozak said the surrounding area was being methodically grid-searched, in an ever-expanding manner, with drones and dog teams.

"We're looking for everything and anything, any

trace, shoe impressions, ground disturbances, indications of a shallow grave. Nothing more has been discovered yet," she said, nodding to Carillo.

"Yeah, all available residential security camera footage is being collected to be studied. It should be noted that there are no cameras along the wooded stretch near the area her car was discovered. So, off the top, we don't have much hope of video evidence yet," he said.

The fenced gate with access to Blueripple Woods was being examined with a mind to who maintained the gate, its lock, and who had access to it.

Kozak continued. "Given its ping-ponging history, we'll ask your help with county, state, and federal agencies, checking employee lists... You know the drill."

"Our Toolmarks Unit can do a lock and key examination, after you process it for latents," FBI agent Gary Dungey said.

Kozak nodded her thanks, saying that case updates had been submitted to all local, regional, state, and national databases, including ViCAP, the Violent Criminal Apprehension Program, and NCIC, the National Crime Information Center. More investigators were being brought in to help with checks with the New York State Sex Offender Registry.

"We're looking at all risk levels of registered sex offenders within a ten-mile radius of the scene, checking alibis. We'll expand it from there," Kozak said. "We're also working with Corrections, checking recently paroled offenders and their where-abouts."

Pictures of Trailside Grove, the Griffins' street and house appeared on the screen as Kozak provided complaint history and patrol logs for the zone that covered the family's neighborhood and those nearby, noting they were being reviewed for reports of suspicious activity, vehicles, people, anything that raised a concern.

"Anything we flag will go into the case database we've established," Kozak said. "It will also encompass information from tips we have coming in from the public. All of it will be assessed and prioritized. It means we've got a lot more work ahead of us." Kozak turned to Becker. "But that covers the major elements at this time."

"Thanks, Claire, Ned," Becker said. "Let's open this up to questions, brainstorming, and theories."

"Any indication of a kidnapping for ransom, or extortion?" Carrie Deakman, with Erie County, asked.

"Nothing so far," Kozak said.

"Sticking to the key facts," said Detective Tony Letto with Buffalo PD, "we need to know how her car got into Blueripple. There's a locked gate and it's driven deep into the forest and concealed."

"We're thinking she was stopped on Ripple Valley Boulevard," Carillo said.

"Was stopped?" said Louise LeBrie, with the state police.

"By someone official possibly."

"Someone with a flashing light," Letto said. "A cop."

"Or someone pretending to be a cop pulls her over?" LeBrie said. "Makes the stop, overpowers her, then drives her car into Blueripple."

"She might've been stopped by someone she recognized," FBI agent James Goldman suggested.

"In the dark? While driving?" Letto said.

"Pulls up beside her, drops the windows, she recognizes the car, the person," Goldman said.

"What about the husband, Claire?" LeBrie consulted her notes and those scrapes.

Kozak typed a few commands and the photos Trooper Menza had taken of Greg's hands, his T-shirt, dirt-streaked face, and messed hair, after he'd reported his wife missing, appeared on the big screen.

"Greg Griffin said the scrapes came from removing a traffic cone he hit at a patch of roadwork on Ripple Valley Boulevard when he was out looking for his wife," Kozak said. "And there are traffic cones and roadwork on the boulevard. We'll process them."

Clint Freely, a veteran homicide detective with Buffalo PD, had been scrutinizing the reports and his notes. "There's financial stress in the home, correct?" Freely asked Kozak.

"An indication, yes."

"Are we taking a close look at his books?" Freely said.

"It's on our to-do list," Kozak said.

"We should check her medical records for any indication of abuse," Freely said.

"In progress," Kozak said.

"Looking at your reports here," Freely said, "we see the husband's business is shaky, they contemplated moving west. Their son says they argued about money, that he thought his parents were getting a divorce. The husband's got a three hundred thousand dollar policy on her. Connect the dots."

"That's a lot of circumstance, Clint," Carillo said.

"So, she leaves the book club around ten thirty," Freely said. "The husband *says* he goes looking for her around 2:45 a.m. No matter the time spread, from the time she left until the time he called it in, he has opportunity to flag her down, dump the car, get rid of her then make the call. Look at those incriminating pictures of him, his hands."

"What about her purse?" LeBrie said.

"He tosses it deep into the bush, makes it look like a robbery," Freely said.

"With all her cash and cards intact? I don't buy that part," Kozak said.

"Or, she was running away," Carillo said. "She escaped from whoever had attacked her. Terrified, no time to even call for help, or her phone was already dead, panicked and fleeing, she loses her purse in the night. That's why everything's there."

"What does FIU have from the scene?" Special Agent Goldman asked.

"No obvious signs of violence or a struggle,"

Kozak said, "but everything's still being processed."

"What about an online hookup?" Letto asked. "She was having an affair, tried ending it, and it got out of hand with her boyfriend, or girlfriend?"

"It's a possibility," Kozak said. "We still have to analyze all their phones and devices. We could get something from that."

"Are we going to search the house?" Freely asked.

"We are," Carillo said.

"Polygraph the husband?" Freely asked.

"We intend to," Kozak said.

Without looking from her notes, LeBrie said: "Her son, Jake, told you that there were times his mother would sit alone, quiet 'like she was sad about something.' What do we know about her mental health? Was she under care, using medication? Could she have harmed herself, had some sort of episode, and run off disoriented?"

"Based on what we know so far, no medication, no treatments, no psychological issues," Kozak said. "We know she had a tragic past. She was the lone survivor after her parents died in a house fire. She was eight at the time."

"Eight?" LeBrie said. "The same age as her son is now. Interesting."

"Maybe she staged this?" Freely said. "Wanted to leave her husband, make this her last goodbye?"

"I don't think she'd leave her son," LeBrie said.

"Been known to happen," Freely said.

The moment that followed was punctuated by Becker.

"Before we close this, I want to say thanks for the help. You're all good at what you do, but indulge me because this needs to be said. Don't get tunnel vision. These cases are not like TV and the movies. You all know how theories, threads, and leads explode in all directions, like a starburst webbing everywhere. Our job is to follow the evidence to the truth."

Freely looked at Becker; they were old friends.

"Did you practice that in the mirror this morning, Phil?"

Soft chuckles went around the table.

"All right, all right," Becker said.

Over the next few minutes, assignments were distributed, tablets, phones, notebooks, and jackets were collected as the meeting broke up. Becker, Kozak, and Carillo were alone in the room when Becker's phone rang and he answered.

"Phil, this is Les McCarren, regional security with Korner Fast Corp. How ya doing?"

"Hey, Les."

"Look, legal cleared things on the video from our store in Ripplewood Creek."

"Good."

"I think your investigators are going to want to see what we've got."

Twenty-Six

Clarence, New York

Jenn walks into the Korner Fast store, passes the newspaper rack, the bread shelves, the snack cakes, the chip displays. She goes to the dairy case at the back. She searches without opening a door then goes to the counter, walking past another customer. Jenn's wearing a mauve turtleneck and blazer looking calm, casual, talking to the clerk before leaving, returning to the night. A few moments later, another customer enters the store.

Kozak, Carillo, and Lieutenant Becker were at Clarence Barracks studying the store security video on the large screen in the meeting room.

Les McCarren sent it to them and had also arranged for Trevor Bara, the clerk who was on duty at the time, to go the barracks. Bara was waiting in a separate room while the investigators examined the footage.

Discovering Jenn had been in the store was a break in the case, establishing the last time she was seen. They replayed the video, watching the

jerky, choppy images that appear to make people
pause as they move. Kozak made notes. The image
quality was strong, crisp, and in color. It was clear
this was Jennifer Griffin. The time of the recording was 10:46 p.m., making it a key puzzle piece,
fitting with the timeline.

"So this narrows it a little," Kozak said. "Whatever transpired, happened between the store and
Blueripple Woods."

"What, how, and who?" Carillo said. "She enters
and leaves the store without incident."

"It comes back to her being stopped somewhere
along that stretch of Ripple Valley Boulevard,"
Kozak said.

"Or anywhere in the area. Let's run the criminal history—" Becker glanced at his notes "—for
unsolved sexual assaults, stalking, burglaries, the
history of everything along the boulevard and the
surrounding neighborhoods. Other thoughts?"

Carillo scratched his chin, then said: "Try this.
She's on her way home but she knows her husband's
asleep, right?"

"Right," Kozak said.

"So she stops off to see a friend, you know, she's
having an affair. An hour or two. Greg won't know.
Then something goes wrong and her lover gets rid
of her and ditches her car?"

Kozak and Becker digested the theory.

"We need names and addresses of everyone in
her circles," Becker said. "Then cross-check them
to who lives in Ripplewood. We talk to people,
alibi them."

"We'll need help with that, Phil," Kozak said.

"Leave it with me," Becker said. "Now, it's time for you to talk to the clerk."

Kozak and Carillo brought Trevor Bara into the large meeting room.

It was just the three of them there.

They began by collecting Bara's basic information. He was twenty-five, had worked at the Korner Fast store in Ripplewood for two years. He was planning to go to college to be a chef. The investigators then went through the drill, asking if he had a record. Kozak and Carillo would run Bara's name before he left, but it helped establish credibility if a witness was truthful from the get-go.

"No, I don't have a record," Bara said.

Before coming to Jenn, they moved on to what Bara did that night.

"My shift ended at midnight. Dallas Peller relieved me."

"What did you do after that?"

"Rode my motorcycle home to Cardinal Hill, watched an old movie with my girlfriend, then went to bed."

"What movie?" Carillo asked.

"Bullitt."

"We're going to play the security video for you, so we can walk each other through it," Carillo said.

Kozak played the video on the big screen.

"Do you remember this woman?"

"I do. She's been on the news."

"Why didn't you come forward to say she was in your store?" Carillo asked.

Bara's face flushed and he shrugged. "I think I sent an email to your tip line."

"You think?"

"Guess I figured you guys would've known."

Carillo and Kozak let it go and moved on.

"What was she looking for? What did she ask you?" Kozak said.

"Yogurt, a certain brand in blueberry. We were out of it."

Kozak was making notes.

"What was her demeanor? Was she nervous, scared, happy?"

Staring at the video, Bara stuck out his bottom lip.

"She was cool. Not scared or nervous. Pleasant."

Kozak made notes.

"So, she purchased nothing."

"Nothing."

Kozak was thinking as they watched the video.

"What about the person who came after her?" Carillo asked.

It was a person about six feet or so with a regular build. The age was difficult to determine. They wore jeans and a dark hoodie, with the hood lifted over a ballcap, obscuring their face.

"What about that person?" Bara said.

"Do you know them? Are they a regular?"

"I don't think so."

"Looks like they bought a can of soda," Kozak said.

Bara looked at the footage.

"It was an energy drink."

"They pay with cash or plastic?" Carillo asked.

Bara nodded to the screen: "Cash. You can see it."

"All right. Thanks, Trevor."

They had him wait out front, then Kozak and Carillo went back to look at the footage one more time.

"Watch. I'll play it a little longer at the end because we missed something," Kozak said, letting the video play out.

"There. Did you see that, Ned?"

"What?"

She replayed the sequence and slowed it.

"Look. Hoodie person at the counter turns their head."

"I see that."

"Ned, they're watching Griffin leave the store."

"All right. They're watching."

"Look to the top of the frame. You can just see her taillights."

"Right."

"It's like they're watching her leave to get the direction she's driving."

Twenty-Seven

Clarence, New York

Later that day, April Kent twisted the straps of her purse while waiting in the reception area of the state police barracks.

An investigator, Carillo, had contacted her about coming in for an interview to discuss the last time she'd seen Jenn.

April was anxious to help, but while driving to the public safety building in Clarence, her conscience gnawed at her. Now that she was here, looking at the framed portraits of police commanders, the memorial plaques and flags, reality pushed down on her.

This was stone-cold serious.

Yet, she was not sure if she should tell them what she knew about Jenn's bruises. April hadn't told anyone about them.

They were the result of playing football in her yard with Greg and Jake.

That's what Jenn had said.

April wasn't convinced that was true.

But if I report this to police, I'd be pointing a finger at Greg. And what if Jenn's explanation is true?

April knew from her nursing experience, from seeing so many cases of abuse, that women were often afraid to report their partners; they stretched the truth, covered it up, made excuses like how Jenn had blamed it on roughhousing.

No, I can't let this go. So much was wrong.

The backs of Greg's hands were scraped. Jenn had bruises. She was missing, and they'd found her car in the woods.

What if Greg did hurt her? My silence would protect him.

"April Kent?"

A solidly built man in his fifties, with clipped gray hair, wearing a button-down-collar shirt, loosened tie, and a navy sport coat that looked off the rack from JCPenney, stood before her.

"Yes."

"Ned Carillo. Thanks for coming in." He extended his hand.

April walked with him to a private office, then at his direction took a seat before taking a breath.

Steeling herself, April decided to tell him everything.

Twenty-Eight

Buffalo, New York

At Tall Elm School, Thelma Clark in admin was working at making sure another school day ran smoothly.

But it was a struggle for her and her colleagues.

Jenn Griffin's disappearance had permeated the office, the halls, and the classrooms like a dark fog, adding to the distress everyone was already feeling for Principal Bickersley. That Jake's mom was missing was now all the staff could talk about, and all Thelma could think of. As cochair of the Parent School Support Committee, Jenn was involved in everything.

She fights the good fight; she's part of our school family.

Swiping and tapping at her phone for the millionth time for updates, Thelma came to a news photo of the volunteers from the school, taken on the first day they helped search in Ripplewood Creek. There was Thelma with the group of teachers and support staff. And there was Porter Sellwin.

Sellwin.

Something was going on between Sellwin and Jenn.

A chime sounded the arrival of a message on her computer from Anita Overhauser with the advisory committee.

Hi, Thelma: Did we receive the forms for the information session on the new report cards?

Yes. They're going out end of day, Thelma responded.

Thanks. You hear anything on Jenn?

No.

We can't give up hope.

No, we can't.

Thelma resumed updating attendance, excused students, tardies, and early dismissals before moving to new teacher requests.

"Hey, Thelma."

Bert Cobb, the senior custodian, was at the counter.

"I wanted to bring you up to speed on the storage request," he said.

Thelma went to the counter, leaning on it with him.

"Yes, for supplies."

"We're clearing the room behind the gym," Bert

said. "Got stuff in there that we don't need. Be ready in a day or two. Are you okay?"

Thelma was touching a tissue to her eyes.

"I'm worried about Jenn. We should be out there searching."

"We'll get out there again and we'll find her."

"It's just so terrible."

"Got to keep the faith," Bert said.

"Sure do," Thelma said, changing the subject. "Is it true? You're really leaving us, Bert? Really moving west?"

Nodding, he took out his phone to show her a picture of a cabin near mountains. "My buddy wants help with his fishing guide business. He's renting me a place to get started."

"Looks pretty there. Oh Bert, we're going to miss you."

"Same here, and with everything happening, it's a bad time to go."

They both glanced through the glass walls of the office at the man approaching. Bert mumbled: "Here comes trouble."

"There's someone I wish would be leaving," Thelma said.

Porter Sellwin.

Looking every bit the school board honcho in his navy suit, tall, with a tanned face and styled hair, he entered the office.

"Hi, Bert. Hi, Thelma." He looked at Thelma. "Is Viv in?"

Vivian White was the vice-principal, currently

in charge because Principal Eugene Bickersley was at Sloan Kettering in New York City.

"Yes. I'll see if she's free to see you."

"Oh, she'll be free to see me." Sellwin flashed his politician's smile and winked. "By the way, have you guys sent out an email to all the school families expressing our support and prayers for Jenn?"

"We're waiting for Vivian to sign off and she's been very—"

"Don't wait. Get moving on it. Send it to me first. Viv will agree with my approval. Now, how's Eugene doing?"

"Latest word from the hospital in New York was no changes."

"All right. Keep me posted." Sellwin then opened the principal's office door, switched on his grin as he stepped inside. "Hi, Viv, I dropped in to—" Sellwin shut the door.

Bert looked at Thelma. "Ain't he a piece of work?"

"He's a piece of something, all right," Thelma said, then her hand flew to her mouth. "Sorry. Please don't tell anyone I said that, Bert."

"I can keep a secret." He smiled. "Gotta go."

Thelma watched Bert leave.

Keeping secrets is a part of my job, too, she thought, returning to her desk and her curiosity about Sellwin and Jenn.

Thelma had only a suspicion that something had happened between Sellwin and Jenn—something disturbing.

It was in the days before Principal Bickersley went to New York City to undergo treatment that the issue—or what she believed was an issue—between them had surfaced.

Jenn came into the office to see Principal Bickersley, privately. Jenn had been crying. Less than five minutes after Jenn had left, Sellwin, looking angry, tense, also met privately with the principal in his office.

Thelma thought hard.

I have no idea what transpired between Jenn and that man but whatever it was, it was not good.

Twenty-Nine

Batavia, New York

Some twenty miles west of the Tall Elm School, Beethoven's *Symphony No. 9* floated in the vehicle analysis garage of the Forensic Identification Unit.

Investigator Serena Krol loved the music for its celebration of life, for how universal love triumphs over the agony of war. It also helped her focus on processing Jennifer Griffin's Toyota for evidence.

Krol had started her work at the scene where the Corolla was discovered. She continued after it was transported to Troop A's forensic building in Batavia. She was an expert at her work, having grown up devouring H. G. Wells, Jules Verne, and Sir Arthur Conan Doyle, which fed her passion for science, forensics, and her successful pursuit of several degrees before joining the New York State Police.

At the scene, in Blueripple Woods, Krol and the other investigators went through the car meticulously. They also examined the environment, the condition of the surrounding undergrowth, and the forest. They took tire impressions and looked for foot impressions both around the car and where Jennifer Griffin's purse was located. When the scene work was completed, the car was covered, loaded onto a flatbed, and transferred to the garage.

So far, not everything collected from the scene had been fully analyzed. A lot of work remained: processing the soil samples, and the casts for the impressions, some of which were not ideal.

The car itself was mechanically sound. The fuel tank was three-quarters full. The tires were all inflated properly, not worn. The service history was up to date. There were no issues with the vehicle.

At the garage, Krol had wriggled into a set of fresh disposable coveralls—the hooded white bunny suit, she called it. Then she put on foot covers and tugged on gloves.

The Toyota's exterior and interior were processed for any latent prints left by any potential suspect. Krol moved between the car and her workstation as she collected then logged, made notes, and passed along for further analysis every item found in the Toyota, including the remote garage door opener, sunglasses, tissues, a charging cord, and the owner's manual. From the trunk, she collected the spare, a small supply of tools, a plastic jug of windshield-washing fluid, and reusable canvas tote bags.

The car's interior was neat and orderly.

Krol inspected the floor, the seats, the door side panels, and the ceiling for any traces of fibers or hairs. Then she vacuumed the carpet and interior.

Her colleagues applied luminol spray to detect any trace amounts of blood.

Nothing of any consequence had emerged from all of their work so far.

Krol and the investigators examined Jennifer Griffin's purse and its contents, her wallet, cash, credit and bank cards, cataloging every item and preparing them to be processed for latents, as well. She knew other members of the forensic team were still examining every piece of digital material extracted from Jennifer Griffin's phone and her computer.

Taking a moment to drink some coffee, Krol leaned against her worktable and stared at the Toyota. She'd missed something. In keeping with her procedure, nothing in the car had been moved or adjusted. Still, something had been overlooked.

Krol turned to her laptop, tapped out a few commands and Jennifer Griffin's driver's license filled her screen, showing her height as five feet three inches.

Krol had a lot of room while working on the driver's-side floor.

Why was that?

With the answer dawning on her, Krol got into the car behind the wheel and discovered she had ample legroom to reach the pedals. In fact, she had to strain to reach them. Krol was five feet five inches tall.

The seat had been pushed back.

Krol double-checked all file notes on the car.

No one from the forensic team had moved or re-adjusted anything in the Corolla.

Whoever moved the seat was the last person to operate the car.

Krol then called on other investigators to suit up and sit at the wheel, colleagues of different heights. Each time, Krol scrutinized their placement, recorded their height then made calculations on her laptop.

Krol had the height range of a suspect.

Thirty

Ned Carillo lived alone in a bungalow built with hope in the gloom of the 1930s. It sat under towering maples at the fringe of Cheektowaga.

Since buying the place ten years ago, he'd put on a new roof and vinyl siding, and installed a new furnace.

He liked this house; he was comfortable here.

Even if I only have ghosts for company.

It was early evening, and Carillo was in his kitchen making a sandwich of super-crunchy peanut butter, banana slices, and iceberg lettuce. He poured a glass of ice-cold milk.

Returning to his desk, the soft echo of the creaking hardwood floor awakened memories, the stillness underscoring Charlie's absence. No padding of his paws, no jingle of his collar, or lapping water from his bowl. He'd been gone for two months now, a friend who'd given Carillo unconditional love for twelve years.

Old age and a weak heart, the vet said.

And Carillo still missed Kelly.

It'd been five years since they broke up. Carillo thought they were happy together and had never envisioned it ending, but it did. He had to smile to himself, because every Christmas, Kelly sent him a card from San Francisco, always writing something like: "You'll always be part of my life. Nothing will change that. Treasure what we had and have a great New Year, Ned."

Carillo had carried on, trying a few dating sites, even went out a couple of times. Nothing came of it.

Enough sentimentality; the past was gone and he was alone. Besides, he had more important issues before him. Settling in at his desk, he bit into his sandwich and got back to work. It didn't matter where he was—in the field, at the office, or home—when he was on a case, he was on it twenty-four hours a day.

A number of leads had arisen in the Griffin investigation. Carillo consulted his notebook and the files on his laptop. The revelation of Jennifer's bruising that her book club friend, the former nurse, had provided needed to be followed. The bruising was a concern when juxtaposed with Greg Griffin's appearance in the time immediately after he'd reported his wife missing.

Carillo called up the photos state trooper Menza had taken. Greg appeared on the screen, face streaked with dirt, hair messed, T-shirt soiled with grime, the backs of his hands marked with bloodied scrapes. Greg had attributed those scrapes to removing a traffic cone wedged under his truck when he was looking for his wife. The analysis was still to come.

Thinking for a moment, Carillo reached down to pet Charlie but he wasn't there. Absorbing the stab of loss, he went to the interview notes, excerpts of statements from the son, Jake.

> *...I heard them arguing about money and stuff. ... They would argue about bills and my dad's business maybe moving to Arizona. ... Sometimes in the last couple of months, she'd just sit alone, not reading a book or looking on her phone, just sitting alone all quiet...like she was sad about something.*

Then he went to statements made by Greg's sister, Kat, about Jennifer.

"I don't know, a feeling, I guess. She just seemed a little sad to me."

When they asked Greg if he and his wife argued, he'd said: *"Yes. Don't all married couples argue?"*

Carillo paged through his notes.

Greg had acknowledged his family was facing financial stress; that he was the beneficiary of the $300,000 life insurance policy on his wife.

Pull these factors together, Jennifer's bruising, Greg's scrapes, and the apparent tension in the household, and the concern deepened.

Carillo scrolled through reports and messages.

They needed data from the Griffins' phones, computers, and devices but the forensic cyberexperts were still working on them.

Finishing the last of his sandwich and milk, Carillo brushed crumbs from his hands and analyzed the disturbing circumstances. Jennifer was last seen at 10:46 p.m. Greg reported her missing some six or seven hours later, giving him a big window of opportunity. There was the mystery hooded figure, their face obscured, who appeared to be watching her in the Korner Fast video. *Was that Greg?* Could be nothing, could be something. Statistically, in these types of missing spouse cases, the "nearest and dearest" were involved.

Carillo's doorbell rang.

He opened the door to Kaylee Treen, his thirteen-year-old neighbor from across the street, standing on his step with a small dog in her arms.

It looked like a white Lab.

"Hi, Mr. Carillo. We just got back from my Uncle Roy's farm and we got some puppies. I thought you might want one and my mom said to ask."

Looking over Kaylee's shoulder, he saw Rebecca Treen wave from the sidewalk.

The pup looked to be a couple months old. It had a sweet face and was licking Kaylee's while squirming in her arms.

"Gosh, well, this is sudden."

"Want to hold him? He's a boy."

Kaylee put the dog in his arms before he could say anything. Feeling his warmth, his excitement, he drew the pup's nose to his, cooed, and returned him to Kaylee.

"Tell you what," Carillo said. "This is a wonderful, thoughtful offer, Kaylee, and I thank you.

I can't say yes or no right now because I'm busy with work. Can you keep him a little while then I'll check back with you?" Carillo smiled then looked to Rebecca, who nodded.

His phone rang.

"That's work," he said.

"Okay," Kaylee said, giggling, almost singing as she left with the pup, "but I know you're going to want him."

"Carillo," he said into his phone, closing the door.

"Ned, it's Resnick in Comms. Buffalo PD called us. They got something on their anonymous tip line concerning your missing mom. I'm sending it to you and Kozak now."

Thirty-One

Amherst, New York

"You're not defeated, Claire."

Pen in hand, staring at her divorce papers, Kozak heard her late father's voice.

Dominic Kozak had come to America from Poland with his parents at age five, learning English at school, then as a teen working as a security guard before becoming a cop and Buffalo PD detective. He'd pass on family history to Claire with stories of relatives who worked as slave labor under the Nazis.

"No matter what you face in life, others have faced worse. You never give up because as long as you're breathing, you're not defeated."

She adjusted her hold on the pen, the same ballpoint she used to make her grocery list and sign off on things for her boys. Then she swallowed and signed her name, ending her marriage to Wade Mitchell Ferron.

Setting the pen down, she shut her eyes to squeeze back tears.

I'm still breathing, Dad.

Kozak slid the papers into the envelope, closed it, and set it aside to return to her lawyer. She touched her fingertips to the corners of her eyes then resumed working on her tablet and the Griffin case.

She scrutinized the key facts: Jennifer Griffin had bruises, her husband had scrapes, there was stress in the home, Jennifer appeared to be dejected, there was a hoodie figure in the Korner Fast video... Kozak came back to the fact that whatever unfolded had happened between the store and Blue-ripple Woods.

Kozak tapped her pen to her chin then went to her emails, messages, and folders, looking for updates, finding nothing new.

Damn, we need the data from the family's phones and computers. There have to be answers there.

Kozak knew it took time to extract digital material, but she knew this case was solvable.

She began looking deeper into Jennifer Griffin's early life. She was the sole survivor of a house fire that killed her parents. Orphaned when she was eight years old, raised by her grandmother.

Could her tragic past have any relevance to the case?

Kozak let out a breath and cautioned herself about getting distracted with aspects that were likely unrelated. Her job was to collect irrefutable evidence and follow it to the truth.

Aiden was sixteen and the elder of Kozak's two sons. He approached her desk, phone in hand. Kozak kept her eyes on her work and said: "Yes?"

"Mom, can I go with Tanner and his family to their cabin in the Finger Lakes next weekend?"

"Where?"

"Seneca."

"You've got a major paper on Mark Twain that's due."

"It's done."

She turned to him.

"Let me see it."

"It's *almost* done. I'll have it done in a couple days."

"You get it done, *and done well*, then I'll talk to Tanner's folks."

"I will. Thanks, Mom." Aiden turned.

"Hold it. I don't hear the washing machine. You guys are falling down on your chores."

"It's Chase's turn."

"I don't care. You two sort it out and if I don't hear the machine going, you're both grounded."

"But Mom, it's not my turn!"

"End of discussion."

Aiden glared at her, stomping away but not before she heard him mutter: "This is bullshit." His intonation matched his father's voice and unleashed in her a whirlwind of pained fury.

"Get back here right now."

Aiden returned.

"What did you say?"

Face reddening, he lowered his head.

"Don't you ever talk to me like that."

"I'm sorry, Mom."

Watching him, loving him, Kozak held on, harnessed and holstered her misdirected anger.

"Now—" her voice softened "—go and do what I told you to do."

Aiden nodded, turned, and left.

Staring at nothing, she collected her thoughts to get back to the case when her tablet pinged and her phone vibrated.

She answered the call.

"Claire, it's Ned. See what Resnick just sent us from BPD?"

She had just received the file and opened it to four photos, taken in a bar from a distance. The first photo showed Greg Griffin with several people, seated in a raised section, close together at a table that was covered with bottles, pizza, and nacho trays. In the second, the woman sitting next to Greg had her hand on his shoulder and was smiling at him. In the third, she had leaned into him and was speaking into his ear. In the fourth, she was smiling at him while, although the photo showed a forest of legs, it was clear that under the table, the woman's hand was on Greg Griffin's inner thigh, nearly on his crotch.

And he was smiling back at her.

Kozak was gauging the significance of the information.

"What do we know about these pictures, Ned? Who sent them and why?"

"The source is anonymous. But enlarge them and look at the big TV screens behind them at the sports scores and the games. One is a Mets-

Toronto game with the score in the seventh inning.
I watched that one. These were taken the night she
disappeared. We need to find out who the girl paw-
ing Griffin is."

Kozak went to her notes where Greg provided
the names of people with him at the bar in Depew.
They hadn't interviewed any of them yet. She went
to the website and other social media pages for
Solid and Strong Contracting, finding photos of
the contracting crew. She studied them, then the
bar pictures.

Bingo.

"Looking at Griffin's company online, the guy
on the other side of Greg looks like Al Clayton,
Griffin's crew leader."

"What do you think, Claire?"

"First, we need forensics to authenticate the photos, make sure they're real."

"And if they are?"

"We'll have a new lead. We'll need the bar's security cameras."

"Did you see the note that accompanied the pictures?" Carillo asked.

Kozak went back to the anonymous note that
accompanied the tip.

It said: "GREG GRIFFIN BEFORE HIS WIFE
DISAPPEARED."

As Kozak continued examining the new evidence, she blinked with satisfaction when she heard
the start of the washing machine.

Thirty-Two

Images and events of the past few days burned through Greg.

Searching alone in the night for Jenn, seeing her Corolla in the woods, the fear in Jake's face, Vince's and Kat's heartbreak and concern, the detectives' accusatory questions, the helicopters, the dogs, the press calls, the TV reports, all the volunteers, the massive effort to find her...

And still not a trace.

Where are you?

Greg was at the kitchen table on his new laptop, looking at Jenn in the pictures her work friends from Crystallo View Optical had posted online. They and the school had established the funding site offering a reward that now stood at $16,000 for information on her disappearance.

Please, let me find you alive!

Greg was lost in his anguish.

Vince was in the basement with Jake, tinkering with the drone. Kat was at the counter, her back to him as she said: "This sounds terrible, I know, but it's kind of like the old days, just the three of us again. And Jake, of course, you know?"

Greg wasn't listening.

Looking at Jenn, his chin crumpled with a sob. Kat turned from the sink where she was cleaning up to see him put his hands over his face.

"Why can't we find her, Kat?"

Drying her hands in a towel, Kat hugged him.

"We'll find her, Greg."

Pulling his face from his hands, he looked at his sister. She stood, straightened, his gaze locked on her, growing colder. Wheels turned within Greg, the memory of a troubling moment bubbled to the surface.

She knows something.

"Why're you looking at me like that, Greg?"

"Early on, you wanted to say what you thought happened—but didn't."

"No, it wasn't like that."

"Yes, it was. Kat, you know something, don't you?"

She shook her head.

"No, Greg, I don't know anything."

"Tell me."

"Greg, please."

"I know when you're lying. Tell me what you know about Jenn!"

"Keep your voice down. I don't know anything."

His chair scraped along the floor as he got to his feet, stepping into her space. Kat was five-ten, but at six feet, Greg stood over her.

"Tell me."

Kat stepped back from her brother.

"All right but sit down. Please," she said. "I don't know anything but I had a thought."

"A thought?"

"Yes. Sit down."

Greg sat.

Kat took the chair across from him. Sadness in her eyes, she reached out, taking one of his hands.

"Greg, do you think it's possible that maybe, just maybe, she was seeing someone?"

Greg pulled his hand away.

"No. What makes you say that?"

"I never told anyone this but—"

"Never told anyone what?"

"I saw—" Kat looked away to find the words to continue. "I saw Jenn with another man, Greg."

"What?"

"A couple of months ago, I had a delivery at Jake's school and I saw Jenn with a man."

"Saw her, how? What're you talking about?"

"Greg, you had to be there. They were in a corner of the parking lot, like they wanted to be alone. He was touching her shoulder gently, smiling."

Struggling to interpret Kat's revelation, Greg said: "Who was the guy?"

"Porter Sellwin."

"With the school board?"

"Yes. I asked Bert Cobb who he was because Sellwin's come out to the searches. You met him, Greg."

Shaking his head, he said: "No, I don't believe

there's anything to this. Jenn's on a lot of committees, dealing with school polices. They were likely talking about school stuff."

"Greg, you didn't see it the way I did, their body language," Kat said.

"Don't, Kat. Just don't."

"Sellwin's a handsome man with a reputation with women."

The muscles in Greg's jaw began pulsing.

"Stop!" He glared at her. "I know you don't like Jenn."

"Don't say that."

"It's been that way ever since I brought her home, and it continued when we got married," he said. "And you want to know why Jenn didn't invite you to be part of our wedding party? It's because you and Neil were coming apart and you were a wreck."

"I was not."

"You were, Kat. You were dealing with so much, you were drinking, and Jenn didn't want to put more on your plate. But since then, you've fought a silent war with her."

"That's not true!"

"It is! And now you tell me this crap."

"Greg, I know what I saw."

"God, Kat, do you hate her that much?"

Tears rolled down Kat's cheeks, and she returned to the counter. Greg drove his hands in his hair, his creased face sagging as he stared at the floor. A tense, quiet minute passed.

"Everyone's stressed. You need to sleep," Kat

said. "Go to bed. I'll finish cleaning up. We can go searching in the morning."

Greg nodded, then said: "I'll get Jake."

Descending the basement stairs, Greg's legs nearly buckled. Wobbling from exhaustion, he gripped the railing and sat on the stairs. After a few seconds, he continued down to see his father had fallen asleep on the sofa with the TV on. The drone was on the table.

No sign of Jake.

"Dad?" Greg nudged Vince. "Where's Jake?"

Waking, Vince groggily looked around.

"Isn't he with you? I thought he went upstairs."

Greg hauled himself back up to the kitchen.

"Did you see Jake?"

"Isn't he downstairs with Dad?" Kat said.

"No. You look around here for him. Jake!" Greg called then started upstairs, where he checked every bedroom, bathroom, and closet.

No sign of Jake.

Greg returned to the kitchen.

"He's not on this floor," Kat said. Vince was next to her.

"I swear he went upstairs."

"But you fell asleep, Dad," Greg said. "Did you see him go upstairs?"

"Maybe. I don't know. I'm sorry."

Greg returned to the basement with Kat and Vince behind him. A sickening new fear twisted in Greg's gut. Maybe Jake had heard him arguing with Kat, became upset, and ran off into the night to Carter's house? In the basement, Greg checked

the man cave again and the spare rooms. Then he
opened the door to the room with their furnace, hot
water tank, boxes and crates of things, what he and
Jenn called their storage room.

Raising his hand for the light switch, he stopped.

The light was on.

Jake was on the floor, asleep on the thick area
rug, next to a couple of stacks of plastic tubs and
older cardboard boxes where Jenn kept their Christmas decorations. Some of the containers were open
and decorations displaced as if Jake had been rummaging through them.

Greg noticed Jake had wrapped himself in one
of Jenn's old sweaters, one she wore when Jake
was a toddler.

Maybe that's what he was looking for?

Lowering himself, Greg took Jake into his arms.
Jake stirred but didn't wake as Greg carried him
upstairs to their bedroom, loving Jenn's scent mingling with Jake's.

Kat and Vince said nothing, shutting lights and
doors behind them.

Exhausted, Greg got into bed next to his son,
his heart racing, staring into the night, thoughts
tormenting him.

*Not knowing if Jenn's alive... Jake in her
sweater... Tearing at my heart—we can't lose
Jenn... Jake can't lose his mother like I lost my
mom. No... Was Jake looking for something in the
decorations, or just for Jenn's sweater? Jenn... Was
she having an affair with Sellwin? Is that why she*

was withdrawn? Will the detectives find out when they look on her phone and computers?

His heart pounded faster.

They have mine, too.

Thirty-Three

Jennifer Griffin couldn't understand her captor's message.

It had come from a printer in bold uppercase.

"YOU'RE NOT READY. BUT SOON YOU WILL KNOW WHY YOU'RE HERE."

Not ready?

How many times had she stared at the words, her captor's first communication with her?

I don't know what this means. Ready for what? To be killed?

Jennifer didn't know how long she'd been imprisoned—three days? Four? She felt time was ticking down on her. *I've got to find a way out.* She stood, wincing because her ankles were sore from kicking at the door.

Breathing hard, she focused on the two lower delivery doors.

That's it!

She opened one, removed the pail then placed her head and shoulders into the space. Tricky, but she could squeeze through. The only thing stopping her was the door on the other side.

She pushed at it. It didn't move.

She got down on her back and inserted both feet, pressing her shoes against it. She pulled her legs back and drove her heels into it. Her ankles hurt. Nothing happened. She kicked and kicked, gritting her teeth, growling.

The door didn't budge.

Grunting and cursing, spittle flying, she kicked and kicked until her feet and legs were inflamed with pain.

It was futile.

Wiping at tears, she continued taking inventory of her cell. She had no tools. Nothing. Moving to replace the white pail in its storage compartment, she picked it up by the handle then stopped.

An idea came.

The bucket had a steel handle. Her captor had used buckets with plastic handles, metal handles, and some with no handle at all.

She worked the metal handle free from the connector bolts on the bucket. The u-loop ends had edges to them. Jennifer tried folding the handle, like a hanger, but couldn't. Positioning it against her lower leg, she used her foot and her weight, clenching her jaw at the pain, as she bent the ends together, then she got a towel and twisted it around forming a grip.

The little metal tool with its looped edging felt good in her hand.

Jennifer then went to the big door.

She looked at the hinges, which were mounted on the inside. Strange, but that's how the room was constructed. She studied the steel hardware of the hinge and bolt assembly. There were two steel assemblies, one upper and one lower, each secured by three flathead star-point screws.

Gripping her new tool, Jennifer got on her knees and began scratching at the wood around the lower assembly. The steel edge produced a tiny curl of a shaving.

She continued scraping.

Another tiny shaving of wood curled from the frame.

Then another.

Thirty-Four

Lancaster / Elma, New York

Kozak and Carillo parked their Taurus among the pickups and vans on the hardened soil in front of the white job site trailer for Phase 2 of Pine Castle Park development.

They went inside and asked for Al Clayton with Solid and Strong Contracting.

Eyeing their badges, project supervisor Pavel Hatch grunted, clamped his teeth on the unlit cigar at the side of his mouth, leaned over a worktable, and ran his finger over a map.

"Solid and Strong's in the upper nine hundreds. You'll find Clayton there. Just go right when you step outside."

"Thanks," Kozak said.

"Wait. You'll need these. Rules." Hatch handed them white hard hats. "You can give 'em back on your way out."

They moved along the evolving neighborhood of houses. Some were finished; some were shells. All had crews working at stages of completion. Lot numbers were spray-painted on fragments of fiber-board leaning in the window frames, or affixed to a stake in the yard. Walking on the new street, uneven with stones and dried mud tracks, Kozak was glad she was not wearing open-toed shoes.

Passing trucks sent dust swirling. The air smelled of lumber, earth, and cement, echoing with the punch-thud of nail guns and the roar of excavation equipment. Earlier that morning, Kozak and Carillo had received some forensic results. They were expecting more soon. For now, they were tracking down witness leads. It was part of the job. You followed them wherever they took you, and Kozak's instinct told her this one was a thread to a hidden truth.

When they reached the high nine hundreds and asked for Clayton, they were directed to a man supervising lots #975 and #976. He had a full beard, a strong build, with the hint of a paunch beneath his flannel shirt and jeans.

"Al Clayton?" Kozak said.

"Yeah."

Introducing themselves, the investigators presented their badges.

"Can we talk?" Kozak said.

"Is this is about Jenn?" His face brightened. "Have you found her?"

"It's about Jennifer and no, we haven't located her."

Clayton's face fell. He nodded.

"Sure, we can talk, but so you know, I got a concrete mixing truck coming to pour at any moment.

Greg wants us to keep the work moving. We have deadlines."

"Just need a couple minutes," Kozak said.

Clayton nodded to a pickup truck and they went to it. Leaning on the fender, he removed his hard hat, dragged his forearm across his forehead.

"First," Carillo asked, "can you show us some ID?"

Clayton pulled his driver's license from his wallet. Carillo took a good look then took a picture of it before returning it.

"We'd like your help," Kozak said, showing him a picture on her tablet. "Is this you?"

It was a tightly cropped shot of Clayton in the bar.

Clayton nodded.

"And this is Greg?" She showed him a frame of just Greg Griffin.

"Right," Clayton said.

She showed him another cropped photo of just Clayton and Griffin with the big TV screens with games in the background.

"Do you know when and where this is?" Kozak asked.

Clayton scratched his beard.

"In the Mulberry Bar in Depew."

"When?"

Clayton hesitated, looked at the detectives.

"The night Jenn disappeared. Why?"

"And who's this?" She showed him a photo, tightly cropped, of the mystery woman in the bar.

Clayton looked at it.

"Brooke Bollman."

"And who is she?"

Clayton hesitated, then cast a glance to the extreme end of the job site, where a mixing truck was signaling to turn.

"She runs a food truck company, has about half a dozen trucks. Why?"

Kozak then showed the full sequence of photos, showing Bollman, Clayton, and Greg, ending with Bollman's hand under the table on Greg. Clayton leaned in, understanding what was happening in the images.

"How would you characterize the relationship between Greg Griffin and Brooke Bollman, the woman you identified in these photos?"

Clayton looked at Kozak and Carillo, then glanced toward the approaching mixing truck.

"This is the first time I've seen these pictures. How do I know they're even real?"

"They're authentic. Our forensic people confirmed it," Kozak said.

"You're making me a little nervous. Maybe I need a lawyer or something."

"All you need to do is tell us the truth," Carillo said. "If you are concealing evidence, or mislead us, it could be construed as obstruction, and that includes keeping our conversation confidential."

Clayton's face whitened.

"Look, as far as Brooke and Greg and those pictures go, I don't know a damned thing and that's the truth. Brooke hangs out with the crew sometimes after work."

The rattle and growl of diesel grew louder as the mixing truck lumbered nearer. Clayton waved it closer to the lots.

"What's the name of Bollman's company?" Kozak asked.

"Excelsior," Clayton said. "I have to go."

"We'll be in touch," Carillo said.

The investigators stepped clear as Clayton talked with the truck driver, then the crew in the foundation. They got busy with the operation, reversing the truck, its back-up beeper bleating, inching it carefully into place as the mixing drum turned, then positioning the chute.

While watching, Kozak went online and found a site for Excelsior Rapid Food Truck Service. Bollman's picture was on the About Us page. As Clayton and his crew worked, the discharge began with the scraping rush of concrete into the foundation of #975.

Stepping away and turning from the roar, Kozak called the cell number for Brooke Bollman.

Thirty-Five

East Aurora, New York

Polly and Vic's Café was at the edge of town near the expressway.

The sign in the window said: Today's Special: Polish Potato Pancakes $4.99.

The place had eight booths, a wraparound counter with twelve stools, and an ever-present aroma of deep-fried food, onions, and garlic.

"Hey, Vic." Carillo waved to the man in the kitchen with a white T-shirt and apron, who waved back.

Brooke Bollman had agreed to meet Kozak and Carillo at the café. The investigators got there early, took a booth, and had ordered coffee when Kozak's phone rang with a call from Lieutenant Phil Becker.

"Sent you a summary update on material FIU extracted from their phones and computers so far," Becker said.

"Anything there?" Kozak opened her tablet, then the new attachment.

"Not much from Jennifer," Becker said. "But

look at those highlighted texts Greg received. Especially the one sent to him about an hour before she was last seen at the Korner Fast."

"I see it." Kozak raised an eyebrow. "And I see who sent it."

"More forensic results are coming, but I wanted to get this to you. Could be something there, Claire."

"Could be. This is good timing, Phil. And what about security cameras at the Mulberry Bar?"

"Poor quality, nothing on the angles we need. We don't know who sent us those photos. Gotta go."

Polly brought the coffee and started pouring.

"You make the best coffee in the state." Carillo winked at her.

She waved off his compliment. "Oh go on, Ned."

As they started on their coffee, Kozak turned her tablet to Carillo and they reviewed the new information.

"Interesting," he said.

For some twenty minutes, in lowered voices, they discussed the investigation when Kozak glanced out the window. A white van parked, and she recognized Brooke Bollman as she got out and walked into the diner. She stood in the doorway wearing a formfitting Bills T-shirt and jeans, sunglasses perched on her head. One hand held the strap of her bag over her shoulder.

Kozak caught her attention, and she joined them.

Bollman was tall, shapely, had long black hair and a bright smile. After quick introductions, Carillo requested her driver's license, confirming her identification and photographing it before giving it back to her.

Bollman asked the first question.

"Have you found Jennifer? Oh my God, everyone's so scared for her."

"No," Kozak said. "Tell us, how do you know her?"

"I don't *know her*. I've seen her briefly, casually, a couple times, you know, at job sites. That's how I know Greg. Why did you want to talk to me?" She looked up at Polly. "Just diet Pepsi for me."

"We only have Coke."

"That's fine, thanks."

Kozak resumed. "And how well would you say you know Greg?"

"Casually, from meeting him on construction sites for a few years. I guess we have a professional friendship."

"Is that what you call it?" Carillo asked.

"What do you mean?"

"Were you with him at the Mulberry Bar in Depew the night his wife went missing?" Carillo asked.

Bollman's face flushed. She didn't answer.

Kozak had the photos cued up on her tablet. She turned it toward Bollman.

"Isn't this you next to Greg Griffin at the Mulberry?" Kozak asked.

Bollman stared at the screen without speaking.

"Brooke? Isn't that you?" Kozak asked again.

"Who gave you those pictures?" Bollman asked as her soda arrived in a glass with ice. She flicked her eyes to Polly in thanks then looked at the detectives for an answer.

"That's not important right now," Kozak said. "We know you sent Greg a text an hour before Jennifer Griffin was last seen."

"Are you involved in her disappearance in any way?" Carillo said. "If you are, now's the time to tell us the truth, Brooke."

Bollman's face reddened; tears stood in her eyes. She looked out the window, shaking her head.

Thirty-Six

Buffalo, New York, Whispering Valley

Greg woke up angry that morning.

It had fused with his fear for Jenn, forcing him to grapple with the ugly possibility that Kat had raised.

Was Jenn having an affair with Porter Sellwin?

The question hammered at him as he showered, dressed, then went downstairs. He was heading for his office and laptop when Kat called him to the kitchen where she was making breakfast.

"Jake's vice-principal called while you were in the shower to say he can go back to school if he likes. Even for half the day," Kat said. "They have a school psychologist there, if he wants to talk her. Or they could send her here. They think it might help if Jake resumed his routine, saw his friends. Makes sense to me. I could take him, if you like."

"Let's ask him." Greg called Jake to the kitchen.

Jake appeared. Greg lowered himself and took his hands.

"Son, would you like to stay home today, or go

back to school? If you want to go to school, even for a half day, Aunt Kat will take you."

"I miss my friends." Jake shrugged. "But what if Mom comes home and I'm not here?"

"I'll be right here to tell everybody," said Vince, who'd joined them from the living room. "Then we'll bring you right home."

"Where're you going to be today, Dad?"

"I'm going to look for Mom."

Jake took his time, looked at everyone and weighed his choices before deciding. "Okay, I'll go to school for a little bit today."

Greg hugged Jake and Jake hugged him back, hard.

"Hey, what were you doing in the Christmas decorations?"

"Mom likes them and I remembered she got a new one, an angel thing. I was looking for it."

"Why?"

"Maybe I could make a wish on it for Mom to come home."

"I see." Greg nodded, glanced back to Kat. She'd covered her mouth with her hand. Greg swallowed hard and said, "Good idea. We can look for it later." He buffed Jake's hair and everyone got on with things.

With Vince returning to the living room to watch news, Greg went to his office and worked on his laptop, going to Jenn's social media pages. He was certain there was something there when he found a group photo of a fundraiser—Jenn with Porter Sellwin. She was smiling up at him as he held up a large check.

Greg went to the school's Facebook page, searching all the photos before finding one of the Parent School Support Committee being congratulated by Porter Sellwin of the board. Sellwin was shaking her hand, another hand on her shoulder. Again, she's smiling at him.

So what? he thought.

But the caption said something about another improved policy. "After many long hours, co-chair Jennifer Griffin and board member Porter Sellwin achieved the new…"

Many long hours.

Greg dug deeper online.

Sellwin was a Realtor with Levey & Warensk Partners. Greg found the agency's site, and its Facebook page, raced through all posted pictures with Sellwin. Many were congratulatory events, house deals, sod turnings, or renovations. In most, he flashed that white-toothed smile with women; with his hand on a shoulder, or arm around a waist, or kissing a cheek.

Has he kissed Jenn?

Uncertain what to make of it, Greg's pulse increased as he replayed Kat's account of what she'd witnessed, her words prodding him.

Greg, you didn't see it the way I did, their body language… Sellwin's a handsome man with a reputation with women.

I can't let this go, Greg thought. *I need to talk to Sellwin, get a better hold on this.*

Greg called Levey & Warensk Partners to arrange to see him.

"Porter's out," the woman who answered said. "Not sure when he'll be back. He's with the school group, searching for the missing woman."

"Do you know which area?"

"I'm sorry, we don't. Who's calling?"

"That's okay."

"If this concerns a property, I can have him call you?"

"No. Thank you."

Greg needed to do this face-to-face. Getting ready to leave, he found his father near the front window.

"Those press people have been out there since Kat left with Jake." Vince turned to Greg. "Want me to go with you?"

"No, you stay here, Dad. Who knows what could happen. Don't talk to any reporters or let them in."

"I won't."

"But keep an eye on the news, alert me to anything, you know."

"I know." Vince took Greg's hand, clutched his upper arm. "Don't give up hope, son. We'll find her."

"Thanks, Dad."

Greg's pickup was in the garage. The absence of Jenn's Corolla meant more room, a cold reality. Greg took advantage of it as the automatic door lifted and he backed out, pulling his ballcap down further.

On the sidewalk, half a dozen newspeople with cameras, phones, and microphones flowed around both sides of the cab calling out his name and questions. He kept the windows up, gave a short wave and drove off.

* * *

Driving through Trailside Grove, Greg battled to make sense of the turmoil swirling in his head.

Was Jenn cheating with Sellwin? Was that why she'd been so cool and distant? Was it my fault? Have I been so consumed with losing contracts I ignored her? Could it all be related to her disappearance?

"No," he said aloud to no one. "No way. She wouldn't do this to Jake."

But what if it was true?

Ripplewood Creek was the first search point Greg went to. While several days had passed, his anguish was as raw as the night Jenn had vanished. Spotting Doug Tucker at the volunteer command post, he asked about Sellwin. Tucker flipped through pages on a clipboard.

"Porter Sellwin, right? He'd be with the school group," Tucker said. "No, they didn't sign in here. Greg, want me to check the other zones?"

"Yes."

Tucker got on a walkie-talkie, enquired with search posts in Trailside Grove, Cardinal, and Noble Haven. Greg glanced around at the activity in Ripplewood. Some of the coordinators waved their support. Greg nodded his thanks, while privately he wondered how much longer before they gave up looking for Jenn.

"Got it," Tucker said. "Whisper Wind Park."

The park was less than two miles south of Greg's home.

It was in the new neighborhood of Whispering

Valley, adjacent to the Harriet Tubman School. He parked at the school, went to the command post, and got directions to find the volunteer group from Tall Elm.

Whisper Wind Park was rugged; large homes backed onto it with the chain-link fences of their backyards bordering the trails necklacing the forest, which snaked through the community.

The dense woods held valleys, waterfalls, ledges, and outcroppings sweeping in dramatic slopes down into ravines and creeks. Here, sunlight was dimmed, the air smelled of moist earth. The murmur of voices, the crack of a branch, and swish of leaves carried through the park. He saw flashes of colors, spotting searchers.

Looking for Sellwin, Greg fought doubts.

Is this the right thing to do? Have I given way to my anger, exhaustion, and guilt? But I got a bad vibe about Sellwin and when I think of him with his hands on Jenn—

"Greg?"

He turned to Bert Cobb.

"Hi, Bert."

Assessing him, Cobb said, "Are you okay?"

"Yeah, I wanted to talk to Porter Sellwin."

"Sellwin?"

"Is the school still letting everyone search? Because Jake went back today."

"They let us rotate in shifts, like half days there and half days here, all to support Jennifer. How're you and Jake holding up?"

"It's hard, Bert."

"I hear you, but you can't give up."

"Thanks."

"Sellwin's down there." Cobb pointed to a small valley, about thirty yards off. "In the blue shirt. I was searching with him."

Finding a branch to use as a walking stick and stepping carefully, Greg made his way, getting near enough for Sellwin to turn in surprise.

"Hello, Greg." He flashed a smile.

Greg looked around quickly to ensure they were alone, tightened his grip while leaning on the branch.

"Sellwin, I want to talk to you about Jenn."

Sellwin's smile faded; his eyes conveyed curiosity.

"What is it?"

"You've worked closely with her."

"Of course, on committees, school policies."

"But it was more than that."

"What do you mean?"

"I have a witness who saw you with my wife."

"A witness? Saw what?"

"You were touching her."

"Touching her? What're you talking about?"

"You know damned well what I'm talking about."

"No, I don't. Greg, you're upset. You look like you haven't slept."

"There's something going on with you and Jenn."

Greg stabbed Sellwin's chest hard with his forefinger.

Sellwin's Adam's apple rose and fell.

"Look," Sellwin said, "I don't know what Jennifer told you but—"

"*What she told me?* What do you mean?"

Sellwin's eyes shifted then came back to Greg.

"Tell me what you were doing with my wife."

"Greg, there's nothing to tell."

"You're lying. I know about you!"

Greg jabbed Sellwin's chest again with his finger. This time, something in Sellwin clicked. His body tensed, his face hardened, his eyes narrowed.

"Be careful, Greg."

"What the hell does that mean?"

"Don't do something you'll regret."

Sellwin's smile detonated Greg's wrath, and he raised the branch over his head.

"You're a lying piece of—"

Greg couldn't move the branch. It was frozen. Bert Cobb had taken hold of it from behind.

Sellwin walked away, shaking his head.

Greg hesitated then let go of the branch, his chest heaving, his teeth still gritted.

"Greg." Cobb watched Sellwin get some distance from them then said, "Calm down. You're stressed." Cobb lowered his voice, ensuring Sellwin was out of earshot. "If you unload on him and he presses charges, where does that leave Jake?"

Letting out a breath, Greg nodded his thanks to Cobb.

In the distance, he saw a TV camera aimed at him. Cursing to himself, he dragged his hands over his face when his phone rang.

It was his Dad. "Get home right now!"

Thirty-Seven

Several police vehicles and news trucks were clustered in front of Greg's house.

So was Kat's Ready Quick Courier van, white with chartreuse stripes. She must've rushed over from work.

Fear for Jake rose in Greg's throat.

Was he home? Oh God, did they find Jenn?

Passing through the newspeople, ignoring questions, Greg got to his front door as troopers wearing latex gloves carried boxes and paper bags of his belongings out of his house. He sidestepped some of the troopers at the entrance where he found Vince holding documents in his hand.

"They got these search warrants, Greg. I had to let them in."

Jake was sitting at the kitchen table, his mouth open wide. A female forensic tech wearing latex gloves was swabbing the inside of his cheek.

"This will just take a sec, sweetie," the tech said to Jake.

Kat held Jake's hand.

"They brought him home from school."

"I rode in a police car, Dad," Jake said when he could speak.

"What?" Greg said.

"They're collecting his DNA," Kat said. "They'll get ours, too."

Greg turned. Carillo had entered the kitchen then led him down the hall. Along the way, Greg saw forensic people taking files, notebooks, and other items from Jenn's office area. In his office, they were doing the same.

"All part of the investigation," Carillo said.

"But you already have our phones, laptops, our fingerprints."

"I assure you, it's standard. We need you in the upstairs bathroom that you and Jenn use."

Kozak was there with another forensic tech at the counter.

"Hi, Greg," Kozak said. "Would you please identify Jennifer's combs, brushes, and her toothbrush? We're taking them for DNA analysis."

The blood drained from Greg's face.

"Did you find her? Is she dead?"

"No," Kozak said. "This is part of the investigation. We'll submit the DNA to all local, state, and national databases to help us locate her. Before we leave, we'll collect yours, as well."

Greg stared at Jenn's toothbrush, her comb, her hairbrush. He glanced at her sink, her mirror.

Suddenly he saw her there, the image breaking his heart.

"Greg?" Kozak said.

He pointed. "Those are hers, obviously."

"Thanks." Kozak stepped from the bathroom with Greg, leaving the tech to collect the items. "The warrants allow us to process your house, for evidence. It'll take a while."

"Why? She's missing from Ripplewood. She never made it home."

"There could be something here that's tied to it," Carillo said. "You wouldn't want us to over-look anything, would you?"

Everything was moving so fast; all of these peo-ple, these strangers, who deal with violence and death, invading their home, swabbing his son, and taking Jenn's things.

"This means we'll need you to leave the house, to find some place for the night," Kozak said. "Our people will watch you collect some overnight things for you and Jake. They'll make a record of it."

Greg stared at them.

"We'll need you to do this now, Greg," Kozak said.

"I don't like this," Greg said. "Maybe I should be getting a lawyer."

"Maybe," Kozak said, "because we'd like you to submit to a polygraph exam as soon as possible."

Thirty-Eight

Lynsey Dowd slid five new twenty-dollar bills into an envelope, wrote, "Jenn" on it, then pushed back tears.

She put the envelope, the deposit bag, and other weekly records into the office security safe on the lower shelf behind her. After locking it, she turned and worked at her computer.

Most financial business at Crystallo View Optical was conducted digitally. Some matters involved cash. A few suppliers and older customers insisted on cash-only transactions. The eye doctors who owned the company accommodated them.

Lynsey made weekly trips to the bank. Her uncle was one of the owners and had asked her if she would split her duties as an optometric assistant and do the initial bookkeeping before passing things to the accountants. She didn't mind because she had done it for his small practice before he partnered with the others.

Lynsey was typing and checking invoices when

an icon for a Buffalo TV station popped up in the corner of her monitor, notifying her of a news story.

She clicked on it, bringing to life a video of police at Jenn's house.

"Mystery deepens in the disappearance of Buffalo-area mom, Jennifer Griffin," the reporter's voice said. "New search warrants were executed late this afternoon at the Griffin home in Trailside Grove..."

The report amplified Lynsey's grief. She whispered another prayer for Jenn. Everyone at Crystallo had volunteered to search, including Lynsey.

Why is this happening? She's such a good person.

The money in the safe for Jenn was an example of her altruistic nature.

Several weeks ago, Jenn confidentially asked Lynsey to divert $100 a week from the direct digital deposit of her salary, and give it to her in cash.

"I want to start a secret fund to save for a winter vacation to the Caribbean for us. Greg works so hard. I want to surprise him and Jake. I can hide it in our household costs. He won't know."

Lynsey was glad that the doctors insisted that Jenn's salary continue because everyone believed and hoped that she was coming home. It meant Lynsey would honor Jenn's secret request and keep diverting and holding the cash for her.

Jenn's face appeared on Lynsey's monitor as the news story ended.

And I won't tell anyone about it, Jenn.

Thirty-Nine

LaSalle in Buffalo, New York

"Yes, polygraphs are common in cases like this, Greg."

Phone pressed to his ear, he sat in Kat's kitchen, consulting with Susan Segretti, a Buffalo criminal defense attorney he'd contacted.

"There are considerations," Segretti said. "I'll outline them…"

It was evening, and listening, with his elbows on the table, Greg gripped his head with his free hand as if to stem his whirling fears. While state police were processing their home in Trailside Grove for evidence in Jenn's disappearance, Greg and Jake had made the half-hour drive to Kat's cozy two-story colonial in LaSalle, near the college. Kat and Vince got a couple of pizzas, but Jake had only taken a few bites because worry had taken his appetite.

"What if Mom comes home and we're not there?" Jake said.

"Police will call us," Greg said.

"But why're they looking in our house? She's not there."

"They're looking for the tiniest things that might help them," Greg said.

"Even in my mouth?"

"It's complicated, Jake. Everybody's doing everything to find Mom." Greg stroked Jake's head. "Have some more pizza."

"Hey." Kat smiled. "I've got some video games you can play with Grandpa after."

"Think you can still beat me at hockey?" Vince asked.

Jake shrugged. "Probably."

Vince winked. "Give you five bucks if you do."

After eating, Greg and Kat had talked alone in her kitchen with the door closed as Greg tried to hold it together.

"So you decided to talk to Sellwin?" Kat said. "What happened?"

"I got a bad vibe off him. I wanted to beat the smile from his face."

"Do you think there's something going on with him and Jenn?"

"I have no proof. And I don't know what Kozak and Carillo know, or found. They've been going through our phones, our computers. They've taken our prints, more stuff, our DNA. Now they want to polygraph me. *God, Kat, they think I hurt her.*"

That's when Kat took control, insisting he talk to a lawyer immediately about the polygraph. After a combination of calls to Kat's friends and an online search, they reached Susan Segretti, considered one of the best. Segretti was aware of Jenn's case—most people in the region were—and she'd returned Greg's call, noting the first consultation, even if it was after regular hours, was free.

"...now, there are advantages and disadvantages to agreeing to submit to a polygraph," Segretti said as she relayed the basics to him.

No matter what investigators say, it's not routine, and Greg should assume he has not been ruled out as a suspect. And while the results cannot be used in court, any statements he makes during the process could be used against him later.

Segretti said that Greg had every right to refuse the polygraph, but refusal would create the perception that he was hiding something, while participating could expedite removing him as a suspect. She said she could be present, acting as his attorney, if he agreed to take a polygraph, and could represent him subsequently, depending on how things went.

Her fee was $300 an hour.

"The decision is yours. Think about it, Greg, and let me know."

The call ended. Greg stared at nothing while Jake and Vince's game playing spilled from the living room.

"Well?" Kat said. "What did she say?"

Greg told her everything, including Segretti's rate.

"I don't know what to do," he said.

"You don't know? Look. I got these while you were on the phone." Kat had cued up Buffalo TV news reports. "These are new."

The first showed volunteers in the ongoing search for Jenn. They turned up the sound to hear the reporter say, "...however, tension apparently surfaced between Greg Griffin, the missing woman's husband, and a volunteer searcher today in Whisper Wind Park..." The footage was blurry but it showed Greg confronting Porter Sellwin. "No one would comment as to the source of the apparent disagreement..."

"And look at this one." Kat hit play on another report showing police at Greg's house as he entered.

"...late today state police investigators executed new search warrants at the home of missing mom Jennifer Griffin. Sources tell us DNA samples were collected giving rise to speculation that people close to Griffin may not yet have been ruled out as suspects..."

At a loss, Greg lowered his head, shaking it slowly.

"This looks bad for you," Kat said as her laptop chimed with a notification. "Oh, this is live news on the case."

Kat clicked on it and a video blossomed of a man at a cluster of microphones, newspeople huddled around him, a woman at his shoulder.

"...to reiterate, my client, Brooke Bollman, is cooperating with police and is not involved in any way with the disappearance of Jennifer Griffin. That concludes our statement. We will take no questions."

All the saliva drained from Greg's mouth, then he cursed.

"Who is she, Greg?" Kat asked.

He didn't answer.

Heart racing, skin tingling, Greg reached for his phone.

His call was answered on the third ring.

"Hi, Ms. Segretti, Greg Griffin again. I will take the polygraph and I'd like you to be there, as my attorney."

Forty

Clarence, New York

Greg took a deep breath.

"That's it, breathe regularly. Remember, treat this as a conversation, but give only yes or no responses." Valerie Vera, the polygraph examiner, checked her instruments.

It was midmorning the next day.

Greg was seated in a comfortable high-back chair with wide armrests. He looked at the sensors connected to his fingertips and chest to gauge his breathing, pulse, and perspiration. Cables linked the sensors to Vera's polygraph and laptop, where she would measure and record the activity.

Earlier, in explaining the exam process, Vera also conducted the pretest interview, which included questions on Greg's physical and mental status, and the use of any medications.

"It's okay to be uneasy. I expect some anxiety, Greg."

Valerie Vera wore red-framed glasses that rested partway down her nose. She was in her early fifties and looked at him through her glasses and over them to ensure he understood as she told him how she would analyze the results and give investigators one of three outcomes: Greg Griffin is untruthful, Greg Griffin is truthful, or the results are inconclusive.

Greg took another breath.

How did this happen?

Here he was at the Bureau of Criminal Investigation offices of the New York State Police, Clarence Barracks, in a meeting room, hooked to a lie detector. Behind him were Kozak, Carillo, their boss, Lieutenant Phil Becker, and Greg's attorney, Susan Segretti.

Centered at the far end of the table, Vera had placed a clear glass lamp with floating globs of luminescent goop for him to watch and stay calm.

"All set," Vera said. "Are you relaxed, Greg?"

"Yes," he lied.

"We'll start with some basics to establish a foundation."

Vera made a quick adjustment of the polygraph and began.

"Are you Greg Griffin?"

"Yes."

"Is your wife Jennifer Griffin?"

"Yes."

"Is your son Jake Griffin?"

"Yes."

"Are you the quarterback for the Buffalo Bills?"

"No."

"Do you reside in Trailside Grove?"

"Yes."

Vera took one second, studying the graphs on her laptop.

"Is your wife missing?"

Greg caught his breath.

"Yes."

"Did you report her missing?"

"Yes."

"Did several hours pass before you realized she was missing and your call to police?"

"Yes."

"Did you first search for her before calling police?"

"Yes."

"Were you the only person searching for her for several hours?"

"Yes."

"Did you enter the Korner Fast outlet in Ripplewood Creek the night she was missing?"

"Yes."

"Did you enter the Korner Fast outlet in Ripplewood Creek more than once the night she was missing?"

What does that mean? Where're they headed?

"Your response?"

"No."

Vera made a notation.

"Do you own a hoodie?"

A hoodie?

"Yes."

"Is it light in color?"

"No."

"Dark?"

"Yes."

"Were you wearing your hoodie the first night you searched for your wife?"

I can't remember. I don't know.

"I don't know."

Vera made a notation.

"Did you injure your hands the night your wife was missing?"

"Yes."

"Was the injury due to removing a traffic cone from under your vehicle?"

"Yes."

"Are you aware your wife had bruises on her neck and wrists the night she went missing?"

Jenn's bruises?

Greg swallowed.

"Yes."

"Have you ever struck your wife?"

"No."

"Have you ever abused your wife?"

"No."

"Did you give her the bruises seen on her neck and arms?"

Greg hesitated.

"But they were from playing football in the yard," he said.

"Yes or no, please, Greg."

"Yes."

Vera made a notation.

"Did you argue with your wife about financial

matters in the time leading up to her disappearance?"

Beads of sweat formed on Greg's brow.

"Yes."

"Do you hold a life insurance policy on your wife?"

"Yes."

"Is the death benefit three hundred thousand dollars?"

"Yes."

"Are you the beneficiary?"

"Yes."

Greg heard movement behind him, and Vera reached for a tablet handed to her by one of the investigators. Vera used it to show Greg a photograph of a woman.

"Do you recognize this woman?"

It was a closely cropped photo of Brooke Bollman in a bar. Greg's stomach lurched. Cold sweat webbed down his back.

"Greg, do you recognize this woman?"

He swallowed hard.

"Yes."

"Do you know this woman?"

"Yes."

"Is she Brooke Bollman?"

"Yes."

Vera cued up another photo of Greg sitting next to Bollman.

"Is this you with Brooke Bollman?"

"Yes."

Vera moved to the other photos of Bollman's

hand under the table on Greg in the vicinity of his crotch, both of them smiling at each other.

Staring at it, Greg's scalp stung, ice coiled up his spine.

Where did they get this photo? Who gave it to them?

"Was this photo taken at the Mulberry Bar in Depew the night your wife went missing?"

Tears brimmed in Greg's eyes.

"Yes."

Vera swiped at the tablet with the photos, then showed Greg a text.

Think about it Greg. We'd be great together.

"Do you recall receiving this text from Brooke Bollman the night your wife was missing?"

"Yes."

"Have you had discussions with Brooke Bollman about entering into a business partnership after she had won a substantial settlement from a construction firm arising from their negligence and an accident on a job site in Lackawanna?"

Greg swallowed hard.

"Yes."

"Are you now, or have you in the past, engaged in sexual relations with Brooke Bollman?"

Greg hesitated.

He'd been tempted to act on Brooke's offer, so tempted, but something echoed in him, taking him to that day he saw Jenn crying alone in high school.

Who'd be stupid enough to break that girl's heart? I couldn't do that to Jenn with Brooke. I couldn't bear hurting her and Jake. I'd forever be a liar in his eyes. I took a vow to love only Jenn. What it came down to, and what I came to realize over the years, is that when I saw Jenn that day in school, I was watching over, and preparing to love, my wife.

"Greg, are you now, or have you in the past, engaged in sexual relations with Brooke Bollman?"

"No."

Vera made a notation.

"Have you ever driven your wife's Toyota Corolla?"

"Yes."

"Is your wife's height five feet three inches?"

"Yes."

"Is your height six feet?"

"Yes."

"Do you need to push back the driver's seat in your wife's Toyota Corolla when you drive it?"

"Yes."

"Did you drive your wife's Toyota Corolla the night she went missing?"

"No."

"Are you involved in your wife's disappearance?"

"No."

"Do you think Brooke Bollman is involved?"

"No."

"Do you think anyone in your family is involved?"

"No."

"Do you think anyone in your wife's social circles is involved?"

"No."

"If you know someone was involved in your wife's disappearance, would you tell police?"

"Yes."

"You were seen arguing with a searcher. Do you suspect anyone is involved in your wife's disappearance?"

Sellwin. Porter Sellwin. Shout out his name. Sellwin with his phony smile, his arrogance, his hands on Jenn. But I have zero evidence. No proof. If I accuse him, I'm accusing Jenn of adultery, of cheating, something I know in my heart she would never, ever do, because it would be a betrayal of who she is, to Jake, to her moral fiber. No, I have no proof. But she's been so cold, so distant—and I'm the one. I'm the one considering Brooke's offer, and every aspect of it—yet—I just don't—

"Greg, your response please: Do you suspect anyone is involved in your wife's disappearance?"

"No."

For nearly an hour, Vera's questions were relentless. Again and again, framing them in different ways, she hammered away on the same areas until she wound it all down.

"Greg, are you concealing any information from investigators that may have a bearing on your wife's disappearance?"

"No."

"Have you been truthful during this process?"

Truthful?

Staring into the lamp with its hypnotic floating goop, Greg traveled back years to the time he was driving with Jenn through the Florida Keys, the road rushing under them, surrounded by celestial turquoise water, windows down, Jenn's arm extended, her hand playing in the breeze, her smile under her sunglasses in a moment of pure happiness.

Now, here in Clarence Barracks, wired to a polygraph, he'd been emotionally eviscerated.

Life was not simple. The truth was elusive.

He'd had lust in his heart and blood on his hands that night.

"Greg?" Vera said. "Have you been truthful during this process?"

He didn't answer.

Forty-One

PEACE THROUGH PERSEVERANCE.

Kozak nodded to the motto under the sign for Sunlit Way Yoga.

"Maybe you should give it a try, Ned," she said as she parked their Taurus and approached the studio. "Connect with your spiritual core."

Carillo shot her a look. "I'd rather get a puppy, Claire."

Kozak smiled and reflected.

"Well, I could use some spiritual mending. I signed the papers the other day, making it official with Wade."

"What?" Carillo's face softened. "Hey, partner, you knew it was coming. Signing was a formality."

"Sadly, yes."

"Remember, when one door closes, another one opens." He held the door to Sunlit Way open for her and winked.

"Appreciate that, Ned."

The studio, on the west side of Williamsville in a

strip mall, was where Jennifer Griffin took weekly
yoga classes. The investigators had come here after
Greg's polygraph because Valerie Vera needed several hours to analyze Greg's responses before the
next case status meeting. Meantime, Kozak and
Carillo resumed following up every thread of Jennifer Griffin's life and routine, looking for anything out of the ordinary that might yield a lead.
In doing the legwork by checking things off, they
ruled things out. Kozak had called ahead to Sunlit Way.

Lori Monroe, Jennifer's yoga teacher, met them
when they entered. She was wearing yoga pants, a
T-shirt under a light yoga sweater. She was bare-
foot, guiding them along the edge of the studio
while a class of mostly women stretched and arched
on mats. The glass-walled office was small, and
Monroe closed the door.

"We're all shocked about Jennifer," Monroe said.
"Some of our people helped in the searches. Our
hearts go out to her family."

"How long has she been taking classes with
you?" Kozak asked.

"About a year and a half. I looked it up before
you came. I also looked up Brooke Bollman, as
you'd requested. She was never a student with us."

"In the time leading up to Jennifer's disappearance, did you notice anything different about her?"
Carillo asked. "Were there any changes in her demeanor, appearance, conversations, anything?"

Monroe started shaking her head.

"Not really."

"What about her routine, anything at all?" Kozak asked.

"Well, she was taking the sixty-minute class up until several weeks ago, when she switched to an express class, which is thirty minutes."

"Can you get the date of the change?" Kozak asked.

Monroe turned to her computer, typed on her keyboard, clicked her mouse, then pointed to a date on the screen and said: "There."

Kozak made a note. "Did she give you a reason for the change?"

"No, I suspected she was busy, or maybe to save money."

"Is there anything else you can think of?"

Monroe crossed her arms in front of her and thought.

"No, that's it," she said. "We're all praying you find her."

After thanking her, Kozak and Carillo walked through the studio and were at the door when they heard the soft padding of bare feet on the floor.

They turned to Monroe, who took them into the hallway.

"One thing I remember," she said. "But it's so small, likely nothing."

"Go ahead," Kozak said.

"Well…" Monroe nodded outside, looking across the street. "Around the time Jennifer shortened her classes, I sometimes noticed her coming out of that building."

The investigators turned, following her gaze.

"Alone, or with someone?" Kozak asked.

"Alone."

"And each time around class time?"

"Yes."

The Five Cloud Professional Center was a four-story stone building.

Kozak and Carillo stood in the lobby reading the directory that showed locations of a pharmacy, a lab, a physiotherapist, accountants, law offices, dentists, architects, and several more tenants.

"Ready for more sleuthing, Ned?"

"No, but let's go."

They began on the ground floor, going from office to office, showing their badges and Jennifer Griffin's photo, asking if she was a customer or a client. It was needle-in-a-haystack work as they went floor to floor. While a number of people recognized Jennifer's face from news reports, most inquiries ended with apologetic headshakes.

"I'm thinking this could be a dead end," Kozak said as they came to one of the last offices on the third floor.

"What was that you were saying about perseverance, Claire?"

They entered the offices of Century & Dilling Architects through the double glass doors. The receptionist greeted them and within seconds had seized their attention.

"Yes, the missing mom. So sad."

"You've seen her on the news?" Carillo said.

"Yes, and on this floor."

"This floor?"

"She comes regularly, maybe every week—I mean she used to."

"She came to this office?" Kozak asked.

"No, the one at the end of the hall. I bumped into her a couple of times in the bathroom. She'd be changing, looked like for yoga. Do you know what happened to her?"

"Thank you," Kozak said.

The office at the end of the hall was for Dr. Anna Bernay and Dr. Stuart Maynart, Psychologists.

It had dark polished floors. The receptionist looked up from her desk. A painting, a large landscape of mountains, filled the wall behind her. The smile she greeted Kozak and Carillo with melted when they identified themselves and showed her Jennifer Griffin's photo.

"Is Jennifer Griffin a client here?"

"I—um—I can't. One moment, please. Have a seat."

The receptionist left her desk, went down the hall, knocked softly on a door, entered, and closed it behind her. The investigators stood, waiting near a sectional couch but not for long. The door opened and a woman in a well-cut navy skirt suit, her dark hair pulled into a ponytail, met them.

"I'm Dr. Anna Bernay. How can I help you?"

"Is Jennifer Griffin a client here?" Kozak said.

Bernay looked at the photo Kozak held out on her phone, then at Kozak and Carillo.

"Please come into my office."

The walls were lined with books, certificates, and degrees. A framed photo of Bernay, a man, and two girls laughing on a beach, stood on her clean desk next to a computer screen. She offered the investigators the sofa chairs in front. There was no couch.

"As you know, communication between a registered psychologist and patient is privileged," Bernay said, tapping her pen on her desk.

"Yes," Kozak said. "But the statute states there are exceptions."

Bernay nodded slowly.

"I can confirm Jennifer Griffin is a client of this office. That's basic information, but that's about all I can tell you."

Kozak leaned forward.

"Doctor, the privilege of confidentiality is not absolute. You're aware about your 'duty to warn' as it pertains to harmful acts."

"Quite aware."

"Are you aware of her location?"

"I'm afraid I cannot answer that question."

"Dr. Bernay, you know Jennifer Griffin's disappearance is the subject of a serious investigation?"

"I am."

"We have reason to believe that she could've been harmed, and if you're in possession of information, such as her location, or treatment records, anything that could have direct bearing on her case, then withholding it could be problematic for you."

"Revelation of such information and records violates a client's right to privacy, violates professional ethics, and could lead to malpractice action and loss of certification."

"And you could face civil action from her family if you do not share information that could help us locate her safely."

Bernay steepled her fingers.

"We can subpoena your records, Doctor," Carillo added.

"What were you treating Jennifer Griffin for?" Kozak asked.

Bernay pursed her lips, placed her pen on her desk then ever so slightly moved her framed photo.

"She's not my client."

"Excuse me?" Kozak said. "But you just said—"

"Leave your cards with me and I'll discuss this with my husband. He's not here at the moment."

"Your husband?"

"Dr. Maynart. Jennifer Griffin is his client."

Forty-Two

Buffalo, New York, Trailside Grove

Dark grayish powder had been smudged and streaked on doorknobs, window frames, walls, banisters, and counters as if malevolent forces had battled throughout Greg's home.

The state police crime scene team had processed the house, looking for more evidence. When Greg returned with Jake, Vince, and Kat, he was taken aback by the aftermath, its intrusiveness, the implication compounding the mental toll of events.

After the polygraph ended, Greg went straight to Kat's house where he refused to answer her questions about it. Kat didn't push things. She made him coffee and a ham and cheese sandwich. He couldn't eat. The stress was gnawing at him. Sometime later, Carillo had called, saying the house had been released and he could go home to Trailside where a patrol unit was waiting with his key. Greg was thankful no media were camped at the house when they'd arrived.

Now, walking through the main floor of his

home, he was shocked by the disarray, by how the furniture had been moved slightly, and how investigators had rummaged through their belongings.

Greg sat on the lower steps of the staircase, trying to recover, while Jake tore past him and up the stairs to his bedroom like he was looking for something amid the chaos.

"Everything okay, Jake?" Kat called after him.

"Leave him," Greg said.

"Look at this stuff." Kat touched a fingertip to a smear near a light switch. "This won't be easy to clean. What is it?"

"I think it's the graphite they use for fingerprints," Vince said.

"I can't believe they would leave such a freakin' mess. Greg, you're going to need a cleaning company to get this stuff out," Kat said.

Greg shut his eyes at the thought of another expense, calculating that the lawyer would cost nearly a thousand dollars for sitting in on his polygraph today then assuring him afterward that police didn't have enough to charge him with anything.

Didn't have enough? God, it was horrible. The questions the polygraph examiner asked, stabbing me with accusations. And those pictures...

"Greg?" Vince touched his shoulder. "You gonna be all right?"

"They think I'm involved in Jenn's disappearance, Dad."

"What?" Vince said, his eyes raking lightning fast over Greg's fading scrapes. "That's stupid. Listen, I watch *Dateline*. They always suspect the husband or boyfriend first. It's procedure. You're smart getting a lawyer so they don't try to pull anything."

"What about Sellwin?" Kat said. "Did he come up?"

"Who's Sellwin?" Vince asked.

Kat flashed her palm to Vince to let Greg answer. "Did you tell them about Sellwin?" she asked again. "You're on the news confronting him."

Greg glared at her, shaking his head.

"What about him, Kat? I lost my mind with him because of what you told me. So, he's a touchy-feely jerk. So what? It proves nothing."

"Greg, I was trying to help."

"Do you honestly believe Jenn would do something like that to me and Jake, and with a creep like Sellwin?"

"I'm sorry—I just—"

They heard sounds of Jake moving around upstairs.

"What's he doing?" Kat said. "I'll go up."

"No, I'm sure he's just glad to be home and is straightening up." Greg stood and let out a long breath. "Thank you for everything, both of you. I need to think. We'll be fine. We need time alone tonight, some space."

Kat and Vince traded looks.

"All right," Kat said. "We'll go."

Greg called for Jake, who came downstairs.

"Aunt Kat and Grandpa are leaving."

Jake hugged and kissed them.

"We'll be back in the morning," Kat said.

"Can you bring some video games, Grandpa?"

"You bet," Vince said.

After they left, Jake started back upstairs, but Greg stopped him.

"What're you doing? Cleaning your room? Don't touch the powder stuff, just leave it."

"No, Dad. I found something."

"You found something?"

"Come up and see."

Greg's phone rang. "Go ahead, son. I'll be right up."

The caller was Al Clayton.

"Got your message to call, Greg. How you holding up?"

"Al, did police talk to you?"

Seconds passed. Clayton didn't answer so Greg prompted him.

"Two investigators? Kozak and Carillo?"

"They told me not to say anything. I don't want to get in trouble."

"Dammit, Al. They had me take a polygraph. You gotta help me here."

Clayton dropped his voice.

"They asked about Brooke. They showed me pictures of her, with her hand on you in the Mulberry that night in Depew."

Greg cursed.

"I said she hung out with us and that's all I know," Clayton said.

"Where did they get those pictures?"

"Damned if I know."

Greg took a moment, digesting matters before he asked Clayton the status of the job.

"Did you get the concrete poured for nine-seventy-five and nine-seventy six?"

"We did. I told you we're on schedule but—"

"But what, Al?"

"I think you should be more concerned about Jenn."

Greg bit his bottom lip.

"Thanks, Al. Keep me posted."

As soon as Greg ended Al's call, he got another one. The number was blocked. Still, he answered.

"Is this Greg Griffin, husband of Jennifer Griffin, the missing woman?"

"Yes, who's this?"

"Tina Thomas, a reporter with FirstWitness News."

"How'd you get this number?"

"It was passed to me by a source."

Anger and anxiety pulsed through him. Did they find Jenn? The reporter could have information he needed.

"Sir, we have a crew in front of your house. Would you agree to an on-camera interview?"

"About what?" Greg thought about going to the window but dismissed it, envisioning footage of him looking like a guilty man under siege.

"Would you agree, sir?"

"I agree to nothing unless you tell me what you know."

"One moment."

Silence on the line. Greg figured Tina Thomas was consulting with another person.

"Sir," Thomas said when she came back, "we

understand search warrants were executed at your house and you've taken a polygraph. Have police indicated if you're a suspect in your wife's disappearance?"

White flashed through his brain.

"No comment."

Greg hung up, sat on the stairs, holding his head in his hands, feeling the walls closing in, his mind swirling, first with his suspicions of Brooke Bollman.

Is she after me, my business? Does she want Jenn out of the picture? Does she want it all? I could call her, find out what police told her. No, I'm entangled in this with her texts, the flirting, and the photos. I was considering following through on Brooke's offer just before Jenn vanished. And how did police get those pictures at the Mulberry? Did Brooke have a friend take them to set me up? Why does she have a lawyer?

Greg recalled that maybe—*I'm not certain*—but maybe he saw someone else at the bar that night. A glimpse of someone at another table, but who? Who was it? He racked his brain but couldn't remember.

Abandoning the effort, his thoughts shifted to the issue of Porter Sellwin. Greg refused to believe Jenn would cheat on him with Sellwin.

Was my anger at him a reflection of my own lust? But when I pressed him on Jenn, he said, "I don't know what Jennifer told you." What was that?

Greg's heart raced.

And those questions during the polygraph, about the life insurance policy on Jenn, my height, her

*Corolla, do I have a hoodie, did I have sex with
Brooke... Did I argue with Jenn? Yes, I did. I lost
it with her after playing football in the yard. I demanded to know why she was so damned cold and
distant for the last few months. I couldn't take it
anymore. Jenn had tears in her eyes but wouldn't
tell me. She walked away. I was so angry I grabbed
her hard. I never hit her but in the heat of the moment I was rough.*

A blood rush roared in his ears with the mon-
strous truth before him.

My wife is missing!

"Dad, are you coming?" Jake stood at the top of
the stairs. "Come up and see."

Greg went upstairs where the disarray continued with sooty blotches on doors and walls. Police
had rifled through closets and dressers. Jake was
on the floor of his own room. Next to him: a box
and several metal pieces.

"See, I found it. Mom's new Christmas decora-
tion thing."

Lowering himself, Greg looked at the orna-
mental pieces, including three winged angels with
trumpets.

"I found it earlier. Mom hid it in the closet. I was
worried the police would take it, but they didn't."

"Looks like an angel chime." Greg picked up
the cardboard box. It was the size of a hardcover
book and contained no markings, no instructions.

"Will you help me put it together with the candles and make it work, Dad?"

"Let's go to the kitchen."

Greg gathered the pieces into the box, taking it to the kitchen table. As he began assembling the chime, he wondered why Jenn hid it, keeping it apart from the other Christmas stuff in the basement.

He began putting it together, the base, the arm, the windmill, the chime bells, the angels, and rods. He inserted the four white candles into the holders at the base.

The finished ornament stood about a foot tall.

"It looks good, Dad. Can you make it go?"

Greg got the butane lighter from a kitchen drawer, the one Jenn used to light the candles on Jake's birthday cakes, and theirs too. He squeezed the trigger and lit all four candles. Within seconds, the heat from the flames caused the three angels to spin, the needlelike rods hanging from them striking the chimes, creating a gentle tinkling in a mesmerizing, glittery carousel.

"Why did Mom hide it?" Greg asked.

"I guess it was special." Jake shrugged. "When she watched it, it made her smile, then she cried and put it away."

"When did she get it?"

"I think a couple months ago. It came in a delivery at the door."

Greg was perplexed, listening and watching the angels. Why would Jenn hide the chime? He glanced up to the smoke detector and sprinkler head. And why would she get something powered by flames when she had an aversion to fire? Greg watched Jake, seeing the candlelight sparkling in his eyes. He'd seemed to find comfort in the chime's connection to his missing mother while Greg grappled with the torment of being suspected of killing her.

"You know what I just did?" Jake said.

"No, what?"

"I just wished on the chime for Mom to come home." The chimes tinkled. "Now, I know we're going to find her. I just know it."

Forty-Three

Some four hundred miles from where Jake and Greg watched the angel chime, Eugene Bickersley was at Memorial Sloan Kettering Cancer Center, in Manhattan's Upper East Side.

All the scans, tests, and second opinions had brought Bickersley to this point.

You live your life, love what you do, then at age forty-nine, fate knocks you to the mat and you're staring at your own mortality. It's foolish to believe we have any control over our lives, Bickersley thought.

Thirty percent.

That was the survival rate for what he had. He was scheduled for two surgeries in the weeks ahead, and Sloan Kettering was among the best in the world. The medical staff was in his corner, like everyone back in Buffalo at Tall Elm.

He turned to the flowers, balloons, cards, and notes from students, drawing strength from the support in a battle he wasn't sure he could win.

He squeezed his wife's hand, smiling at her, knowing he'd be adrift without her. He heard her phone vibrate with another message.

"It's Viv again," Clara said. "Everyone at the school is sending you more good thoughts."

Bickersley nodded, then asked: "Any news on Jennifer?"

"No. I'm sorry, Gene."

He turned back to the TV, which played the movie *The Treasure of the Sierra Madre* on mute. With the help of Thelma and Vivian at the school, Clara had tried to shield him from Jennifer Griffin's situation. He was dealing with so much, they didn't want him to know that one of his school's moms was missing.

It didn't matter.

Bickersley had learned about it from a New York City TV news report he watched when Clara was out of the room.

Now he demanded updates.

Clara, and the others back in Buffalo, thought it was out of Bickersley's concern for Jennifer.

His interest ran deeper.

Jennifer Griffin's tragic situation had given him one more reason he needed to win his fight. But in his heart, he knew he had to brace for reality. He needed to make a critical decision.

Should I tell police what Jennifer confided to me, before it's too late?

Forty-Four

What had come to be known as the Griffin task force came together early the next morning for a case-status meeting.

"We've got a lot to cover," Lieutenant Phil Becker said to investigators. "You've got your summaries. Let's get to it. Go ahead, Claire."

Sitting upright as investigators from several agencies settled in, Kozak started. Again, she worked from her laptop, which was linked to the large screen on the wall at the end of the room.

"Off the top, as you can see, we have compelling elements pointing to Greg Griffin and Brooke Bollman. But it's circumstantial at this stage, nothing solid, according to the Erie County District Attorney's Office. We need more evidence and—this is key—we need to rule out all other possibilities."

Kozak moved on.

"We've recently learned that Jennifer Griffin was seeing a psychologist. The reason is unknown, but we're pursuing it."

Eyebrows went up, acknowledging the development as Kozak continued.

"Valerie Vera submitted the results of Greg Griffin's polygraph exam. They're inconclusive," Kozak said. "She speculated that Greg could be harboring guilt over issues with his wife, or *other unrevealed matters*."

Kozak went to the updates from the Forensic Identification Unit's analysis of the scene where the Toyota Corolla was located. They showed some partial shoe and tire impressions. Further investigation was ongoing to determine if they were consistent with Greg or Bollman.

"No significant trace, blood, hair, or fiber has yet been recovered from the car," Kozak said. "However, one key fact has emerged. The last person to move it was five-ten, or taller."

"What points to that?" someone asked.

"Jennifer is five feet three inches," Carillo said. "The driver's seat was pushed back, and FIU says anyone under five-ten would have had trouble reaching the pedals."

"How tall is Greg?"

"Six feet."

"Now," Kozak said, nodding to FBI agent Gary Dungey, "Gary will give us the FBI's analysis of the padlock on the gate to the section of Blueripple Woods where Griffin's Toyota was driven."

"Our Toolmarks Unit determined the padlock is a cheap, substandard model, sold everywhere." Dungey read from his tablet. "It has a four-pin style keyway. The lock is keyed to a key code used for one of the most common keys in the country. Just about anyone who owns one of these locks could, with a little finesse, open the one on the gate."

Dungey nodded to the Erie County deputies. "In working with Erie County, we know Public Works and their contractors have used the Blueripple Woods site to store equipment and supplies. We're confident most contractors would have the style of key that could open this padlock. We are still investigating to confirm if Solid and Strong Contracting had access."

"Thanks, Gary."

Kozak continued with updates on forensic analysis of the Griffins' phones, computers, and other items arising from the search warrants. It frustrated investigators that information extracted from the phones and computers, including browser histories, had not presented any clear leads.

"Other than communication between Bollman and Greg, including the night Greg reported Jennifer missing, there's very little to go on."

"Anything else from the warrants on the house?" Detective Tony Letto, with Buffalo PD, asked. "Complaint history, strange calls, trades, or service people?"

"A couple things," Kozak said. "In the spring, SparkleThru, a student window-washing service, did all the windows, and two months ago, the Griffins' cable went out. Their provider, Distinctly Connex, sent a cable guy to repair it. No incidents. And there's this."

Kozak tapped her keyboard to replay the video

of Jennifer at the Korner Fast store. They watched
her looking for something before leaving. Then the
figure who entered the store after she did, about
six feet tall, wearing a dark hoodie, the hood lifted,
their face obscured by a ballcap, watching Jennifer exit. "Among Greg's clothing, we found a dark
hoodie," Kozak said. "It proves nothing, but there
it is." A photo of Greg's hoodie appeared on the
screen. It was unclear if it matched the one in the
video.

"And," Carillo added, "the forensic people who
looked at all of the Griffins' finances found that
in the last few months, about one hundred dollars
a week from Jennifer's salary is unaccounted for."

"That's odd," Louise LeBrie, with the state police, said.

"Yeah, what's up with that?" Letto asked.

"Let's get through the rest and we'll discuss theories," Becker said.

Kozak resumed by noting that monitoring of all
local, regional, state, and national databases, including ViCAP and NCIC, had yielded no useable
response to queries and cases in other jurisdictions.

"No links, or similarities, have surfaced. No unidentified female remains have been discovered
that fit the description."

Carillo added that investigators assigned to
check with Corrections on the locations of recently
paroled offenders, and those in the New York State
Sex Offender Registry, had presented no leads of
suspects.

"To date, we've followed up on over half of the

listed offenders within a ten mile radius of the car and nothing has emerged," Carillo said. "All have been alibied for the night of Griffin's disappearance."

Carillo said every anonymous tip has and is being followed.

"The photos of Greg and Bollman are the strongest leads to come to us that way so far," Carillo said. "We don't know who sent them. Anonymity is absolute through the tip line and servers."

"What about security cameras in the bar?" Letto asked.

"A washout, nothing useful," Carillo said.

Reported crimes and complaint history, particularly concerning Ripplewood and Trailside, had not shown any leads, as well as the extensive canvassing of the entire region.

"I can't believe that in this digital age with phones and cameras everywhere, that we didn't get something more than we got," Letto said.

"There are no cameras along the curving stretch through the forested area adjacent to where her car was discovered. However," Kozak said, tapping at her keyboard, "one home security camera on Ripple Valley Boulevard recorded what we believe to be Griffin's Corolla heading east at the time. We need to review it further."

A short grainy recording encompassing a partial view of a vehicle passing along a street at night played.

"All right," Becker said. "Let's kick around theories, bearing in mind that it is crucial that we not get locked into making something fit."

Clint Freely, the homicide detective with Buffalo PD, leaned forward.

"Look at the car's location and the hard facts," Freely said. "Financial stress in the home, Greg's got another woman, and he argues with his wife. She has bruises. He's bleeding the night she disappears. The car seat's pushed back. His poly is inconclusive. Connect the dots."

"But," Carrie Deakman, with Erie County, raised her finger. "There were traffic cones on a repair section of Ripple Valley Boulevard." Deakman checked her tablet. "Blood traces on one cone match Greg's blood type, indicating he truly ran over it."

"So," Freely said. "He could've done so purposely to disguise his injuries."

"What if Bollman assisted Greg that night?" LeBrie asked. "They were together in the bar in Depew. We've seen the photos. Then Bollman sent him that text. How tall is she, Ned?"

Carillo looked at his notes: "Five nine and a half."

"Bollman could've moved the Corolla into Blueripple," LeBrie said.

Freely began nodding big nods. "You've got Bollman throwing herself at Greg, got her willing to offer him money for his business. And there's the insurance policy."

FBI agent James Goldman was studying the notes on his laptop and tapping his pen to the side of it, then said: "Let's consider Jennifer Griffin's movements and actions in the time leading up to her disappearance."

Goldman went over how in the months before she went missing, Griffin altered her routine. She shortened her yoga classes, she began visiting a psychologist. But after investigators painstakingly scrutinized the family's expenses they found that $100 a week from her salary was unaccounted for.

"Have we asked her employer, Crystallo View Optical, about the money?" Goldman said. "They could enlighten us."

Kozak patted her notebook. "On our to-do list."

"Because," Goldman said, "taken together, these aspects could point to something, or nothing, but it's worth a shot."

"Did she have a gambling problem?" Letto asked. "Or maybe she was buying drugs with the money?"

"We found no evidence of either," Kozak said.

"Did Greg reveal Jennifer was seeing a psychologist?" Letto asked.

"No," Kozak said.

"From the case notes," Deakman said, "it appears he didn't know."

"It's possible," LeBrie said, "Jennifer discovered Greg's relationship with Bollman and sought counseling?"

"Right. She could've discovered Greg was cheating on her with Bollman, staged her own disappearance," Letto said.

Freely shook his head. "Like in the movies? I don't think so."

"Been known to happen," Letto said.

"Could be that Greg was abusing her and she was saving getaway money," Deakman said. "Or that she actually ran off and is in hiding, surviving on the cash she stashed?"

"Would she leave her son?" Carillo said. "It doesn't fit. Look how rooted she is, with Jake, with her friends, the school, the community."

"It would be good to know what was going on in her head before this happened," Goldman said.

For nearly an hour, they challenged each other's theories and suppositions before Becker glanced at the time.

"All right, I think we're done here," he said. "This is good, but it's crucial we keep an open mind to all possible scenarios. If history has shown us anything, it's that there are too many cases where investigations were laser-focused on the wrong subject. We rule out nothing and no one. Until then, we follow the evidence, wherever it points. Thanks, everyone."

Detectives, agents, investigators, and deputies collected their belongings. Navigating through patches of parting conversations, Kozak left the room, battling to clear her mind. By the time she'd returned to her desk, her phone vibrated with a text message.

This is Dr. Stuart Maynart. You wanted to talk to me about one of my clients. May I suggest we meet in my office at 2:00 p.m.?

Forty-Five

Buffalo, New York

Later that morning, Rhonda Baker, a dispatcher at the 911 call center in the Erie County Public Safety Campus in downtown Buffalo, sipped coffee.

Her job was stressful.

Every minute of every shift she faced tragedy, aiding people at the worst moments of their lives—*what could be their last moments*. The margin for error didn't exist for her.

But after nearly six years at her job, Baker remained calm and focused. Her meditation exercises had helped her deal with the horrible incidents she'd been through—*the heart-wrenching screams and cries for help that haunted her*. Baker embraced the fact that today she'd been assigned to handle nonemergency calls.

So far, the calls had concerned a stolen snow-blower, a dumpster fire, and, "my drunken idiot neighbor's dog won't shut up."

Sitting before the large computer monitors horse-shoed at her workstation, Baker contemplated her upcoming break and getting more coffee when her console lights illuminated, signaling an incoming call.

Key information related to the call appeared on her screen.

"Erie County Call Center. How can I help you?"

"Hi. I'm calling to um—um…" The female caller's voice trailed to nothing, then she came back. "No, this call's a mistake. I'm sorry I—"

"Wait. It's okay. Why don't you tell me about it?"

Baker read the basic information on her screen. The call was originating from a landline in Cardinal Hill. She had the address and names of the two adult residents, Laila Price and Darrell Price.

"I don't know if I can. This is hard. Maybe it's nothing."

Baker absorbed the caller's tone, her emotion, her hesitation.

"Sometimes it helps to talk to someone to sort things out, right?"

"Um, right."

"Listen, my name's Rhonda. Let's start with you telling me your name, all right?" Baker needed to verify the caller's identity.

Dropping her voice, the caller said, "Laila."

"Thanks, Laila, and your last name?"

"Do you need it?"

"It helps me."

"Price."

"Good. I just need a few more little things." Baker's keyboard clicked softly as she worked, verifying Laila's address and phone number then continuing. "Laila, I need to ask you some questions and I need you to answer yes or no. Can you do that for me?"

"Yes."

Baker glanced at her screen. The police, medical, and fire agencies that served the caller's location were there. If she needed to send police, it would be District 2 deputies.

"Are you under any threat by someone in your residence right now?"

"No."

"Do you require any assistance from fire, police, or paramedics right now?"

"No."

"Are you safe right now?"

"Yes."

"Good. Thank you, Laila. Please, tell me why you made this call."

Baker heard Laila swallow a breath, then let it out as her voice cracked.

"Oh, I'm going to sound foolish."

"You won't, I promise."

"I'm also a little scared because I don't want to get anyone in trouble."

"Don't be afraid. You're brave to call, just let me know what it is and I can take it from there. Maybe all you need is to talk to someone, Laila."

Laila took a breath.

"It started when our cable and internet went out in our house..."

Laila recounted every detail to Baker concerning the cable guy, what he did with her underwear and how he made her feel. The keyboard clicked softly as Baker took down everything, listening intently, professionally, with empathy, pausing Laila to check information.

"...his name is Zoran Volk, the company is Distinctly Connex, he drove a white van..."

Laila confirmed the details, some of which she had on her electronic copy of the invoice. She also gave Baker a physical description of Volk.

"Let me go over things one more time, Laila," Baker said as she typed. "Did he touch you inappropriately in any way?"

"Well, he brushed his finger on mine when I signed the thing..."

"Did he say anything threatening to you, or imply a threat?"

"No."

"Okay, give me a moment." Baker typed. "That just about does it."

Laila stayed on the line, listening as Baker typed. When she finished, she said: "I can send a car to your house to take a statement, then our people will probably go to the cable company, talk to Zoran Volk and his employer, advising them of the complaint."

"Would he face a charge?"

"I can't tell you that. It's up to the deputies and if you want to pursue this further with them."

"You know what, Rhonda," Laila said. "I don't. Please cancel my call, complaint, whatever."

"Are you certain?"

"No, but I feel better talking to you. Maybe he's just a creepy jerk, you know?"

Baker believed Laila was just scared, uncomfortable, but it was ultimately her choice to pursue this.

"I understand. Think it over. You can always call me again."

"Thank you, Rhonda, for listening."

The call ended, leaving Baker staring at her screen with the details and information of Laila Price's complaint. Baker thought that with a couple of strokes she could delete it, cancel it, as Laila wished.

Thinking about it, that it was in Cardinal Hill, not too far from Trailside and Ripplewood Creek, where a woman disappeared, Baker typed a few commands, saving the complaint about Zoran Volk, submitting it to the regional database.

For good measure, because you never know.

Forty-Six

By 2:11 p.m., Kozak and Carillo were back at the Five Cloud Professional Center in the office of Dr. Stuart Maynart.

The door was closed.

They were seated at a table across from Maynart and his lawyer, Violet Chen, who was wearing a tailored navy suit that Kozak liked.

Maynart wore a sport coat over a pin-striped shirt. His face held a few days' growth, his hair a little mussed, his expression taut behind his frameless glasses. He had a file folder, tablet, and phone on the table. Chen's clasped hands rested on a legal pad.

All business and ready for battle, Kozak thought, glancing at Carillo.

His jaw muscles were bunched. Not a good sign.

"Thank you for agreeing to assist us," Kozak said.

"To be clear," Chen said, "this is extremely confidential. My client's cooperation is voluntary out of concern for the safety of his client and others given the grave circumstances. While he will discuss therapy, he will retain all records, unless subpoenaed, which we will challenge. But hopefully you will not find such action necessary."

"Yes," Kozak said. "To start, you confirm Jennifer Griffin is your client?"

"I do," Maynart said. "And I want to reiterate that this discussion must be held in the strictest confidence."

"You have our assurance," Kozak said.

"Jennifer has been a client for some two months," Maynart said. "She insisted her treatment be confidential. She told me that her husband did not know. I suspect that's why she chose not to use her insurer. Instead, she paid me in cash, as some clients do. So there would be no record in her household. We also adjusted her weekly sessions with me to fit with her yoga classes across street, which I encouraged her to maintain for their calming value."

"What were you treating her for?" Kozak asked.

Maynart thought for a moment. "Her situation was a complex combination of what appears to be abnormally prolonged grief disorder over the deaths of her parents during childhood, and, something related to it, something I suspect was a recent trauma of some sort."

"A recent trauma?" Kozak repeated.

"Yes, but I can't yet identify it."

"What about her recent disappearance?" Carillo asked.

"Your point being?"

"Were you concerned when she was reported missing?" Carillo asked.

"Certainly."

"If that was the case, then why didn't you come to us?" Carillo said.

"The issue of protecting her privacy prevented me."

"Really? Given that she may have been—" Carillo was interrupted.

"I think it's clear," Chen said, "the circumstances concerning Dr. Maynart's client were fluid. They deteriorated, becoming exceptional, reaching into his duty to warn, for the safety of his client and others. Therefore, he is cooperating. Fully, Detective Carillo."

"Dr. Maynart," Kozak said. "We have a range of concerns to ask, if we could just cover them first?"

"Of course," Maynart said.

"Concerning the possibility of Jennifer experiencing a recent trauma, did she mention stress in her marriage?"

"No."

"Did she indicate she suffered abuse of any sort from her husband?"

"No."

"From anyone else?"

"No."

"Was she facing financial struggles?"

"Yes, they were concerned about finances and had considered relocating. To Arizona, I believe, but I don't think it was a serious consideration."

"Did she suspect her husband of cheating on her?" Carillo asked.

"It didn't come up."

"Was she having an affair or contemplating a divorce or separation?" Kozak asked.

"She never raised that with me."

"Was she being stalked, threatened, harassed in any way by anyone?" Kozak asked.

"No."

"What about drugs, illicit or prescribed?" Carillo asked.

"No."

"Any addictions, like gambling or did she have any debts?" Kozak asked.

"No."

"Did she give you any indication that she might want to run away?" Kozak asked.

"No."

"Was she at risk of self-harm?" Kozak asked.

"I don't think so, out of love for her son and husband, but there are never guarantees."

"Could she have any kind of disorder where she may have become disoriented and wandered off?" Kozak asked.

"No, not from my observations."

"In your opinion," Carillo said, "could she have staged her disappearance? Would she have the inclination and a reason?"

"Highly unlikely."

"Did she have any fear of anyone or anything?" Carillo asked.

Maynart began shaking his head. "No. As I said, her situation was a very complex one."

"Tell us about her treatment," Kozak said.

"You're aware of her tragic childhood," Maynart said, "how she was orphaned at age eight after her mother and father died when their house burned? Jennifer was the sole survivor. She had no brothers, no sisters, no other family but her grandmother who raised her."

"Yes," Kozak said. "We know about her parents' deaths in the fire."

"The cause was a dropped cigarette," Carillo said. "But that was nearly thirty years ago."

"Correct," Maynart said, "but when Jennifer came to me a couple of months ago, she was experiencing inner turmoil related to the tragedy."

"In what way?" Kozak asked.

Maynart folded his arms.

"It was perplexing to me. Our sessions dealt largely with her groping to remember her parents and their happiest times. On occasion, Jennifer drifted into the nightmare of the fire, questioning why she alone survived. At first I thought she was struggling with a form of prolonged grief disorder. You see, speaking clinically, normally, the deepest forms of grief last about a year, even two, but usually lessen after key anniversaries have passed. This generalization might not be true in all cases. The duration and intensity of grief may vary. The closeness to the deceased person, age, and circumstances of death, say an older person's long illness, versus the unexpected, sudden death of a young person, are factors."

"So what happens with this prolonged disorder?" Carillo said.

"In a prolonged grief situation, a person, or survivor, can ruminate over how the tragedy could've been prevented, or struggle with bouts of self-blame. It could encompass thoughts of not deserving to live and have a life. They may be tormented by a sense of failure over things they'd done, or hadn't done, with regard to the deceased. A sense of, if only I had done this, or said that, the deceased would be alive. This can go on for years."

"Is this what happened in Jennifer's case?"

Maynart let out a breath.

"She was experiencing these feelings, I'll get to that, but in her sessions, my advice to her, concerning the tragic loss of her mother and father, was that the burden of her carrying any guilt for having survived, while understandable, was not warranted because she was a child at the time of the tragedy."

"So she was seeing you to deal with these old feelings, but what brought them on after thirty years?" Kozak asked.

Maynart nodded and pointed to Kozak.

"Precisely," he said. "What brought them on? From our sessions, it emerged that Jennifer, while having memories of her parents and the tragedy throughout the years, had succeeded in placing them appropriately within the context of her life. I encouraged her to draw comfort in the fact that she had survived in a way her parents would have wanted, raised by a loving grandmother, going to college, getting married, becoming a mother, engaging in her community, living a full and meaningful life."

"So why did she come to you?" Kozak said.

"That's the question I was working to resolve with her because she wanted to resolve it, and was receptive to therapy, although it was challenging for her. While we were making progress, she was still having enormous difficulty getting to the core of her problem. As if it was a dark, concealed room in her life she kept locked and feared to open."

"Why?" Kozak asked.

"I'm not sure. You see, grief can come suddenly, with an unexpected pang of pain brought on by a song, a smell, an object, a memory, a location, anything that evokes a connection to the deceased person and, or, the circumstances of their death."

"And in Jennifer's case, it was…?" Kozak asked.

"She never reached the point where she could tell me, other than saying it came upon her with the sudden and powerful force of a tsunami, which led me to conclude that in the time before she started seeing me, she experienced a triggering incident."

"A triggering incident?" Carillo said. "Like what?"

"I don't know," Maynart said, "but before she was reported missing, at our last session, she indicated she was prepared to bring me something to discuss."

"Like what?" Kozak said.

"I don't know if she meant it figuratively, or if it was an actual object she planned to show me and talk about, something that might have brought us closer to whatever she kept locked away."

The investigators looked at Maynart as if expecting more.

"I'm afraid that's it," the psychologist said. "Her treatment ended there, without us getting to the truth."

Forty-Seven

Location Unknown

Jennifer Griffin worked at the hinges, rasping with her makeshift tool.

Scratching at the wood around the metal assembly until her wrists, arms, and shoulders weakened, forcing her to pause again.

Her hope was to remove the hinges from the wall to loosen the door and force it open.

How long has it been now? Five or six days?

She was encouraged that her captor hadn't realized one of the pail handles was missing. But her progress was disappointing. She'd gouged nearly a fraction of an inch deep into the wood that anchored the screws of the lower and upper hinge assemblies. She curved her fingertips around the metal edge of the upper hinge and pulled.

The screws held firm.

Gritting her teeth, she pulled again but they didn't budge.

Jennifer then tried for the thousandth time, pushing with her tool at the end of the steel bolt holding the hinge together.

It didn't move.

Again, she tried wedging her tool under the bolt's head.

It didn't work.

She groaned, releasing an exhausted sob.

Her notes in the bucket exchange pleading to her captor were futile or at best, the response was unsettling.

One day her captor wrote: "I NEED YOU TO UNDERSTAND WHO I AM BUT YOU ARE NOT READY."

She wrote: "I am ready! I want to know! Please help me understand!"

A day later her captor wrote:

"SOON."

It was hopeless.

She had to keep working. She had no choice.

I can't sit here, waiting to die.

Taking a deep breath, she resumed, her arms throbbing as she dug into the wood. Tears rolling down her face, she worked through her pain.

Please God, help me get out of here.

BOOK TWO

ONE MONTH LATER

Forty-Eight

Cleveland, Ohio

She ran in the night.

Fear slamming in her chest like a frenzied bird in a cage.

Her pursuer's vehicle was gaining on her, chasing her into a desolate realm of the metropolis.

No help in sight.

The woman fled through a vast wasteland of abandoned appliances, stumbling around cast-off tires, furniture fragments, and mounds of earth embedded with trash and weeds.

Close by, she saw the elevated multilane freeway, a webbed network of on-ramps, off-ramps, curving overpasses, humming with lighted streams of the traffic it carried. A near yet distant world of life flowing by.

A quarter-block away, brakes creaked.

She glanced back.

Her pursuer had stopped, got out of their vehicle, hurrying in her direction, forcing her deeper into the lot. Breathing hard, the woman navigated around pyramids of cinder blocks and twisted rebar clawing the night like skeletal fingers.

A sudden burst of brightness nearly captured her in a white halo as the hunter swept a flashlight, probing the terrain.

Her pursuer was closing in.

Moving around a chest-high heap of rubble and wood, the woman dropped to the ground. Inhaling the rotted earth, she crawled carefully under a torn mattress that reeked of urine.

The hunter was close.

The ground crunched with footfalls.

They slowed.

They stopped.

Trembling, the woman prayed.

Blazes of light filled the seam between the earth and mattress.

The woman pressed her hand over her mouth, feeling her face damp with sweat and tears.

She waited and prayed.

Oh God, help me! Help me, please!

No sound but the freeway's hum, echoing.

One minute. Two minutes.

Please help me!

The light vanished.

Footfalls crunched on the ground then faded to nothing as her pursuer abandoned the pursuit.

The woman didn't move.

Minutes passed.

Five. Ten.

Maybe twenty, before she slid slowly from under the mattress, relieved by the cool night air on her skin. Her pulse still throbbing, she weaved through the empty lot. Adrenaline pumping, she was nearly out when there was an abrupt snap and swish of air. A hand combed over her arm. In white-hot hysteria, she smashed her fist into her attacker's stomach.

The attacker swayed.

The woman bolted, running toward the freeway.

The hunter staggered to the vehicle.

Running for her life, now with no escape, the woman entered an on-ramp, while a distance behind her, the vehicle's door slammed, its motor turned.

Blood roared in the woman's ears as she ascended the ramp.

Caught in the hunter's headlights, she kept running.

Her throat raw, she reached the freeway, waving at cars and trucks, the air rushing, pummeling her, the deafening traffic racing by, headlights streaking like shooting stars.

"Help! Please! Somebody help!"

Her pursuer's vehicle climbed the ramp.

The woman ran down the freeway's shoulder toward the lines of oncoming traffic. Waving frantically, losing her mind to her fear, she looked back at the pursuing vehicle while at the same time, without realizing, she had run into the traffic lanes.

Horns blared; the woman turned her head and, in a heartbeat, the horrific ballet played.

Tires screeched, drivers swerved, missing her, setting off a chain of collisions. Twisting chunks of jagged metal and plastic burst into the air, spreading a debris field over all lanes. Hoods flew open, side panels crumpled, windshields fractured, vehicles were spinning, sliding.

A double tanker rig, hauling some ten thousand gallons of fuel charged through a gap. The tanker driver's eyes widened at the woman standing on the freeway ahead.

She was paralyzed with fear.

In a millisecond, before his brain issued the order to brake, before his jaw opened, before his hand spasmed on the wheel, before he could form the cognitive command to act, he knew it was too late.

Still, he yanked the wheel, his rig began jack-knifing, his mind flailed; his tanks had so many safety valves and rollover devices but nothing to prevent this horror of the woman he was going to kill.

His brakes screamed, rubber began thudding and shredding, the tanks shook, breaking free of the hitch, rolling over debris, puncturing sections, metal sparking on the asphalt, the guardrails, fuel spilling, igniting a tidal wave of fire. The woman held up her hands as she was engulfed in flames in the second before the truck's rear axle assembly rolled over her.

On the shoulder, some distance down the freeway, after watching the tragedy, the hunter's vehicle, which had New York State license plates, drove away, returning to Buffalo.

Forty-Nine

Cleveland, Ohio

The flames rose more than a hundred feet, licking the night sky with a column of fire that could be seen for miles.

Freeway traffic halted in torrents of brake lights.

Scores of 911 calls inundated the Cuyahoga Emergency Communications System.

Drivers who'd witnessed the crash had stopped safely then risked their lives by confronting potential explosions and blistering heat to rescue injured people from the wrecked vehicles scattered across the lanes.

Within minutes, sirens sounded the arrival of emergency crews; fire, police, paramedics, and other groups dispatched to the scene, including the Cuyahoga County Medical Examiner.

Taking brave action despite the heightened volatility and heat of the blaze, firefighters and police removed all surviving crash victims from the scene, including the truck driver. Bleeding, he had first dragged himself from his overturned cab, which, after breaking away, had slid some distance from the fire. He was dazed but walking as they aided him through the strewn metal and wrecked cars, to the back of an ambulance.

"She was standing there! Nothing I could do!" said Leroy Vine, the forty-two-year-old truck driver from Corbin, Kentucky. His face stitched with blood, soot, and sweat as he gave his statement to Ohio State Highway Patrol trooper Brandon Caster. "There was no way I could miss her! No way! Why was she there?" Vine's cheeks glistened with tears as he looked to the fire.

Responders worked fast, cordoning a large area, keeping people away, detouring traffic, getting alerts broadcast for drivers to avoid that section of the interstate, and evacuating residents within a blast radius in case of additional explosions.

Firefighters attacked the inferno from a distance with unmanned equipment using fire-suppression foam then cooling operations, deciding the best strategy was to let it burn itself out and consume all the fuel—even though it would rage for hours.

Drones were employed throughout the night to assess the status and scope of the incident. Mindful of statements given by the injured motorists, investigators determined that a total of ten vehicles and sixteen people were involved. Miraculously, fifteen survived with injuries ranging from fractures to abrasions to lacerations.

A testament to airbags and seat belts, one official told reporters.

All the people in the crash were accounted for.

Except one.

The terrified woman witnessed running into freeway traffic.

A dog barked behind the cordoned zone.

Shadow, the canine half of a state police K-9 unit, stared at the heaps of blackened, twisted metal, eager to get to work while his handler, Annie Gaynor, held his leash and stroked his coat.

"Hold on, buddy," Gaynor said softly as firefighters continued their work.

It was dawn when the fire was finally doused, cooled and the destruction zone deemed safe for Gaynor and Shadow to probe it. They'd been called to the scene to find the woman, believed to have been entombed and incinerated in the wreckage.

Shadow, a Labrador retriever, had been trained as a cadaver dog. He had the ability to find human remains. Even after an intense fire, he could detect bone, blood, and tissue. Gaynor knew that Shadow had confidence, good nerves, and the soul of a hunter.

A weary-faced fire captain waved to Gaynor, giving her the all clear. She lowered herself, then unclipped Shadow's leash.

"Show time," she said into his ear.

Shadow trotted to the devastation, panting as he poked around the charred vehicles then picked his way through burned fragments and scorched chunks of debris, dripping with foam and water, and coated in ash. The air was thick with a riot of smells, chemical, gas, oil, engine fluids and components, the competing odors of burnt rubber, plastic, and broiled asphalt.

Debris crackled under Gaynor's boots as she followed Shadow.

He darted here and there, sticking his snout into this area then that, his tail wagging as he worked. He'd stop, think, then dismiss a scent before moving on. Gaynor knew he was contending with so many smells, challenging him to pinpoint anything human.

Shadow inserted his nose into a blackened tangle of wreckage, withdrew it, reinserted it, then released a deep bark.

Bingo, Gaynor thought as she went to him.

"Got something, buddy?"

Tugging on latex gloves, Gaynor bent down.

She lifted a hunk of metal to reveal a piece of human skull no bigger than an orange peel.

A few minutes later, Gaynor was joined by Jasmine Sharp, from the medical examiner's death scene investigation unit.

Together, they soon discovered other bone fragments but so damaged they were nearly unrecognizable. A partial outline of a human form emerged in the debris and ash. Sharp took control of the scene, taking photos, video, measurements, making notes, swabs.

It took time before Sharp could make a preliminary examination to determine the remains, what little there were, had been pulverized, cremated and baked into the pavement and debris.

* * *

The remains were removed from the scene and transferred to the Cuyahoga County Medical Examiner's Office at University Circle.

A short walk from the Cleveland Museum of Art, the stone and glass building housed several services. Among them: the crime lab, the morgue, and autopsy suites, which were located on the top floor.

In one of the suites, the remains from the freeway tragedy had been placed on a table where forensic pathologist Dr. Lynn Narlow prepared to examine them, to determine the cause of death and identify the deceased.

Police investigators needed as much information as possible to determine who the person was and the circumstances that led to their death.

Gowned and gloved, Narlow looked through her face shield, surveying what she had on the table. The medical examiner's office examined nearly two thousand bodies each year. Narlow knew the team was good.

But with so little to work with, this one's going to be a challenge.

She glanced at her primary tools nearby. They were basic—a scalpel, scissors, forceps, a ruler, a probe, and a large knife.

Taking a deep breath, she set out to work.

All of the deceased's skin was gone, so fingerprints, scars, and tattoos were eliminated as a means to help in identification. The impact forces of the crash had crushed the small pieces of jaw that had been recovered. The few surviving tooth fragments were extremely damaged. Dental identification would not be possible. No surgical implants, or jewelry, clothing, or pieces of identifying information had survived.

Narlow continued working.

From the fragment of rib cage she determined from the lumbar curve that it was female. Her observation was reinforced after she examined pieces of the pelvic region and the triangular bone found in the upper section of the pelvic cavity—the sacrum.

It was wide and circular.

Definitely female.

Narlow worked for as long as she could before concluding that cause of death was likely due to catastrophic force of the truck's rear axle assembly causing body separation followed by incineration from the ensuing fire.

The deceased was an adult female, approximate age ranging from thirty-five to forty-five, approximate height estimated to be between five feet two inches to five feet five inches.

Other than that, Narlow concluded that identification of the deceased was not achieved at this stage.

So she moved to the next step in the process, a Hail Mary effort.

Narlow set out to collect DNA.

As she worked on swabs, she reflected on proper sourcing and how samples from crime scenes could be degraded, depending on the environment from which the swabs were collected. So it may be difficult for DNA analysts to interpret results for a profile.

But we live in hope.

Narlow prepared the DNA collection kit to submit to the state's Bureau of Criminal Investigation's laboratory. The lab would create a profile for comparison with profiles existing in the state's DNA database.

Analysts there would also check it against the Combined DNA Index System, known as CODIS, the national database managed by the FBI, which would also compare it with offenders and missing persons from across the country.

Then we wait. But this is our best shot, Narlow thought, looking at the remains on her table as she concluded her work.

Blinking, her heart broke as she imagined the woman in life.

Someone knows you. Someone loves you. They deserve to know why you came to this end.

Fifty

Later that day, two hundred miles east of Cleveland, Greg Griffin finished placing apples, mayo, and butterscotch ice cream, the last of his groceries, on the belt of the checkout at Saving Shelf Grocery.

He was unshaven; his hair needed trimming.

While the cashier scanned his items, he stood at his cart in his T-shirt and torn jeans, drained from little sleep, of once more driving in the night, searching for Jenn, like he was trying to catch the wind.

It had been over a month since she had vanished, a month of going through the motions of life without her, of not knowing what happened.

"Sir? That's ninety ninety-two," the cashier said.

As if waking, Greg looked at the cashier. "Mandy," her name tag said. He caught her sideglance to the couple next in line, a woman in her sixties with stylish glasses and a man in a plaid shirt and ball cap with the word *America* on it. Keeping her eyes on Greg, the woman whispered to the man: "That's him, the husband."

Behind the couple, Greg saw that other shoppers were holding up their phones, aiming them at him and recording. Their accusatory expressions, murmurings, and finger-pointing burned into him.

He paid and left the store.

The sun was setting when he pushed his cart through the lot to his pickup.

Jenn's disappearance was an amputation, as if part of him had been severed. In the time since she vanished, the searches had all but stopped. Her story had faded from the news and social media.

There were other, newer tragedies.

Police had few updates for him.

Kat came by when she could but was unable to be with him and Jake all the time. She had to return to her job. Vince continued helping where he could. Jake resumed school and Greg went back to work. At home, Greg battled to keep a semblance of their normal lives, struggling with the daily things that Jenn had taken care of, the laundry, groceries, and cleaning.

As time went by, even though police had long since searched the house, it felt like Jenn was not gone. Greg came upon reminders; her makeup and perfume on the bathroom counter, her clothes in the closet, her favorite brands of yogurt that had expired in the back of the fridge, the books she'd read, and new ones she'd planned to read, waiting on her night table. A couple of new ones that she'd ordered online had arrived.

And there was the empty space in the garage for her Corolla.

The investigators were still keeping her car.

But each passing minute created a new layer of time and distance from Jenn, terrifying Greg, eating at him, because for him to go on every day felt like a betrayal.

But I have to do it, for Jake.

Greg reached his pickup, started loading his bags when out of nowhere an unseen voice called: "What did you do to your wife, asshole?"

Greg climbed behind the wheel and drove home.

He cleared the parking lot, absorbing the taunt, relieved that Jake was not with him. Still, Jake couldn't escape being ridiculed either. The previous morning, Greg had made one of Jake's favorite breakfasts, waffles. He'd stacked three on a plate, set it before him.

Jake only stared at them.

"That's not the way Mom makes them," Jake said. "There's no whipped cream."

"Sorry, buddy."

Greg got the can from the fridge. It hissed as he squirted a swirl on the waffles. But Jake continued staring at them without moving, tears rolling down his face.

"Did I forget something else?" Greg said.

Jake shook his head.

"But you wanted waffles. Are you not hungry anymore?"

Jake shook his head.

Greg lowered himself and put his hand on Jake's lap.

"What is it?"

"The kids at school say things."

Greg froze for a moment.

"What kind of things?"

"That you and Mom had a big fight, that you hurt her because you have a girlfriend."

Greg cursed to himself.

"It's not true, son. How many times have we talked about this? You have to believe me, it's just not true."

Jake said nothing.

"Those kids don't know anything," Greg said. "We have to be strong and wait until Mom comes home."

"But when, Dad? I miss her so much!"

Jake cried and Greg held him tight.

Now, driving home, Greg bit back on his anger at the memory of Jake's agony, and that he was helpless to do anything, and because an unreal fog of torment had enveloped them, refusing to lift from their lives.

When Greg got home, Vince was in the living room watching news.

"Need some help?" Vince turned from the TV.

"I got it, thanks."

Greg could see the screen from the kitchen and while putting groceries away, he paused when a news anchor said: "…and now, some dramatic pictures from our affiliate in Cleveland, where one woman was killed and several people injured, after a tanker truck exploded in a multicar pileup on Interstate…"

The screen filled with footage focused on a rising pillar of fire on a freeway, amid gridlock and a sea of emergency lights.

"That looks bad," Vince said before the newscast broke for a commercial.

"Where's Jake?" Greg asked.

"In the backyard with his drone." Vince nodded. They saw him through the glass doors to the patio. Vince shut the TV off then joined Greg in the kitchen. "You hear anything?"

It had become a routine question in their lives, punctuating the beginnings of nearly every conversation.

"No, Dad. You?"

That's when Greg noticed Vince had a slip of paper in his hand and was sliding on his glasses to study it.

"Yeah, Nicole Pitcher, one of the teachers at Jake's school, called on the landline. She wants you to get back to her about a new fundraiser for the reward offered on the website."

Greg glanced at the message then put it in his pocket.

"Thanks, I'll call later."

"Want me to stay?"

"No, we're good. Thanks for helping, Dad."

"Day by day, son," Vince said. "That's how we hold on."

Greg nodded, they hugged, then Jake came inside with his drone and said goodbye to his grandfather.

For the rest of the evening, Greg and Jake watched a *Star Wars* movie in the man cave. When it ended, Greg hugged Jake.

"Want to try sleeping in your own bed again tonight?"

"Okay, but did you remember at the grocery store to get more candles for Mom's chime?"

"Yes."

"Can we start it for a little bit? Please?"

Greg knew how much it meant to him.

"Go get it, and put it on the kitchen table."

Jake ran upstairs with Greg walking wearily behind him.

Greg had kept the chime on Jenn's desk. It seemed the best place given how Jake wanted to light it every night.

Carrying the chime with such care it bordered on reverence, Jake set it on the kitchen table. Greg opened the new box of candles, inserted them, then lit the wicks, and, because Jake insisted, he shut off all the lights.

They watched the three angels, spinning above the flickering flames, captivating them with the delicate ringing.

The angels twirled in the twinkling carousel, pulling Greg back weeks ago to the time when Kozak and Carillo came to him as if they'd discovered a new development in the case. They were tight-lipped and cryptic, asking again if anything about Jenn had seemed out of the ordinary in the months before she'd vanished.

"Anything new, or sudden?" Kozak had asked. "Anything, large or small, that seemed to bring on a change in her?"

Greg could think of nothing, until, shrugging,

he'd mentioned the angel chime. The investigators asked to see it. They looked it over, asked about it, then questioned Jake before requesting Greg allow them to take it with them.

"Why? It's just a Christmas chime she had delivered. I mean, sure, take it, but why the interest? Is it connected?"

"For processing," Carillo said, "just a standard thing."

There had to be more to it. Greg believed the detectives knew something they were not revealing to him. But any apprehension he had melted a few days later when they returned the chime with their thanks, leaving Greg to think it couldn't be linked to Jenn's disappearance.

Now, watching the candlelight reflected in Jake's eyes, seeing how the chime comforted him, warmed Greg, giving him hope.

"Okay, blow out the candles, son. Time for bed."

First, Jake clenched his eyes. Greg knew his ritual. He was making his wish-prayer for Jenn's return. After Jake gently blew out the candles, Greg tousled his hair then turned on the lights.

"Upstairs now and brush your teeth. I'll be up after I take care of this."

Greg put the extinguished candles in the sink, touched the chime to ensure it was cool then took it back to Jenn's desk when the phone rang and he answered.

"Is this Greg Griffin?"

"Yes, who's this?"

"Nick Rivers, with *USA TODAY*. We're doing a

news feature on your wife's disappearance. Could I set up an interview with you?"

"I don't know about that."

"The attention could help, and I'd be happy to share whatever we learn."

Greg searched for an answer among the books on the shelves above Jenn's desk. He'd dealt with a number of media people and was accustomed to their pitches. There were pros to agreeing to talk to Rivers. *USA TODAY* had a big reach, and it could indeed bring attention to her case as it was growing colder. But there were also cons.

People still suspect I'm involved.

"Let me think about it, Nick."

"I'll keep in touch."

Upon hanging up, Greg drove his hands into his hair, then froze.

Staring at Jenn's old college textbooks on the shelf, he noticed a large brown envelope slivered between them. He wasn't familiar with it. Police must've left it after their search.

He slid it out.

The envelope bore no writing and wasn't sealed.

Looking inside, he pulled out several newspaper clippings.

The first bore a large news photo of a child in a firefighter's arms, under the headline:

Girl Rescued After Parents Perish In Fire

This is odd, Greg thought.

Jenn had never shown him these clippings—ever.

Why was she keeping them?

Fifty-One

Clarence, New York

Four people had been shot to death in their home in Rochester, New York.

They were a doctor and her husband, who was an FBI agent, and their teenage daughter and son.

The homicides took Kozak and Carillo away from the Jennifer Griffin investigation because the two men suspected of murdering the Rochester family had fled to the Buffalo-Niagara region. Every law enforcement agency across Western New York was pulled into the case.

Kozak and Carillo helped by canvassing, pursuing leads, and pushing their informants.

Buffalo police and Erie County deputies had found evidence that the fugitives were in the greater Buffalo area but had fled. The manhunt ended two weeks later when one suspect died during an armed standoff with the FBI in Tennessee and the second suspect surrendered to police in Boston.

It soon emerged that the tragedy of the Rochester

family was a drug deal gone wrong and the family was the wrong target.

"A doctor, an FBI agent, and their children. This world makes no sense, Claire."

Carillo shook his head at his monitor after reading the latest out of Rochester. Then he sipped coffee and resumed work with an undercurrent of disquiet.

For now, this morning, Kozak and Carillo returned to the Griffin investigation, picking up where they'd left matters. A month had passed since Greg Griffin had reported his wife missing. The case was growing colder, and they were no closer to clearing it.

Kozak and Carillo also knew that with each day that ticked by, the chances of them finding Jennifer Griffin alive grew increasingly unlikely.

They collected files, their tablets, and phones, then moved to the empty boardroom. Settling in at the big table, Kozak recalled how in the first days of the case, the room would be crowded with investigators.

"All right." Kozak went to her notes. "Dr. Maynart said Griffin was experiencing unusual prolonged grief, arising from surviving the fire that killed her parents, leaving her an orphan with no other family but her grandmother. Then some thirty years later, and two months before she went missing, there was some sort of triggering incident, which led her to seek therapy."

"But we don't know what triggered it, and we can't tell Greg she was secretly seeing a psychologist," Carillo said, "and not just to protect her privacy."

"No. Greg could've been the reason she was seeking help."

"So, what could this triggering incident have been?" Carillo said.

Reviewing their notes, interviews, files, and reports, the investigators analyzed the question. Barring something random or unforeseen, they started with the most likely areas of Jennifer's life.

Nothing had emerged from her job at Crystallo View Optical, other than the fact she had arranged to secretly divert $100 cash weekly for her therapy sessions.

Her community and social work had yielded nothing of apparent consequence. At the time of her disappearance, her Parent School Support Committee was working to adjust a lunch program policy and was being challenged by a school board member, Porter Sellwin.

At home, nothing stood out in terms of contractors in the months prior to her disappearance. The windows had been washed by SparkleThru, and their cable service had been repaired by Distinctly Connex with nothing to indicate a problem on that front.

"That brings us to this." Kozak cued up photos of the angel chime on her tablet. "This could've triggered something related to her prolonged grief. Look at what her son Jake said."

Carillo read his notes from their interview with Jake, quoting what he'd told them about the chime.

"'It came to the door. When she started it, it made her smile, then she got real sad. She cried then put it away.'"

"But our search of all invoices, all deliveries, all credit and bank card charges, failed to show delivery of a chime or ornament," Kozak said. "She'd ordered several books. But we found nothing for the candle chime."

"Maybe young Jake was confused about a delivery?" Carillo said. "Maybe she got it at a flea market, yard sale, something like that?"

"And our FIU pulled no other clear latents from it but hers, Greg's, and Jake's," Kozak said. "So I don't know how, or if, the chime is a triggering incident, or how it could be tied to the fire that took her parents."

Carillo reached for a copy of the report on the fire they'd obtained from the Buffalo Fire Department. It came out of their archives and was made by a fire company that had since been disbanded as part of the department's fiscal reorganization.

"Once again." Carillo scanned it. "The cause was a lit cigarette smoldering between two sofa cushions. Smoke alarms were not maintained. Wait. I missed this. A neighbor reported seeing someone running nearby at the time of the fire. However, it was never determined to be a factor as arson had been ruled out. And," Carillo said, closing the report, "there were two fatalities and one survivor."

Kozak tapped her pen on the table.

"You know, Jennifer going to see a psychologist to deal with a past trauma may be a coincidence, unrelated to her disappearance. It could lead us down a rabbit hole. I don't know, Ned."

"Let's look at all the other factors."

They surveyed the tips—now dwindling to a trickle—that had come in. All had been pursued and nearly all had been dismissed.

Tips like: "I saw Jennifer Griffin bowling in Tonawanda, but caller named a nonexistent location." Or: "Guy drinking at a bar said he knew what happened to Jennifer Griffin. Caller could not name the man, or recall the bar or time." Or: "Caller said Jennifer Griffin had drowned in Lake Erie. Caller said information was 'spiritually channeled.'"

"It brings us back to the evidence and her situation at home with Greg," Carillo said, listing the key facts.

A book club friend, a retired nurse, had seen bruising on Jenn. Jake said his parents had argued. There was financial tension in the home, and those photos of Greg with Brooke Bollman in Depew the night he reported Jennifer missing; add to them Bollman's offer of a business partnership with Greg and it was incriminating. Greg had bloodied hands the night his wife went missing, and a hoodie was discovered when the Griffins' Trailside home was searched. His polygraph was inconclusive.

"The DA says it's just not strong enough," Kozak said. "It's all circumstantial."

A knock sounded on the door where Lieutenant Phil Becker was standing.

"Come to my office. I want to show you something."

A short video was cued up on Becker's monitor.

"This just came in. It's from the home security system of a resident in Ripplewood Creek. He sent it to his brother, a sergeant with Buffalo PD, and an old friend of mine. He sent it to me.

"Now, the resident was on an extended vacation, but he got our flyer. That's why we're getting this now. And, keep in mind, the resident lives a long way down Appleleaf Road, but his cameras picked up something arising from the Korner Fast store."

Becker played the video.

It was dark, grainy, but in the distant corner, a tiny set of headlights shine and head east on Ripple Valley Boulevard. A short time later, a second set of headlights surface and also move east along Ripple Valley Boulevard. Not enough detail existed to define the makes of the vehicles. In all, it lasted about forty seconds. Becker replayed it a few times.

"The time of this residential video fits with the time of the Korner Fast security footage we have of her in the store," Becker said. "It isn't ironclad, but it takes us closer to the possibility that the hooded person could've played a role in her disappearance."

Fifty-Two

Buffalo, New York

Lorena Jo Tullev tossed gnawed chicken bones into the plastic garbage bag as she cleaned up her house east of downtown Buffalo where she lived with her boyfriend.

The coffee table in the living room was a disaster. She grabbed the stinking pizza box, dotted with dried remnants, then the crushed beer cans. Her eyes shot across the room, burning on her boyfriend's soiled socks, T-shirt, hoodie, and jeans heaped on a chair.

Lorena was sick and tired of coming home from work and picking up after him and concerned with his growing lack of consideration for her.

He belched, drawing her attention to the spare room he called his office. The door was open, his laptop keyboard clicking. Still holding the trash bag, she went in, taking stock of him in jeans, shirtless, his muscular body laced with tattoos. Finally, she said: "If you ever helped me clean up, just once, I'd die, Zoran."

He gulped beer from the can next to his keyboard.

"You still haven't told me where you were the other day," she said.

Eyes on his monitor, he swallowed beer then held his empty can to her.

"Get me another one."

She didn't take the can.

"We need to talk, Zoran."

He crushed the can.

"You need to get me another beer."

"Zoran?" She took a breath then said: "Are you seeing someone else?"

"I don't have to answer to you."

"Show a little respect and talk to me."

He tossed the crushed can to the floor then turned to her.

"If you're not happy, leave," he said. "I meet plenty of women on my job every day, and you know what? Most of them want me."

Lorena took the blow and retaliated.

"I meet a lot of men at my job and *all of them want me.*"

He ran his eyes over her.

"Because they know what you are, *Skye.*"

Lorena kicked the crushed can to the wall then strode to the kitchen for sanctuary. Skye was her stage name, which she never used in their home. Zoran knew that. Lorena was an exotic dancer, and she was not ashamed of it. She was good at it, and she made good money without working overtime or doing specials, as some girls called it.

But Lorena was more than Skye.

She'd studied dance in college with dreams of being in a big production. She moved to New York City, got an agent, went to casting call after casting call, always coming close but never making the cut. She took whatever work she could to pay her bills while her dream eluded her. She did not find a life in a show on Broadway; she found it dancing on tables and laps in Buffalo.

It seemed like a million years behind her.

Now, in the kitchen, fighting tears as she made tea, she thought back to when she met Zoran about two years ago. He'd come to her apartment to fix her cable. He was good-looking, well-built, and even shy. He was accepting of the fact she was an exotic dancer, even proud of her. He was kind and considerate. And in bed, well, he rocked her world. They got a place together, talked about getting married, kids, a house in the suburbs, she'd open a hair salon.

A new dream for Lorena.

Zoran's job was secure because his uncle owned the cable contracting company, Distinctly Connex. But it wasn't long before Lorena found herself facing Zoran's dark moods, his drinking and addiction to online porn. Despite her profession, despite the things she'd experienced, Lorena was uneasy with Zoran's obsession. They'd argue about it. She wanted him to get counseling, but to no avail.

Zoran couldn't stop.

And in the last few months, things had gotten worse. He'd disappear for days, going to his fishing cabin. That's what he told her. But she couldn't tamp down her fear that he was seeing someone else.

Now, the way Lorena saw it, she had two choices: Leave. Or try to salvage the relationship.

In her heart, she knew Zoran was abused as a child. One time, after his father caught him stealing a Hershey bar, he held a lit match under his fingers. One winter night, when Zoran was eight and wet the bed, his father dragged him into the backyard and made him stand naked in waist-high snow while a blizzard blew off Lake Erie.

Zoran was damaged, flawed, but still a good man, Lorena thought.

But she was fed up with his crap. If things were going to work out between them, he needed to work on himself and get help.

We're going to have this out right now.

Heading back to his office, she heard his phone ringing.

"Let it go, Zoran. We're going to talk."

Ignoring her, he got up from his laptop to search for his phone in the clothes he'd left on the chair in the living room.

Holding back on her anger, Lorena went into his office to wait for him while she heard him talking in the living room to someone at work. Drumming her fingers on the back of his chair, she glanced at his screen, still lit, expecting to find porn.

But it wasn't porn. Instead, she saw the face of a woman.

I've seen her somewhere.

But before Lorena could focus on the image, Zoran returned, went to his desk and calmly closed his laptop.

"Who's that woman?"

"No one."

"Zoran, tell me who she is."

He turned to her.

"I told you. No one."

Fifty-Three

London, Ohio

At the Ohio Bureau of Criminal Investigation's Laboratory, located about twenty-five miles southwest of the state capital of Columbus, Ben Abbott concentrated at his workstation.

He was with the CODIS Unit, tasked with developing and processing DNA profiles from samples submitted from law enforcement agencies across the state. He'd been dealing with one that had been sent by the Cuyahoga County Medical Examiner, and it challenged him.

It could've been because Abbott, nicknamed "the rookie" by his colleagues, had been hired as a forensic scientist three months ago, right out of Yale. Or, it could've been because the Cuyahoga sample was slightly degraded, making the results difficult for him to read.

But Abbott was not giving up. He wanted to prove himself.

He'd already gone through all the major steps in the process, extraction, then cleaning up the sample, removing anything extraneous to make a pure profile, then counting and amplification, then making copies. The result, not as strong as he would prefer, was a profile he could work with.

Abbott had clearance to access CODIS, the national DNA system administered by the FBI, which held DNA profiles collected across the country. He could also access Ohio's DNA databank and local systems across the state.

He started by running a computerized comparison of the Cuyahoga profile through all of the local and state databases holding offender profiles.

Nothing came up.

Abbott then did the same with all local and state databases holding missing person profiles.

Nothing.

He'd keep trying because new samples were added every day, and you never knew when you may hit on one.

Abbott wasn't finished, though. He moved on to CODIS. First, he searched for comparisons with offenders.

Again, nothing.

But the FBI's system encompassed several other federal databases, including the National Missing Person DNA Database, which compared DNA records stored in the Missing Person, Relatives of Missing Person, and Unidentified Human Remains Indexes.

Abbott's terminal pinged.

Really?

He caught his breath.

The notification was an indication of a match.

He entered his security code to access the profile.

It was a missing person case, which included direct reference samples from the missing person, and a sample from a close relative.

Abbott took a long breath then studied the information.

Yes, the genetic information was limited but it was there.

This was it. His first hit.

He had more work to do, more steps in the process.

He looked at all the information of the submission, growing excited as he anticipated calling Lynn Narlow, the forensic pathologist at the Cuyahoga County Medical Examiner, to say they'd solved the case.

And maybe provide some comfort to the family involved.

Fifty-Four

Buffalo, New York, Trailside Grove

A house engulfed in flames, black smoke curling into the night sky, fire trucks and emergency crews battling the blaze.

News stories on the fire that had killed Jenn's parents were fanned out on Greg's kitchen table. Again, he puzzled over them, the same questions swirling.

I didn't know she'd had these. She never talked about the fire. It was too painful for her. So why keep these clippings tucked away?

The envelope had no markings and held nothing else but the nearly thirty-year-old news articles.

Could it be related to some kind of anniversary, or why she had withdrawn from me over the last few months?

The doorbell rang.

Greg collected the clippings into the envelope, set it aside, then went to the door, wondering who it might be. It was the weekend, late afternoon. Jake was at Carter's. Greg was alone. Looking through the window for a media truck, he saw Kat's purple Jeep and let her in.

"Hey," she said.

They went to the kitchen. Kat got coffee then made small talk. When they sat down at the table, she hesitated then changed the subject.

"Look, the real reason I dropped by this morning is—" Kat stopped.

"Is what?"

"There's something I haven't told you, Greg— I'm sorry."

"What?"

"I never told you everything after I saw Kat with Porter Sellwin."

"Come on, Kat. We're not going down that road again, are we?"

"Just listen. After it happened, I spoke to Jenn, telling her what I saw. Because I suspected she was cheating on you—"

"Kat, I don't believe she would do that—"

"Listen to me, Greg. After I told her what I saw, I said if she didn't tell you, I would. She told me I didn't understand, said I should mind my own damn business. We argued and it got so bad that I—"

Greg's phone rang. Holding up his hand to pause Kat, he answered.

"Greg, this is Claire Kozak. Are you home now?"

"Yes."

"Are you home alone?"

"My sister's with me. What is it?"

"There's been a development. We'll be right there. We're on your street."

After the call, Greg, taken aback by Kozak's urgency, stood in silence.

"Who was that?" Kat asked.

"Kozak. There's a development and they'll be here any minute." Greg looked at Kat. "What were you going to tell me?"

The impending arrival of the investigators had forced Kat to reconsider.

"Let's talk after police are done."

"Go on. Finish what you were saying."

"It can wait."

Kat began clearing the table, going to the counter, preparing fresh coffee.

"Tell me, Kat."

"I want to wait until after they go."

She got the coffee started then retreated to the bathroom, leaving Greg not knowing what to think.

Minutes later, Greg opened the door to four people: Kozak, Carillo, and two women he didn't know.

"Hello, Greg," Kozak said, "this is Dr. Rochelle Clemmons and Nora Singer, with our victim services section."

In that instant, Greg registered their sober expressions, sending something in his chest plummeting to the pit of his stomach.

They went to the living room. Everyone found a seat while Kat brought coffee then sat at Greg's side.

"This is my sister, Katrina," Greg said to the others.

"Where's Jake?" Kozak asked.

"He's at his friend's house," Greg said.

Kozak nodded, glanced to her colleagues, their faces telegraphing dread, tripping an alarm, a faint clanging in a corner of Greg's heart.

Kozak's eyes locked on to his. She said: "Jennifer has been located—"

"What?"

"—she's been located, but she was hurt. Badly hurt."

"How bad? Where is she? What happened?"

"Greg, it was a terrible accident. Jennifer didn't survive her injuries." Kozak swallowed, tears now in her eyes. "I'm so sorry."

"What? *What?* No, no!" Greg's voice shattered into an agonizing moan, the alarm grew into a scream. He clasped his hands together to keep from coming apart, holding them tight, twisting them until his knuckles whitened.

"Oh my God!" Kat threw her arms around her brother. Then to Kozak: "Are you certain?"

"Yes, we're certain. I'm sorry."

"What happened? I want to see her. Where is she?" Greg managed.

"Cleveland," Kozak said.

"Cleveland?" Greg said.

Kozak took a moment and a small breath. "Nearly two weeks ago, she was seen running onto a freeway at night. She ran into a traffic lane. Drivers attempted to avoid her, but it resulted in a multivehicle collision. She was struck by a tanker truck after it jackknifed, rolled, and exploded. The medical examiner said Jennifer was killed instantly, that she didn't suffer."

Greg buried his face in his hands.

Carillo was watching him intently.

Greg lifted his head. "Cleveland? How did she get there? Why was she on the freeway? This makes no sense."

"We're going to find the answers," Kozak said. "We're working with detectives in Ohio. We're going to find who, if anyone, is responsible, and bring them to justice."

"Greg, I'm sorry," Carillo said, "but we have to ask. Is there a connection that Jennifer, or you, have to Cleveland?"

Greg shook his head.

"No, none."

"Did you have any reason to be in Cleveland recently?"

"What?" Greg stared at him. "No! This makes no sense! You found her car a couple miles away in Ripplewood. Now you're telling me this thing happened in Cleveland? It's not Jenn. It can't be Jenn! It's a mistake!"

Kozak glanced at Carillo, at the others, then Greg.

"Remember, we collected Jennifer's DNA and Jake's, too," Kozak said. "Those samples were entered into FBI databases. A comparison was made through the Ohio Bureau of Criminal Investigation and the Cuyahoga County Medical Examiner. Jennifer's DNA matched the DNA of the woman on the freeway. I'm so sorry, Greg, but it is Jennifer."

Kozak was wrong.

He wanted to push the words back into her mouth. But he didn't move.

Staring at the floor as if it were an abyss, Greg went numb as if floating out of his body. It couldn't be real. Until he saw Jenn, it wasn't true.

"Greg," Dr. Clemmons said, waiting for him to look at her. "We know your pain is overwhelming. We're here to help you, to talk to you and Jake." Her voice was soft, almost soothing. "It doesn't have to be now. It can be whenever you're ready. It's important you know that you have someone to talk to who can help, Greg."

Then Nora Singer reached into her bag for a crisp brochure folder that gave a soft snap when she opened it slowly to a printed page.

"Greg." Singer cleared her throat. "When you select the funeral home, give them this information. They'll contact the people at the medical examiner's office in Ohio to arrange to bring Jennifer home."

Her eyes filled with compassion, Singer extended the folder to Greg. He made no move to accept it. Singer glanced to Kat, who took it.

"Thank you." Kat's voice was a whisper.

"I can also give you an electronic copy of the information," Singer said.

"You also need to know," Kozak said, "that in a few hours, news releases updating Jennifer's case will be issued here and in Ohio. It's a requirement under our policy. Media will respond. We'll make an appeal for the press to respect your privacy, but there are no guarantees they will."

"Is there anything we can do to help you at this time?" Singer asked.

"We..." Kat found her voice. "We need to get Jake and tell him. His friend's house is nearby. And I need to call our dad to come here."

"We can help you, if you like," Clemmons said. "We could get Jake and tell him. Or would you prefer to tell him?"

"I'll tell him," Greg said. Then to Kat: "Tell Dad to get Jake at Carter's and bring him home. I'll be upstairs."

Greg stood and left the room.

He climbed the stairs slowly as if climbing Everest in the thin air of The Death Zone, not feeling or hearing anything but the roar of blood in his ears, alarm throbbing in his gut, his head, his fingers, as if he were going to burst into a million fragments.

He made it to the bedroom, to Jenn's side of their closet. His chest heaving, looking at her clothes hanging neatly, the things she wore every day. He opened his arms wide, closing them around her tops, her sweaters, her pants, her skirts and dresses, holding the soft fragrant bundle tight as if it were a lifeline. Metal hanger hooks straightened, then plastic hooks snapped from his weight as he dropped to his knees hugging her clothes, plunging his face into them, inhaling her scent, sobbing with such fury his grief thundered against the walls.

Greg didn't know how long it was before he heard Jake and his father downstairs.

He pulled himself up, went to the bathroom,

splashed water on his face then dried it just as Kat brought Jake to the bedroom door.

Greg sat on the corner of the bed and gestured to Jake.

Kat left, closing the door behind her.

But Jake stood there, his face a portrait of fear. He stared at his dad.

Greg recognized that even if Jake had not been told, he must have sensed what had happened, must be reading it in his face. Greg also recognized the cruel tragic repetition of horror, for in that moment he and his son were looking at each other, Greg was catapulted back to that day when he was ten and his principal, Sister Mary, took him from the classroom…

…*Walking down the hall with Sister Mary… Hearing Sister Roberta's voice spilling after them in the hall, telling his class: "Stop your work, please. Now we're going to pray for Greg."… Arriving at the principal's office, seeing Kat, her face broken, looking so much older, seeing his dad, still in his work clothes, his big hands crusted with dried mortar, his face white as if all the blood had been drained from him, and he was now a shrunken ghost of himself. They had come to tell him that his mom was dead…*

Now here was Greg, staring at Jake, suddenly seeing how much he looked like Jenn.

"This is about Mom," Jake said. "That's why all those people are here."

"Sit with me, son."

Jake got up on the bed with Greg and he put his arm around him.

"I have something very sad to tell you."

Greg gave Jake a moment to brace himself before he continued.

"Mom won't be coming home."

Jake blinked, absorbing the words.

"Ever?"

Greg's Adam's apple rose and fell.

"No, son. Not ever."

"But why? Is she mad at us?"

"No." Greg brushed Jake's hair. "Mom was in a bad accident, she was hurt bad, so bad that she—"

Greg couldn't say it. He cleared his throat and tried again.

"That she—"

He struggled until Jake said: "That she what, Dad?"

"That she died, son. Mom died."

Jake stared at him, eyes probing his.

"But how? What happened? She didn't have her car?"

"Jake, it's—there was an accident in Cleveland—"

"Cleveland?"

"Yes, the police will tell us more when they find out."

After listening to all that his father had told him, Jake had not shed a tear while processing it, as if it were a math problem that didn't add up. Jake shook his head.

"Everybody's lying, Dad. Just like when the kids at school say things. It's not true. Mom's not dead."

"It is true, son. I know it's hard to understand, but it's true."

"No, Dad. It can't be true. It can't!"

"Son."

"It can't be true because I wished for Mom to come home. I wished on her angel chime."

"That's where Mom is now, son, with the angels."

"No, no." Jake's voice grew small, weak. "She's supposed to come home to us, Dad. God wouldn't do this. God wouldn't let Mom die."

Jake's body spasmed against Greg's as he sobbed, the two of them holding each other in a whirlwind of agony, spiraling with images of a house fire thirty years ago, to Sister Mary's office, to Jenn and Greg's bedroom. Jake and Greg stayed that way for a long time until Jake asked Greg if they could start Jenn's chime.

Greg brought it into the bedroom, set it on the night table, started it, and shut off the lights. They watched the angel carousel spin with the gentle, calming tinkling, with Jake making his wish.

Kozak and the others had left.

Kat and Vince stayed with them that night but respecting Greg's insistence on being alone with Jake.

Downstairs, the news of Jenn's death brought calls and messages from media, friends, and neighbors. Kat told reporters that the family was devastated, thanked all of the volunteers, but had nothing more to say. She and Vince accepted condolences from friends and neighbors, thanking them for all of their support, explaining that they'd let them know about plans for Jenn's funeral service.

Upstairs, Greg and Jake passed the evening on the bed watching family videos on Greg's tablet. Jake's face was etched with sadness as birthdays, Christmases, and vacations rolled on the screen. The pictures on the tablet resurrected other images of their life. They played in Greg's memory where he saw Jenn in high school, where he fell in love with her, then getting married, Jake's birth, this house—"Our forever home"—in Trailside Grove. Where All Your Dreams Come True.

But this is not our dream.

Now here was a video of a vacation they took together in Florida. Here was Jenn walking in the sun on the beach. Greg was walking with her, recording her. Jake was in the distance behind them, building a sandcastle.

Jenn fills the frame, radiant and shapely in her bathing suit, beautiful, glowing in the sun, saying: "Come, Greg. Stop recording. Walk with me."

This is not how our story's supposed to end.

Jenn's holding out her hand to him but he keeps recording.

"Walk with me, Greg."

You were supposed to come back. I always believed you would come back to me. I needed you to come back to me.

"All right." Jenn smiles to the camera, withdrawing her hand in mock disappointment, giving him a playful dismissive wave.

Greg is suddenly chilled because he can't remember his last moment with Jenn, the last thing he said to her.

"That's it, buddy," Jenn says, walking a little faster ahead on the beach.

You can't leave me like this without me telling you how much I love you.

"So long," Jenn says, turning, smiling with a final wave. "Bye."

Fifty-Five

From a hill overlooking the freeway, Greg could see the blotch of blackened asphalt.

It was the day after Kozak had told him Jenn had been killed on that very spot.

Greg and Kat made the three-hour drive to Cleveland, to this grassy ridge. He needed to see the site of Jenn's death. Nothing yet honored the location, nothing signifying Jennifer Griffin's life had ended here but a scorched stain stretching across several lanes.

Seeing cars and trucks rushing over it was an indignity.

Greg adjusted his grip on the bouquet of a dozen red roses, Jenn's favorite. But he got plastic ones, so they would last longer. He gestured to Kat. They got into her Jeep, made their way to an on-ramp and entered the freeway, driving to the location. Kat activated her Jeep's emergency lights, stopping on the narrow shoulder.

Greg got out.

Horns blared from traffic in the rush whipping past within feet of Greg while he zip-tied the flowers to a signpost near the spot. He said a prayer for Jenn before returning to the Jeep.

They headed for University Circle, guided by Kat's GPS.

"How did she get from a book club meeting in Ripplewood to that spot in this city?" Greg asked. "Why was she on the freeway?"

Kat nodded sympathetically.

These were the questions Greg had been asking all morning. During the drive from Buffalo, he'd put them to Kozak in a phone call. Then he put them to an investigator with the Ohio State Police, then a deputy with Cuyahoga County, then an FBI agent because Greg was told all agencies were involved in the investigation.

But no one had answers, frustrating him, so that by the time he'd reached a Cleveland police detective, he'd run out of patience.

"I know it's early in the case." Greg had raised his voice to the detective. "But why can't you guys tell me what the hell my wife was doing out there? Someone must've seen something! How did she get to this city?"

"Mr. Griffin, we're working with the other agencies. We're talking to people who survived the crash. The freeway traffic cameras are live, but they don't record. We're working to obtain any dashcam, or security video footage, and we're canvassing. But you have to understand," the detective said, "it happened near an industrial area, with empty lots and vacant warehouses. It's a challenge, sir."

So is having my wife go missing only to die alone on a freeway, Greg thought, grappling with his pain as they arrived at the Cuyahoga County Medical Examiner's Office.

Greg had requested a meeting to get more information. Forensic pathologist Dr. Lynn Narlow greeted them in the lobby. The air and atmosphere of the building evoked a hospital as she led them to her office.

With great sensitivity, including how identification was confirmed using DNA, Narlow explained the process used in Jenn's case. When she finished, she asked Greg if he had questions.

"I want to see her."

"I understand—" Narlow's tone was kind "—but I'm afraid that's not possible. I'm sorry. At this time, the remains are about to be transferred to the funeral home vehicle for delivery to Buffalo."

"Show me the pictures you took, the scene, the autopsy, everything. I want to see them."

"I can't. They're part of the investigation, and..." Narlow leaned forward, eyes glistening with empathy. "Even if I could, Greg, I would strongly recommend you not look at them."

But Greg read the concern written in Dr. Narlow's face.

Jenn had died in a god-awful way in a god-awful tragedy.

Before they left the office, Kat's quick thinking

resulted in Narlow arranging for them to follow the funeral home's vehicle back to Buffalo.

So, in a lonely two-car cortege, Kat drove her purple Jeep close behind the dark blue Cadillac hearse from the Lansing and Elklend Funeral Home as they traveled east on I-90.

Along the way, Greg and Kat sank into their thoughts. Kat tuned in an FM station playing classical music; she kept the sound low. The soft strains were soothing until Greg's phone rang.

It was Vince, who was back in Trailside with Jake.

"Hey, Greg," Vince said. "Sorry if I got you at a bad time but Jake wants to talk to you."

"Okay, Dad, put him on."

He heard the muffling of the phone being passed.

"Hi, Dad," Jake said.

"Hi, son."

"Did you find Mom? Is it really true?"

Greg swallowed hard, staring at the back of the hearse.

"Yes, and it's really true. We're bringing Mom home now."

A few seconds passed before Jake said: "Okay, Dad. I love you."

"I love you, too. Stay strong now, buddy. I'll see you in a few hours."

Ending the call, Greg dragged his hand over his face.

"How's he holding up?" Kat asked.

"He's stronger than me. Has more faith than me. He's like her."

Kat nodded.

Greg's thoughts hurled back to the site where Jenn died, the old news photos of Jenn's home burning in the night, again the vile replay of horror, her parents' deaths by fire, Jenn's death by fire, Greg and Kat losing their mother, Jake losing his mother...

Dear God, please help us.

He stared at the road rushing under him, stared at the hearse carrying his wife. Blinking back tears, he turned to Kat.

"Thank you for being such a good sister, for helping me through this, through everything."

She patted his hand, took a breath, and nodded.

"What is it that you were going to tell me, Kat?"

"What?"

"The other day, about Jenn and Sellwin, you said you never told me everything."

"Oh, Greg, it's not important now."

"No, I want to know. I deserve to know. You said you'd argued with Jenn and it got bad. Tell me, Kat. It's just you and me here."

She tightened her grip, looked straight ahead at the hearse.

"We argued about Sellwin and what I saw. Things were said. Later, I felt so bad, I couldn't leave it alone."

"What do you mean?"

"I wanted to apologize, you know. So I drove over to your house."

"When was this?"

"That night."

"The night she didn't come home?"

"Yes. I wanted to see her and clear the air."

"I went to your door but nobody answered. Nobody was home."

"Then what?"

"I drove home."

"That's it?"

"Yes."

"I thought you told Kozak and Carillo that you were home all night."

"I was. Coming to your house was not even worth mentioning, in the whole scheme of things."

Greg stared at Kat.

"That's it, Greg. Quit looking at me like that."

He swallowed, then looked at the hearse ahead of them.

Fifty-Six

Greater Buffalo, New York

The smell of candle wax, flowers, the calm, lush tone of the pipe organ, and the creaking of the oak floors and pews blended in the church.

The brick building sat on three acres of serene countryside at the edge of the city where it was built in the 1800s by settlers who attended services in horse-drawn carriages.

This church was where Greg and Jenn were married.

Now, it was where her funeral was taking place, and where she would be buried, near her parents.

Consumed with torment grinding to his marrow, Greg was constrained in his tight-fitting dark suit, battling to hold himself together for this day.

Gently, he gripped Jake's knee, his son sitting beside him in his new dark suit. *Jenn would love it.* Kat had taken Jake to W.C. Supersuits to pick it out. Now, sitting on the other side of Jake, she held his hand. Vince, a tissue crushed in his fist, sat next to Greg.

Here they were, the survivors of a small family.

No other living relatives.

Just us now, Greg thought as the organ's peaceful, rich timbre floated above the mourners crowding into the main floor and the balcony.

Outside, cars, including a sprinkling of media vehicles, lined the shoulders of the two-lane rural road. The newspeople were set up a respectful distance across the road with their cameras concentrated on the entrance and the cemetery, which was adjacent to the church.

Inside, Jenn's closed casket was displayed at the front.

She would've wanted something plain, simple, Greg had told the funeral director. The model he and Kat had chosen was the Celestial Rose, made of 20-gauge steel, finished in glossy white. They'd kept it closed during both showings, and Greg ceased pursuing his attempts to see Jenn's remains. The funeral director, his voice a whisper, had said: "There will be some difficulty, Mr. Griffin, but I assure you we'll do all that can be done for her."

Jenn was radiant, smiling at the mourners from her framed photo atop a bed of roses on her coffin, positioned between two large sprays of flowers.

The organ stopped, the reverend began the service, then later, one by one, people stood over Jenn's casket and eulogized her. The president of the school board praised her, "as the embodiment of altruism." A tearful teacher acknowledged all Jenn had accomplished, calling her "a warrior angel." A longtime friend and colleague at Crystallo View Optical spoke of the care Jenn took in helping people improve their vision, especially children. And Holly Wiley, their neighbor, said Jenn was "the kind of mom all moms wanted to be, completely devoted to her family."

Greg struggled to absorb the words but while listening, he turned to the light streaming through the stained-glass window, observing how it spilled on her casket with such horrible beauty that...*it couldn't be...no...no, this is not real.*

In an instant, Greg thought, no, this wasn't true. This funeral was imagined. Jenn didn't die in a fireball on a freeway in Cleveland. She came home that night from her book club and they started the next day the same way they always did. Jenn had even caught him drinking milk from the bottle and got mad, really mad: "Greg, come on! How many times have I asked you to stop doing that? It's so gross!" He expected her to walk into the church, to wake him up, take him back to their life now. Oh God, he'd give anything to get back to what they had.

Because Jenn's death was not real.

But it was real.

His twisting stomach underscored his pain as he took stock of Jenn's casket, the packed church. He knew the press was outside. At one point, Greg was certain he'd seen Kozak and Carillo among the mourners. He recalled how in a true-crime documentary he'd watched on Netflix, the detectives had said that to avoid the distraction of getting emotionally involved, they never attended a victim's funeral—*unless they thought the suspect was among the mourners.*

Vince tapped Greg's knee.

This part of the service had ended.

It was time to bury Jenn.

Juan Perez and Charles Stanton, two teachers from Jake's school, and Nate Wiley and Ahmed Karim, men who were neighbors, along with Al Clayton, and Greg, served as pallbearers.

They took the casket through the church doors, leading the procession over soft green grass beside the church, then through the wrought-iron gates of the burial ground. They moved among the head-stones to the plot that was one row from the graves of Jenn's mother and father.

Jenn's stone wouldn't be ready for some time.

Following the funeral director's instructions, they aligned the casket over the open grave, plac-ing it on the straps of the aluminum lowering de-vice. Once everyone was assembled, they remained standing and the reverend read a passage from Ec-clesiastes. When the reverend finished, the funeral director released the brake on the device.

Greg's knees buckled but he caught himself, holding Jake tight to him, as much to steady him-self as to comfort his son, tears rolling down their faces as Jenn's casket descended slowly into the earth, disappearing into the grave.

And with his next heartbeat, Greg saw Jenn on the Florida beach, smiling with one last wave: *So long. Bye.*

After Jenn's burial, a reception was held at the Cedar Winds Community Center, two miles down the road.

Many of the volunteers who'd helped search for her in the first days were there, helping load tables with an array of sandwiches, buns, cold cuts, salads, vegetables, dips, fruit, cheese, crackers, chips, pastries, cookies, and cakes, spread out buffet-style. The book of condolences was set up on a table at the entrance for those who hadn't yet signed it. It was a casual atmosphere for friends to share memories and celebrate Jenn's life.

Ties were loosened amid handshaking, hugging, and cheek kissing. Children rushed to the dessert table as people, nearly two hundred in all, found places to sit and talk.

The volunteers guided Greg, Jake, Kat, and Vince to a table reserved for them, where they offered to bring them food, drinks, and coffee. Vince opted to take Jake to the food table. Kat sat with Greg, who declined all offers as he watched.

How can anyone eat? he thought. He supposed it was a matter of closeness. Those who'd come with others but were insulated from grief because they didn't know Jenn were inclined to eat. Greg thought there was a healing quality to it; that life went on. But not for him, not now, for he was lost in a haze, where all he could hear was one, prolonged scream. It took every molecule he had to go through the motions of being alive as people approached him with their condolences.

Among the first was Nicole Pitcher, a teacher at Jake's school.

"I'm so sorry, Greg." Pitcher hugged him. "Jenn was treasured by everyone who knew her."

Then his neighbors, Holly and Nate Wiley.

"Oh, Greg." Holly hugged him, sobbing.

"If there's anything you need," Nate said, "anything we can do. We're here for you, Greg."

Next, Bert Cobb, a custodian at Jake's school.

"My condolences, Greg." Cobb took his hand in a warm, firm grip, his face ashen and his voice soft. "Not long ago, I lost my sister." He swallowed. "You just got to take it one day at a time."

Greg nodded his appreciation.

Liz Miller, from Jenn's book club, and her husband, Calvin, were next.

"I just don't know what to say." Crimson veins webbed Liz's eyes. "I'm so, so sorry, Greg." She embraced him.

When the Millers left, Porter Sellwin stood before Greg.

"My condolences," Sellwin said. "I know this is a hard time and I can't begin to imagine what you're going through. Jennifer will always have a special place in my heart. She worked selflessly for the well-being of the kids. I'm so sorry, Greg."

Greg stared at Sellwin for a long moment. Something about him seemed off. But he dismissed it and shook his outstretched hand.

Across the hall, at the food table, Jake surveyed all the offerings while his grandfather fixed himself a coffee.

Jake's face was blank. He had no appetite. But he was thirsty.

He plucked a can of orange soda from a punch bowl filled with iced drinks, turned, and collided with a man holding a paper plate with a sandwich and coleslaw, causing him to drop it on the floor.

"Oh," Jake said, recognizing the man. "I'm sorry, Mr. Cobb."

Cobb collected napkins, bent over to scoop the spillage onto the plate when he saw Jake was on the verge of tears.

"It was an accident," Jake said. "I'm really sorry."

"Hey." Cobb's voice was soft as he quickly disposed of the mess in a trash can then wiped his hands before lowering himself to look into Jake's face. "Hey, hey, it's okay, Jake. No big deal at all."

Jake nodded as tears rolled down his face.

"Hey, you know, I like your suit," Cobb said.

Jake nodded.

"I know this has to be the toughest day ever, right?" Cobb said.

Jake said nothing, looking at his feet.

"Well, you did good today, Jake. Real good."

"Thank you, Mr. Cobb," Jake said.

"You bet, you bet."

At Greg's table, the stream of people offering their sympathies was dwindling.

He thanked Juan Perez after he offered his condolences. Then Lynsey Dowd, who worked with Jenn, hugged Greg.

"She was such a good person. I'm so sorry," Dowd said.

Al Clayton, among the last mourners, embraced Greg.

"There are no words, Greg, no words. I'm so sorry."

Then, Brooke Bollman was standing at his table in a formfitting dress, her eyes glistening.

"I didn't know if I should be here, Greg, but I wanted to pay my respects."

He nodded.

"I'm so sorry for what happened. You have my condolences."

Bollman hugged him and when she left, Greg looked across the near-empty hall to a table where Kozak and Carillo were alone, finishing their coffees.

Watching.

Later, with the reception ended, Greg and Kat thanked the volunteers and left with Jake and Vince.

In the parking lot, while walking to Kat's Jeep, Greg saw a state police patrol car, an Erie County deputy's car and a familiar unmarked Taurus in a far corner. The trooper and deputy were talking to Kozak and Carillo.

Leaving his family to wait at the Jeep, Greg approached them.

As he drew nearer, he overheard pieces of conversation about "recording all license plates," then the detectives turned to Greg.

"Excuse me," Greg said.

Kozak's face creased with concern.

"Greg, we're sorry for your loss."

"I don't know if I should thank you for coming," Greg said, "or curse you."

Kozak and Carillo traded a quick look.

"I have only one thing to say," Greg said.

Carillo lifted his chin to receive it.

"You find out why my wife is dead."

Fifty-Seven

Cleveland, Ohio

Claire Kozak's gloved hands lifted the shattered screen of a discarded TV to find a rat's carcass infested with maggots.

Dropping the frame, she moved on, the rhythmic thrumming of the freeway underscoring the futility as she and Carillo searched the vast, abandoned lot.

They weren't certain what they were looking for—a piece of evidence, anything pointing to answers as to how and why Jennifer Griffin went from a quiet evening at a book club meeting in Buffalo to dying here in Cleveland, some one hundred yards away from where Kozak now stood.

They'd arrived in Cleveland last night, driving from Buffalo shortly after Jennifer's funeral, checking into the same Hyatt they'd used in the days after she was first identified.

Because she died in metropolitan Cleveland, Cuyahoga County had taken the lead on the investigation, building on the work done so far by Kozak and Carillo. This morning they'd attended a new case-status meeting downtown at the Justice Center on West Third Street in the Detective Bureau of the Cuyahoga County Sheriff's Department. Again, the group included people from the county, Cleveland police, Cleveland FBI agents, investigators from Ohio's Bureau of Criminal Investigation, and the highway patrol.

Again, leading that morning's meeting with updates was Marge Bayne, a detective with the county.

"We re-created what we know of Jennifer Griffin's final steps, based upon interviews of crash survivors, witness motorists, and canvassing the area," Bayne said, consulting her laptop.

"And video?" Carillo asked. "Where're you with that?"

Bayne shot him an icy glance and continued.

"As mentioned previously, the freeway cameras monitor live traffic. They do not record. Following a public appeal to witnesses for any recordings, we received some dashcam footage and reviewed it. Here it is."

Several video recordings of varying quality from varying perspectives played in a montage on a wall-mounted monitor. It showed Jennifer emerging in the night from the on-ramp and running into traffic, then the fiery explosion.

"Like she came out of nowhere," one of the Cleveland detectives said.

"We canvassed the area several times and searched it with dog teams and drones," Bayne said. "On one side of the freeway, there are several apartment blocks. On the other, several empty lots. Our efforts have yielded nothing to date."

"We moved on the new warrants," Kozak said.

"Yes, in response to our request, our New York colleagues executed warrants on any existing and new phones and devices for Greg Griffin and Brooke Bollman. We were specifically interested in tracking movement from Buffalo into the Cleveland area in the period leading up to and immediately following Jennifer Griffin's death. Now, we know Greg came to Cleveland with his sister to meet with Dr. Narlow at the ME's office after the fact, but aside from that, nothing else surfaced in Ohio."

"Greg and Bollman could've gotten new burners," an FBI agent said.

"It's possible," Bayne said.

"What about LPRs?" Carillo said. "You've got license plate readers in the city and about twenty other Cleveland suburbs?"

"We have searched them for New York plates of all vehicles linked to either Greg Griffin or Brooke Bollman without results," Bayne said. "We're still searching, but to what end? The LPRs are not on every access point. So they can't read every potential plate."

"They just have to read the right one," Carillo said.

Bayne looked at him.

"That's a hope and a wish, isn't it?"

Bayne's hair was tied into a tight ponytail, accentuating her taut expression. She glanced to her

sergeant, then the other county detective. Tapping
her pen on a thick file folder, she looked at Carillo
and Kozak then made a pronouncement.

"You know, we've looked extensively at your
case, at the key facts and every aspect you've provided us," Bayne said. "Given all the evidence
against the husband, Greg, who stands to gain
several hundred thousand dollars in insurance
money—well, to be frank, we, and our prosecuting
attorney, are wondering why you haven't charged
him."

"We've gone over it all a hundred times," Kozak
said. "It's all circumstantial. A charge would not
hold up."

"It seems apparent to us," Bayne said, "that she
was running from an abusive situation with an unfaithful spouse."

"But at this point," Kozak said, "we don't have
a solid piece of evidence linking him to her disappearance. And you cannot place him here at the
time of her death. Nothing we have is conclusive.
And, *to be frank*, it's dangerous to form a conclu-
sion then try to make the circumstances support it.
We cannot rule out other avenues."

"Really?" Bayne's eyebrows climbed a little.

"I think," Bayne's sergeant said, intervening,
"all of us need to keep working and following up."

"Look, Detective Bayne," Carillo said, "maybe
there's something we all missed along the line.
Maybe it's in New York. Maybe it's in the area
where she ran onto the freeway. Maybe we missed
something there?"

Bayne gave him the beginnings of an eye roll.

"That area's been thoroughly searched." Bayne closed her laptop. "But you're welcome to go poke in it again."

So here they were, picking through the desolate region of vacant lots, with their heaps of earth, bricks, long-dead appliances, furniture, cast-off car tires, and mufflers, in an urban graveyard of long-forgotten dreams.

A sudden rattling of metal and glass sounded nearby.

Kozak waved to Carillo and they walked to it, passing around several mounds, coming to a figure in a long, heavy coat over torn jeans, boots, and a pulled-up hoodie, plucking cans from a pile, dropping them into a shopping cart.

Aware they were being watched, the figure stopped to look at Kozak, with Carillo behind her.

The can collector was a man. Deep lines were carved into his leathery weatherworn face, disappearing into a wild beard. His age could've been anywhere from thirty to sixty, Kozak thought.

"Can you help me?" she said.

Shaking his head, the man worked, cans clattering in his cart.

Kozak reached into her wallet, extended a twenty-dollar bill. The man glanced at it, ignoring her. Then she produced her phone, stepped closer. He took a step back.

"It's okay," she said, holding out the phone with Jennifer's photos. "Please take a look at this woman. Have you seen her around here?"

He stepped closer to look. A breeze delivered the strong reek of alcohol. He looked and Kozak swiped, showing him more photos. But the man shook his head, stepped back, resumed his work.

Kozak thought for a moment, extended the twenty.

"This is yours." She smiled. "Thank you for your time."

He stopped, raised his arm, and pointed. Kozak and Carillo followed his direction to an underpass about a hundred yards away with a patch of blue at the summit, where a sloping retaining wall met the underbelly of the multilane overpass.

"She might know," the man said.

"Up there?"

The man nodded.

Kozak and Carillo assessed what appeared from the distance to be a makeshift tent.

"All right, thank you," Kozak said, holding out the twenty. "Please, this is yours."

The man accepted the bill and the detectives trekked to the underpass. They trudged over a downed chain-link fence amid the rumbling of traffic on the elevated freeway before coming to two shopping carts at the base of the small encampment. Leaning forward, she started up the great, sloping retaining wall.

"You want us to climb up there?" Carillo said.

"Got to pursue all leads, partner. Stay there and guard the carts if you can't make it."

"Hang on. I'm right behind you."

They ascended the incline, fast-food bags fluttering nearby, pushed by the whine, gusts, and flow of the traffic rushing above them. The air was heavy, the retaining wall stained with guano, sewage, water, and urine. They reached their destination, a collection of heavy blue plastic tarps forming a lean-to shelter. A thick foam mattress serving as a floor stuck out. Blankets fixed to a line of twine made for the curtained entrance.

The detectives stood a few yards away, Carillo catching his breath as pigeons cooed and the traffic thundered overhead.

"Hello?" Kozak called.

Nothing but the traffic and the crackling of the tarps lifting in the wind.

Kozak moved closer.

"Hi, if you're in there, we need your help."

Nothing.

Carillo nodded for Kozak to open the curtain but before she could, there was movement, then the blanket was drawn and a woman's face appeared.

She might have been in her fifties, gray hair curled under a woolen cap, a coat over a clean plaid flannel shirt and turtleneck. She was alert, with sharp eyes behind glasses. Kozak caught the smell of something pleasant, like laundry detergent.

"What do you want?"

"Only your help."

Her quick eyes took stock of Kozak and Carillo.

"You want *me* to help *you*?"

"Yes."

"Help you with what?"

Kozak held out her phone with Jennifer's photos.

"Have you ever seen this woman in this area recently?"

As the woman leaned closer to study the photos, Kozak watched her face as she swiped the photos for her. The woman scrutinized them carefully as Kozak kept repeating the gallery.

After a long moment the woman shrugged.

"I don't know, maybe."

"Maybe? Maybe where?"

"At the shelter, maybe, I don't know."

"Which one, where?"

"The Sheltering Halo. That way." She pointed her chin.

"Thank you. You've been helpful. Can I get your name?"

She shook her head.

"Who are you, anyway, to come up here?"

"Police."

"I don't want to talk to police."

"That's all right." Kozak was going to take her picture but changed her mind and reached for her wallet while nodding to Carillo. They held out fifty in cash for her.

Tears came to the woman's eyes as she looked at it, making Kozak wonder what had happened in the woman's life that had led to her living under a freeway. The woman took the cash, grunted her thanks then retreated into the tent, closing her curtain.

Fifty-Eight

Manhattan, New York

Eugene Bickersley's eyes watered above his breathing tube at Memorial Sloan Kettering Cancer Center.

Jennifer Griffin's death, and her funeral, which he was unable to attend, was a wound that went deep. But his secret shame and regret for not acting on what he knew about her went deeper.

His Adam's apple rose and fell.

He turned away from the TV, muted on a Western movie—a wagon train moving across the great plains. His head rustled against his pillow when he looked to his wife, Clara.

There was little left to say.

Dread filled the room and their hearts.

A few days ago, their hopes were high. The possibility he could go home to Buffalo was real. But then Bickersley had experienced a troubling setback.

Now, as they waited for the latest test results, he

pretended to watch a movie while Clara was scrolling through family photos.

Soft sounds of activity in the hallway spilled into the room when the door opened and Dr. Samuel Khalid entered.

Bickersley braced. Clara set her phone down and held a breath.

The doctor stood near them both.

"We have the results of the latest tests." He slid his hands in the pockets of his white coat and looked directly at Bickersley. "I'm afraid there's no easy way to say this, Eugene. The results are not what we'd hoped for but rather what we feared."

Clara groaned and Bickersley took her hand.

"We'll carry on with some therapies," Khalid said in a soft British accent. "But the progression is closing the window. The situation is all but untreatable."

"What are my chances?" Bickersley said. "You had me at thirty percent. Where does this put me now? Give it to me straight."

"As this stage, survival rate is at ten to fifteen percent."

Bickersley shut his eyes. Clara sobbed, crushing his hand in hers. He could feel her trembling.

Bickersley cleared his throat.

"And the time, Sam? How much?"

"Three to six months."

Bickersley took a moment to absorb and process the information as the doctor put his hand gently on his shoulder.

"Never abandon hope," Khalid said. "There is

cutting-edge research underway, a joint study with Johns Hopkins in the US and Cambridge in the UK. It's at the experimental stage with new drugs, but it's showing promise. We're endeavoring to get you enrolled as a participant. With your permission, of course."

"Yes," Clara said.

"Yes, you have my permission," Bickersley said. "Thank you, Sam."

Khalid nodded, tapped Bickersley's shoulder with encouragement, touched Clara's shoulder, then left.

As Clara tugged a fresh tissue from the box on the stand, Bickersley turned to the muted movie, which he'd left on, and reflected.

Time was running out for him. Yes, there was hope, but the odds against him were growing with each passing minute.

"We have to pray Dr. Khalid can get you in that study and put you on new drugs," Clara said.

"We have to prepare for the worst."

"Gene, please, we can't give up hope."

"There are no guarantees."

"Gene."

"I want to be in the study. I'll keep fighting, but I've decided there's one thing I must do while I still can."

"What?"

"It's something I cannot and will not carry with me."

Clara's eyes searched his as she fought to understand.

"Gene, what are you talking about?"

"It's about Jennifer Griffin."

"But she's— Gene, I don't understand."

"Clara, I'm going to tell police what I know about Jennifer Griffin."

Fifty-Nine

Buffalo, New York

*W*ho was that woman on Zoran's laptop?

For days the incident had eaten at Lorena Jo Tullev.

She'd only glimpsed the screen when he answered his phone that day, yet Lorena felt she knew the face. But she didn't get a good look because Zoran had closed his laptop, as if she'd caught him red-handed at something beyond his porn obsession.

It has to be something new he doesn't want me to know about, maybe involving that woman on his laptop.

Lorena placed four cans of peas in her shopping cart and continued grappling with her predicament.

This laptop thing increased her unease over their increasingly rocky relationship, eroding her trust. For all she knew, Zoran could've been looking at something totally harmless and was offended by her suspicions. His refusal to talk about their issues fed her concern that it was something more serious.

If he's cheating on me, then it's over.

But if it's something else, I'll move heaven and earth to save our relationship because deep down, I have to believe that the Zoran I know is a good man.

As she shopped in the frozen food section, she began working on a plan. She needed to get into Zoran's laptop to find the truth.

I can do that.

She had his passwords. He'd changed them recently. He hadn't been very creative, or careful, with them. She'd surreptitiously watched him jot them on a piece of paper, crumple it, and toss it into the trash. That slip of paper was now in her wallet, tucked between two credit cards.

The problem was, Zoran took his laptop wherever he went; to work, and to his fishing cabin.

The cabin.

He'd been spending more time there. If he was cheating with another woman, that was the most likely place he'd take her. It's where he used to take Lorena in the first months of their relationship.

For a moment she'd drifted into memories of her time there with him. It was a beautiful, secluded spot, isolated in the woods west of Buffalo in Pennsylvania.

Almost halfway to Cleveland.

By the time Lorena had reached the checkout, she had a strategy.

The next time Zoran went off alone to his cabin, she'd follow him. She'd either catch him in the act, or find a way to gain access to his laptop when he was out of the cabin.

"Will that be cash or credit?" the cashier asked her after she'd rung in Lorena's groceries.

"Credit card."

Reaching into her wallet for her card, she took comfort seeing the slip of paper she needed.

One way or another, I'm going to bring this all to an end.

Sixty

Greater Buffalo, New York

Greg slipped from the tentacles of sleep.

It was still night.

In the ambient light under the sheets beside him he saw a shape.

Jenn was there!

Comprehension and joy blossomed in his chest.

Jenn's not dead! It was a horrible nightmare. It never happened.

His heart racing, wanting to take her in his arms, he drew back the sheet slowly but not to Jenn. It was Jake, asleep. Reality hit Greg in the gut with sledgehammer force.

Jenn was dead.

Head sinking into his pillow, he choked down a sob because part of him had known it was futile to deny she was gone.

He looked at the clock: 1:20 a.m. Practically the same time he woke that awful, awful night. Then, as he had every night in the time since he had buried Jenn, Greg lay there in bed, his eyes open. Again, his grief had overpowered the sleeping pills, taking him hostage, torturing him with lightning flashes of memory.

Jenn's empty side of the bed, driving into the night searching for her, searching all night, Brooke's hands all over him... "We'd be great together..." Jenn's blue Corolla entangled in the woods, the detectives' accusations, the polygraph, Kozak telling him: "Jennifer didn't survive her injuries. She's dead." TV news reports—"A woman was killed"— the fiery freeway explosion, finding images of charred remains, carrying her casket with... Jenn smiling and waving on the beach. "So long..." Her last wave. "Bye."

Her casket descending into the ground...

Over and over, the images tormented him until the hour before dawn and he hefted himself from bed. Body aching, he made his way into the bathroom and started a hot shower.

As steam clouds rose around him, he slammed his back against the wall, slid down to the floor, lifting his face to the needles of water and sobbing for Jenn.

Greg and Jake began the day, going through what had become the semblance of a morning routine for them.

Jake got up, got dressed. He had started going back to school. He wanted to because in some way, he felt his mother's presence there, found comfort in being with his friends, the teachers, the cafeteria workers, and the custodians.

366   *Rick Mofina*

Downstairs, in the kitchen, Jake got his own breakfast, a bowl of frosted flakes with milk. But he ate little, reading the promotion for a game prize on the back of the box. Jake hardly spoke at home anymore. *His shirt looks bigger on him. He's losing weight,* Greg thought, when he made coffee for himself and toast for both of them.

Greg could only manage a few bites. Jake didn't touch his slice.

"I'm running out of clean underwear, Dad."

Greg looked at him, stunned Jake had said so much at once. Forcing himself to deal with the issue, Greg, up to now, had just kept buying new underwear for them. When Kat found out, she'd taped instructions to the washer and dryer for Greg, for the times she couldn't be there to help.

"I'll take care of it later," Greg said. "Brush your teeth when you're done, and I'll drive you to school."

Rolling through the neighborhood in his pickup, Greg glanced at his son. Wounded by the loss of his mother, Jake had become muted. He even looked older, and it pulled Greg back to when his own mother had died.

Your world is never the same. It's like you can't trust the earth not to collapse under your feet.

Greg stopped at the school. Jake hugged him tight.

"I love you, Dad."

"I love you, son."

Jake grabbed his backpack and climbed out of the truck.

"Remember, Dad, underwear."

"Got it."

Greg watched Jake join his friends in the school-yard. Seeing he was safe among the living, he drove off to the job site.

He hadn't fully returned to work, but when he was up to it, he'd drive past Depew to Pine Castle Park where he would see his crew, and Al Clayton would update him on the status of the project. Sometimes he heard what Al was telling him, other times, he heard nothing but a dull thudding at the back of his skull. He would thank Al, then walk alone around the site, then leave.

Greg drove off, thinking how he and Jake had been drained of the essence of their lives. The pain was immobilizing, leaving them weakened to mimic the motions of everyday life. His driving was an effort to outrun the guilt, anger, and sorrow whirling inside him, but he couldn't outrun them because they were interwoven with his soul. A horrible force had clawed through the web of his existence, leaving it in tatters. He'd defined himself through Jenn. Now he was lost.

He was her husband.

Now he was a widower.

Today Greg had, once again, driven to the edge of the city, coming to the church in the countryside where Jenn was buried.

He parked in the empty lot.

No other vehicles in sight. No sign of anyone.

He got out, walked over the soft green grass, passing through the gates of the cemetery. He came to the fresh mound of earth that was Jenn's grave. The monument maker had told him that it would be some time before the engraved granite headstone would be ready for installation. Until then, the cemetery's rules allowed for a wooden cross to be placed on the site. Greg swallowed then tenderly touched it, an oak cross grave marker with her name professionally carved into it:

Jennifer Marie Griffin.

As breezes flowed through treetops stirring birdsong, he stood there alone, his heart quaking as he struggled to understand.

How did this happen?

He was not sure how long he stood there, bound to his grief, the pain scraping his insides, until he dropped to his knees, wanting to gouge at the grave and crawl into it with her.

I'm sorry for what happened. I'm sorry it ended this way.

Huge tears streamed down his face. He sobbed and his body shook with such great spasms he steadied himself by hugging the cross.

I'm so sorry, Jenn. Please forgive me.

At that moment, his phone began buzzing, vibrating.

Greg ignored it until it stopped.

He couldn't let go of the cross.

If he did, he'd fall off the face of the earth.

Sixty-One

Around the time Greg was driving Jake to school, Meredith Martin was catching up on her work at the FBI's crime lab complex.

Only yesterday she and her husband were taking sunset walks on the beach in Ocho Rios.

Or so it seems, Martin thought, glancing out her small office window at the Virginia woods west of Washington, DC.

It was coming up on a week since she'd returned from her vacation in Jamaica, and she had cut down the backlog that was waiting for her. Sipping tea from her new mug with a hummingbird on it, she turned back to her computer monitor.

As a supervisory biologist with the CODIS Unit, Martin was performing more random quality assurance checks. She focused on recently completed cases of samples that had been submitted from law enforcement agencies across the country for comparison to DNA profiles in the National DNA Index System.

She'd examined two cases yesterday, one from California and one from Texas. Both were matches. Step by step, she'd scrutinized the work done. Everything in the process had been followed correctly. Martin affirmed the findings. Another sip of tea. She'd signed off on those cases, and this morning had moved on to another recently completed submission that had been a match.

Martin glanced at the Originating Agency Identifier, or ORI, of the profile in one of the national databases then pulled it up. Then she called up the submission.

Martin had a PhD and nearly fifteen years of experience in analyzing DNA with the FBI. She had testified in several court cases and had been recognized as a leading expert in her field.

After several long minutes of examining her monitor, her brow furrowed.

She reached for her phone and called her colleague, Abby Ross, to come to her office to consult on the submission.

A moment later, Ross joined Martin at her desk, looking at the monitor.

"All right." Martin pointed with a pen to the monitor. "See that?"

"Sure. The mt is consistent," Ross said.

"That's correct. The mitochondria DNA is inherited solely from the mother." Martin's pen hovered in a new area. "Take a real close look at the STR sequences."

Ross drew her face closer to the monitor.

"See it?" Martin said.

Ross began nodding. "There's a variance in the repeats."

"It's almost imperceptible, easy to miss, but it's definitely there."

"Oh jeez."

"Yup," Martin said. "And this was identified as a match."

"Oh no," Ross said. "Who handled it?"

Martin shook her head.

"Doesn't matter right now." Martin clicked back to the ORI with all the contact information. "What matters right now, is we got some calls to make."

Sixty-Two

Several long minutes had passed before Greg released his hold on Jenn's cross and got to his feet.

He was thankful that no one else was at the church or in the cemetery.

The solitude was a gift.

He sat on a bench in the shade of a maple tree, wiping his face with his sleeves, pulling himself together. He took out his phone from his pocket. It had vibrated twice while he mourned at Jenn's grave, but he'd ignored it. Checking it now, he saw it was not Jake, or his school. It wasn't Kat, or his father.

No messages.

The number was blocked.

It could've been media, a spam call, or anybody.

He was sliding the phone back into his pocket when it vibrated and buzzed in his hand.

The number was blocked.

Dragging one hand over his face, he cleared his throat then said, "Hello?"

"Greg, it's Claire Kozak."

He hesitated, then sniffed. "Yeah?"

"Are you driving right now?"

"No. What is it, Kozak?"

"Greg, we're in Cleveland and we wanted to reach you the moment we had this confirmed and before it got out to the press."

The last time Kozak called like this it was to prepare him for the most devastating news of his life.

"Before what got out?"

"The woman killed in the crash here was not Jennifer."

A sensation thundered through Greg's entire body, and he sat there in numbed silence.

"Greg, listen, it's complicated, but it was when they were analyzing the DNA—something got misinterpreted. Then the FBI's experts in Quantico reexamined it exhaustively several times before alerting us with the confirmation that Jennifer was not the woman killed in the crash in Cleveland."

"She wasn't?" Greg's voice broke as if reluctant to accept the news.

"No. I'm so sorry for what you've been through."

Greg adjusted his grip on his phone.

"You're sorry? What the f—" He stopped. "What—I just buried—dammit, Kozak!"

"Greg, it was a mistake."

"But how—who was the woman killed?"

"The FBI tells us that from their analysis of the dead woman's DNA, and the DNA we collected directly from Jennifer and Jake—you know, her toothbrush, comb, and Jake's cheek swab—that the woman killed in Cleveland is a relative of Jennifer's."

Shutting his eyes, his heart sank. He was shaking his head.

"But she has no relatives! It's another damned mistake!"

"No, we told the FBI that she has no other relatives, but they were adamant. The person killed in Cleveland is a relative."

"Listen to me. I've known Jenn for more than twenty years, since we were kids in high school, and I'm telling you she absolutely does not have any other relatives."

"The FBI is one hundred percent certain that it's a relative."

"I—can't do this—this is all—this can't be true—don't do this to me."

"Believe me, we pushed back hard on the FBI and with Ohio and they assured us that it's true, Greg. Jennifer did not die in that crash."

Greg said nothing.

"Alert your family, Greg. Press statements are going out soon in Ohio and New York."

He stared at the cemetery, at the headstones and the wooden cross bearing Jenn's name. He tightened his grip on his phone and pounded his fist on his knee with as much force as he could.

Wake up! This is another nightmare.

His disbelief, fear, and anger erupted.

"Kozak, if this is true then tell me—who did I bury?"

"We're working on that. And we're hoping it will lead us to Jennifer."

"And if it's true—" Greg stood and gulped air "—then it means Jenn is still alive."

"Yes, she very well could be."

Sixty-Three

Location Unknown

Will I ever get out of here? Will I ever see Jake and Greg again?

Jennifer Griffin's neck, shoulders, arms, and hands were numb from digging at the wood using the same repeated motions.

How deep are those screws anchored?

She'd progressed about a full inch into the wood around the top hinge, and maybe half that around the lower hinge, and still the assembly hadn't loosened. It was rock-solid.

She looked up at the naked bulb hanging from the ceiling, dimming and flickering.

Like her hope.

How many weeks have I been kept here?

She had never seen her captor. Her captor had never spoken to her, except through those rare notes that made no sense to her.

They were cryptic, torturing her, deepening her fear that if she didn't escape, she was going to die.

Accepting that these could be her last days, Jennifer ached to be with Jake and Greg.

To hold them and tell them how much I love them.

She reached for her notepad, to start a farewell letter to them.

"To My Sweet Son, Jake and Dear Darling Husband, Greg: Whatever happens to me, please know that I love you..." she began as tears stained her paper and she stopped.

How would Jake survive my death?

Jennifer knew the horror of losing her mother and father. Setting the pad down, reflecting on her life, on how Jake was nearly the same age as she was when her parents died in the fire, she knew that the scars of that kind of tragedy never heal.

She closed her eyes.

Her scars were sliced open in the months before she was taken when she found a small cardboard box on her doorstep.

It held an angel chime.

Seeing it had staggered her, thrusting her back across time to the fire.

Who sent this?

Why?

There was no message. No markings on the box.

Home alone, she had found the courage to start the chime, watching it, her joy and agony spinning like the angels. But staring into the dancing candle flames, she reeled with a thousand emotions.

She stopped the chime and hid it.

Telling no one about the chime, she struggled

to get on with her life. Right up until the time she was abducted, she was grappling with her problems with Greg, Porter Sellwin, Kat—even that cable guy thing still bothered her. All the while, Jennifer had tried maintaining the facade of normalcy when in reality, she had plummeted into a black hole of despair.

She went to a psychologist, Dr. Maynart.

Her secret weekly sessions with him helped but were difficult. She wasn't prepared to tell him everything at first. He understood. She told him what she could, little by little, and eventually, he told her that she appeared to be grappling with prolonged grief disorder over her parents' deaths, and possibly, a recent trauma of some sort may have triggered it. She had progressed in her sessions to the point where she was ready to reveal the chime, bring it with her to a session and explain its significance in the tragedy—hoping that Dr. Maynart could help her unravel the mystery.

Why was the chime left anonymously on my doorstep?

Or did I give it to myself for reasons buried deep inside me?

And now, as her eyes went around her cell, she wondered:

Could the chime be related to why I was brought here? How? No one could possibly know its meaning in my life.

Sixty-Four

Surfing channels, Greg found a Breaking News report from a local station.

"…has been a twist in the case of missing Buffalo-area mom, Jennifer Griffin," the news anchor was saying. "We have pictures for you now while our Anika Shimo brings us the latest. Anika?"

"That's right, Cora. Police in New York and Ohio have just confirmed that Jennifer Griffin, the missing Buffalo woman thought to have been killed in Cleveland, was misidentified and did not die in the freeway crash there after all. This turn of events comes after her family recently held a funeral…"

Shimo related the history of the case, and the TV screen in Greg's living room filled with news images of flashing lights of police units at the church where yellow tape cordoned off a section of the cemetery. Jennifer's face filled the upper right corner of the screen, above her name and the words:

MISSING MOM WRONGLY IDENTIFIED AS DECEASED.

Then came more images from early in the case of Jenn's Corolla in Blueripple Woods, of Greg being interviewed, police scouring the forest, graphics, arrows, maps, helicopters, dog teams, and volunteer searchers.

"...and our sources tell us that early in the investigation, Greg Griffin, the missing woman's husband, took a polygraph but police have not released the results. And police won't say if Greg Griffin has been ruled out as a suspect..."

Greg wondered if Jenn was alive, if she was watching, if she'd been abducted, wondered if whoever took her was watching, or maybe saw the news and went ahead and killed her.

Oh God.

There was footage of the fiery freeway crash in Cleveland with Shimo ending her report saying: "Jennifer Griffin was first identified by DNA as the person killed in that incident but later analysis by the FBI found the first results had been misinterpreted and now the FBI confirms that Jennifer Griffin was not the victim. The person killed has yet to be identified, and investigators have not provided further details. Meanwhile, the mystery surrounding this case deepens. Back to you, Cora..."

That was the latest TV news report.

Staring at the screen, Greg absorbed the enormity of events, not yet fully comprehending what had happened.

Only that it had.

Triggered by Kozak's call to him at the cemetery, Greg had acted fast and pulled Jake from school. He was grateful that Kat was able to leave work, pick up Vince, and get over to the house. In the brief calm preceding the storm, Greg had sat them down and told them that Jenn could very well be alive because she had not died in Cleveland; the person they buried was someone related to her.

"So she really could be alive?" Vince asked.

"Yes, that's what Kozak told me."

"But this can't be," Kat said. "She has no relatives."

"I know, I can't believe it," Greg said. "I've known Jenn since we were kids. I spent so much time with her at her grandmother's house. I never saw or heard of any other family members, and they both told me there were no other relatives, just Jenn and her grandma."

Jake said nothing, his face tensing in his effort to understand what he was hearing. Kat put her arm around him, pulling him close to her.

"If they made a mistake with the DNA the first time," Vince said, "then maybe this is a mistake, too?"

"Kozak assured me it's not," Greg said. "She said it had been checked and rechecked and checked again by the FBI's experts in Quantico."

"Then we should thank God," Vince said. "Isn't this what we prayed for?"

Jake nodded with a sudden realization. "My wish on the angel chime came true! Mom is not dead!"

Greg brushed the top of Jake's head.

"We have to remember that this also means that someone else died. Someone related to Mom."

"But who?" Vince asked.

That's when the calls started. The first was a reporter with the *Buffalo News*, then a local radio station, seeking Greg's reaction. Then Al Clayton, then their neighbor, Holly Wiley, then Liz Miller from Jenn's book club, then a teacher from the school, all of them wanting to know if it was true. A producer from CNN called, requesting Greg give a live interview with one of the network's anchors in New York City. Greg declined. The doorbell rang. Vince went to the window.

"It's the press. Two—no, three—news trucks out front, and another one arriving."

"Kat, get the door. Tell them we can't comment at this time," Greg said. "Don't answer any questions, leave it with me."

Then Greg turned on the TV.

Jumping from channel to channel, he found the first of the breaking news reports while his landline phone continued ringing. Kat answered the calls. Now, she was holding the cordless receiver when she came to Greg and he turned to her.

"It's the *New York Times*," she said.

Greg shook his head, stopped, changed his mind and took the phone.

"Is this Greg Griffin, Jennifer Griffin's husband?"

"Yes."

"Sue Williams, *New York Times*. We're doing a

story on the development in your wife's case and
I'm seeking your response."

"I'm shocked, like everyone."

"Mr. Griffin, how did you learn of the misread-
ing of your wife's DNA?"

"A detective on the case called me."

"Where were you and what were you doing when
you got the call?"

"Visiting my wife's grave."

"Really? You were at the cemetery just before
police declared it a crime scene?"

Greg said nothing as Williams continued.

"What thoughts went through your mind when
the detective informed you that your wife had not
been killed in Cleveland?"

"Disbelief." Greg took a moment. "While it com-
pounds the tragedy, it breaks our hearts because
it raises so many questions. At the same time, it
gives us hope. I really have nothing more to say."

"But Mr. Griffin, do you have any idea who was
killed in Cleveland?"

"No."

"One last thing. Mr. Griffin, do you feel police
still consider you a suspect in your wife's disappearance?"

Anger surged but Greg got in front of it.

"Ask them," he said. "That's all I have to—"

"Mr. Griffin, there are sources in New York
and Ohio who tell us that some investigators feel
strongly that you should be charged. What's your
reaction?"

Greg hung up.

He sat on the sofa, staring at the phone, holding one hand over his face. That's when he saw Jake at the window, curtain pulled aside, looking at the growing collection of newspeople out front. Greg saw the cameras, on tripods, on shoulders, one photographer in a white van with a long lens, all of them aimed at the house, aimed at Jake. Likely zooming right into the living room like powerful, prying eyes, Greg thought.

"Jake, close the curtain and get away from the window," Greg said, then resumed staring at the phone in his hand.

Vince took Jake into the kitchen and Kat joined her brother on the sofa, placing her hand on his knee.

"What is it? Does that *New York Times* reporter know something?"

Greg shook his head, shifting his thoughts.

"The thing with Porter Sellwin," Greg said, "when you saw him with Jenn."

"Did the reporter know something about that?"

"No. But for some reason I was thinking back to what you said about it."

"I said I was sorry about that."

"No, not that, but it just struck me again."

"What?"

"A couple of things Sellwin said to me were weird. Like when I first confronted him after you told me. One of the things he said to me was 'I don't know what Jennifer told you.' It was odd, out of place, almost like he was expecting to be confronted, you know?"

"That is weird."

"Then at the funeral, he offered condolences then said, 'Jennifer will always have a special place in my heart.' It just struck me, given the tone he used, as an odd, rather intimate thing to say. I just don't—"

"I don't know what you're getting at," Kat said.

"I don't know myself. All right, so maybe Sellwin's a touchy-feely creep with a reputation. I mean, you suspected Jenn was cheating with him and argued with her about it, right?"

"Yes, but I wanted to apologize to her." Kat cupped her hands to her face. "Greg, I'm sorry I said all those things. That day I saw Sellwin touching Jenn, I don't know what I saw, okay?"

"But that's just it," Greg said. "With the things you saw and the things Sellwin said to me, I just—I just got a real bad vibe about him and—" Greg shook his head. "I mean, who could've taken Jenn? And if she's alive, where is she? I'm just so lost, Kat."

"Greg, listen to me. Since Jenn's been missing, you've been through hell. We all have. Then this news that she may not be dead comes and you're in shock. We all are. Nothing makes sense."

"They're saying that Jenn has a relative, and we know it can't be true."

"I thought about that," Kat said, "and I have an idea. There might be a way we can check that out."

"What do you mean?"

"Did you move any of Jenn's stuff? Make any donations?"

"I couldn't bring myself to do anything like that. It's all so raw."

"Come upstairs. I'll show you what I mean."

As they went up the stairs, Greg thought of how Jake had said he'd wished upon the angel chime then Greg tried to decipher what the chime meant to Jenn. But it was in vain. Upstairs, he followed Kat down the hall to a storage closet, one he seldom used. She opened it to shelves of extra sheets, towels for guests, cleaning supplies, and an assortment of storage totes and boxes. The U-shaped storage area was large enough for a person to walk into and close the door behind them.

Kat reached to the corner of a top shelf and pulled down an aged cardboard box that Greg was not familiar with. It was about the size of a milk crate. It had wispy traces of fingerprint powder.

"I think police gave this a cursory look," Kat said. "It looks like they didn't pay much attention to it when they searched the house in the early days. Guess it wasn't important at the time."

She set the box on the floor in the hall where she began sifting through the contents: an album with a few old photos, bundles of cards, letters secured with ribbons.

"The pictures are mostly of Jenn's parents at their house." Kat flipped through it, then she untied the bundles, shuffling through the collection. "These are birthday cards and sympathy cards, saved from the funeral after the fire. I think her grandmother kept all of this and Jenn saved it."

Greg looked through everything with surprise.

"You never saw this stuff?" Kat said.

"No. In Jenn's office downstairs, I found some clippings and things she'd kept on the fire, but I never saw this all tucked away in here. I never go in here, never look in here."

Greg stared at Kat, rummaging through the box.

"How did you know about this?"

She stopped, a little smile coming to her face.

"You won't believe me."

"Tell me."

"A couple of years ago, I was here in the house, watching Jake while you and Jenn were out. He loved playing hide-and-seek. I hid in here and when he found me and opened the door, I raised my hands up high and jumped to scare him. I hit the shelf and knocked some boxes down. They spilled out. I tidied things up and put them back. That's how I knew what was here."

Greg held his sister in his gaze for a long moment as if deciding whether to believe her. Feeling his stare, Kat turned to him.

"It's the truth, Greg. Jesus."

Sixty-Five

Cleveland, Ohio

Claire Kozak steadied her fingers over her keyboard and began typing messages while waiting for the emergency meeting to begin at the Justice Center.

That Jennifer Griffin was not the woman killed in the freeway incident had shocked investigators on the case; others were pissed off. There were mutterings about a "massive, embarrassing screwup," as people took their seats around the table in the Cuyahoga County Sheriff's Department.

As problematic as the misidentification was for law enforcement, Kozak considered the anguish for Jennifer's family, especially her son, Jake.

The boy was only eight and had faced what he thought was his mother's death and funeral.

Her stomach fluttering, Kozak pressed Send. She started another message on her tablet, to her lieutenant in Clarence, adding to the strategy she'd outlined for him yesterday following the turn in the case. On an urgent front, it meant Kozak and Carillo had stayed another night in Cleveland to attend that morning's meeting.

Kozak typed quickly, read what she wrote, then sent it as Sergeant Frank Renner started. His jawline pulsing, he undid his collar button and loosened his tie.

"No need for a roll call. Let's get to it," Renner, the senior officer with Cuyahoga County, began. "Finger-pointing and venting won't get us anywhere. We pick things up from here. Before I hand off to Detective Marge Bayne, let me say that much of the work we've done remains unchanged. Marge."

Bayne, her face tight, unsmiling, went through work done on the investigation, noting what would stand, and what was needed.

"The focus is obvious," she said. "To identify the victim killed on the freeway and investigate for links to the missing New York woman."

She turned to the two Cleveland FBI agents at the table.

"We reiterate that Quantico's analyzed the DNA extensively," Special Agent Alice Jordan said, "and confirms the DNA from the fatality does not belong to the missing woman, but the two profiles are genetically related. In our effort to identify the freeway DNA, the FBI is processing it through all federal databases, and will extend the search to DNA databases in Canada and Europe. Warrants are being prepared to search commercial genealogical DNA databases, as well. This will take time, but we're moving on it."

Bayne nodded to the agent, then turned to Kozak and Carillo.

"And," Bayne said, "given that the grave in Buffalo could now be considered a crime scene with buried evidence, we need you to—"

"Already on it," Kozak said. "We're securing the cemetery and posting a patrol. We'll also initiate the exhumation process. It will take time."

"Additionally, Detective Bayne," Carillo said, "our case analysts are working with county and state officials in New York to review hospital, divorce, birth, death, and any records concerning Sofia Ann Korvin."

"Who is that?" a Cleveland detective asked.

"Jennifer Griffin's biological mother," Kozak said. "Sofia and her husband, Leo Korvin, Jennifer's biological father, died in a house fire almost thirty years ago in Buffalo. We provided a report on the fire in the case files we shared with you. Jennifer was their only child, the sole survivor. She was raised by Leo Korvin's mother, who was Jennifer's grandmother."

"We believe investigating Jennifer Griffin's family history," Kozak said, "could lead us to identifying who was killed on the freeway, and possibly to Jennifer."

"Of course." Bayne's smile was cold. "But nothing changes the overwhelming evidence that Jennifer Griffin was running from an abusive situation with an unfaithful spouse."

"That case still has to be made to support a charge," Carillo said.

"Maybe Erie County's prosecution team lacks the confidence to proceed," Bayne said.

"Proceed with what?" Carillo said.

"Detective Bayne," Kozak said, catching Sergeant Renner shifting uncomfortably in his chair, "to debate your point would be an exercise in futility."

"Would it?" Bayne said.

"That fact is," Kozak continued, "the misidentification serves to underscore that we must pursue all investigative avenues so that nothing is missed."

"Yes," Renner said. "I think we can all agree on that."

"Right," Kozak agreed. "So we'll tie up some loose ends here before we head back to Buffalo to resume work there."

Renner collected his notes and folders, signaling the meeting's end.

"I think we've covered everything for now, so we can all get back at it. Thank you, everyone."

In the elevator to the lobby, some investigators made small talk about the Browns and Cavaliers. Kozak and Carillo said little, waiting until they were alone in their Taurus where Carillo took the wheel while Kozak scrolled through her messages.

"What did you do to that Marge Bayne?" Carillo smiled.

Kozak waved a dismissive hand, her eyes on her phone, reading a message from Chase, the younger of her two sons.

Aiden's making me do his chores. When are you coming home?

I'll talk to Aiden. I'll be home in time for supper. We'll get pizza. OK?

OK.

Love you, honey.

Love you, Mom.

Kozak then sent a message to Aiden.

Go easy on Chase. I'll be home today.

He's such a lazy baby.

Do it for me. Show me it was not a mistake to leave you two on your own. Can you do that, honey?

Sure. Can we get pizza tonight?

With wings?

Yes!

Relieved, Kozak looked away from her phone and took a long, slow breath, looking at Cleveland's skyline.

Carillo had been following directions on the GPS to take them back to the area near the deadly, fiery freeway crash. He glanced at Kozak.

"You're up for this?" he asked.

"Yup."

"It'll likely be nothing."

"We have to try, Ned."

He nodded as the Taurus accelerated onto the freeway, taking them closer to a potential lead in the case.

Sixty-Six

Cleveland, Ohio

The Sheltering Halo Community House was an abandoned brick school that had been slated for demolition. But it was rescued by a coalition of nonprofits and converted into the sanctuary it was today.

Walls along its entrance held Halo's mission statement, its pledge to help those in need. Also posted were requirements for guests to report all communicable diseases. And there were rules, such as instant eviction for possession of weapons, disruptive behavior, and/or the use of contraband, including alcohol or illegal drugs.

The floor smelled of cleaner.

Sheltering Halo provided free recovery and rehabilitation programs for those with addictions. It also offered help finding employment, Colleen Golinka, the shelter's director, explained while leading Kozak and Carillo to the dining hall, which had been the school's cafeteria.

In coming here, the investigators had taken into

account the revelation that Jennifer Griffin was not the person killed in the freeway tragedy. But, if the DNA identified the victim as her relative, then maybe the dead mystery woman bore a resemblance to Jennifer. And if the woman living nearby had seen a woman who looked like Jennifer, well, wasn't that a potential lead?

A lot of "ifs," but Kozak wanted to pursue it before they left Cleveland.

The dining room was empty, but for volunteers cleaning up. Golinka chose a table near the kitchen, where people were working amid the sounds of running water and the clatter of pans. The air held the aroma of fresh-baked bread.

"Would you like some coffee, Detectives?"

"No, thank you," Kozak said.

"So, you're from Buffalo. How can we help?" Golinka said.

Kozak showed her photos of Jennifer.

"It concerns this woman," Kozak said.

Studying them, Golinka nodded.

"Oh, yes, the woman killed on the freeway not far from here, a terrible tragedy. I understand she was from Buffalo."

"Well, yes, but there's been a new development, which may not be widely known yet," Kozak said. "Aside from that, we understand that she, or someone resembling her, might've stayed here?"

Golinka thought then slowly said, "No, I don't think so. I recall that shortly after the accident, Cleveland police were here, asking about her."

"And what came of their inquiries?" Carillo said.

"To my knowledge, nothing. We don't think she was here. However, while we do operate like most shelters, in some ways, we don't."

"What do you mean?" Kozak asked.

"People come and go with us all the time. We respect their privacy and only record names and Social Security numbers if they wish to provide them. Some people, for a number of reasons, may not provide their information or true name."

"We figured that," Carillo said.

"And," Golinka said, "we also help women and children in abusive relationships. So anonymity to protect them from a vindictive partner is a priority, as well."

"We understand," Kozak said. "Now, you say many guests come and go. Is it possible some, who may have resided with you around the time of the crash, may not have been interviewed by Cleveland police? Or they may, for their own reasons, have been reluctant to talk to them?"

"It's possible. In some cases, our guests are acquainted with local law enforcement."

"Would any of those people be with you now? Anyone we could talk to, given we're from Buffalo and our interest is not related to local criminal history but to the mother missing from Buffalo and her family there?"

Golinka blinked.

"We assure you, it's our only interest at this time," Kozak said.

Golinka thought for a moment.

"All right. I'm going to my office to check," she

said. "Please stay here. Have coffee. It might take a little while."

Kozak and Carillo went to the counter, got chipped ceramic cups, and filled them with coffee from the carafe. Carillo sat down while Kozak looked at crayon drawings posted on the wall of stick people families living in houses with dogs, cats, under sunshine and rainbows. Some children in the pictures had balloon comments: "Will Santa come back?"

"Why do we not have more food in the fridge like my friend?"

"Why does Daddy hurt Mommy?"

The detectives had finished their coffees and were contemplating a refill when Golinka returned. A man and a woman were with her.

"This is Donnie and this is Annie. They're willing to help you."

After initial greetings and handshakes, Kozak asked them if they'd spoken to Cleveland police about the freeway death.

"No," Annie said. "I wasn't here when they came. I'm in a program."

"What program?" Carillo asked.

Annie hesitated.

"I have a gambling addiction."

Kozak nodded.

"And you, Donnie?"

"No," he said. "I wasn't here when they came."

"Where were you?" Carillo asked.

"I thought," he said, glancing at Golinka, "I thought you didn't care, that talking to you wouldn't come back on me? I'm trying to do some good, here."

"That's right. I'm just curious; it's no problem."

Donnie gave the detectives another assessment.

"I'm under APA supervision."

"Parole?" Kozak said.

"Yeah. I used a credit card that wasn't mine to feed my kids. Times are hard, you know?"

"We understand," Kozak said. "It's okay."

She showed them photos of Jennifer Griffin, asking if they'd seen her.

"Her face was all over the news," Annie said. "I think she was here."

Donnie nodded. "Yeah, there was a woman like that here with us."

Kozak and Carillo shot them an intense look.

"You're certain?" Kozak opened her notebook.

"Well," Annie said, "she looked a little different than those pictures."

"Yeah," Donnie said.

"What do you mean?" Kozak asked.

"She looked older, but the same around her eyes, mouth. But older."

"Yeah," Donnie said, "like she'd been living in the world for a stretch."

"Did you talk with her?" Kozak asked.

"A little. All three of us sat together for meals right here," Annie said. "She was at Halo off and on before that crash on the interstate."

"Did she tell you her name?" Kozak asked.

"No."

"Did she tell you anything about how she got here?"

"Not really," Annie said. "But one time she starting tearing up, telling me that her life got messed up when she was a kid, growing up in Buffalo."

"In Buffalo?" Kozak repeated.

"Yes."

"How was her life messed up?" Carillo said.

"Somebody died. I don't know, she didn't say, and I didn't push it. We mind our own business here."

"And you, Donnie?" Kozak pressed. "Did the woman talk to you?"

"I heard the same stuff Annie just told you."

Kozak thought for a moment, asked more questions before ending things, thanking them and closing her notebook.

"One thing I forgot," Donnie said. "One time, I was outside having a smoke, and I saw her way down on the corner. She was talking to somebody who was sitting in a van, then she started yelling at them, like they were bothering her, then she walked back fast to Halo."

Kozak opened her notebook.

"Did she tell you anything about it?"

"She was upset. Didn't make much sense 'cause she was pissed off."

"Who was in the van?" Kozak asked.

"She never said."

"What about the van? Who was driving? Man? Woman? Did you see a plate, any markings, or damage?"

Donnie shook his head.

"I think it was a white van. There was glare on the windows, so I couldn't see anybody. That's all I remember."

"Do you remember the date, or location?" Carillo asked.

Shaking his head, he said, "Northwest corner of the block, maybe a couple days before the crash."

"You're certain about this?" Kozak asked.

"I am."

"Why didn't you go to police with this, Donnie?" Carillo asked.

"Like Annie says, we mind our own business. Besides, I got my own troubles, but I'm telling you now. So there you go."

Thanking Donnie and Annie, Kozak closed her notebook.

Once they were outside, the investigators walked to the northwest corner of the block. They scanned the area for security cameras but didn't find any.

Kozak's phone rang. It was Lieutenant Phil Becker in Clarence.

"Claire, I just got a call from the NYPD. They've assigned two detectives to collect a statement on the Jennifer Griffin case in Manhattan."

"In Manhattan? Who's giving the statement?"

"Hang on," Becker said, "I'm getting a follow-up email now." A few seconds passed as he read it, then said: "This could be something."

Sixty-Seven

Manhattan, New York

That same morning, before Kozak had alerted Greg that Jennifer had not died in Cleveland, two New York City police detectives stepped from an elevator at Memorial Sloan Kettering Cancer Center in Manhattan.

Nicky Petro and Carl O'Shea from the 19th Precinct badged their way to Dr. Samuel Khalid, who'd been expecting them.

"Yes, this is a good time. He's lucid and has most of his strength," Khalid said, leading them into Eugene Bickersley's room.

After quick introductions, the television was switched off, and at the request of the detectives, they were left alone with Bickersley. They positioned a tablet and a phone to video record, then began.

Petro and O'Shea stated their names, the date, and their shield numbers, along with Bickersley's identification, date of birth, address, the date and location of the recording, and his position at the Tall Elm School in Erie County.

"Mr. Bickersley," Petro began, "you may proceed with your statement concerning the missing person case of Jennifer Marie Griffin, now under active investigation by the New York State Police and the Cuyahoga County Sheriff's Department in Ohio."

"Yes. Not long before Jennifer Griffin was reported missing, there was an incident, a confidential matter, to which I was a party."

Giving approximate dates and times, he continued, his voice rasping.

"As a parent with her son enrolled in the school, Jennifer Griffin participated in a number of committees, working closely with board members.

"She was cochair of the Parent School Support Committee that was working to broaden a lunch program policy to include more students. There were many long meetings that went into the evening. The committee was being challenged, chiefly by a school board member, Porter Sellwin, who objected to the cost."

Bickersley paused to drink some water.

"The day following a late night meeting, Jennifer, very angry, came to my office to speak confidentially about the behavior of Mr. Sellwin, alleging that he had made unwanted sexual advances. Specifically, she claimed that after the previous night's meeting, Sellwin approached her alone by her car in the parking lot, stated that her passion for improving school programs conveyed her underlying attraction to him, and that she didn't need to hide it any longer."

Bickersley paused, then resumed.

"Jennifer said she told him he was mistaken but he laughed, saying that's what 'his women' always tell him. Then he kissed her on the mouth while groping her buttocks. She said she slapped him and drove away. She said she hadn't told another person, that she wanted my advice about filing a formal complaint with the board."

Bickersley drank more water.

"I advised her that she had every right to file a formal complaint to the board, and that she could even go to police. But whatever she did would be a serious step. I said because the alleged incident happened on school property, I would need to speak to Mr. Sellwin. She said she wanted time to think it over and was going to the office we had in the school for parental committees."

Bickersley paused again.

"After she left my office, I considered calling Mr. Sellwin, but he came to my office shortly after she'd left, stating he had seen Jennifer leave my office looking upset. I was taken aback by the sense that he'd been watching her.

"Mr. Sellwin then demanded confidentiality before proceeding to give his account of the incident. He stated it was a misunderstanding, that Jennifer Griffin had invited his advances, then changed her mind. I told him that she may proceed with a complaint or go to police."

Bickersley stopped to collect his thoughts.

"That's when Mr. Sellwin became angry, his face got red as he suggested to me, incorrectly, that he had gotten me my position as principal. He then said that if Jennifer Griffin went ahead with her complaint it would be, 'unpleasant for all of us,' because he was talking to well-connected people about running for the New York State Assembly, that Jennifer Griffin was not going to stand in his way, and that I had 'better damn well bury this problem,' or he would."

Bickersley glanced at the ceiling briefly.

"Later, after he left, I saw him approach Jennifer Griffin in the parking lot. They appeared to have a conversation where he touched her shoulder and she smacked his hand away before driving off."

Bickersley blinked several times, looked at the detectives, and swallowed.

"As far as I know, Jennifer Griffin never filed a complaint," Bickersley said. "I wish to God I had told you this sooner but—my condition—I wasn't thinking. I'm sorry."

Sixty-Eight

Interstate 90 between Batavia and Buffalo, New York

The image of the woman moaning pleasurably played in Porter Sellwin's mind while driving west on I-90 to Buffalo.

Traffic was good.

He stole glances at his burner phone, sitting in the center console of his car. The video recording was there.

I can't wait to watch it.

He relived it…the woman, her top unbuttoned, braless and naked from the waist down. She was straddling Sellwin on the bed. It'd been her idea to meet in a motel outside of Buffalo, at the edge of Batavia, to further discuss Sellwin's political ambitions.

She was a moaner and held her own with her beauty, her body, and performance, *for a gal her age*, Sellwin thought, watching the road and smiling because she was unaware he'd recorded them last night.

Sellwin had told his wife the truth. He'd gone to Batavia for a meeting about his political plans with key players in the party, one of them being Lyyindelle Smith, who headed the nomination committee for his district.

Sellwin used his looks and charm to make a pass at Smith.

She accepted.

On the bed, while watching Smith unzip her skirt, take off her pantyhose and unbutton her shirt, Sellwin called his wife on the hotel phone, so the number would show and left her a voice mail. He'd told her his meeting was a success but had run late, and he'd had a few celebratory drinks so he thought it best to stay over.

A short time later, she'd texted him back.

You work so hard, sweetheart. I'll see you in the morning.

His wife sent an immediate second text starting: OMG! Did you hear on the news about the mistake in the— But he'd been too busy to read further at that moment.

Now, enjoying the memory of Smith's sighs, Sellwin agreed.

I do work hard.

Smith had guaranteed that the party would endorse him as its district candidate for the state assembly. She would arrange for the party's volunteers to collect signatures for the petition and help him establish his campaign account and launch fundraising.

Taken by Sellwin's time in the military, his take-charge personality, Smith had told her committee members that he'd proven he was a strong contender. In his time on the school board, he'd demonstrated fiscal responsibility, like his recent opposition to proposals for costly program expansions. Ever since Lyyindelle Smith had let him know that she and the party were impressed with his record, it had been smooth sailing for him.

Relatively smooth sailing.

There had been some challenges.

This video was insurance.

Smith's husband, Raylen, was on the party's national committee. This video would destroy them. It would hurt Sellwin too, but he was willing to play that card because his ultimate goal was the US Congress and a shot at the White House, and he was determined to get what he wanted.

Sellwin thrived, living on the edge, playing by his rules, letting nothing—*and no one*—get in his way.

Remembering Smith moaning and pumping astride him, he thought: *I wish it was Jennifer Griffin on top of me.*

Jennifer was so beautiful.

She was so many things—*I bet she's the kind of woman who likes her hands bound. Good thing I always keep—*

His thoughts were interrupted by his phone—his business phone—ringing in his chest pocket.

He didn't recognize the number but answered. "Hello?"

"Porter Sellwin?" a woman asked.

He warmed his tone. "Yes?"

"Claire Kozak, State Police."

He caught his breath, tensing.

"Yes, Detective Kozak."

"Mr. Sellwin, could you meet us today at Clarence Barracks?"

"Meet you—may I ask why?"

"We have a few follow-up questions concerning Jennifer Griffin."

Sellwin looked ahead at the highway, thinking.

"But I already talked to you, gosh, it was a while ago."

"Yes, sir, but we've had a few recent developments."

"What's happened?"

"We'll explain when you come in. We just need to follow up and clarify a few things. Can you meet us at the barracks this afternoon at four?"

Staring ahead, thinking for a moment.

"Yes, I'll be there."

After the call, he'd kept one hand on the wheel while tapping his phone to his chin with the other and thinking.

What could this be?

A memory niggled at him from the back of his mind. A text his wife had sent, something about news of a mistake.

A mistake? What was it? I'll find the text.

His mind had been on Lyyindelle Smith and Batavia. He hadn't been paying attention to the news. He started scrolling through his phone, keeping one eye on his driving. He couldn't find it and he didn't want to call his wife. He'd search news sites.

Why talk to me again about Jennifer? What do they know?

A droplet of sweat trickled down the back of his neck.

Take it easy. It's all good. Relax.

Jennifer.

She was all he could think of.

She was a lot of things to him. She'd been a pain in the ass in the battle over the lunch program. But she was so much more. Why did she deny the truth? Over the course of all those intense late night meetings, she'd developed a thing for him. He knew it, yet when he tried to move on her, she got all gun-shy after someone spotted them. Trying to cover her ass, she ran to Bickersley to complain.

To ruin me. No way was I going to let that happen.

He'd put a stop to that.

Then, in a twist of fate, Bickersley's on his death bed and Jennifer Griffin becomes one more thing to Sellwin.

A solved problem.

But God, what a glorious beauty.

How he'd ached to own her, to possess her.

Sellwin slid his phone in his pocket then reached to the central console for his burner—the phone where he hid all his secrets—scrolling to his private photos of Jennifer Griffin. The ones he'd taken of her without her knowledge.

He drank them in.

Why's the car shaking?

In an instant, the right side was vibrating because Sellwin had taken his eyes off the road before going into a curve, drifting.

Now his car was leaning and thudding over the dirt and grass embankment. He twisted the wheel, overcorrecting, making it worse as the car rocked. One side became airborne, the car rolled over. Sellwin gripped the wheel, cursing, the world spinning, airbag deploying, windshield exploding, window, dirt, and grass churning, seat belt cutting into him, debris flinging in all directions, his burner phone flung from the car, catapulted dozens of yards into the rushes and reeds of a large marsh.

The car came to a stop upside down in the muddied water of a culvert.

Pain shot through Sellwin. He was pinned, suspended upside down. He couldn't move. Feeling the top of his head wet from the cold water flooding through the broken windshield, the car slipping on the mud deeper into the water.

"Help!"

Sellwin screamed as his temple, then ears, sank into the cold, then his nostrils, water filling them as he made his last gurgled scream before his entire head was submerged.

Sixty-Nine

Location Unknown

Jennifer Griffin felt a clock ticking down.

Scraping and scratching at the wood, choking back a sob, she prayed to see her family again, to get her life back, even if it wasn't perfect before this happened.

Greg was consumed with the business, said someone was interested in investing, forming a partnership: Brooke Bollman. She owned a food truck company. Jennifer had seen Brooke a few times and thought she was a strong, intense person.

And pretty.

In fact, when Greg had recently grown cold toward Jennifer, it gave rise to her suspicions that he may have been seeing someone—like *Brooke Bollman*.

Another issue for Jennifer was Porter Sellwin. It wasn't that he'd fought her committee on every key issue to help students from families who were struggling; no, the man was a disgusting jerk.

Sellwin considered himself God's gift to women.

He chose Jennifer as his next conquest. She was not interested. His groping and unwanted advances had humiliated and infuriated her. She'd made it clear to Principal Bickersley that she wanted to make a formal complaint and even press charges against Sellwin.

She didn't want to talk to Greg about it. She was so shaken, gathering the courage to act on it. Then things got complicated with Eugene Bickersley's sudden cancer diagnosis.

It was terrible.

While all this was happening, Kat got involved. Having seen what she'd seen that day in the parking lot, Kat got in Jennifer's face.

"Why're you cheating on Greg? He's too good for you."

Jennifer knew Kat had always resented her for coming between her and Greg. It was something Jennifer never understood and couldn't stomach, especially then, with Kat's accusations. So she'd unloaded on her.

"You've always hated me for marrying Greg. You've always been an interfering bitch. You have no idea what was going on in the parking lot and you have no right to accuse me, Kat!"

It was a bitter, epic battle.

Now, Jennifer brushed at her tears, regretting all the mean things she'd said to Kat, wishing she could take them back.

Needing to rest, she sat on her mattress, shaking her head at the turns her life had taken. If her issues with Greg, Sellwin, and Kat weren't enough, there was the strange thing with the cable repair guy, who'd come to the house a few months earlier. After his service call, Jennifer was certain that in the days and weeks that followed, she had seen him in other places, like Walmart or the mall. In the distance, stealing glances, or staring.

Now, goose bumps rose on her arms because she wasn't sure—but she thought she saw him at the Korner Fast store the night it happened.

Her life had been taken up in a whirlwind that seemed to have started when the candle chime arrived on her doorstep.

Who put it there? Why?

It pulled her back to her childhood, memories of her mom and dad, and their small frame house. How her mother worked so hard as a cashier, standing on her feet all day then coming home to rest, have a cigarette, and sip rum and Coke. And how sometimes Jennifer saw her mom sitting alone on the sofa, staring at nothing and crying. And if Jennifer came into the room, her mom would take her into her arms.

How in her arms, Jennifer felt the weight of her mother's sadness as though she were carrying something unbearable. She would search Jennifer's eyes, stroke her hair, on the brink of unburdening herself of some great pain, as if on the edge of a revelation, but all her mother said was: *I love you more than anything in the world, honey...*

Then she remembered how her dad worked long, long hours, driving his cab. Coming home, having a beer, smoking his Lucky Strikes, one always tucked in the corner of his mouth while he showed her card tricks.

Jennifer remembered that year. It was winter. Her mom had retrieved a box from her stored Christmas decorations that Jennifer had never seen before. It held a candle-powered angel chime.

Her mother set it up, struck a match, lighting the candles, dimming the lights in the house, showing her how it worked.

The heat from the candle flames propelled the three angels to spin like a carousel, the tiny metal sticks striking the tiny bells, making a pretty chiming as the angel shadows danced across the room.

Jennifer thought it was magical.

"This chime was my mom's, Jenn. She gave it to me, and now it's yours. But only a grown-up can light the candles for you. Promise me you'll never play with it by yourself."

"I promise, Mom."

Jennifer loved her chime, watching it for hours while the winter winds swept over Lake Erie, bringing heavy snowfalls. With her mom and dad working so hard, it came as a blessing when one day a teenage boy knocked on the door and offered to shovel their small driveway and sidewalk for twenty bucks.

He did a good job. Her mom liked him, and he came around every time it snowed. Whenever he finished, her mom invited him to get warm and have hot chocolate while Jennifer showed him how her chime worked.

They would sit together, not speaking, her mom

smoking and having a couple glasses of rum and Coke, the boy and Jennifer drinking hot chocolate while all of them watched angels spinning. The boy was quiet, shy, almost self-conscious, always insisting, despite her mom's protests, on leaving his wool cap on his head, pulled down over his forehead, and his scarf loose around his chin. Still, the candle flames would glow in his eyes as he watched them flickering in Jennifer's and her mother's eyes too.

Jennifer loved that time in her life, right up until the horrible night she woke in her bed, hearing her mother and father screaming, inhaling the suffocating smoke, feeling the heat, the horror of her home on fire. The sirens, the noise, no way out, Jennifer could find no way out…

But I did get out. I did survive.

A firefighter smashed her window and saved her life.

Now, wiping at tears, she looked around her prison.

I have to get out of here. But no firefighter's going to save me this time.

Seventy

"I don't believe it."

Kozak looked at Carillo then at Lieutenant Phil Becker after he'd told them about Porter Sellwin's crash on I-90, east of Buffalo.

"They've airlifted him to Erie County," Becker said. "He's got life-threatening injuries."

Digesting the information, Kozak leaned forward in the chair at her desk. She and Carillo had returned to the barracks from Cleveland less than twenty minutes ago. While driving home, they'd read the emailed statement that Eugene Bickersley had given to the NYPD, which prompted her to call Sellwin.

"I spoke to him, what, an hour ago?" Kozak told Becker. "He agreed to come in."

"Maybe his crash has something to do with the call?" Carillo said.

Becker kept checking his phone while standing before them as the three investigators broke down recent events. The school principal's statement had been so troubling that they had moved immediately on warrants.

Even before Kozak and Carillo got back, Becker had reached out to a judge and sent her emails. Becker presented a case of exigent—life-and-death—circumstances in the suspected abduction of Jennifer Griffin based on the statements and actions of Porter Sellwin. Becker also indicated to the judge that additional warrants would likely be needed.

The judge agreed that probable cause existed to issue the initial warrants, which concerned all of Sellwin's credit and banking card transactions around the time of Jennifer's disappearance.

The response by the security branches was swift with Becker now flagging a transaction.

"Look, this one just came in," Becker said. "About an hour before Jennifer left her book club meeting, Sellwin purchased gas, duct tape, and a flashlight at a Sunoco, close to Ripplewood Creek."

"This raises questions," Kozak said.

"If he knew her routine, he could've been lying in wait for her." Carillo typed on his keyboard, finding Sellwin's driver's license. "He lives in Ripplewood Creek. He's six feet even. His height fits for the person who moved Jennifer's Corolla."

"Sellwin's crash could've been a suicide attempt," Becker said.

"Or he could've been distracted, looking at his phone, maybe desperate to remove anything incriminating before meeting us?" Kozak said.

"I've already requested our guys at Sellwin's

crash site and Genesee County treat it as a crime scene, not a traffic accident. FIU is rolling on it," Becker said.

"Good. Want a quick debrief on a lead we got in Cleveland?" Kozak said.

"Put it aside for now," Becker said. "Get over to Erie County for a dying declaration from Sellwin while there's time."

"On our way," Kozak said.

Walking through the barracks, Kozak and Carillo were approached in the hall by Melinda Hyland, the lead data analyst assigned to the Jennifer Griffin case.

"There you are. Do you have a sec for me to update you?"

"Walk with us to our car, Mel," Carillo said.

"Okay." Hyland, who was in her twenties, and had a tiny, silver loop nose ring, nudged her black, square-framed glasses.

"What do you have?" Kozak asked.

"Nothing so far proving that Sofia Ann Korvin gave birth to any other children besides Jennifer."

"We gave you her Social Security number, right?" Carillo said.

"Yes, and we have records for Sofia giving birth to Jennifer, but here's the thing. I've been working with vital records in Albany and county records. In some cases, over the years at some hospitals across the state, fires, moves, and water damage hampered complete collections of records. It's slow going. We'll also take our search outside the state."

"Start with Ohio and Pennsylvania," Kozak said.

"Keep working on it, Mel," Carillo said.

They passed through the doors and were outside.

"What about your analysis of tips, statements, reports?" Kozak asked.

"Working on them as they come in and also going back, double-checking, cross-referencing," Hyland said.

"Thanks, Mel." Carillo opened the driver's door of their Taurus.

"Keep us posted," Kozak said.

"This case is like one of those Russian nesting dolls, Claire," Carillo said as he drove.

"How so?"

"Greg Griffin, his girlfriend, Jennifer seeing a shrink for some past trauma, DNA, phantom relatives, now Sellwin. So it's like we open up one doll, there's a smaller one inside, open that one, and there's another, open that one, then we find something else."

"That's the way it goes, Ned. Cases get complicated."

Carillo rubbed the back of his neck as he drove. Starting in Cleveland that morning, it'd been a long day and it was far from over.

"I could use a coffee," Carillo said.

"Me too." Kozak was texting her sons when her phone rang.

"It's Becker," she said to Carillo before answering.

"Forget the hospital," Becker said. "Sellwin never recovered. He's deceased."

Kozak took a second.

"All right. That's that." Then to Carillo: "Sellwin's dead."

Carillo shook his head. "We keep opening nesting dolls."

"Soon as we can," Becker said, "we'll get warrants and move on his house, office, everything for anything linked to her. Head to the crash site and see what the crime scene people find in his car."

"Will do." Then to Carillo: "Get on ninety, and head east."

Traffic inched its way around the cluster of emergency vehicles, their lights flashing, on the shoulder of the westbound lane of I-90 between Batavia and Buffalo.

People rubbernecked at the overturned vehicle, half submerged in the culvert. As forensic people worked on the wreck, K-9 teams and a drone swept the immediate area.

Kozak and Carillo observed from the embankment, pleased when the forensic team recovered a flashlight and a roll of duct tape. Then Becker texted Kozak, alerting them that Sellwin's cell phone had been recovered from the emergency medical staff and was seized as evidence.

But a couple dozen yards from Sellwin's car, under three feet of murky water thick with rushes and reeds, was Sellwin's burner phone.

The one no one knew existed.

Its charge weakening, the phone was dying, taking all of Sellwin's secrets with it.

Seventy-One

Buffalo, New York, Trailside Grove

"Deepest Condolences."

"Thinking Of You At This Time", "Our Thoughts And Prayers Are Of You."

Dozens of old sympathy cards were on the kitchen table where Greg and Kat continued trying to determine if Jenn had relatives.

The cards were still in envelopes, addressed to Jenn's grandmother. Using the senders' names and return addresses, they'd worked to locate people who knew Jenn's parents. They went online, consulted street maps, directories. Kat got a colleague to check her courier company's databases. They did all they could to pinpoint names, then make calls.

Greg and Kat's work had yielded a few leads, but they dead-ended. It had been thirty years. People had died or moved. Those they'd reached couldn't remember many details about the lives of Sofia and Leo Korvin, except for the tragic way they'd died.

"We need to go to her old neighborhood, ask around there," Kat said.

Greg agreed.

They went to Vince.

"Kat and I need to go check something in Jenn's old neighborhood," Greg said. "Stay here with Jake and don't talk to anybody, okay?"

Vince nodded but Kat and Greg caught something swirling behind his eyes, sorrow and fear, as if his concentration had taken him elsewhere, like the time their mom died.

"Are you okay, Dad?" Kat said.

Vince touched his jaw. "Got a sore tooth."

"Sore tooth?" Greg and Kat traded a quick look. Then Greg said: "Want to go home, Dad? I can get someone else to come over."

Vince's focus shifted. He'd returned, looked at them, and shook his head.

"No. I'm good. Jake and I will be fine," he said.

Media people were still waiting outside, shouting questions as Greg and Kat got into her Jeep. She reversed slowly, easing through the pack as Greg waved them off before Kat shifted into Drive and sped away. Then he watched his side mirror.

"Some of them are following us."

"I'll lose them."

They got onto Sentinel Trail, with its four lanes running through the suburb's commercial stretch. Kat threaded through the traffic. Some news vehicles had quit the chase. Then Kat turned into a Burger King drive-through but veered from the lane, using the parking lot's rear exit to get onto another side street.

"As a courier driver, you have to know short-cuts," she said.

Greg checked his mirror. Kat's maneuver had worked. Except for a white van, which seemed to trail them for several more blocks before abandoning its pursuit.

The neighborhood was east of downtown in an old working class district north of the interstate, bordering the Hydraulics and Larkin area.

This was where Jenn had grown up until her parents' deaths in the fire.

A small apartment building now occupied the lot where Jenn's house had been. The building had also swallowed a few lots next to it. The apartment had been there a long time, and it had been years since Greg had even driven by here. Neat frame houses built with the optimism that followed the Second World War still lined the street where Jenn spent the first eight years of her life. Greg imagined her skipping rope, or learning to ride a bike along the tree-shaded sidewalk.

Kat parked.

They got out, intent on going to the few names and addresses taken from the cards that they hadn't crossed off, and since they were here, every home on the block. House after house, door after door, the responses they'd received varied but soon began to blur with head shakes and dismissals.

"No, don't know anybody named Korvin."

"Who? What? Naw, never heard of them."

"Is that about the woman on the news? No, sorry, we just moved here last year."

"Not us. Try the Galassos, the house with the hedge. They've lived here forever..."

But the older man trimming the hedge at the Galasso house shook his head.

"You might try the Krynskis," he said. "Second place from the corner."

As they headed toward it, Kat reached into her bag.

"I think we have a sympathy card from the Krynskis. Yes, Marek and Celina."

They rang the doorbell, heard movement inside before a man in his twenties opened the door, a question rising on his face as he assessed Kat and Greg.

"Sorry to bother you," Kat said. "We're looking for anyone who may remember a family who lived nearby a long time ago. Leo and Sofia Korvin. They had a daughter, Jennifer?"

The man started shaking his head.

"The parents died in a house fire about thirty years ago," Kat said.

The man shrugged.

"A sympathy card was sent from this address." Kat showed it to him.

Studying the card, he began nodding as they heard barking from inside.

"Wow, yeah, those are my parents and this is, or was, their house." He handed it back. "But they died a few years ago, and I'm living here now with my family."

"So you didn't grow up here?" Greg said.

"I don't know anything. Sorry, I can't help you."

"Well, could you tell us if—"

The barking grew louder. The man glanced at his phone in his hand.

"I'm sorry, I have to go," the man said, closing the door.

Cutting short what had appeared to be a hopeful lead drove home for Greg the futility of their effort as they turned from the house and started for the sidewalk.

What are we doing? Jenn had no relatives. The DNA analysis has got to be a mistake. And if it is... then Jenn is really dead.

He glanced at Kat.

Did she really tell me the truth about knowing where Jenn had kept her mother's things?

A glint, a reflection caught Greg's eye, and his focus went beyond Kat, down the street, way down by more than a block.

Was that a white van and a camera lens?

"Excuse me?"

Greg and Kat stopped and turned.

The young man had returned to his front door and called to them.

"I think I know someone who might be able to help you."

Seventy-Two

Clarence, New York

Melinda Hyland's keyboard clicked in staccato bursts, halting only when she paused to nudge her glasses over the bridge of her nose.

She'd been making requests and studying databases for records confirming Jennifer Griffin's biological mother gave birth to another child.

Come on, show me something.

Okay, so the FBI's experts at Quantico stated that the DNA of the Cleveland victim did not come from Jennifer Griffin, but belonged to a relative from the same biological mother, Sofia Ann Korvin.

Hyland had found records confirming Sofia Ann Korvin gave birth to Jennifer Marie Korvin in a Buffalo hospital. Leo Korvin was listed as Jennifer's biological father.

But so far, Hyland's search of available records throughout all of New York had found no documents for Sofia having another child. It was entirely possible that the birth was not registered, or had taken place in another state, another country. It could've been a home birth. Sofia could've abandoned, or given up the child, had an affair. Any number of scenarios came to mind.

It's also possible Sofia Korvin changed her name.

Hyland knew that in most states, like New York, legal name changes were public record. However, if a person felt their safety, or their children's safety, was at risk, the court would seal the name change so that it would never be public. This happened in cases of domestic abuse. But police could access the change if needed.

Hyland put in a call to her contact in Albany for help with sealed name changes. Hyland left a message.

She then returned to another aspect of the investigation, her continual examination of statements, tips, and reports that had come in on the case, cross-referencing them, double-checking them with local, regional, and statewide databases for any potential links to other cases.

Hyland mined the latest information, using keyword searches, or dates—whatever was required. She also had a checklist of facets of the case she continually checked for updates.

Kinda like panning for gold.

Consulting her list, she went to service calls made to Greg and Jennifer Griffin's home in the months prior to her going missing. Again, there were only two. Starting with SparkleThru window washing service, Hyland submitted the company name and names of the workers in all the databases.

Nothing new came up.

She submitted the name of the cable repair company, Distinctly Connex. Waiting for the results, she reached for her coffee when her computer pinged with a hit.

She froze.

What's this?

Her screen filled with the summary of a recent complaint that was actually withdrawn because the caller had changed her mind. *This is interesting.* It came from a woman in Cardinal Hill concerning the cable repairman, his offensive behavior with her underwear in her home and his suggestive comments.

It made Hyland's skin crawl.

When she checked the database for Jennifer Griffin, it showed the same company, Distinctly Connex, had sent the same man to restore their service *and that Jennifer was alone in the house with him at the time.*

Hyland swallowed.

The repairman's name was Zoran Volk.

Hyland sat up, her keyboard clicking as she typed.

We've got a new lead here.

Seventy-Three

Elk Creek, Pennsylvania

Gravel ricocheted under Lorena Jo Tullev's Ford Escape as she drove deeper into the woods of northwestern Pennsylvania.

Lorena couldn't remember the last time she and Zoran had been here together. She took in the tranquility of the forest with its gentle slopes and streams. The region was paradise for people who liked to fish.

Or wanted privacy.

Coming to the eagle-like rock formation that marked the turn for Zoran's cabin, Lorena slowed down but kept driving. Passing by the acreage, staring through the interlacing of trees, branches, and leaves, she saw a corner of the cabin, a flash of chrome, a reflection of glass, and she identified Zoran's white van.

He's there.

She didn't see a second vehicle.

If Zoran was cheating, maybe he would meet the other woman here, or maybe he'd picked her up? He had enough time. Lorena had waited nearly two hours before she left Buffalo, heading west on I-90 after he said he was going to his cabin to fish for a couple days.

Now, having spotted Zoran's van, she drove around a bend, then a little farther until she'd come to the mouth of an unmarked entrance to a neighboring property. Its grassy pathway was nearly invisible in a thicket. She parked her Ford there, on the side, grabbed her bag, and got out, satisfied her SUV was concealed by the shrubs and branches.

She walked back down the road then left it, entering the forest. Staying off the pathway, she stepped carefully through the woods making her way to the rear of Zoran's cabin. Constructed of logs, it sat some forty yards from a wide, twisting expanse of Elk Creek.

She went to the cabin's back wall, stood next to it, listening for voices. A long minute passed. The leaves in the treetops moved in a little breeze, birds chirped. There was the soft peaceful flow of the creek.

But no voices.

What am I doing? This is silly. I should go home. No. I have to do this. Something's going on with Zoran. Something's not right.

Suddenly Lorena heard movement inside, someone walking. She slipped into the bushes, positioning herself to see the front door that faced the creek.

Zoran had stepped outside.

Carrying a rod, a tackle box, and a plastic

bucket, he locked the door then took a trail that cut into the woods.

When he was out of sight, Lorena went to the door, got her key from her bag. She'd secretly made a duplicate months ago when she first suspected Zoran was cheating at the cabin.

She slid her key into the slot, hoping he hadn't changed the lock.

She turned it.

Nothing happened.

She tried again, shoving it in all the way, jiggling, and turning.

It clicked.

Stepping inside, the air smelled of lumber with a hint of fried bacon.

Lorena could feel memories stirring as she inventoried the place. It had one private bedroom and one small bathroom with a shower. The rest of the interior was a large open area. In one corner, the kitchen, in another, sofa chairs faced the stone fireplace.

On the table was Zoran's big backpack, a couple of empty beer cans, and an open bag of Doritos. The chairs were draped with his jeans, his hoodie, a T-shirt, and socks.

Lorena went to the bedroom door.

When she opened it, she stopped in her tracks.

A tripod with a video camera stood at the foot of the bed.

Chains with handcuffs reached from the headboard and footboard.

He's making his own porn here. Or he's cheating with someone who's into bondage. Or both.

Anger surged through her.

Who's he doing this with? Who?

Lorena thought.

His laptop! Yes, I came here to find it.

A quick search of the bedroom—the dresser drawers, the closet, under the bed, under the mattress—resulted in no laptop.

Lorena returned to the living area, scanning it for answers, looking at the table. She went to Zoran's backpack. If it wasn't in there, if he'd locked it in his van, she'd be out of luck.

Rifling through his backpack, she found mostly packaged food, then something hard and flat.

Bingo! Laptop.

She placed it on the table and fired it up.

As it came to life, she reached into her bag for her wallet and the slip of paper with Zoran's password.

Everything worked.

She was in.

He had a galaxy of folders. The first she went to were listed as "JOBS," and she opened a few randomly. They looked like work orders for repairs and connections.

Another was labeled "SPORTS" and seemed to contain team stats, probably for his gambling on games.

Next she found an array labeled "FUN" that appeared to be porn, purchased or at least downloaded. He was not in the few videos she'd zipped through, and she didn't recognize any of the women.

Lorena shot a glance to the window, listening for Zoran's return. Biting her lip, she continued opening folders, finding records on his taxes, banking. She kept hunting, then found a folder hidden within a folder, within a folder, following it until she found one labeled: "PROJECTS."

Projects?

The next one she came to had a folder labeled "LP Cardinal Hill."

It contained a mundane-looking work order with a date, address, and name.

Then she found a series of short videos.

One was taken inside a house, showing a woman's folded laundry on a large bed, specifically underwear. Then she found footage of a woman, a rather pretty woman, in the house, that seemed to have been recorded without her knowing. Then there was video taken from a dash-mounted camera of a car being followed in traffic. Then the camera angle changes to show the woman driving the car was the same one who'd been in the house.

What is Zoran doing?

Lorena went to another folder, one labeled "J.G. Trailside Grove."

Opening it, she saw a collection of news stories and headlines:

Missing Woman Investigation Continues

Mystery Surrounds Mom's Disappearance

One Month Later Woman's Case Baffles Police

Then she played a video of TV news reports showing Jennifer Griffin, the mom missing from Trailside. There were more files of news reports, photos, videos, showing her car in the woods, the search, and her anguished family...

What is this?

Lorena's fingers shook as she went to more videos and played them.

Her hand flew to her mouth at what she saw.

Seventy-Four

Jennifer knew there was little hope of escaping.

But a grain of hope was all she had, so she kept digging at the door's hinges while her tattered mind went back to the chime.

Who gave it to me and why?

The angel chime had signified her happiness and her horror.

Its arrival was an omen, a triggering incident, just as Dr. Maynart had said. But he didn't know the whole truth. No one did. It was a secret Jennifer had carried ever since the night of the fire...

How I loved the chime Mom gave me, loved its soothing, soft ringing... I was enraptured by the flash and glaze of the golden angels, their carousel of shadows, mesmerizing, as if casting a magical spell. I could watch them for hours, forever...

...and that night, that night I couldn't sleep. All I could think of was my chime. I yearned to watch it. From the muffled snoring in Mom and Dad's room, I knew they were asleep... I tiptoed down

the stairs to the chime in the living room, set it on the coffee table, got the candles and matches from the kitchen. I'd seen Mom light the candles so many times...

I put the candles in their holders and took the matchbox with a voice in my head, a warning... I was breaking the rules. I was never to play with the chime alone. It was wrong but I couldn't stop. I felt a rush of rebellious adrenaline as I struck the match. Its flame flared with a hiss. Feeling its heat, I lit the candle wicks just like Mom, fanning out the match and blowing on it, putting it on the metal base... I was thrilled I did it all by myself... Soon, the carousel began turning, creating the glorious chiming with shadows dancing around the room, and on our Christmas tree, a real one, in the corner. I watched with delight, until I fell asleep on the sofa, waking to find the candles nearly burned down...

I blew them out, put the chime away, placed the cold, burnt matchstick and burned-down candles in the trash, hiding them under potato peelings, tiptoeing back to bed, falling asleep...

The screams woke me. The loud cracking and snapping of wood, of walls collapsing, the smoke, the stinking, thick choking smoke, the flames and searing heat, my home on fire... I'm going to die. Then, a face at the window, a firefighter, saving me. Only me. Not my mom, not my dad... My world, my life, burned to the ground, destroyed... Shock. Horror. Waking in a hospital bed, feeling Grandma's arms... "You'll live with me now..." A lit ciga-

rette left burning between the sofa cushions in the living room caused the fire. That's what they told Grandma, that's what she told me. No. No, that's wrong. Not true. I didn't tell her. I didn't tell anyone. I couldn't tell them the truth. I kept it to myself because I broke the rule...it was the chime. I started the fire...

I killed my mom and dad...

And then the chime shows up mysteriously at my door.

Who put it there?

Why?

It comes like payback, like a toll to be exacted for what she did, ripping open her wounds, triggering her overwhelming guilt.

I was only eight. It was an accident. I'm so sorry.

Jennifer froze, hearing a faint, distant sound on the other side.

Scattering the shavings on the floor, she sat on her mattress. She tucked her tool under it, keeping it within reach, bracing herself.

If the door opened, she would use it to stab her captor.

The door of the viewing port slid open.

Jennifer stared at the eyes watching her.

Then there was movement at the small doors, buckets were transferred, food was left—and a folded page.

She set the food beside her mattress, opened the page to find a new note:

ONE MORE PIECE TO PUT IN PLACE BEFORE I SHOW YOU EVERYTHING.

Jennifer's stomach lurched.

What more could be coming? Oh God. I'm going to be killed!

She took up her tool.

Sobbing, she returned to the hinges and clawed for her life.

Seventy-Five

Greg and Kat returned to the young man's front door.

"I'm sorry," he said. "You came at a busy time. I was waiting for word on a job I'm up for."

"That's okay," Kat said. "Hope you get it."

"I did." His face was warmer. They could hear the dog start up again. "I'd invite you in but my dog's sick. Wait, I'll put him in another room."

They could hear yelping and his one-way conversation with his dog. "Did you take a nap, Barney? You need to take a nap, buddy." A moment later, he returned.

"The fire you're talking about happened before I was born," he said. "But my older sister lived here then."

"So she would know about it," Greg said.

"She and my mom knew the family. They'd talk about it sometimes around Christmas."

"Can we talk to your sister?" Kat said.

"She lives in Toronto."

"How can we reach her?"

"Give me your information and I'll pass it to her."

Seeing that the man was still gripping his phone, Kat said: "Be easier if you give me your phone. I'll put it in for you."

The man hesitated. "Wait. Are you cops?"

"No," Greg said.

"Who are you? And why're you asking about an old fire in this neighborhood and stuff?"

"I'm Greg Griffin. This is my sister, Kat. My wife, Jennifer, is missing. She grew up in this neighborhood and we're trying to learn more about her family, like, if she had any sisters or brothers."

"Your wife's missing?" The man looked at Greg until recognition dawned. "Wait. Is your wife the woman from Trailside? The one in the news?"

"Yes," Greg said.

Realizing the significance, the man blinked, thinking. Kat waited a moment then indicated the man's phone.

"So you're going to help us get in touch with your sister?" she said.

"Sure, sure."

He swiped his phone, cued up an email to himself, then passed it to Kat and she typed in all of her and Greg's information.

"Thanks." She returned his phone.

"No problem," he said. "I'll reach out to my sister and tell her to get back to you. It might take a while. We haven't spoken for a bit, but I'm sure she'll want to help you."

Seventy-Six

Westfield, New York

"My boyfriend killed the missing Buffalo woman!"

"What woman?"

"Jennifer Griffin! He's got these videos. I saw them." The female caller's panicked voice trembled.

"Okay, slow down." The Chautauqua County emergency dispatcher was calm, professional. "Tell me where you are."

"I'm at a McDonald's in Westfield, in my car, in the parking lot. God, I just saw these videos on his laptop in his cabin and I just drove away!"

"I need to confirm you're at the McDonald's in Westfield, New York?"

"Yes, I think it's the one on Main."

"Your name and date of birth?"

"Lorena Jo Tullev," she said, before giving her birth date.

"And your car's model, color, plate number?"

"Ford Escape. Blue." Lorena then recited her license plate.

"Okay," the dispatcher said. "A unit is on the way to you. Should be three minutes. When it gets there, go to the deputy and identify yourself."

"Thank you."

Lorena's heart raced while studying the activity in the parking lot and the drive-through. Waiting there, she tried to make sense of what she'd discovered in Zoran's cabin only an hour ago.

Those videos and pictures on his laptop, the camera, tripod, chains and handcuffs, and what it all meant. Barely able to think, she'd shut down his laptop, replaced it in his backpack, taking nothing, leaving everything as it was, and left. Hurrying through the woods to the road, she ran to her SUV.

Driving from Elk Creek, she got on I-90 driving east, her nerves throbbing, her thoughts spinning. Finally, thankfully, she'd gained enough distance and clarity to pull over in Westfield and call police.

Now Lorena scrutinized each vehicle entering the McDonald's lot; cars, pickups, SUVs.

She caught her breath.

A white van rolled slowly by the parked cars.

It's Zoran.

Slouching in her seat, Lorena kept her eyes above her dash, examining the vehicle as it eased by the front of hers. The driver was a woman. The van was not Zoran's.

Exhaling, Lorena sat up.

A moment later, an SUV with Chautauqua County Sheriff's markings wheeled into the parking lot, stopping in front of her Escape.

The deputy dropped the front passenger window and Lorena went to it.

"You called our emergency dispatch?"

"Yes."

"Can you show me your driver's license?"

Lorena took it from her wallet, passed it to the deputy. She glanced at it, gave it back.

"All right. Get in the front with me and I'll take your statement."

Lorena locked her car, went with the deputy who then parked in a far, isolated spot, under the shade of a tree. Lorena began relating her story while the deputy typed notes on her laptop, pausing to ask the occasional question then letting her continue.

"I took as many photos as I could of what was on his computer." Lorena swiped through them on her phone before sending them to the deputy. Tears filled Lorena's eyes as she finished. The deputy passed her tissues.

"He'd just been acting so strange lately," Lorena said. "I'm so scared."

"You're safe now. Things will move very fast once this gets blasted through the system."

Lorena looked at the deputy, who was now scrolling through the photos that Lorena had sent her on her laptop. They were pictures of Jennifer Griffin, at the mall, another of her shopping for groceries, a series of others taken in her home.

Zoran had given each of them a number with the same label:

She's Next

Seventy-Seven

Pennsylvania and New York

A state police helicopter circled over Zoran Volk's cabin in the northeastern woods of Pennsylvania.

On the ground, Erie County deputies sealed access roads to the property while a heavily armed state police SWAT team descended on the building, taking points around it before calling out Volk.

His van was not there but they took no chances.

Receiving no response, they entered the cabin.

Finding no trace of Volk or anyone else, they cleared it in seconds.

Lorena Jo Tullev's discovery and her report to police—backed up by the photos she'd taken—had set in motion a law enforcement operation that moved on several fronts across three states.

The FBI, working with state and local police, led the response at the cabin. Once it was secured, an FBI Evidence Response Team, dispatched from Cleveland, began processing it.

County and state police K-9 units searched the woods for Jennifer Griffin while deputies, troopers, and agents walked through the forest, shoulder to shoulder, in grid patterns, looking for anything that would lead them to her. Police divers entered the water at various points in Elk Creek while police boats used sonar to search for body mass.

The helicopter continued thundering overhead.

The investigation also encompassed a dragnet that reached into Ohio and New York where a break in the manhunt soon emerged.

Checking plate readers at the Lackawanna and Williamsville toll booths of the New York Thruway, police found that Volk had returned to Buffalo.

Buffalo PD and New York State Police along with county deputies used unmarked units to set up an outer perimeter reaching for several blocks. Focusing on a white van bearing Volk's plate, they monitored traffic in Volk's neighborhood.

At this stage, no news releases had been issued by any agency at any point in any of the involved states. They all agreed on the strategy to move fast enough to locate and arrest Volk before he became aware he was wanted. Still, they expected it was only a matter of time before their efforts got out to the media.

With something this big, a leak was inevitable.

Volk's house was at the edge of North Buffalo, on a calm street of small frame houses with well-kept lawns. Volk's house filled the crosshairs in the scope of a Buffalo SWAT sharpshooter, who was flat on his stomach behind the shrubs of the house across the street.

Neighboring residents in the line of fire had been quietly evacuated by plainclothes police and sheltered in a church at the end of the street.

After nearly an hour, a white van rolled into Volk's driveway, the brakes creaking when it stopped.

Volk shut it off and got out, shouldering his backpack and gripping a six-pack, shutting the door, pausing to listen as the engine ticked down.

The air in the neighborhood seemed still.

Too still, he thought.

The Buffalo SWAT commander, watching unseen from the house next door, whispered into his headset: "Go!"

Dark-clad SWAT team members sprung from hedges, house corners, garage corners, guns drawn, instantly putting Volk facedown on the street and handcuffing him.

"What the f—"

"Zoran Volk, you're under arrest. You have the right to remain silent..."

Seventy-Eight

Clarence, New York

Within forty-five minutes of Zoran Volk's arrest, Buffalo PD transferred him to the state police who'd put him in custody.

He sat alone in a secure holding room at Clarence Barracks.

Not far from Volk, in another part of the building, Lorena Jo Tullev waited with a female trooper in an empty meeting room.

Down the hall, Kozak and Carillo, who now had the lead on questioning Volk, worked at their desks.

While forensic teams searched the Pennsylvania woods and processed Volk's cabin, Volk's van, and the house in Buffalo, Kozak and Carillo had dug into his background, running his name, again.

Again, they found no arrests, convictions, or warrants.

But earlier that day, before everything broke out of Pennsylvania, they were reviewing the report Melinda Hyland, the analyst, had found concerning a Cardinal Hill woman's complaint about her cable repair man. Hyland showed them that the same man had made a service call to Jennifer Griffin's home.

His name was Zoran Volk.

Now, taken with Lorena Jo Tullev's alert to police, and events that were still unfolding that same day, it was becoming clear that Zoran Volk was responsible for Jennifer Griffin's disappearance, Kozak thought as she and Carillo joined Tullev in the meeting room.

They dismissed the trooper.

Taking their seats across from Tullev, Kozak noted the woman's fingers were pulled into fists, whitening her knuckles, and her eyes were blank as if refusing to believe what she had seen.

"Would you like coffee, water, anything?" Kozak asked.

Tullev closed her eyes and shook her head.

They began with a number of questions as Tullev, squeezing a tissue in her hand, related her history with Volk, their relationship, then her concerns, her fears, her suspicions, and finally, her discovery at the cabin.

Kozak typed on her tablet, calling up the security video recorded in the Korner Fast store the night of Jennifer Griffin's disappearance.

"We'd like you to watch this with an eye to the figure in the hoodie," she said.

Tullev drew her face close to Kozak's tablet as she ran the video several times.

"Does Zoran have a dark hoodie like that one?" Kozak asked.

"Yes."

"Does he have a ballcap?"

"Yes."

"Does he like energy drinks?"

"Yes."

"Judging by the build of the figure in the video, the posture and walk, could that be Zoran?"

"Yes," she said, her voice breaking.

Then Carillo produced Zoran's laptop, one of the first items seized from his backpack upon his arrest. In keeping with the chain of custody for evidence, the lab technician had affixed a bar code to the device. After switching it on, Carillo requested Tullev log in and show them the folders.

Nodding, she guided them to the folder marked "PROJECTS" and the photos and videos inside.

The evidence against Volk was overwhelming.

When it was over, Tullev sat there, crushing the tissue in her hands.

"I wanted to marry him." Her voice was shaky. "I wanted to have a family with him." She stared off, to a dream that had twisted into a nightmare. "He killed that woman!"

Kozak reached out and touched her hand.

"We don't know that yet," Kozak said. "What we know, is that what you did is one of the bravest things a person can do. Remember that, Lorena."

Seventy-Nine

Clarence, New York

By early evening, Zoran Volk was handcuffed, escorted to a harshly lit small white-walled interview room, and put in a chair.

A chain was affixed from the steel loop in the table to his handcuffs. He rested his arms on the table.

Kozak worked on an apple, Carillo was finishing off an egg salad sandwich as they studied Volk through the one-way mirrored glass of the wall separating the two rooms.

On their side, the lighting was soft, calming.

Kozak was glad that nothing had been leaked to the press, so far.

However, reporters from Buffalo, Cleveland, and Pennsylvania had been calling law enforcement agencies much of the day with rumors of a break in the case of the missing Buffalo woman.

No agency had commented or confirmed anything, only that a statement might be forthcoming. Kozak didn't expect that would keep the press from getting the story for much longer. But it would do for now, she thought, because the investigation was close, so close, to the truth behind Jennifer's disappearance.

She and Carillo got sandwiches and fruit, which passed for supper, while working flat out. After their interview with Lorena Jo Tullev, there were quick calls on the status of the ongoing work in Elk Creek, and preliminary forensic results arising from Volk's devices, the van, and his house. There were more reviews of case reports and statements, then a round of discussions with Wendy Reade in the district attorney's office.

"It's all there. You've got enough to talk to him," Reade said. "Has he been Mirandized?"

"Yes," Kozak said. "Hasn't asked for a lawyer yet."

"Do it again," Reade said. "Do this by the numbers, Claire. We don't want anything to come back on us."

Now, tossing the apple core with the napkin she'd used into the trash, as Carillo took a last gulp of water from a bottle, they gathered their tablets, phones, files, and left.

Zoran's eyes strolled over Kozak when she and Carillo entered the room, taking the chairs across from him, putting their things on the table.

"Mr. Volk, I'm Investigator Claire Kozak. This is my partner, Ned Carillo. Before we proceed we want you to know that the camera lens in the upper corner, with the red light, means our conversation is being recorded."

Volk glanced at it then back at Kozak.

"You were given your Miranda rights earlier, but we'll give them to you again," Kozak said. "You have the right to remain silent. Anything you say can and will be used against you in a court of law. You have the right to an attorney. If you cannot afford an attorney, one will be provided for you. Do you understand these rights?"

"Yes."

Kozak took a page from a folder. "This document states you've been advised of and understand your rights. We need you to sign at the bottom."

She set down a pen. Volk looked at the document then picked it up, his chain clinking as he signed and she noticed his muscular, tattooed arms.

"We'd like to talk about Jennifer Griffin." Kozak took the signed document and pen. "Understanding your rights, do you wish to talk to us?"

Volk remained silent.

Carillo leaned forward.

"Let's get to it, Zoran. You won't be free for years, if ever."

Volk looked at Carillo with a sharp glint in his eyes.

"As we speak," Carillo said, "we have people combing through your cabin, your house, your van, your laptop, your life. We know Jennifer Griffin was one of your projects."

Volk's jaw muscles bunched.

"We've got videos you took of her when you were in her house, when you followed her in the mall. We've got video of you in the store that night.

We know about your cabin, the camera, and chains on the bed."

Volk said nothing.

"You selected her, stalked, and hunted her," Kozak said.

"Where is Jennifer Griffin?" Carillo said.

Volk stared at Carillo, then at Kozak.

"Mr. Volk," Kozak said. "You have the right to remain silent and to end this interview at any time and request a lawyer. If you do, we're required to inform the district attorney that you're not cooperating. The consequences of that decision can be profound."

"Zoran." Carillo drew his face closer. "You're facing life in prison. But if you help us, if you cooperate, you may get a shot at parole."

Volk said nothing.

"Do you want to die in prison, an old man?" Carillo said.

Volk swallowed.

"Where is she, Zoran? What did you do to Jennifer Griffin?" Kozak asked.

His handcuffs jingled as he clasped his hands together.

"Get me a lawyer and I'll help you find her."

Eighty

Zoran Volk's tattoos writhed along the muscles of his glistening skin as he did push-ups in the holding cell while waiting for his lawyer.

Grunting in time with his piston-like pumping, Volk thought of Project Griffin and his hunger for women.

Real women in the wild.

Over the years, he'd refined his methodology. Each time he entered a home on a call, he scoped it for opportunities, absorbing photos, personal information left out, like bills, bank statements. He'd eavesdrop on conversations, read notes on kitchen calendars, such as birthdays and appointments.

And book club meetings.

Jennifer Griffin was one of his more enjoyable projects.

He'd practiced with others but had only gone so far with the work. When he first saw Jennifer Griffin, he knew she was the one. He'd selected her to be his first completed project, observing her for months, learning everything about her, until the night when he'd moved one step closer to going fully operational for the first time.

It was her book club night and he'd gone to Ripplewood, waited unseen before following her, even daring to walk into the Korner Fast where she'd stopped.

Oh the thrill of getting so close to her.

If she recognized him, he'd play it as a coincidence.

After he'd spotted her leaving the store, he was emboldened to continue. He followed her in that Corolla into the night, recording with his dashcam. This was going to happen. Driving behind her down that remote curving stretch of the boulevard, his heart bursting with anticipation when…

Someone knocked hard on his holding room door.

Volk stopped the push-ups and got his shirt.

His attorney had arrived.

Volk was handcuffed and escorted from his cell.

Robert J. Storemer wore a navy sport coat over a blue button-down dress shirt, a five o'clock shadow, and round, frameless glasses.

He was stone-cold serious.

Storemer had once worked for Volk's uncle, who told him: "Zoran, if ever you get into trouble, you call R. J. Storemer. He's the best GD lawyer in town. That should be on his business card."

This evening's after-hours visit was costing Volk $1,500.

They talked in the same interview room where the investigators had questioned Volk. Again, he was handcuffed to the table as he watched Storemer go over the notes he'd made on his yellow legal pad after first talking with Kozak and Carillo.

"The evidence against you is compelling," Storemer said. "They're not required to reveal at this point how they got on to you. I suspect it arose from a complaint, or you made a mistake along the line."

Volk grinned.

Storemer looked at him, sighing with exasperation.

"Zoran, they have your setup with chains at the cabin, and thanks to your video collection, they have you in her house. They have you stalking her at the mall and other places. They have you following her into and out of the Korner Fast. You are the last person to see her. It's significantly damning."

Volk shook his head slowly.

"After she was reported missing," Volk said, "I watched all the news reports. I see mistakes the cops made. I knew something like this could happen to me, so I took precautions, and you're going to get me out of here."

"I don't think that's achievable. You're not appreciating the gravity of your situation." Storemer looked at his notes. "The best we could do is a plea and confession."

Volk slammed his palms on the table.

"You're not listening. I told you I took precautions."

"What precautions?"

"There's a golf course in East Amherst where I had a call. Give me your pad and pen. I'll draw you a map."

"A map?"

"You'll need to go there right away."

"Why?"

"I want outta here. Look, there's a dirt service road here at the southern border of the course, a fence line, and here, there's a fallen oak. This is what you do." Volk sketched. "At this spot here, under the rock, I buried…"

Eighty-One

Buffalo, New York, Trailside Grove

While the investigators worked in Clarence, Greg was at home with Jake, eating the tacos he'd picked up for their supper.

It was good to see Jake biting into his food.

Living on the hope that Jenn is alive.

They were downstairs in the man cave, sitting at the coffee table in front of the TV because Jake wanted to watch videos online about his drone, which was on the floor beside him.

"Danny at school said there are new ones on how to make the flight time last longer, Dad."

"We'll see them after we're done eating, okay?"

Greg took up the remote to watch the news. *For anything about Jenn.* The broadcast began with reports on local, then state political issues.

The news bored Jake. Between bites, he fiddled with his drone. Half watching the reports, Greg glanced at his phone on the table.

Still no messages from Toronto.

No messages from anybody at the moment.

The last time Greg had talked to Vince, he'd seemed out of sorts with a toothache.

Shrugging it off, Greg's thoughts shifted to Kat. She was home and would have contacted Greg if she'd heard anything arising from their efforts in Larkin earlier that day. That young guy with the dog said his sister knew Jenn's family, said he'd get her to call from Toronto.

Greg checked his phone again.

Nothing.

He thought about how he and Kat had pored over the sympathy cards for Jenn's mom and dad, made calls before door-knocking in her old neighborhood. He needed to know if she had a relative so he could find out who died in Cleveland, find out who he buried, and how it was connected to his wife because—emotion tore through him—*because maybe it will help me find Jenn and bring her home...*

Turning away from Jake, Greg swallowed hard, holding himself together.

"Hey, Dad," Jake said, "that man used to talk to Mom at school a lot."

Greg looked at the TV. A photo of Porter Sellwin filled a quarter of the screen with the graphic Fatal Crash on I-90. Greg grabbed the remote and increased the volume.

"...has learned that the victim in that fatal single-vehicle crash has been identified as Porter Sellwin, aged forty-four, a Buffalo Realtor..."

News footage showed emergency vehicles, traffic, a car overturned in a swamp, the area cordoned off with tape.

"...Sellwin, the sole occupant of his car, was killed when it left the westbound lane and overturned, coming to a stop in a culvert between Batavia and Buffalo. Sellwin was also a school board member for the district that included..."

Not knowing what was coming next, Greg hit record on the remote then switched to a sports channel.

"What's going on, Dad?"

"A terrible accident, I guess. I'll finish watching the news later." Greg wiped his mouth with a napkin. "Are you done? Go wash up, then we'll work on the drone videos, son."

Gulping the last of his tacos, Jake plodded upstairs to the bathroom. Greg then played the rest of the Sellwin story he'd recorded, checking to see if it reported anything linking Sellwin to Jenn.

It didn't.

Still, Sellwin's sudden death weighed on him as he recalled Kat's account of him with Jenn in the parking lot and what Sellwin had said after Greg had accused him of being interested in Jenn. *I don't know what Jennifer told you.* Then what Sellwin said at the funeral: *Jennifer will always have a special place in my heart.*

All of it was weird, puzzling. Greg didn't know what to make of it—and now Sellwin was dead.

Will I ever know the whole truth? Jenn would never be unfaithful. I just know it.

"All done, Dad."

Jake came back and for the next couple of hours,

they played the videos and made adjustments to his drone. When they finished, Jake begged to fly it outside.

"It's late. Bedtime for you, pal."

"Okay, but can we start the chime for a little bit, Dad?"

Greg set it up on the kitchen table, dimming the lights. Jake was enraptured by the dancing flames, the tinkling, glittering angels with their mesmerizing shadows twirling. Greg's thoughts cast back to Jenn's old neighborhood, thinking of her growing up there a happy child until her world collapsed around her.

Some fifteen minutes passed before Greg put out the candles and Jake went upstairs to brush his teeth, put on his pajamas, and get into bed.

"I wished again on the chime for Mom to come home," Jake told Greg when he tucked him in.

"Me too."

Greg kissed him good-night and returned to the kitchen.

He started taking care of the chime when his phone rang.

"Is this Greg Griffin?"

"Yes."

"This is Frances Penney. My brother Louis in Buffalo told me to call you at this number."

"Oh, yes. Thank you for calling. My wife, Jennifer—she was Jennifer Korvin then—grew up near your house…" Greg sat at the table as he explained.

"First, Greg," Frances said, "I'm so sorry Jennifer is missing. Louis told me. I looked at reports online, and I said a prayer for you before I called."

"Thank you."

"Yes, I remember Jennifer. Such a sweet little girl. We talked sometimes, but not too much. I was older. She would be skipping, or riding her bike. But she had no relatives, except her parents and grandmother. No brothers and sisters. She was an only child."

"What about her mom? Was she married before? She must've had other children?"

"No, I don't think so. My mom worked with her, Sofia Korvin. They worked at the Colby Food Mart before they turned it into a call center. Mom said Sofia was never married before. We talked about that, after."

"After?"

"The fire. Awful. We saw it, the flames and smoke. There was nothing we could do. I remember my dad telling the firefighters he thought he saw someone running from the house just before it went up. Nothing came of that because the arson guys said the cause was a cigarette left smoldering in the sofa. It was Christmas, such a horrible tragedy, leaving her an orphan. And to think, she was only eight."

"Yes, Jenn doesn't like talking about it."

"I remember how one day in the aftermath, the cleanup crews just gave some of the things they recovered to my mom for safekeeping. The guys put it all in cardboard boxes, and my mom kept it until Jennifer's grandmother came for them."

"Do you remember what things?"

"Mementos, like collectable spoons, commemorative coins, souvenirs, like a statue of liberty, a jackknife, keepsakes, trinkets, a jewelry box."

"I see. And they all went to Jenn's grandma?"

"Yes," Frances said. "I'm sorry I couldn't be more helpful."

"You were very helpful, Frances. If you think of anything else, please call."

"I will, Greg, and I'm praying Jennifer will be reunited with her family. She's been through so, so much."

Greg sat for a long moment, processing Frances Penney's call and looking at the chime, remembering Jake saying it had arrived at the door, like a delivery. How when Jenn started it, it made her smile then made her cry and she put it away.

She practically hid it. Why? Too many sad memories? But why did she order it? Or who would send it?

Greg was at a loss and he was exhausted. He needed sleep. He drank a glass of cold water and started for the stairs and bed when his phone vibrated.

It was a text from Bob Lugoski, a reporter with the *Plain Dealer* in Cleveland.

How the media got Greg's number, he didn't know.

"Mr. Griffin, have police told you about the latest developments in your wife's case?"

Greg thought then responded.

"Sellwin, the school board guy? No, but it's on the Buffalo news."

"No. Trying to confirm rumors of an arrest and crime scene."

Greg froze.

Arrest and crime scene?

Eighty-Two

The sun was rising when Storemer returned to the Barracks from East Amherst.

He went to the bathroom, washed out the dirt under his nails, patted his face with cold water, then squinted at his reflection in the mirror.

What happened? I was home reading Marcus Aurelius with a glass of chardonnay. What am I doing?

What Storemer just did near the golf course was wrong on so many levels. But he was following his client's wishes, working on a solid defense, and doubling his bill.

The aroma of fresh coffee filled the hall as Storemer entered the meeting room with Kozak and Carillo.

All parties had insisted on working through the night if necessary.

Before they'd taken their seats, Carillo glared at Storemer.

"What were you doing in East Amherst, counselor?"

The lawyer stared back before accepting the fact he'd been followed.

"Did Volk tell you what he did to Jennifer Griffin?"

Storemer said nothing.

"Did he put her in the ground near the golf course? Because we're going to seal and search the area and you're looking like an accessory."

Storemer held up his palms.

"My client wishes to have any consideration of charges against him dismissed because we have evidence that will remove him as a suspect."

Kozak and Carillo traded glances as Storemer withdrew his laptop from his briefcase.

"And how will that happen?" Kozak asked.

"First, you must agree to dismiss any pending charges."

"The evidence we showed you is irrefutable," Kozak said.

"Mr. Volk committed no violent crimes," Storemer said. "What you have is circumstantial. The best you can do right now is what? Video voyeurism or unlawful surveillance? My client wants a guarantee from the DA there will be no charges, none of any kind, in exchange for his cooperation."

"Where's Jennifer Griffin?" Carillo said.

"What I have here will help you find her." Storemer took in a deep breath and let it out. "Before I show you, may I please get some coffee?"

Eighty-Three

Greg's calls, texts, and emails to Kozak and Carillo went unanswered.

Arrest and a crime scene?

Through the night, he'd tried reaching the investigators, his sleep coming in fits and starts. He woke and checked the Cleveland *Plain Dealer*'s site for reports of an arrest and crime scene, finding nothing, and seeing no responses from Kozak and Carillo.

Greg rose just before dawn, made coffee, and took a hot shower.

By the time he dressed and went down to the kitchen, he'd received a new text from Julie Nash, with the Associated Press in New York.

May I speak with you over the phone, Mr. Griffin?

Even though he knew, he texted back: About what?

A possible break in your wife's case.

What break?

A crime scene, possibly in Pennsylvania. It's unconfirmed. That's all I have. Hoping you know more.

Fingers squeezing his phone, he wanted to question the reporter, wanted her to tell him what she knew about Pennsylvania.

But a part of him didn't want to know.

If I don't know she's dead, then for me, she's still alive.

He'd been through this before.

I can't comment. I don't know anything.

Greg's heart beat faster, his fear rising.

A crime scene in Pennsylvania. An arrest. The implications.

Something was happening; the press always knew.

Greg heard Jake upstairs, getting up, going to the bathroom as he continued checking online for reports. Here was an item posted fifteen minutes earlier on Twitter by a TV news station in Erie, Pennsylvania. It came with video of a LIVE BREAKING report.

Greg played it and saw aerial footage of a wooded area, a river, the camera tightening on activity around a cabin, search teams and dogs in the forests, police boats, divers in the water while a reporter said…

"…they began yesterday. This morning is the second day of probing this corner of Elk Creek.

Again, we stress this is unconfirmed, but we're learning from a source that this operation is related to the case of Jennifer Griffin, who went missing from her Buffalo…"

Greg's stomach twisted.

This was real. This was happening.

Anticipating more news coverage this morning, he was fearful of seeing a tarp covering Jenn. *I can't let Jake see his mother like that. We can't go through this again.*

Greg reached for his phone and made a call.

As it rang, he moved to the front of his house, driving his free hand through his hair when Holly Wiley answered.

"Holly, it's Greg. Sorry it's so early, but I need a favor."

"No problem. We're up. What is it?"

"Could you take Jake? Keep him out of school today? Something's happening."

"Of course, I'll take Jake. What's going on?"

Greg watched a Buffalo TV news truck and another van turn down his street.

"Greg? Is everything okay?"

"Some news is breaking. Media are coming to the house. It could be bad, Holly."

"Oh no—"

"Can you come get Jake? Come through the back way?"

"Yes, I'm on my way. Be there in five."

"Thank you. And Holly, keep him outside, away from any news, please."

"I will. Nate's off today and I'll keep Carter home, too. What is it? What's happening?"

"I don't know. I'm trying to find out."

Greg turned. Jake was dressed, walking downstairs to the kitchen table.

"Who're you talking to, Dad?"

"Carter's mom." Greg fixed Jake a bowl of cereal, went to the fridge for milk. "I've got some things to do today, so how would you like to go to Carter's and fly your drone there? Maybe make a video with your phone?"

"What about school?"

"Carter's staying home today and I'll keep you out today, too."

"Why?"

"Something's come up. I'll call the office."

Jake hesitated before saying: "Okay, Dad."

He returned to crunching on his cereal. Carter had a big backyard. Jake would be able to fly higher and get a better view with his drone. Something he'd wanted to do ever since he got it. Greg made toast for both of them, and they ate together at the table.

"When you finish eating, brush your teeth. Carter's mom is on her way over to get you."

The front doorbell rang, and Jake moved to get it.

"Don't answer," Greg said. "It's reporters again."

Jake strained to see the front windows, then looked at his dad while they finished eating. Jake sensed something was happening.

Kids could read the truth in the air.

Eighty-Four

Buffalo, New York, Trailside Grove

After Holly and Carter left with Jake down the back way to their house, Greg turned on the TV, grabbed his phone, and searched online.

Starting with local outlets, the *Buffalo News* had just posted a breaking story with the headline: Suspect Arrested In Missing Trailside Mom Case.

The item was short. Greg raced through it, reading of yesterday's arrest of Zoran Volk, a cable repair contractor, at his residence in the North Buffalo area. He was taken to state police barracks in Clarence for questioning. A grainy video recorded by a neighbor showing SWAT team members putting Volk in handcuffs accompanied the story.

All the blood drained from Greg's face.

Jenn had been home when a cable guy came to the house a couple months before.

He swallowed hard. The doorbell rang; his phone vibrated with more requests from news reporters. Greg didn't respond. Instead, he texted Claire Kozak again.

It's Greg Griffin. Media says arrest made? What's happening?

Sorry, can't talk now.

PLEASE! I'M BEGGING YOU. DID CABLE GUY KILL JENN?

Kozak didn't respond.
Greg texted: IS SHE DEAD IN ELK CREEK?
Kozak didn't respond.
Greg texted: WILL GO THERE IF YOU DON'T ANSWER!!
Another moment passed before Kozak responded.

Don't go. Stay home. Hold on, Greg.

Eighty-Five

Carillo got Storemer's coffee, muttering as he set it on the table before him, the contents swaying dangerously to the brim.

"So what's your evidence?" Kozak said after texting with Greg Griffin and putting her phone down.

Storemer drank some coffee then held up a USB key. "This is my client's, what I retrieved from the golf course."

Storemer inserted it into his laptop.

"It was recorded from the dash-mounted camera of his van the night Jennifer Griffin disappeared. It's date-stamped. Your forensic team will authenticate it."

He typed a few commands then turned his laptop to them.

"This view is while traveling east on Ripple Valley Boulevard."

The screen came alive with the point of view of a vehicle moving through Ripplewood Creek at night, past the colorful signs of Trader Joe's, the

Citizen Bank, the Rite Aid, the town hall, moving beyond its commercial center, past the Bluebird Retirement Manor and Wood Creek Apartments, then beyond the houses lining the boulevard, leaving the developed area.

The headlights switched to high beams as it entered the long curving stretch through the woods, illuminating the lonely road and the trees of the thick forests towering on either side.

Suddenly, there emerged the taillights of vehicles on the shoulder of the road ahead, and Volk's van slows, the camera recording showing the first vehicle to be a white van, bright red and blue emergency lights pulsing in what appears to be a police traffic stop.

Volk's van slows to a near crawl. The dash-mounted camera turns so it captures the stopped vehicle, a Corolla. It zooms to the driver. The interior dome light is on, illuminating a woman behind the wheel, who, for a split second, looks at the camera.

Jennifer Griffin.

The camera continues recording through the night. Storemer accelerates as it shows Volk never stopping, driving through the city, parking in his driveway in the North Buffalo area, leaving the camera on until the sun rises the next day, proving he had nothing to do with Jennifer Griffin's disappearance.

Kozak flicked a glance to Carillo.

Both of them thinking the same thing.

It's a cop.

Eighty-Six

Clarence, New York

Kozak accepted the USB key with the video from Storemer.

The thought a cop was involved in Jennifer Griffin's disappearance thundered in Kozak's mind, and she used that anger to focus on her job. She documented the evidence with Storemer's signature, telling him that they'd talk to the DA later, but would hold Volk while they investigated.

Storemer informed his client, drove home, passed on the chardonnay, drank two shots of whiskey, and collapsed on his sofa.

At the barracks, Kozak and Carillo set aside Greg Griffin's messages—thinking Volk's arrest must've leaked to the press—and pushed ahead, copying Volk's video to their devices, running it, studying the sequence with Lieutenant Becker.

"Why the hell do we not have any record of her being pulled over that night?" Becker said. "I don't get it. Who made the stop?"

"Look, the plate's right there but we can't make it out," Carillo said.

For an instant, the license plate of the van flashed. Replaying the footage, freezing the frame and zooming in didn't help. The van's plate was not clear enough to read. Rubbing his lips, Becker went to his office, made calls, then returned.

"Our video forensic experts in Albany might be able to get the plate," Becker said. "But they need the original key. Do the chain of evidence paperwork. I'll get an evidence tech and a unit to deliver it to them ASAP."

Moments later, a state police patrol car, siren wailing, lights flashing, raced to Buffalo Niagara International Airport. The key was delivered to a waiting state police Cessna 206. The plane lifted off for the one-hour flight to Albany to get the key to the New York State crime lab.

At the barracks, the investigators moved fast, reaching out to Erie County, Buffalo PD, every area state and federal agency and security firm with service vehicles.

They'd requested urgent checks of unit logs, duty rosters, calls, traffic stops, and checks of fleet records that would identify and put a van in Ripplewood Creek at the time of Jennifer Griffin's disappearance.

Time ticked by, the responses started coming back with one after the other being negative.

They'd go back, review what they had, and request any commercial security video for a white van in the area at the time.

They considered the possibility the van was part
of an undercover operation. Still, it was unlikely to
make a traffic stop.

"What about car service companies, towing
companies, couriers, repair contractors?" Carillo
said.

"The lights they use are usually yellow," Becker
said.

Kozak searched on her tablet.

"You know," she said, "anybody can buy emergency red and blue police lights online." She slid
her tablet for Carillo and Becker to see a display
of models for sale. "They could easily pass for the
real thing, to convince someone to pull over."

"It could've been someone posing as a cop," Carillo said.

Kozak cupped her hands to her face.

She took a long breath, glanced at Jennifer Griffin's photo on her phone, praying against the odds
that she was alive.

Eighty-Seven

Jake placed his Firelight Mega Striker drone on the grass.

He exchanged excited glances with Carter.

This was the first time they were going to fly it in Carter's backyard.

It was twice the size of Jake's, with a lush green lawn bordered by a chain-link fence and an unlocked gate that opened to a forest strip. Save for the sporadic wink of chrome, the trees hid the traffic flowing on Wild Orchid Lane, an artery with no residential or commercial development that paralleled the woods.

Jake and Carter went through the drone's pre-flight checks. The propellers were secure. The battery was in place. The drone's camera lens was clean.

Jake secured his phone to his controller, connecting it to the feature that let him view and record whatever his drone's camera captured.

He extended the controller to Carter.

"Want to go first?"

Carter gave a nervous laugh.

"No, you go. You're a better flyer than me. I'll watch."

"Okay."

Jake switched it on and the quad's propellers hummed to life.

Carter's dad, Nate, was near the garden shed cleaning his lawn mower; he looked up and smiled at the boys as Jake piloted the drone's gentle liftoff.

Jake had it climb about twenty feet and hover there.

When he flew it in his yard, he did so many lift-offs, squares, circles, figure eights, never climbing much higher than the rooftop of his house.

But the short flights sharpened his flying skills.

Today he'd put them to the test.

Today he'd use his drone to try searching for his mom because something was happening. Jake could tell by the way his dad seemed so tense this morning, like he was up all night, and by how even when his dad talked, his voice sounded worried.

"See how high you can go," Carter said, now standing with him, watching the view on Jake's phone.

Easing the controller's sticks, Jake sent the drone shooting straight up to nearly a hundred feet with a fantastic view of the neighborhood.

"Whoa! Awesome!" Carter said. "Are you recording?"

"Yup."

"Go over your house."

The drone picked up all the vehicles now collected on the street in front of Jake's house. Jake then had it descend to capture the huddle of TV newspeople with some looking up and aiming cameras at it.

"What's going on at your house?" Carter said. "Looks serious again."

Jake studied the screen without answering. All he knew was that something was wrong. His mind held one thought.

She's not dead! My mom can't be dead.

Maneuvering the control sticks, Jake pulled the drone away fast, directing it to fly over the forest to look there.

Maybe she fell back there? Maybe she's hurt? We have to find her.

Carter, his eyes on the small screen, didn't see the tear rolling down Jake's cheek as they watched the traffic moving on Wild Orchid Lane on the other side of the woods. That's when they saw a vehicle had pulled off to the shoulder at the edge of the forest directly behind Carter's house.

As the boys studied the roof of the vehicle, their view became obscured with branches.

"No!" Jake said.

He hadn't climbed high enough; the drone was brushing treetops. The screen went crazy, branches and leaves spinning before it froze.

"I'm crashing!"

Jake looked to the forest as they heard the drone falling in the trees.

"You stay here." Jake gave Carter the controller. "I saw where it fell. I'll get it."

Jake ran, opened the fence gate, and disappeared into the forest.

Nate looked up at Carter.

"It's okay, Dad. The drone crashed. Jake went to get it."

Nate hesitated but kept working while keeping an eye on the forest for Jake. Carter stared at the phone and the image of leaves frozen on it, expecting to see it move as soon as Jake retrieved the drone.

Minutes went by.

The screen didn't change.

More time passed.

The image on the screen hadn't changed. Holding the controller, Carter walked to the fence, expecting to see or hear his friend in the woods.

"Jake!"

More time passed with Carter turning to his dad at the garden shed.

He wasn't there.

Nate had run through the open gate and into the woods to find Jake.

Eighty-Eight

Erie County, New York

Some twenty-five miles outside Buffalo, near the edge of Erie County, all but cut off from most of civilization, was a long-forgotten acreage.

To find it, you traveled along winding country roads, where neighbors were separated by more than a quarter mile.

Starting in the 1800s, the farm produced potatoes, corn, cabbage, apples, and other crops, with the operation surviving until the 1950s, when descendants of the people who'd toiled there abandoned it.

Taxes were paid by the generations that followed. But the place was neglected.

A rusted gate with a No Trespassing sign wired to it guarded the entrance. It didn't stop the few people looking for privacy over the years—hunters, partying teens, and those who were up to no good.

Access was by a rutted dirt road overrun with wild grass as it cut through a dead apple orchard to where the main buildings once stood.

Decades ago, the farmhouse had collapsed into

a heap of rotted wood, enshrouded with clumps of shrubs, akin to a burial mound. Birds chirped while streaking over it, and butterflies flitted in the breezes that carried to the barn.

It was nearly wrapped with overgrowth. Many of its boards were missing, the gaps leaving it a leaning, sagging, weather-beaten skeleton at risk of crumpling to the earth.

But it had endured.

Inside, there were the vestiges of a tractor, pieces of a wooden wagon, and rows of livestock stalls. To one side, the way to the barn's cellar beckoned. A wooden trapdoor led to a staircase.

A naked lightbulb cast the steps in gloomy light.

Someone had expertly altered the wires of the old system to bypass safeguards and illegally siphon off electricity from an existing source that had long been shut off.

The damp, foul cellar reeked of the grave.

The electrical cable snaked along the walkway leading to a new corner room, solidly built with fresh-cut lumber.

Light spilled from the room.

The door was wide open.

Its hinge assemblies had been carved away, ripped from their hold on the doorframe.

The windowless room held a mattress, pillow, blankets. T-shirts, plastic water bottles, and plastic utensils were scattered everywhere, along with overturned buckets.

No one was inside.
The room was empty.
Blood was splattered on the floor.

Eighty-Nine

The USB key from Clarence Barracks arrived at the Forensic Video Unit where Rose Kemp signed the chain of custody documents.

This new piece of evidence had been given top priority.

"Consider this one a life-and-death matter," Kemp's supervisor had said. "Guys in Clarence need the plate on the van in the video, like now."

Kemp cleared her workstation, inserted the key into one of her computer towers. As it loaded, she ran a mental checklist of what she would do. In her seven years in the field, she'd worked on more than a thousand cases, presented expert video analysis in criminal trials and was considered one of best video forensic analysts in the state.

It didn't take her long to authenticate the new material, confirming that Zoran Volk's video had not been altered or manipulated.

That was easy. Now for the hard part.

She played the video several times, focusing on

the split-second image sequence that had recorded the rear plate of the van. She was relieved that its rear license plate lights were working; there was illumination. The light from the headlights of the passing vehicle was inconsistent.

She replayed the video, keying in commands.

A brilliant rectangle of a New York state license plate filled a monitor at Kemp's workstation.

But the plate's digits and letters were not clear.

The poor quality could be due to several factors—the resolution, the angle recorded, the environment, especially given it was recorded at night from a moving point of view. Zooming in didn't work. She couldn't enhance or extract something from nothing.

If the data's not there, it's not there.

But there were ways Kemp could make some elements clearer using the array of her unit's state-of-the-art hardware and software.

This might take some time.

Kemp played the video sequence again. It appeared the slow-frame rate was making it hard to see. She slowed the sequence, stopping the footage and selecting the best quality frames to make stills of the best five. Using the latest software, she layered the stills, overlapping them, combining them into one enhanced frame.

When she was ready, she entered several commands into her system and waited as her monitor displayed the result.

Kemp sat up.

Oh my, I think we've got something here.

Ninety

At home, his heart racing, Greg ached to do something when his phone rang.

He checked the ID. It was Kat.

"I've been trying to reach you!" she said when he answered. "I just heard the news about an arrest. What do you know about it?"

"Nothing."

"Where're you?"

"Home. The media's out front. I don't know what's going on."

"I'm calling my boss. I'll be there soon."

"What about Dad?"

"He's at the dentist. Just hold on, I'm coming."

Greg peeked through the curtains at the crowd out front. His doorbell rang constantly. He didn't answer. His phone vibrated with messages from newspeople, but he didn't respond. He was screening calls, waiting for Kozak or Carillo to confirm that they'd found Jenn.

Or to tell me she's dead.

Until they did, until he had absolute proof this time, to him, she was still alive.

I don't want to hear it from the press with cameras aimed at me.

Greg returned to the TV, continuing to surf for any news updates—*maybe Kozak and Carillo were on camera*—when he heard thudding, frantic hammering, at his back door.

Cursing, he strode to it, thinking that if a reporter was at the back then they'd trespassed. But it was Holly Wiley.

He opened the door for her.

"Jake's missing!"

"What do you mean?"

"He ran into the woods! We can't find him!"

Running through the back way, Greg barely heard Holly's words, her voice trembling as she tried to keep up with him.

"Jake's drone fell in the trees... He went looking... Nate called nine-one-one..."

Gooseflesh rose on Greg's arms, his scalp prickled, he struggled to take in what was happening.

Arriving at the Wiley's backyard, he saw Nate using his BBQ grill table like a desk, his phone wedged between his ear and his shoulder, talking, typing on his laptop. A police scanner squawked with dispatches, and a walkie-talkie used for the neighborhood watch was also on the table.

Carter was standing nearby, still holding the controller, staring at the forest as if expecting Jake to emerge with the drone.

"Greg!" Nate turned. "State police are sending

units. They're putting out an Amber. We're blasting it out to the neighborhood watch teams in Trailside, Ripplewood, Cardinal, and Noble Haven. Many of our guys are retired, so we'll get a lot of eyes out there."

Without stopping, Greg charged into the forest, branches slapping and pulling at him as he searched at top speed, calling Jake's name. A flash of color. He found Jake's drone caught in a thicket and untangled its propellers from the branches. Then he studied the traffic on Wild Orchid Lane before returning to the yard, his heart pounding, mind racing.

"It crashed and Jake just went looking for it!" said Carter, his chin crumpling, still holding the controller.

"Were you guys recording a video before the crash?" Greg said.

Carter nodded.

"Let's replay it."

Carter passed the controller to Greg.

Replaying the video with Nate watching over Greg's shoulder, their focus went to the van parked on the shoulder of Wild Orchid near the forest directly behind the Wiley's house.

"Damn, that's got to be it," Nate said.

Greg copied the video, sending it to Nate's and Holly's phones.

"Holly," Greg said, "take Carter. Go to my house, bring the press here, show them what happened, show them the video. Tell police what happened when they get here. You've got pictures of Jake."

"Okay, Greg."

He turned to Nate. "Get your radio stuff. We gotta find that van!"

Ninety-One

Clarence, New York

Tension had turned Kozak's neck to stone.

She rubbed it, drank more coffee, and looked at the clock on the Barracks wall before returning to reports.

It was well into the morning; they'd been at it all night.

Come on, something's got to give, she thought.

Her email chimed; her phone pinged.

So did Carillo's.

It was Rose Kemp at the Forensic Video Unit in Albany. "Your subject's plate is New York RFD 9Q114, registered to—"

Kozak wrote down the name and address.

"Here we go." Carillo sat up at his keyboard, clicking as he ran the name.

The break unleashed an investigative blitz.

In anticipation, they'd already drafted affidavits for warrants. Lieutenant Becker entered their office, tie loosened, in need of a shave, phone to his ear. He was talking to a judge who was standing by to email them sign-off on warrants for the subject's residence, vehicle, and phone.

"We've got ECSO SWAT moving on the address now for a potential rescue," Becker said.

Unit #75 was a double-wide at the end of a pot-holed street in Sweet Lake Breezes Mobile Home Park.

Garbage had been strewn in neighboring yards by dogs picking through discarded table scraps.

The commander of ECSO's—Erie County Sheriff's Office's—SWAT team assigned two members to move neighboring residents and the dogs to safety before the unit took points around #75. Then, using a bullhorn, the commander ordered the occupants to exit the residence, showing their hands.

No response.

They listened for movement inside.

Silence.

No vehicle on the parking pad.

No assumptions were made.

A patio door smashed and a bedroom window disintegrated as flash-bang grenades exploded inside and SWAT members rushed into the home, checking all rooms, closets, crawlspaces, knocking on walls, the ceiling, and floor, checking for body mass.

"ECSO says no one's home at number seventy-five. No sign of Jennifer Griffin," Becker told Kozak and Carillo. "Deputies will canvass."

Becker's phone rang with another call, and he turned away to take it.

At the Barracks, the investigators' efforts to find Jennifer mounted. They'd found no record, no arrests, or warrants for the subject.

Kozak was working with the phone carrier who was motivated by the warrant to cooperate. They were moving fast to help locate the subject by tracking the mobile phone when the case analyst, Melinda Hyland, came to the investigators, flagging a new piece of information.

"The plate came up on the list of vehicles observed at the funeral," Hyland said. "The vehicle was there."

Kozak looked at Carillo; his jawline had tightened.

Becker lowered his phone.

"Jake Griffin went missing moments ago near his home in Trailside Grove."

"What?" Kozak's eyes widened.

"They're issuing an Amber," Becker said. "Greg Griffin's called us and sent us drone video of the suspect's vehicle—don't ask me how they got it. You should now have it with a summary."

Her keyboard clicking, Kozak studied the drone video, showing the white roof of a van pulled to the shoulder of Wild Orchid Lane. Blinking at a quick thought, she got back on the line with the tech working on the subject's phone. Kozak gave her the location and time of Jake Griffin's recent abduction.

"We have new information," Kozak said. "Does the phone track to this location in Trailside?"

"Hang on," the tech said, working at her end. "Hang on. Yes. It was in the area at the time. And I've got the current vicinity coming up. Your target is moving."

Kozak relayed the information to Becker, who punched a number on his phone.

"I'm getting air support. Keep tracking. You guys get going!"

As they trotted to their unmarked Taurus, Kozak's thoughts whirled.

How did we miss this? It was there all this time.

Ninety-Two

Buffalo, New York, Trailside Grove

Houses blurred by Greg's passenger window as Nate Wiley's Dodge Ram pickup rocketed through Trailside.

"Get us on Wild Orchid," Greg said, studying the drone video showing the white van pulled over on the westbound lane. There was a barrier dividing it from the eastbound lane, so they reasoned that the van had gone west on Orchid.

Tires squealing, Nate turned onto Wild Orchid, the Ram's V-8 Hemi engine pushing the truck over the speed limit, coming to the spot that was behind the Wiley house.

As they expected, the white van was gone.

They continued roaring down the long street, passing slower cars.

Nate slammed his palms on the wheel, shaking his head.

"It happened so fast. Jake just ran into the woods. I'm so damn sorry, Greg."

"Now's not the time. We've got to find him."

Panic numbing him, Greg knew the odds.

What chance do I have? How much of a lead did the van get?

His thoughts were jolted to voices crackling on Nate's radio scanner.

"All units, ten-forty in progress in Charlie Sector...standby..."

"A ten-forty's an abduction." Nate reached for his scanner, adjusting it. "I think that's us."

Their phones clanged with the Amber Alert for Jake. *That was fast*, Greg thought, his hopes rising.

"All units, this from investigators: The ten-forty is related to a previous ten-twenty-two—"

Greg looked at Nate who knew all the codes from his role in neighborhood watch.

"That's a missing person," Nate said. "They're saying it's tied to Jennifer!"

"What?"

The radio dispatch continued: "—suspect vehicle tag, New York Romeo Foxtrot Delta Nine Quebec One One Four, a late model white van—approach with caution..."

Nate repeated the plate number to Greg to note while blasting around slower cars. As they rolled farther along Wild Orchid past a Sunoco station, Greg glimpsed an Excelsior food truck, one of Brooke Bollman's people. The driver leaning on the fender talking on a phone was not Brooke.

That's weird, Greg thought, his mind flashing to Brooke, trying to recall if she still had her van, wondering if seeing the food truck meant anything.

He was trying to remember when new dispatches burst over the scanner.

"All units, the subject in the ten-forty, ten-twenty-two, tracking showing last known vicinity at Chestnut Shade Avenue and Moss Creek Road. Standby…"

"Hey—" Nate tightened his grip on the wheel "—that's four or five miles due west. We're heading in the right direction."

The Ram accelerated.

Greg took deep, controlled breaths and prayed.

Ninety-Three

Erie County, New York

Vibrating with adrenaline, turning in a slow circle, Jenn surveyed the property.

There was the dilapidated barn that was her prison.

There was a collapsed house, the remains of its roof atop fingers of decayed wood, jutting from rubble overgrown with weeds.

No signs of life in this abandoned property.

Where am I?

Her chest heaving, tears and sweat trickled down her face, her arms, to her hands, mixing with blood from the scrapes, splinters, and skin-piercing wounds she'd received in breaking free.

Jenn looked around for anyone who might help—*or threaten*—her.

How long had it been since her captor was here?

After the last time she saw eyes at the door's portal, she realized that her captor hadn't discovered her work to escape. But from the notes left for her, Jenn feared the time on her life was running out.

She had clawed nonstop at the hinges, pulling and digging, until finally, they began to loosen. She grabbed and twisted the metal hinges and bolts until her fingers were raw and her muscles were on fire. She took up her tool, gouged and kicked. The door loosened then shifted slightly.

Unrelenting, she kicked and pulled, creating a gap, wedging her fingers and hands, tugging at the door, leveraging it with her foot, her shoulder against the locked side, the wood frame cracking and splintering until the gap widened, and with a half cry, she squeezed through it.

No trace of another person.

She stood in the narrow, low-ceilinged walkway, gagging, the air stinking of bird guano, the dim light leading to the stairs. But the door above was sealed. Jenn climbed up and found it was locked.

It rattled with loose boards. Positioning her back against it, using all her strength, she pushed the door, growling and thrusting until the wood cracked, splitting and giving way.

Yanking at broken pieces, she wedged herself through the hole, painfully scraping her skin in her birth to freedom.

Now, she stood on the abandoned property, stunned and bleeding, her body aching, her clothes torn and soiled.

Drinking in the fresh air, wiping at her face, she spotted the lane and began limping through the dead orchard, thinking of her family.

Jake. Greg. I love you. I'm alive.

Ninety-Four

Erie County, New York

"...Subject tracking at Clinton and Four Rod Road..."

Nate Wiley's police scanner crackled with an update.

"That's due south," Nate said, signaling to turn at the next major intersection.

"And far ahead of us," Greg said.

Nate's walkie-talkie came to life.

"Doug Tucker, Trailside watch captain. I'm heading south on the Amber, who else we got out there? Over."

Nate picked up his radio, keyed his microphone.

"Doug, this is Nate Wiley. I got Greg Griffin with me. We're moving south. Over."

"Thanks, Nate," Tucker said. "Anyone else? Watch captains only, to keep chatter to minimum, please. Over."

Nate's walkie-talkie hissed.

"Jensen from Noble Haven. Our team is rolling. Over."

Seconds passed.

"Zelinski, Cardinal Hill. We've got eyes out there, too. Right behind you, Doug. Over."

A long moment of static silence passed.

"Roger that," Tucker said. "Thanks. Got more people coming. Stay sharp out there. Over."

Greg's phone vibrated with a text from Kozak.

We're putting up ECSO helo. Keep the faith, Greg.

Absorbing Kozak's message gave Greg some assurance, knowing several police agencies and volunteers had assembled an army.

But the van was miles ahead.

It could disappear anywhere.

Anything could happen.

Among the neighborhood watch volunteers monitoring his walkie-talkie and police scanner was Bert Cobb.

The watch captain was right, Cobb thought as he drove.

Got to keep alert; the situation has changed dramatically.

Cobb had seen it all building on the news: Jennifer wrongly identified as dead, later a suspect was arrested, a crime scene in Pennsylvania, and now this: Jake was missing.

And police are tying it to Jennifer's disappearance.

Listening to dispatches and transmissions on his police scanner and walkie-talkie, Cobb adjusted his grip on his steering wheel, thinking of events unfolding and the agony.

It's been going on for so long. It's been so hard. Everyone's been through so much. I know their pain. I lost my sister.

Listening to his radios as he drove, Cobb searched hard.

Sounds like they're getting closer.

Ninety-Five

Wincing with each step, Jenn shambled over the deep grooves in the dirt road, the tall grass brushing her legs as she moved through the orchard.

Fearing her captor was behind her, she cast a glance back to the buildings. Then she looked down the lane winding through the dead trees for the way out.

No signs of life anywhere but for the birdsong and occasional breezes hissing over the acreage. Stumbling, she stifled a sob, got up, wiped her raw, bloodied hands on her shirt, and kept moving.

Nearing the property's entrance gate at the end of the lane, her heart lifted to the hum of tires on asphalt. A car approached. She saw it, knowing it could be her captor. Her heart pounding, she whispered a prayer, took a risk and waved from behind the gate.

"Hey! Help! Hey!"

It sailed by, disappearing down the long narrow country road, taking her hope of rescue with it.

She clenched her eyes.

Don't give up. Keep going.

Steeling herself, she opened her eyes. The rusted gate was secured with a chain and lock. Gritting through her pain, she gripped the metal frame, climbed, and hefted herself over it, staring at the No Trespassing sign. The chain and lock were new.

She looked in both directions.

Where am I?

The road was lined with stands of trees, scrub, and stretches of cleared farmland.

No traffic.

No buildings.

No mailboxes.

Nobody.

Which way to go?

The car had vanished to her left.

Go left.

Dragonflies whirled over the tall grass as she walked along the side of the paved road. Breathing hard, her body stiff, she wiped her face on her shirt. She'd gone about a hundred yards when the sun glared on a windshield.

A distant vehicle was approaching.

Jenn stood in the middle of the road.

As it drew closer, she waved her arms, her tears flowed, waving and begging, praying, willing it to stop.

It slowed, came within ten feet of her and stopped.

Jenn stood there, face in her hands, sobbing.

I've been saved! Thank you, God, thank you!

Ninety-Six

Concentrating on the police dispatcher's tracking updates, Greg used Nate's binoculars to examine the plate of every white van they saw while speeding south.

In the distance, they heard sirens as the dispatcher guided patrol units closer to their target's path of travel.

Commercial buildings and neighborhoods began disappearing from view, the urban landscape melted into rural when Greg's phone vibrated with a text from Al Clayton.

Greg, just heard about Jake, everything. The crew wants to help.

He texted back.

We're heading south near Colden, Glenwood. Should be a police chopper to follow.

On our way.

Greg looked to the sky for the police helicopter when his phone rang. It was not blocked, and it was not police or media.

"Greg, it's Brooke Bollman."

"Brooke." He couldn't hear or see the chopper. "Not a good time."

"I just heard the news. How can I help? What can I do?"

Greg's attention shifted to Brooke, thoughts charging through his mind. How she'd wanted to partner with him, her hands all over him in the bar, battling the temptation, his urges, her text the night Jenn vanished—*We'd be great together*—showing up at the funeral in her formfitting dress... *I didn't know if I should be here, Greg...*

His jaw tensed.

"Do you still drive a white van, Brooke?"

She didn't answer.

Nate's police scanner issued a static-filled update.

"...all units on the ten-forty, ten-twenty-two, subject now tracking near East Concord..."

"Brooke," Greg repeated, "do you still drive a white van?"

A long moment passed.

"You know I do. What—"

"Brooke," Greg said, squeezing his phone. "Did you take Jenn and then Jake?"

It took several seconds for Brooke to respond.

"Why're you asking me this? It makes no sense, Greg."

The line went dead.

Ninety-Seven

Standing on the road, sobbing into her hands, Jenn didn't realize the vehicle door had opened until someone touched her shoulder.

She raised her face.

"Bert?"

Bert Cobb, the custodian at Jake's school, stood before her, worry in his eyes. She threw her arms around his neck, crying and shaking.

"Jennifer, how did you—what—are you hurt?"

Cobb opened the passenger door, left it open, got Jenn into the seat. He uncapped a bottle of water, passed it to her, touching a towel to her free hand then the other, while looking up and down the road.

"Where did you come—"

"I don't know—oh, thank you for saving me, Bert!" she cried, glancing to his police scanner and walkie-talkie. "How did you find me?"

"I'm with the neighborhood watch. I was helping police look for you. It's all over the watch network, something was happening this way. You're going to be okay. I gotta call police, tell them I got you."

Cobb withdrew his phone and called while Jenn drank water, weeping softly, looking around.

"Yes... Bert Cobb... I got her..." he said. "We're at..."

Jenn saw blankets heaped behind her, did a double take, thinking they had stirred, exposing a spark of metallic glint when Cobb placed his hand on her shoulder.

"Yes... She's right here in good condition... alert...yes...will do." Cobb ended the call and returned to Jenn. "The police are telling us to get out of the area and meet them a couple miles down the road. Let's get you comfortable."

He fastened her seat belt, lowered the right armrest of her seat and placed her forearm on it while reaching behind his back. Fast as a cobra strike, a metal handcuff closed on her wrist, sending the water bottle flying, spilling as the other cuff closed on the seat's lower metal frame.

Jenn's eyes widened. "What're you doing?"

Cobb slammed her door, got behind the wheel. He revved the engine, tires squealing as they drove off.

"Bert!" Jenn strained her cuffed wrist. "Please, what're you—"

"Relax. It's a long, long drive," he said. "We're taking you home."

"We— But I don't—"

Cobb reached behind him, snapping away the blankets for Jenn to see.

"Jake! Oh God! Jake!"

He was curled on the rear floor, his ankle handcuffed to the frame.

"Mom!" Jake shot his hand to her—reaching for each other, their fingers entwining, both of them sobbing. "Mr. Cobb told me he knew where you were and that if I went with him right away, we could save you, but it was dangerous so I had to hide and be quiet no matter what I heard. Then he clamped this on me. He said to keep me safe."

Jenn looked at Cobb with anger, fear. Dispatches burst from the radios. She tried to decipher them, realizing he'd faked his call to police to give her false assurance, keep her calm, get her into the van.

Adrenaline coursing, she tried to think.

"Bert." Her voice tremoring, she struggled to appear composed. "Bert, you did a good thing. You found me and Jake. Let's stop and call police, call Greg. I'll tell them how you did a great thing, Bert, please. Please."

Cobb accelerated.

"Listen," he said, patting her arm. "It's going to be all right now. We're together now, the three of us, that's all that matters."

"Bert, please stop. Please."

"You're not listening, Jennifer. We're going to our new home."

"What home?"

"I got a place for us, out west in Montana."

"I don't understand."

They sped down the strip of empty road with

Cobb checking his mirrors, then looking ahead. They were coming to a railroad crossing.

"It's a lot to take in, but I told you in my note you'd know everything. Now you do and here we are together, a family."

"I don't understand. Please just stop."

"Jennifer, I sent you the chime to remind you."

"You—to remind me?"

"I was there the night your house burned."

Shaking her head, tears rolled down her face. Turning to check on Jake, she saw him crying quietly.

"Jenn, I'm your brother. Jake's my nephew. We're family."

"What? No, Bert. No, I have no brothers, no sisters."

"You're wrong! Dead wrong."

"Bert, please stop!"

The bursts of staccato chatter from Cobb's radios sounded more urgent, underscoring the horror, how nothing made sense, nothing was real, and yet it was happening.

Suspension vibrating, they rattled over the railroad crossing tracks.

Cobb's focus went to the sudden flashing of the red engine warning light on his instrument cluster. His van stalled and he brought it to stop on the other side of the tracks.

"Damn fuel pump fuse! I shoulda fixed—"

He got out and lifted the hood, blocking his view of the interior.

"Mom, I'm scared," Jake whispered.

"Everything's going to be all right, honey," Jenn said soothingly. "I'm so happy to see you— so happy. It's going to be all right."

Reaching for Jake's hand, Jenn glimpsed an object in her periphery and caught her breath. A small key had fallen from Cobb's pocket to the far side of the driver's seat—*the handcuff key*.

Jenn reached but it was too far.

"Jake," she whispered. "Come close. Can you see the little key on the driver's seat?"

Jake moved, twisted, then nodded his head.

"Reach for it and give it to me."

The radios squawked, then the air outside was pierced by the whistle of an approaching train.

"Hurry," Jenn whispered.

Moving his arm around the base of the seat, reaching with his fingers, Jake accidentally tipped the key to the edge. Gasping, Jenn glanced to the slit of view under the hood, seeing Cobb still working, then back to Jake, straining, stretching until his shaking fingers touched the key, dragged it slowly back until he snatched it and gave it to his mother.

The train's whistle grew louder with the hammering of its engine.

Jenn moved fast but was careful, angling her hand to insert the key correctly, opening her cuff with a tiny click. She then reached back to free Jake from his cuff.

They moved quietly as she opened her door, bringing Jake to the front, slipping out just as Cobb noticed the shift of weight and glanced around the side to see them out of the van.

Eyeing the train, Jenn ran toward the tracks, about fifty yards away. Her pain flared but she was intent to cross the tracks, putting the train between her and Cobb.

"Run, Jake!"

He was ahead of her, nearly at the tracks, the train nearly at the crossing, its whistle blasting as Jake cleared it safely. Seeing vehicles coming toward him from the distance, he turned to see his mom clear the crossing, with the train bearing down.

Cobb cleared it too.

The passing freight train began thundering by, with Jake running down the road toward the vehicles racing toward them.

Cobb gained on Jennifer, seizing her wrist, pulling her to him.

"Don't run! Our sister ran and it killed her! Stop! We're family!"

Jenn struggled in vain. Overpowering her, Cobb manhandled her back toward the train as the first vehicle arrived, stopping within yards.

Greg got out and ran to Jenn and Cobb. Jake ran to Nate.

"Let her go, Cobb!" Greg shouted.

A posse of citizens and police vehicles arrived, and the helicopter circled overhead. Kozak and Carillo ordered Greg to stand back as they approached Cobb, weapons drawn.

"Release her!" Kozak said.

"There's no way out!" Carillo shouted.

Cobb turned to the freight train still passing,

looked above then at the growing force continuing to arrive.

Loosening his hold on Jenn, Cobb held up his hands.

Jenn flew to Greg and Jake, their arms locking around each other in a fierce, trembling embrace.

It was over.

BOOK THREE

THREE MONTHS LATER

Ninety-Eight

Jenn squeezed Greg's hand.

He ran his thumb over her rings.

"You're sure you want to do this?" he asked.

Nodding, she looked at the cold stone walls warmed by colorful artwork made by the children of inmates at the Wende Correctional Facility.

Since her rescue, Jenn had worked to take back her life, to be Jake's mom and Greg's wife, first, by doing the little mundane tasks that comforted her, restored order to her life, like cleaning her house, getting groceries, all while loving the people who loved her.

It helped her find herself again.

She'd reconciled with Kat; they'd grown closer. And Jenn assured Vince she was going to be okay but needed time.

She had returned to her optometric assistant's job at Crystallo View Optical. She resumed her role on committees at Jake's school, happy to learn that Principal Bickersley's experimental treatment was working. She reconnected with her book club friends, who'd resumed their monthly meetings after Jenn told them she was ready.

Jenn had Greg drive her and pick her up for the first one. Each time they traveled the long wooded stretch where it happened in Ripplewood, it made her uneasy. On the night after the first book club, with Jake at Kat's for a sleepover, Greg and Jenn went to a McDonald's where Greg told Jenn everything about Brooke Bollman, the whole truth, and how nothing had come of it.

"And nothing will come of it. Ever," Greg said. "Our business is picking up. We'll be fine."

Jenn told him everything about Porter Sellwin, how she'd planned to make a complaint against him, and how it didn't matter now.

But Jenn hadn't told Greg everything yet—she still was not ready.

Recovering from the abduction had exacted a toll. Jenn had nightmares, would sob unexpectedly, and nearly panicked the first time emergency lights flashed behind her while driving alone.

What had happened had left her with a black hole of uncertainty in her life, she told Dr. Stuart Maynart after she'd resumed her sessions with him.

"Cobb said things that day," Jenn told Maynart. "I still need answers."

Jenn and Greg had learned through the district attorney's office that Cobb had pleaded guilty to all charges, but was awaiting sentencing. Investigators in New York and Ohio were still digging deeper into the case and his past, including his claims of being Jenn's half brother and that the unidentified woman killed in Cleveland was Jenn's half sister.

Then Kozak and Carillo alerted Jenn that Cobb wanted to talk to her. They told Jenn the decision to see him was up to her but that they would be interested in knowing what he had to say.

"I want to see him. I need answers," Jenn told Greg after discussing it with Maynart.

"Talking with him might give you answers," Maynart had said. "He could also try to confuse you with truth and falsehood, mislead or wound you with his statements, so be prepared, Jennifer."

They went through the steps of a prison visit.

Cobb put Jenn and Greg on his visitors' list. There was an option for a video visit, but she wanted to look Cobb directly in the eye. They completed a visitor application and on their scheduled day, drove some twenty-five miles east of Buffalo to the institution. Bordered with high fencing, topped with razor wire, it was a grim, two-story structure with high red brick walls. Inside, Jenn thought it smelled clean, like a hospital with a hint of high school gym.

They followed the visitor rules—the irony taking Jenn back to the bucket rules in the cell Cobb had made for her. They brought ID. Jenn didn't wear tight, revealing clothing. She wore no jewelry, except for her wedding and engagement rings. They brought no contraband items and submitted to a pat down before being directed to the visitors' room, a common area with tables and chairs.

"It's a no-contact visit. He won't be restrained.

He'll sit across from you and I'll be right here," a corrections officer advised them.

Now waiting with Greg, Jenn looked at the children's finger paintings, depicting dreams of happy families and hope.

A door opened, and inmates filed in and found their loved ones. Cobb, wearing jeans and a T-shirt, sat at Jenn and Greg's table.

The guard stood a few feet behind him.

Cobb looked at Jenn as if seeing her for the first time while Jenn tried to understand what she saw sitting across from her: Cobb, the custodian, a kind man, beloved by the kids. A man she considered a friend.

Now he was what? A disturbed, dangerous man...my half brother?

She glanced at Greg.

The vein in his neck was pulsing like he wanted to jump over the table and beat Cobb for what he'd done, but Greg knew better.

"Thank you for coming," Cobb said. "I'm sorry for what I did to you."

"Tell me why you did it," Jenn said. "Why you said what you said."

Cobb looked at his hands and let out a long breath.

"Your mother had two families. One in Buffalo, one in Syracuse."

"No."

"It's true. I'm her son from her first family, the Telfers. And I had a sister—your sister, well, half sister—Heather. But our mother walked out on us.

I chased her on my bike that day while she walked down the street with her suitcase. She told me she'd send for me and Heather, but she never did. She lied. Yes, Heather and I knew that Dad pushed her around, but the guy worked hard and she had a mean streak with him too, and sometimes with us. Still, how could she do what she did? You're supposed to love your children, not abandon them. Not long after, I found my dad, Clark Telfer, in the garage, hanging by an electrical cord, their wedding picture on the floor under his feet. Heather and I were separated, put into foster homes. Somewhere along the line we were given new last names. When Heather got older, she ran off to the street, like me. I got into trouble searching for her in vain. My anger at my mother kept me going.

"Then I met this juvenile services case worker who hinted she had information on my family—my real family. Once, when the worker left her office, I looked in her files. I couldn't find information on Heather, but I found my mother's address. Her name was now Sofia Korvin, and she was married to Leo Korvin. And you were their daughter, Jennifer. Her new family.

"I found you all, living in that house in Buffalo, around Larkin. I had so much rage inside me. I could never forgive her. I wanted to destroy her life like she destroyed ours. I was in my teens then, on my own, living in a men's shelter when I came to Sofia's house, offered to shovel snow.

"She invited me in, but being half drunk, she had no clue it was me, her son. I met you, playing with your candle chime, my little sister, Jennifer. I got to know that house. I watched our mother, always half drunk. I hated the way she was acting all nice when I knew she wasn't. She had to pay for what she did. So one night, I snuck into the house. I put dead batteries in the smoke detector and placed a burning cigarette in the sofa. I went outside and watched the flames in the downstairs windows.

"Then I thought of you and it hit me. This was wrong! What was I thinking? I didn't want to hurt anybody. I tried rushing into the house to stop the fire, but it was too late. Then I heard sirens. I got scared, ran away with the house still burning. Seeing the firefighters, I figured you would all be saved. From down the block, I watched the fire, smoke billowing, praying no one would know what I did. They'll be saved! It'll be okay! The next day, I saw the news that my mother and her husband had died in the fire but that you were rescued. I was so ashamed of what I'd done, I left the shelter and drifted to other cities."

Tears rolled down Jenn's face.

"I was never caught, but as I drifted, I was haunted. For part of my life, I was addicted to alcohol, drugs. I lived on the street. But I got myself clean, got jobs, got married a couple times, and divorced, but guilt still gnawed at me and I had anger issues. I felt I wasn't worthy of love because of what I'd done. Relationships never worked for me. I had no family, no one, like I was invisible, not even here. Then one day, I realized that I did have a family—you and Heather were my family.

I couldn't find Heather, but I found you and Jake. I knew then that you survived that fire for a reason. It gave me hope for a family.

"I wanted to be near you, be a part of your life. It was hard, but I got a custodian job at Jake's school. I was good at it. It felt like I could watch over you, be a part of your life, be needed, sort of like family again. And I was searching for Heather, doing all I could to find her. I didn't know when to tell you about my plan for us to be a family, or even if I could. Then I learned from the kids at school that you were going to move to Arizona. I couldn't let that happen, not after all I did. I had to act fast.

"That's when I saw the chime in a store window, the exact same kind as the one you had as a kid, and took it as a sign. I sent it to you, to remind you and plant the idea that we needed to be together. I had saved some money, had a small place on a piece of land in Montana, made up a cover story about a fishing buddy there. Then at last, with help from a welfare case worker, I found Heather living in a shelter in Cleveland as Heather Katherine Brady. I approached her, told her I was her brother, Bert, from Syracuse. But she was not well and didn't believe me. Somebody was watching me, so I gave her some money, told her I'd be back to rescue her.

"I had been watching you closely. I knew everything about you and Greg and decided that if I could get you alone, to explain the truth, you would understand. And that night, I followed Greg to the Mulberry Bar in Depew, to make sure he was out of the way. That's when I saw him with that woman. I took pictures. It confirmed to me that I was doing the right thing, that he didn't deserve you. I decided to send pictures to police so they would know what kind of man he really is, kind of like our mother."

Cobb stared hard at Greg, who stared back.

"Then I stopped you that same night in Ripple-wood." Cobb turned to Jenn. "To rescue you and keep you safe, to set things up for us to go to Montana after I got Jake, too. But first I went back to Cleveland, to explain to Heather that it was time to be together, to be with her family. But she didn't understand. She was too far gone because our mom had destroyed her. So Heather fled, running to the freeway."

Tears rolled down Cobb's cheeks.

"I knew at the funeral it was Heather and not you because I was keeping you safe."

Jenn thrust her hands to her face.

"They tell me I will likely never be released from prison for the things I've done. I was only trying to save you and Jake," Cobb said. "I just wanted you to know the truth about your mother—*our mother.*"

Cobb turned to the guard, got up, and left.

Jenn didn't remember walking from the visitors' room, or leaving the prison, only being in the truck with Greg and crying so hard she thought she would come apart. All Greg could do was hold her as she gasped, choking on her words.

"All this time, I never told you. I never told any-one. I thought I'd killed my parents with my chime in the fire. When the new chime arrived at the house, I was horrified. How could anyone know? I didn't want anyone to know! It's why I went to see Dr. Maynart, because I thought the chime came to remind me that I'd killed my family, that someone knew my horrible secret."

"But Jenn, Cobb said he started the fire, not you," Greg said.

"Yes, but now, after thinking all my life that I killed my loving mother and father...now Cobb tells me *he killed her because she was a monster.*"

Ninety-Nine

Buffalo, New York, Clarence and Trailside Grove

The case was not closed.

Not all the way.

Kozak and Carillo were firming up charges on Zoran Volk while pursuing unresolved aspects on Cobb.

Guided by the statements Jennifer and Greg Griffin had provided after their prison visit, the investigators worked with Melinda Hyland, the case analyst, to verify Jennifer's family history with the aim of identifying the woman who was killed in Cleveland.

"I went through what Cobb told the Griffins." Hyland leaned on Carillo's desk as she updated them. "It was all new with names, locations—more than we had before."

"Right. So where does that leave us?" Kozak said.

"To verify it, I reached out to Children and Family Services in Syracuse and requested they send us old records, unsealing them if they're sealed. Our

DA will help with warrants if we need them. I'm waiting to hear back from Syracuse."

"Nice work, Melinda," Carillo said.

Hyland saw Carillo's screen saver. "Cute puppy. Is that Trigger?"

"Yeah."

"Ned's actually a softy," Kozak said.

"So Claire," Carillo said. "How'd your date go with the FBI guy?"

"It was just coffee."

"And that's how it starts," Carillo said.

"It shouldn't be long before we hear from Syracuse," Hyland said before leaving.

Jenn sat alone in her kitchen, gazing into her cup of tea.

Cobb's claims had left her flailing in a whirlpool of disbelief and despair.

Was it true? Was my mother cruel, wicked?

Visiting Cobb had shaken Jenn. She was contemplating her next appointment with Dr. Maynart when her doorbell rang. She went to the window; a FedEx truck was pulling away.

She opened the front door to a package addressed to Jennifer and Greg Griffin, from a Frances Penney in Toronto.

She texted Greg.

She used to live in your old neighborhood and was helping us. Open it, he wrote back.

Frances.

Memories flooded back with images of an older, kind girl, who lived down the street from Jenn.

The accompanying note said:

Dear Jennifer and Greg:
I was so happy to hear of the rescue and re-union, that your prayers were answered. After talking with Greg, I began looking into all of the things my mother left us after she'd passed. I'd mentioned to Greg how after the tragic fire, my mother held some of the re-covered items for a short time before they were given to Jennifer's grandmother. Going through my mother's things, I recently discov-ered something that was missed, something that belonged to Sofia Korvin, your mother, Jennifer.

I enclose it here because now it belongs to you.

With warmest hopes and prayers for you,
Frances Penney

Jenn slid her fingernail along the seam of the wrapped item, unfolding the paper to reveal a small book. It was tattered, its edges blackened and scorched. It had a red, hardboard cover with stitched binding.

She opened it to find handwriting on lined paper.

It was her mother's journal.

The request to Syracuse by the New York State Police had come back to Melinda Hyland sooner than expected—and with documents from several agencies.

The state's regional office of Children and Family Services, the office of Onondaga County Children and Family Services, and the Syracuse Child Welfare Division searched their archives. Going back more than three decades, they found records for the case of Clark and Sofia Telfer and their children, Bertram and Heather of Syracuse.

Hyland pulled together a quick summary with key points to share with Kozak and Carillo that read:

After she was assaulted by her husband, Clark Telfer, Sofia Telfer immediately fled her home without her children. Police were called but her husband, who knew the senior responding officer, reported Sofia Telfer to police and to social services, claiming that she had abandoned her family after he found that she was unfaithful and abusing their children. He claimed that "she was so cruel and threatening that the children would deny it for fear of reprisal."

Shortly after that, Clark Telfer committed suicide in his garage. His death was discovered by his son, Bertram. But Clark Telfer's allegations against his wife, Sofia, became part of the record and were investigated.

In keeping with policy, nothing was made public.

Investigators determined that the children, Heather and Bertram, said that their dad often struck their mom; but their mom was always yelling at him and had slapped him, too, leaving the children traumatized by the violence in their family.

Sofia Telfer and her attorney, along with lawyers

for the child protection agency, appeared in court. The children were not present. Upon consideration of key points of the family's heart-wrenching tragedies—the abuse, real and/or alleged—in the home, the fact the mom did walk out, and that the allegations of abuse against her could not be entirely dismissed, the judge in the case, known to be strict, decided that in the interest of protecting the children, the mother was forbidden to ever have contact with them again.

The children were swallowed by the foster care system.

Records show that Sofia Telfer later moved to Buffalo where she married Leo Korvin, a cabdriver. They had one child, a daughter, Jennifer Korvin.

Highland wrote that a note found in the records indicated that Sofia continued legal efforts, searching the foster care system for her children, Bertram and Heather. It went on for years without success. Then one day, a child care official, thought to have been sympathetic to Clark Telfer's claim and believing she was protecting the lives of Sofia's children—*"lives the mother ruined"*—put an end to Sofia's inquiries by telling her "to cease her search efforts" because her children had passed away. She told her one had drowned and the other had died of illness, and she could provide no other information.

"Damn." Carillo lifted his fist to his mouth after he and Kozak had read the records.

"Horrible," Kozak said.

"This supports the DNA, and that Heather was

Jennifer's half sister and Bert Cobb is her half brother," Carillo said.

"Yes," Kozak said. "We'll have to work with the Cuyahoga County Medical Examiner in Cleveland to let them know our Jane Doe on the freeway is Heather."

Then Kozak was silent, rereading the report.

"What is it, Claire?" Carillo said.

"It's so tragic, so sad." She began closing folders. "Let's go. We need to tell Jennifer Griffin."

Alone at her kitchen table, afraid of what she might find in her mother's journal, Jenn stared at it.

After nearly two full minutes, she opened it.

A small puff of air, like a gasp, floated up to her, smelling of an old book and charcoal. Jenn fanned the pages then went to the beginning, tracing her fingers over the words, written in clear blue ballpoint pen. Her mother's handwriting was beautiful. Judging from the dates, she'd made her first entries when she was in high school.

Swallowing hard, Jenn read.

"Toby Wheeler's in my math class. He's so cute." Days later another entry: "Dad's shouting at Mom again downstairs. I put on my headphones." Another day and an entry read: "Some kids like the new groups, but I'll love The Beatles and Supremes forever." Then later another day: "History test tomorrow yuck." Then: "Does Toby like me?" Scanning ahead Jenn came to: "Dad shouted at Mom all night. He's drunk again. He always yells at her."

Skimming ahead a year or so, turning pages,

Jenn stopped cold, reading: "Mom's dead. I can't stop crying. The world has stopped turning. I'm numb, can't think. Dad says she fell down the stairs. Do I believe him? I have to get out."

Jumping ahead to: "We buried Mom. It hurts so much. My mom is gone. I want her back."

Jenn snapped through pages of short entries. "Sad." "Miss Mom." "Rained all day." Then she came to: "Dad drunk again. Super mean. Argued with him. It was bad. Left home to live with my friend and her big sister. Dropping out of school. What's the point? I'm flunking anyway."

Flipping through years of entries about low-paying jobs and dates with men "who only want one thing," Jenn read that her mom was working as a waitress in Dombrowski's Bowling World when: "Started dating Clark Telfer, a heavy equipment operator. Bowling champ. Nice cologne. Nice smile. Really like him. Could get serious."

Racing ahead Jenn stopped at: "Pregnant. Scared." Then pages later: "Married Clark at city hall. He says 'we'll make it work. It's all good.'" Scanning ahead to: "Had a perfect baby boy, named him Bertram." Then several weeks later: "Baby's crying all night. Clark drinks, shouts at me to shut him up, or he will. I worry about everything."

Jenn paged ahead, skimming years, reading: "Our money's stretched. I juggle bills. Yet Clark bought expensive bowling shoes, a ball, and pays league fees. Dreams he'll turn pro. I beg him to stop drinking. Tell him I'm pregnant again. He shouts at me, blames me, hits me. I slap him back. He goes to the bar."

Flipping ahead Jenn read: "Our daughter Heather was born yesterday." Years later: "Clark's pro bowler dreams are gone because he drinks. His job hangs by a thread. We argue. He hits me. I never tell anyone. All couples fight, don't they? But it's getting worse. Some days, I drink to stop all the pain."

Turning pages, Jenn found: "I told Clark he needs help, AA, a church group, something. I said I'll go with him. But he exploded, said I'm cheating on him, pushed me to the wall, punching me. I fought back but he knocked me down and dragged me by my hair across the floor. It's so bad. Later, I hurt everywhere and decided I can't take it anymore. I can't fall down the stairs like my mom. I had to leave, right away, bruised and sore. Bert followed me on his bike, crying breaking my heart. I told him I'll be back to get him and Heather."

Jenn flips ahead: "At the women's shelter they urge me to call police and report Clark. My hands are shaking as I write. I can't believe it. The officers who investigate are Clark's bowling pals and they believe his lies. Clark says I abused the children, that I was unfaithful, that I drink, that I struck him. Liar!"

In the following pages: "Clark hung himself in the garage. Bert found him…oh dear Lord…my poor boy…he'll never be the same…"

Then: "They won't let me see Heather and Bert. Child services have taken them from me. I have to go to a family court thing." Jenn noticed the next pages were dotted, crinkled, as if they'd been wet then dried. Tears?

She continued reading: "In court the judge believed Clark's lies and ordered that Heather and Bert be taken from me and placed in foster homes; and that because I may be a danger to them—based on Clark's lies—I am forbidden to ever see them again. My heart is bursting. It's just not right. It's killing me. How can they do this?"

Jenn scans pages of months, years of her mother's anguish: "No matter what I do, the courts won't let me be with Bert and Heather." Then Jenn read how her mother moved to Buffalo, met Leo Korvin: "Such a kind, gentle man." She got married again and had a "beautiful daughter, Jennifer."

Jenn read how her mother made several trips to Syracuse to see child welfare people, pleading they help her locate Bert and Heather: "A case worker, who didn't like me, told me I can stop with my inquiries because Bert had drowned a year earlier and Heather had cancer and died six months before that. They say I collapsed on the floor."

Jenn's eyes filled with tears at the cruelty of the system and what it had done to her mother, and to Bert and Heather, too.

Collecting herself, she continued reading some of her mother's last entries: "After learning about Bert and Heather, my heart had been ripped out of me. I'm going through life like a robot. Alcohol helps. And I have Leo and Jennifer to hang on to, but a part of me is gone forever. I know I can never be forgiven for what I've done. I have to carry the pain of the horrible mistakes I've made. At times, I light my mother's chime, the twirling, twinkling angels give me comfort. Because I know who those angels are…"

Jennifer closed her mother's journal.

She absorbed the truth, her mother's anguish, her half sister, Heather, lost to the world, her half brother, Bert, destroyed by her family's tragedy, its tentacles reaching across years, killing her mother, her father, her half sister, reaching to destroy her, Jake, and Greg.

Jenn traced her fingers over the journal until it blurred from her tears.

Her phone vibrated and rang with calls from Greg, then Kozak. They would give her more answers.

In the time after, Jenn worked with Dr. Maynart to heal.

And one day—when she was ready—they went to the cemetery in the country where everyone thought they had buried Jenn.

Kozak had helped with officials in Erie County and in Ohio to make the confirmation and make everything legal.

The headstone meant for Jenn was now engraved with the name of Heather Katherine Korvin, her half sister. Jenn set flowers on the stone for the sister she only knew in death.

As more time passed, there was a moment, an innocent moment, that came to mark a turning point for Jenn.

Jake had begged to play a game of family football in the backyard, their first since the "bad time," as it had come to be known.

"Just like before. I play on Mom's side, then I play on Dad's," Jake said.

The game progressed, and Jenn was winning by a lot when she noticed something was wrong.

"You're not even tackling me, Greg."

"You're just too fast."

Sensing he was being overcautious, maybe feeling the need not to hurt her on any level, she knew what she had to do.

"That's a lie. You're not even trying. I'm tougher than you think, buddy." Jenn laughed. "Chicken."

"Yeah, Dad, you're a chicken!" Jake said.

Reading the deeper meaning of "tougher than you think," and the gleam in Jenn's eyes, Greg grinned, rubbed his hands together, and said, "Okay, baby, look out."

On the next play Greg tackled her with Jake piling on, his little fingers digging deep into her. Jenn said, "Oww!" to the pain, wincing while loving it.

"Are you all right, Mom?"

"I'm fine, honey. It's okay," she said to both of them. "It's okay!"

And it was okay.

For little by little, Jenn, Jake, and Greg got on with their lives. Things would never be exactly the same for Jenn because, in the wake of the horrible truth, her life was now a different one: one she came to treasure even more.

Some nights she would wake, turn to Greg, loving him for who he was. Then she'd get out of bed, go to Jake's room and watch over him as he slept, loving him more than she could imagine.

Theirs was not a perfect life.

It was a real life.

And some nights, in their home in Trailside Grove, Jenn, Jake, and Greg would light their chime, just like Jenn's grandmother and her mother had done, listening to the gentle tinkling while watching the angels.

* * * * *

Acknowledgments & A Personal Note

My goal was to make *Her Last Goodbye* a compelling, realistic story.

Still, I took immense creative license with police procedure, jurisdiction, the law, technology, and geography. Many places mentioned in *Her Last Goodbye* do not exist. However, for me, and I hope for readers, they ring true. Above all, I aimed for a story that affirms Maykov's observation at the front of the book: that no matter how dark the night, hope endures.

In bringing this story to you, I benefited from the hard work, generosity, and support of a lot of people.

My thanks to my wife, Barbara, for her invaluable help improving the tale.

Thanks to Laura and Michael.

My thanks to the super-brilliant Amy Moore-Benson and the team at Meridian Artists; to the outstanding Lorella Belli, at LBLA in London; to the ever-talented Emily Ohanjanians; and the incredible, wonderful editorial, marketing, sales, and PR teams at Harlequin, MIRA Books, and HarperCollins.

A special thanks to Anastasia Knyazeva, at the Dostoevsky Museum in St. Petersburg, Russia. She helped clarify that the epigraph at the front of the book does not—as many incorrectly state—come from Dostoevsky's *Crime and Punishment*, but rather from the Russian poet Apollon Maykov.

This brings me to what I believe is the most critical part of the entire enterprise: you, the reader. This aspect has become something of a credo for me, one that bears repeating with each book.

Thank you for your time, for without you, the story never comes to life, and remains an untold tale. Thank you for setting your life on pause and taking the journey. I deeply appreciate my audience around the world and those who've been with me since the beginning who keep in touch. Thank you all for your kind words. I hope you enjoyed the ride and will check out my earlier books while watching for new ones.

Feel free to send me a note. I enjoy hearing from you. I have been known to participate in book club discussions of my books via Zoom. While it may take some time, I try to respond to all messages.

Rick Mofina

www.rickmofina.com

https://www.instagram.com/rickmofina/

http://twitter.com/RickMofina

http://www.facebook.com/rickmofina